spicy sapphic christmas

EADA FRIESIAN

spicy sapphic christmas

i'm dreaming ...

bunny

"Don't you ever just want a break?" Piper asked.

Bunny jerked her head up, making eye contact. A shiver ran through her because this conversation was coming up. Again. Just about this time of year, every year, Piper wanted them to take a break from work, stay off the road, stop doing so many gigs. Then January would hit, and she would be right back on track to work every single day throughout the year.

"Not really, no." Bunny rolled her shoulders as she stepped into the dressing room, Piper following her.

This venue was much smaller than their normal ones, but Siena, their production manager, had scheduled them here and cranked up the charge on the tickets to make it a more intimate affair. And it had paid off. The seats were full, they'd been able to interact with fans in ways they normally couldn't, and it had been amazing.

But this time, when Piper asked that question, a small tug pulled at Bunny's heart. Was she ready for a break? Or at least to slow down? If they could do more of these intimate affairs, then would it ease the heavy weight on her shoulders to make everything a huge production and more?

"I don't believe you," Piper whispered into Bunny's ear.

Wrinkling her nose, Bunny pulled at the zipper on her leather jacket and jerked it down harder than she intended. "You say this every year."

Piper snorted. "I never get Christmas with my family. I know you don't want that, but some of us people out here do have decent families you know. You're always more than welcome to come home with me."

Bunny gave Piper a flat look and shook her head. "I've done that."

"Yeah, and it went great."

Great wasn't the word that Bunny would use. She'd ended up in bed with Piper's brother's wife after a lot of peppermint schnapps. And at the end of it all, the secrets were too hard to keep. When she'd gone back the next year, she had spent the entire time pining and trying to avoid another insane disaster.

Rolling her eyes, Bunny hung up her jacket in the travel wardrobe that went with them everywhere. She was really missing having separate dressing rooms right about now. Bunny never was much of a talker after playing a big show, but Piper would let that energy course through her for days.

The knock on the door was swift, and it opened right away. Which told Bunny exactly who it was. The only person who wouldn't get their hand cut off for that move. Siena stepped inside and held her hands out for a hug from Piper and then from Bunny.

"You two killed it. Like always." Siena's eyes were bright, but wary. She seemed to be carrying an undefined weight on her shoulders lately. As much as Bunny wanted to pry, she didn't. She wasn't the friendly one; she'd sic Piper on Siena some other time.

"Thanks," Bunny said as she gave Siena a quick side hug before stepping away. Her hands tried and failed to find pockets in her pants as she stood back up. She really wanted to get out of the sweaty concert clothes and into something more comfortable.

"I have a favor to ask you two."

Bunny pinched her face.

"What is it?" Piper chimed in, lounging on the chair and drinking a cold beer. She always did that after a show.

"There's another duo, up and coming, and I was hoping you two could check them out for me. They've requested my services, but I'd love your opinion on their style, blend, workability. Just your overall feel."

Bunny rolled her eyes. "Don't we keep you busy enough?"

Siena jerked her head back in surprise. "Yeah, but I have more than just you in my client base."

"Do we not pay you enough?" Bunny put her hands on her hips.

Piper slowly lowered the bottle of beer from her lips, her eyes wide. "Why are you being an ass?"

"I'm not." Bunny faced Siena again. "I just want to understand why she's looking to replace us."

"Oh my God! No!" Siena's face turned beet red, her eyes wide. She shook her head side to side, her dark brown hair moving with her. "I'm not looking to replace you at all. I'd never dream of that."

Bunny's stomach churned. She wasn't convinced. They had worked with Siena as their production manager for a long time now, but that didn't mean she wasn't tired of them or didn't see bigger and better things over the horizon. Bunny shifted a glance to Piper. And if Piper kept talking about taking a break, that would mean Siena would have to take a break and she would have to fill the time with someone else.

"You're being a worrywart, Buns."

"Don't call me that," Bunny growled. She wasn't overly fond of her name to begin with, but she didn't need Piper to add to that trauma. Rolling her shoulders, trying to loosen the tightness in her muscles, Bunny looked Siena over again.

"I promise I don't want to replace you." Siena tried again, her hands out to her sides as if she'd stepped in the biggest pile of dog shit.

Bunny shrugged slightly, not quite sure where to go from there. She pulled off her loose white tank top and threw it into the laundry basket to be washed for their next concert. It, no doubt, had a gallon of her sweat dried in it. She turned toward the back wall and flicked the clasp of the bra she'd been told too many times she had to wear and pulled on the sports bra she much preferred, sliding it over her head and positioning her breasts in it just right.

When she turned back around, Piper and Siena were eyeing each other, some sort of silent conversation going on between them.

"I think we should go," Piper chimed in.

Bunny turned on her sharply. "Amusing," she said dryly.

"Come on. We can use a break, and we haven't had fun out on the town in forever, just you and me, under the radar."

"If we walk into a club, which is where I'm assuming this is—" At Siena's nod, Bunny continued, "Then we're not exactly going to be under the radar. Unfortunately we're at that stage in our career where someone is bound to recognize us."

"But a break!" Piper jumped up and wrapped an arm around Bunny's shoulders, squeezing her arm lightly. "Think about it. You and me, one night out. If you find someone to dance with, it'll give me a full four-minute break from your insanity."

Bunny scoffed. Her? Dance with someone? Like that would ever happen. The more likely scenario would be that Piper would jump off and dance with all the pretty ladies and gorgeous men, leaving Bunny to sit at the table, watch their drinks, and scowl at the foolish idiots who tried to come near her.

"I'm assuming this isn't a queer club."

"No, unfortunately not," Siena answered, her voice dropping as she no doubt knew exactly what answer Bunny was going to give.

"Exactly." So now Bunny would be warding off the men who thought they could turn her their way and the men who mistook Piper's femme charm for something other than just being the sweet flirty woman she was. Ugh. It just disgusted her.

Bunny found the loose racerback tank she'd been hunting for, slipped it over her head, and smoothed out the material. This was exactly what she'd wanted. Comfort. Ease. A night of rest before they dove right back into the next show in a few days. Bunny straightened her back and pulled at the buckle on her belt.

Every time she went out with Piper, some kind of drama went down. She absolutely wasn't going to do it again.

"You owe me," Piper whispered into her ear.

Bunny immediately frowned. "No, I don't. If anything, at this point, I think you owe me."

"Nope."

Piper had that look on her face. The one that told Bunny she wasn't going to win this one, that she was going to be railroaded into doing whatever Piper wanted. Because she knew exactly what Piper was about to pull.

"Yes, you do." Piper softened her tone. "Remember that Christmas, with my sister-in-law…"

That was all Piper had to say. Because yes, Bunny remembered it. Yes, Bunny had fucked up. And yes, Bunny had desperately needed Piper to figure her way the hell out of it. And still, all these years later, Piper held it over her head in moments like these.

"Exactly," Piper gleefully chimed.

Siena looked at them curiously, as if she didn't understand the conversation that was happening. But she'd been around long enough that she had heard the full story already, multiple times actually. Bunny had drunkenly told Siena all about it when she and Siena had gone out to get shit faced after Siena's divorce was final.

To love lost.

Bunny shook her head, throwing her hands up in the air, her belt buckle hanging from her pants. "I'm not doing this."

"You are!" Piper said loudly.

Bunny glared. She pulled her belt off, unzipped her tight black jeans, and shoved them down her legs. She hated the tight clothes, but sex sells, so she always dressed in ways she didn't like. Bunny tossed the pants into the basket with her shirt and grabbed the loose pair of jeans from her own personal stash. She cinched the belt a bit harder than necessary.

When she turned around again, both Piper and Siena had their eyes locked on her, as if awaiting the answer.

"No."

"Yes!" Piper bounced in her toes. "Where are we going, Siena? When's their set up?"

Siena glanced at the ever-present watch on her wrist. "In thirty minutes."

"You're kidding me." Bunny tensed. "This place better be fucking close if you think we're going to make it there in time."

"It's just down the road." Siena sounded nervous now. "I really could use the extra assessment. There's something about them… I can't quite put my finger on it. I can't decide if it's a good something or a bad something."

Bunny grunted and shoved her boots on her feet. "Fine."

"Fine as in we're going?" Piper's glee couldn't be contained.

Bunny loved giving into her, but she resisted because it

wasn't always the best for either of them. But what could this hurt? And if she did go home, then she'd just be stalking around her apartment attempting to sleep when she knew she wouldn't be able to.

Piper bounced in her shoes, clapping her hands together. She still had all of her stage makeup on. Bunny tossed a wet towel to her. "Get that shit off your face."

"Yes, ma'am." Giggling, Piper walked toward the mirror and started to clean her face up.

Bunny sighed and looked directly at Siena. "Text me the information. And if I'm out until dawn, I'm calling you to pick her sorry ass up."

"Deal." Siena clapped her hands together and spun around. "There's some details we need to talk about for the spring. I'll set up a meeting for next week. But there's also something I wanted to talk to you two about for the upcoming winter."

Bunny hated this business to personal to business flip-flopping. It was so hard to keep up with sometimes. "Yeah, sure."

She was already far more comfortable now that she was in her own clothes. Ready to take on the world again. Piper started to slip out of her clothes and pull out the extensions in her hair. Bunny had never let them do that to her.

Piper quickly changed, throwing on some slinky dress she had stashed away as if she'd anticipated they were going to go out tonight.

Wait.

Had she?

Bunny eyed her carefully, looking for any sign that the conversation between them and Siena had been preplanned. But she couldn't quite say one way or the other if it was. Screw it all. She just wanted to get this over with. She was tired of owing Piper for helping her clean up the one mistake she'd ever made. Though it had been a good one.

The sex was hot and heavy.

The spark burned into a raging inferno that died very quickly.

And despite the drama that had followed, it had so been worth it.

Not that Bunny would ever admit that to Piper. Shoving her wallet into her back pocket, Bunny waited for Piper to be ready to leave.

"You've got ten minutes, Sleeping Beauty."

"I'm not Sleeping Beauty." Piper popped around the corner of the bathroom. "If anything, I'm Cinderella on her one night going to the ball."

"Fuck, why did I say anything?" Bunny rocked back on her heels, hands shoved into her pockets, and she bit her tongue. The more she teased Piper, the longer it was going to take her to get ready. And then they really would be late, and what the hell would be the point of going? Siena would be disappointed, they'd break the promise of scoping out this new group, and they'd be right back where they started.

Then again… that wasn't a half-bad idea.

"Let's go!" Piper looped her arm in Bunny's. "I expect you to buy me a drink."

"I always buy you a drink," Bunny muttered under her breath.

Piper did always say the best part about having a butch for a best friend was that she got the best of both worlds. She could date whoever she wanted and still know that Bunny would be there to take care of her when she got back.

"What's the name of this group? Siena never said."

Bunny snorted. She'd read the name about three times on her phone, wondering if it could be a better name. Then again, it wasn't like her own band had the greatest name on the planet. But they'd branded it that way and they weren't changing it now. "Sole *S-O-L-E* Sisters."

"What?"

"Yeah. I can already tell you that'll be the first thing Siena will want to change."

"No shit, that's awful."

"The worst."

Piper rested her head on Bunny's shoulder as they walked through the back hallway to the back door of the concert hall. They had one more big fan eruption ahead of them, and then they could escape to the club. All Bunny had to do was put on her extroverted face for another ten minutes and then they'd be gone.

She could do this.

She had to.

Because she had nothing but her career to show for her pitiful excuse of a life.

bea

Bea watched as Jo raced back and forth in the small space they were using as a changing room. There was barely room for their suitcases, let alone room enough for Jo to have this much energy. It wasn't as though it was their first gig. In fact it wasn't even their first gig at Julianna's. The club was small and a little too heteronormative for Bea's liking, but she'd agreed easily enough with coming back. Last time hadn't been anything special, but they had walked away with a decent sum for the evening.

But now, watching Jo flatten down her shirt for the fourth time, alarm bells started to sound in Bea's mind.

"Jo?" Bea asked. Something else was going on. Bea knew her sister like the back of her hand.

Jo didn't stop her fussing. She didn't even seem to hear her name repeated.

"Jo?" Bea tried again, a smile stretching over her face. She had no idea what had turned Jo into hyper-Jo before tonight's performance, but she couldn't help smiling. That had always been one of Jo's gifts. She had this electric energy. It didn't matter what mood people found her in, they couldn't help but get swept up in that energy. And being her big sister had never made Bea immune to it.

"Jo." Bea spoke a little louder, the word coming out crisp and sharp. She had to get Jo's attention because she was going to pour out all that energy into this instead of the show.

Jo had leaned forward at the dresser, rolling back her lips to check her teeth for the tenth time. But her shoulders stiffened, her eyes darting away instantly when they met Bea's in the mirror, and that was all it took to confirm to Bea that something else had happened. Something Bea didn't know about yet. But she would find out. She always did.

Quickly going through her options of how to get this information out of Jo, Bea decided a soft, caring approach was going to work the best for tonight. Her stomach flipped. That look on Jo's face rarely left her in a good mood. Usually it would cause at the least tension and frustration. At its worst, that look had caused the only fights they'd ever had in the business side of their life. The personal? Well, they were Irish twins, and fighting like cats and dogs was part of the rules.

Bea closed her eyes and breathed deeply. She had been looking forward to having some time off over Christmas, but that look. That look warned her that plans of taking it easy and putting her feet up might be on hold before they even began.

"What's going on, JoJo?" Bea kept her tone as light as possible, but if Jo was really paying attention, she'd hear the underlying worry there.

"Ugh." Jo turned around, her long blonde locks flying around her head, the snarl she would no doubt one day be famous for lifting the left side of her top lip. "I hate that name."

Bea burst out laughing because what else was she going to do? She couldn't exactly tell Jo that she might actually be able to use JoJo as a good marketing name. The words were on the tip of her tongue before she swallowed them back down.

But Bea also knew her sister very well, and the reaction wouldn't distract Bea for long.

"What's going on?" Bea asked again, putting her hands to the sides of her body, palms up, as she awaited an answer.

"What do you mean?" Jo's snarl turned into a sweet wide-eyed look of innocence. A look that the handful of fans they had were already in love with. Jo was the traditional girl-next-door beauty. Her blonde hair glowed under the spotlights, and her delicate features made her look far more innocent than Bea knew she was capable of being. It also helped that she had a natural hourglass figure that she spent very little effort to maintain. She was the stunning one of the two, and Bea was the plump older sister who had a chip on her shoulder and business on her mind.

It always relieved Bea to be the sister so many people skimmed over. She didn't mind her own slightly darker blonde hair, or the squarer cut to her jaw. It had never bothered her to look in the mirror and see herself looking back, though she had thought about whether or not they should look more alike to sell themselves better. But that could be a conversation for a different day.

"Jo?" Bea narrowed her eyes, her tone steady. She wasn't going to let Jo get away with avoiding answering her again.

Jo batted her eyelids and shrugged as she stretched the smile wider before turning back to the mirror. Her eyes stayed conspicuously away from Bea's.

Bea took a deep breath. "Okay."

There were a few ways she could play this. Jo had been nagging her again about loosening up, about meeting women and maybe even trying that thing called S-E-X. Yes, Jo had specifically spelled it out as though Bea were a former nun and the word still offended her delicate ears.

Which was bullshit. Bea'd had sex before, many times. It just wasn't something she typically shared the details of with her sister. Because that would be weird.

Bea bit back a groan. Surely, Jo hadn't tried to set her up again?

She watched Jo as she rolled her shoulders and moved her head as she went through her pre-show warm-up.

No.

It couldn't be a setup. Jo would be excited and energized, sure, but she wouldn't be primping herself repeatedly and refusing to look Bea in the eye. Her normal MO had always been to butter Bea up with compliment after compliment.

It had to be something to do with the show.

"I'm not really feeling it tonight," Bea said, blowing her breath out between limp lips.

"What?" Jo spun so quickly Bea wondered if she felt dizzy.

"Yeah. It's just… I dunno." Bea shrugged and dropped onto the dark two-seater couch that lined an entire wall of the room. "Maybe it's the club. There aren't really many people here, and the energy just isn't working for me."

"Of course it's working. You have to give it a chance." Jo perched herself at the edge of the couch, scooping up one of Bea's hands as she did. "There are lots of people out there."

"Doesn't sound like many more have come in since we arrived." Bea wasn't the biggest fan of playing these games, but she also knew demanding any harder with Jo would get her exactly nowhere.

"Oh, there will be." Jo smiled so wide that Bea was certain her head shook with the excitement.

"It's Julianna's. It doesn't exactly pull a crowd." Bea wrung her fingers together, twisting her hands in her lap. These games never made her feel good.

Jo looked down at her hands, teeth pressing down on her

lower lip. There would definitely be lipstick on her pearly whites now.

"It'll be a great show. I promise. And you never know who might show up. I've heard that agents of all levels frequent the smaller clubs looking for new talent."

Bea closed her eyes. Jo was a truly terrible liar. In truth, that was one of her saving graces. Bea knew when she could trust Jo's words and when there was a second layer of truth hiding beneath.

"Oh, Jo." Bea gave up the act and pinned Jo with her eyes as she looked up. "What've you gotten us into this time?"

"What makes you think I've gotten us into anything?" Jo's hand reached up to her ear, gently tugging on the lobe.

"That." Bea smiled as she pointed at Jo's hand.

"Damn it." Jo pulled her hand away from her ear, glaring at it as though it were the enemy.

"So what did you do?" Bea asked as she stood and stepped up to the mirror. She had already checked herself and felt comfortable to step on stage. But she used the movement to bite back the frustrations that always rose in her head at how her looks compared to Jo's.

As much as she told herself she was comfortable with the way she looked, she wasn't.

And the deeper they got into the business, the worse the pressure to conform became.

"It's not a bad thing." Jo was right behind her. Her energy now had a nervous edge to it, which meant she was worried Bea was going to be angry.

Bea felt Jo's breath on her bare neck and closed her eyes.

"What isn't a bad thing?" She was resigned to whatever this new drama was.

"You know Siena Frazee?"

"The agent that represents Bunny and Piper?" Bea turned

to stare at Jo, but not before she caught her own wide eyes in the reflection.

"The one and the same." Jo grabbed both of Bea's hands in her own and squeezed. "Well, she's supposed to come here tonight and check us out. See if she wants to take us on as her new client."

"What?" The word boomed out around the room and bounced back to Bea's ears with a dissonance that made her wince.

"It's a good thing," Jo assured, though she still worried her lower lip. "She's at least heard of us, which is amazing. It means we're finally getting some traction, and if she likes us tonight, this could be it. This could be what we've been working for."

Bea stared at Jo, not squeezing back with her hands, not saying a word, and not blinking. Panic swelled in her chest, swirling around and moving into the pit of her belly and forming a vortex of bile. It was exactly what they'd wanted. But that didn't mean Bea was ready for it. Slow steady steps to the top. That had always been her goal. She didn't want to be a one-hit wonder and then die out quickly. She wanted a career that would last a lifetime.

"Bea?" Jo asked, a small tremble in her voice. "I promise. It's going to be great. This is an amazing step forward."

"Yeah, except you've only just told me." Bea's voice rushed out as she hurried to her suitcase and opened the lid. Beside hers, Jo's suitcase lay open with clothes half hanging out and no organization to be seen. "I can't go out there like this. I didn't even bring any of our fancier outfits. How could you do this, Jo? We barely have *Kick it in the Ass* ready for a live performance, and yet it's the third song in the set tonight."

"What?" Jo tilted her head and furrowed her brows.

"Don't you give me those puppy dog eyes. You knew I'd want to make sure tonight was perfect for this, and you haven't given me nearly enough time to be prepared. We're not ready for something like this."

"You aren't mad I convinced her to come?" Jo asked.

"Oh no." Bea stopped searching through her clothes and looked up. "What did you tell Siena? Tell me you didn't lie to the best agent in the business. The agent you know I want for us more than anyone else. Tell me you didn't."

The knock on the door gave Jo an easy out.

"They're ready for you!" The voice called out before footsteps hurried away.

"This isn't over," Bea snapped, turning to Jo as she slapped her suitcase shut.

"It's going to be fine. I promise." Jo smiled with that hyperactive energy. Whatever chagrin had shown on her face as Bea ramped up for a lecture had disappeared in an instant.

Bea closed her eyes and took a deep breath. Slowly, she counted to ten before opening her eyes again and looking at Jo. Their eyes met, and while a fissure of anger lingered in Bea's chest, she knew she would forgive Jo. She would correct whatever lie had gotten Siena here, even if it meant they wouldn't be her client.

Because now she saw the energy that vibrated off of Jo for what it actually was. Jo was nervous and scared.

And now so was Bea.

But that no longer mattered. Despite her palms sweating and her heart racing in her chest, Jo was scared, and it was Bea's job to make sure she wasn't.

It had always been Bea's job to protect her little sister. And she wouldn't let her down tonight.

"You're so lucky I love you. Even if I don't like you very much right now," Bea said but ended her words with a wink.

The wink was enough to shake whatever fear Jo felt as she squealed with happiness and wrapped her arms around Bea's neck.

"But that love is conditional on you not squealing like that again and getting your ass out there before they cancel our set."

Jo laughed and let Bea go.

Bea took several more deep breaths as she followed Jo from the room. Jo's feet barely touched the ground. She bounced more than she walked as the excitement built the closer to the stage they got.

Bea's own excitement was difficult to find, let alone pull to the surface.

She knew they were good. She knew they had worked their asses off to get this far, but they weren't ready for Siena.

Bea wasn't ready for this to be her make-or-break moment. She bit the inside of her cheek to stop herself from racing down any more of the dark paths she knew her brain would take if she didn't put a stop to it.

She was still angry at Jo, but she also understood why Jo did it.

If it were left up to Bea, she couldn't honestly say she would ever feel ready for Siena. Bea wished she had the natural energy and confidence that poured out of Jo, but then again, who would be the one to reel them back?

At the steps to the stage, Jo turned back and looked at Bea.

Bea put on her best smile and gave Jo a thumbs up. The smile she received back was worth it. It would also be worth the tumultuous sensations in her stomach.

In the end, Bea should have known better than to let her panic and fear get the better of her, for even a moment. Because the moment she stepped on stage, the world disappeared and the music was all that mattered.

She forgot about Siena who might or might not actually show up. She forgot about her self-doubts and fears. She even forgot about the unknown lies Jo had told Siena to get her interested.

The only things that mattered were the moment, the music, and the people.

And her baby sister.

With that wicked, excited grin on her face.

That's why they were here.

Together always.

bunny

Siena led the way into the backstage area. Bunny followed closely, worrying her fingers back and forth. She hadn't been to Julianna's in close to a decade, but it had been the exact spot that Siena had discovered them all those years ago. She rolled her shoulders and shot Piper a look of mixed frustration, annoyance, and curiosity as she held the door for both Siena and Piper to walk through.

Bunny put her hand at the small of Piper's back as they walked through the thin hallways. This place had produced more A-list bands and musicians than any other in town. Whoever this duo was, if they were here, they must be at least halfway decent. Which Bunny could attest to. She'd seen them on stage only moments before, sweating and putting their hearts into the music they'd written themselves.

Siena knocked on the dressing room door.

Seeing her acting proper and polite was odd. They'd known each other so long that she was their third band member and had full access to them by now.

"Who is it?" A strong voice slid through the doorway.

"Siena Frazee."

It was a long second until the doorknob turned and cracked open a bit. Inside, Bunny caught a glimpse of chaos, which was exactly what their own dressing room looked like on a good day following a show. She bit the inside of her cheek to keep from making any comments as Siena was allowed inside.

The woman at the door was short, her curves voracious and alluring. Bunny's insides immediately started churning with arousal. She shifted in her boots, more than a little uncomfortable. She trailed her gaze from head to toe over this woman, her dark blonde hair in soft ringlets to her shoulders, the line of her collarbone that disappeared under the edge of her bright red shirt, her full breasts just begging to be touched.

Nope. Stop that, you idiot.

Bunny flicked her gaze up to the woman's face and canted her head to the side.

Stare at her face like you're not some horny dog.

Come on. You've got this.

Bunny kept her lips sealed shut as Siena walked farther into the room and Piper followed closely. Seeing this woman close up instead of on stage was entirely different. The lighting hadn't done her any favors. Bunny's initial thought was that this one wasn't the star of the show and the other could easily sell more tickets without dragging her sister around.

"It's good to meet you two, officially." Siena held her hand out to shake each of the women's hands. "I hope you don't mind, but I brought Bunny and Piper with me to check out your show. This is Bea and Jo."

Bunny barely flicked her gaze to Jo. She was utterly entranced with Bea—with the way she moved, with the sour-puss look on her lips, with the annoyance in her eyes. She had a resting bitch face for days, and it was like she didn't even know it.

"Oh my gosh!" Jo squealed and clapped her hands together. "I'm so excited to meet you two."

Bunny's shoulders stiffened when Siena's phone went off, *Free Bird* playing loudly into the room, startling Bea. Bea flicked her gaze to Siena and then back to Bunny, as if she couldn't look away, too scared of what Bunny might do.

Siena excused herself to the hallway. Bunny would do that too, considering who was calling. Siena had changed the ring tone for her ex-wife as soon as she'd filed for divorce. She had yet to change it back, but it made it really obvious who was calling and when. It was now Bunny's turn to step into the lead role and make sure that Bea and Jo understood why they were there.

Which wasn't to secure them a contract with Siena.

"I can't believe she brought you guys!" Jo again was squealing.

Bea cut her a look that said shut up, and Bunny had to hold back her snort of laughter. She'd given Piper that look far too many times to count. Piper stepped forward, her hand extended. "Well, it's good to meet you."

Jo bounced in her shoes as she took Piper's hand. "I didn't think she'd bring you."

"Siena likes to get a second opinion when she's scouting new talent," Piper said, shoving her hands into her tight jeans.

Bunny had barely been able to take her eyes away from Bea. She was stunningly gorgeous, and so far had also remained quiet through all the introductions.

"So you're sisters?" Bunny said, cringing at the stupidity of the question. She already knew the answer from Siena who had filled them in during the set. Bunny's shoulders tensed. Why was she always such an idiot when it came to women? But she couldn't take her eyes off of Bea, and when Bea turned on her, those stunning blue eyes alight with annoyance, Bunny nearly melted.

"Yes," Bea answered.

Bunny's mouth went dry, her tongue swelling up in her

mouth and making it impossible for her to speak. She wasn't the suave person that most of the news outlets and fan bases thought she was. She was a clumsy idiot when it came to women. Not to mention, she didn't really want anyone to know that she was a lesbian.

Nope. That couldn't happen at all.

"I'm so sorry. I have to run." Siena popped her head in. Her cheeks that were normally rosy were ashen.

Bunny immediately tensed. "What's wrong?"

"It's Harley." Siena stared down at her phone. "You'll have to call a ride. I'm so sorry."

"Family is important." Bunny put her hand on Siena's arm and led her out of the dressing room and toward the back door. "What happened?"

"She fell out of her bunk bed and broke her arm. Might have a concussion. I told Tori those bunk beds were a bad idea." Siena's voice wavered with leashed emotion.

Bunny wrapped an arm around Siena's shoulder and tugged her in slightly. "I'm sure she'll be fine."

"I can't decide if I'm more worried or pissed." Siena snorted. "Tori's taking her to the emergency room right now, so I'm going to meet them there."

"All right." Bunny squeezed Siena in a side hug. "Let me know how everything turns out, okay?"

"Yeah." Siena worried her lower lip. "Sorry about ditching you."

"Don't be. That's what family is for, right?"

"Yeah." Siena managed a small quirk of her lips before she slipped farther down the hallway and out of sight.

With her gone, however, Bunny and Piper were going to have to step in and figure out if Bea and Jo were worth Siena's investment. And that was going to take some tact, which Bunny wasn't known for. With a heaving breath, she turned on her toes and walked back to the dressing room.

Jo and Piper chattered away amicably. Bunny shoved her hands into her pockets and rocked back onto her heels. "Can we buy you some drinks?"

Bea's lips parted in surprise. "Is everything okay with Siena?"

"Yeah. Her kid needs her."

"How old is she?"

Bunny clenched her jaw. She was always wary about giving out more information than necessary, always the tight-lipped one. But since Siena had brought Harley up, by name, what could an age hurt? "She's five. She just started kindergarten this year."

"Oh, five?" Jo seemed to practically melt. "I love little kids."

Fuck, Jo and Piper had the same energy levels. Bea, it seemed, was the balance to that. Bunny kept her hands in her pockets, trying to drag her gaze away from Bea.

"So drinks?"

"Sure. Sounds delightful." Bea dragged out the last word, as if drinks with them would be anything but.

Bunny shuddered as the full force of Bea's grumpy attitude hit her. Why did she always go for the ice queens? Cringing, Bunny turned toward the door, holding it open for everyone as they left. Julianna's would be open for another two hours and the adrenaline from their own show was still coursing through Bunny's veins. A nice drink to round out the night would be pleasant, even if the company was icy.

Jo practically bounced in her shoes as she headed for the bar. They ordered drinks and found a small, quiet table in the corner. Piper eyed Jo over like she had found her new best friend. Perhaps she had, though their bond wasn't one that easily broken.

Bunny rocked back in her seat, looking Bea over again. "So you want to sign with Siena?"

"Yes," Bea answered.

At least business was something Bunny could manage to talk about. "And you think we'll give you the okay?"

"I don't think she needs your approval to make her own decisions."

Oh, this one is feisty, Bunny thought. She had to hide her smile in her beer. She loved a good challenge. "Siena doesn't, but she asked for it. Which means there's something about you that she's not certain of yet."

Bea's full lips parted, her eyes widening. She curled her hair behind her ear and then turned her glass in front of her, staring at it instead of Bunny.

Fuck.

Bunny had already screwed this up. "What's your angle?"

"Excuse me?" Bea jerked her head up.

"What's your angle? Everyone has an angle. Why do you want to work with Siena?"

"Because she's good at what she does." Bea clenched her jaw. "Not everyone has an angle, you know. We want to be represented by someone who understands the business, who has experience working with duos, and someone who is queer."

That last word sent a shiver of panic through Bunny. Did they know? Did the whole world know at this point, and was she just oblivious to the fact that she'd been outed somewhere? Bunny had to resist the urge to get on her phone and check every news site to see if she and Piper had been found out. If Jamie Kettlehouse had gotten hold of some information again, Bunny would have her head. The rumors of them being together would run amok, and it couldn't be further from the truth.

"We want to do this right. And Siena Frazee can help us do that." Bea gave Bunny a firm look. "Isn't that what you did?"

"Kind of." Bunny fingered the dewdrops on her chilled

glass as they fell toward the tabletop. "So you want to be as famous as us? Or more?"

"I want to earn a good, healthy income, and I want to make music."

Bunny nodded along, having heard all of this before, so many times. Yet it was rare for someone to make it into their level. It was rarer still for someone to make it above them. Bunny wasn't stupid. She and Piper had a fantastic fan base. They made enough money to earn a respectable living, but they didn't bring in billions every year either. That had never really been their dream.

"And you want to work with Siena because she's queer?"

"Yes, wouldn't you?"

"Wouldn't I what?" Bunny tensed. She probably shouldn't have brought up this conversation, but she wanted to know for sure. Was Bea queer?

"Want to be represented by someone who gets you." Bea canted her head to the side, her curls falling over her shoulder.

Bunny leaned in, her hand flat on the top of the table as she lowered her voice so that Bea had to lean in and hear her. "I don't have to be a lesbian to understand lesbians."

"It's easier sometimes." Bea's lips pulled upward as if in a half-smile. "At least I find it easier to work with other people from the community."

Confirmed!

Internally, Bunny leapt for joy. But on the outside, she kept the same calm, cool, collected persona that she always had. She gave Bea a grin before pulling back and taking a long sip of her cold beer. "How do you plan on marketing your little duo?"

"Many ways." Bea's eyes lit up. "But I'm not sharing any of our trade secrets."

Bunny snorted hard, the beer coming back up into her nose and burning it. She hated when that happened. She couldn't fault Bea though. Trade secrets were just that—secret. It wasn't like Bunny was willing to share any of her techniques for getting to where she was. Not yet anyway. Not with someone she'd just met and couldn't quite trust.

"Duly noted." Bunny raised her chin at Bea and then glanced at Piper and Jo, both of whom were staring at the two of them like they were deer caught in the headlights. "What?"

Piper shrugged. "Nothing."

Bunny narrowed her gaze suspiciously. "Seriously. What?"

"Nothing," Piper said again. "Jo and I were talking about dancing for a bit."

"So go dance. You know that's not my thing." Bunny waved her hand, trying to convince them to go. She'd nearly forgotten they were even at the table.

"Order us a second round, will you?"

"Sure, sure." Bunny waved her hand again. Piper needed to burn off that energy, otherwise she was going to be up texting Bunny all night. And Bunny strongly suspected Jo was the same way.

When she turned back to Bea, Bunny froze. Bea had a wide expression in her eyes, as if something had just clicked that hadn't before.

"What?" Bunny asked, frowning. A deep line creased in her forehead, and she tried to shake it off. She shouldn't be this concerned about what someone else thought of her. Then again, most people had awful opinions of her.

"You two aren't together." Bea said it like a confirmed statement.

Bunny tensed, fear racing through her, and then she paused. Bea hadn't accused her and Piper of being together. In fact, it was the complete opposite. Bunny spun her drink on the table, keeping her eyes locked on Bea's. She wanted to catch any little expression that she could.

"No, we're not. Why would you think we are?"

"Oh, just… rumors." Bea muttered the last word, her cheeks pinking with embarrassment.

Was she a fan?

Fuck, please say she's not some crazed fan.

"We're absolutely not in a relationship." Bunny rolled her shoulders, trying to settle herself from that immediate upset.

"Well then, I suppose that leaves opportunities for others."

"I'm not looking for a relationship." Bunny chugged the rest of her beer and then looked around to see if she could find a waiter to get everyone refills.

"Who said anything about a relationship?"

Bunny jerked back sharply. "Excuse me? You did."

Bea laughed lightly and nodded toward Jo and Piper on the dance floor. "You think I don't know a lesbian when I see one?"

"Fun fact." Bunny leaned in, her lips so close to Bea's cheek. She tilted her head down slightly so that her breath would wash right over Bea's neck and down into her cleavage. "Piper's not a lesbian."

"You didn't deny you being one."

Bunny sighed. "What's it matter to you?"

Bea's look was wickedly sexy. The raised eyebrows, the parted full lips, the tongue peeking out from the edge of her mouth. Her cheeks were curved with deliciousness, and Bunny wanted nothing more than to bury her face in Bea's neck and pepper as many kisses as possible against her skin. What was so enthralling about this icy woman?

Oh right.

She was sexy as hell.

"Oh, it matters." Bea lowered her voice and turned her head. "Because if you look at every woman that walks in your direction like you're looking at me now, you're in absolute, utter denial."

A chuckle bounded its way up Bunny's chest, into her throat, and out her lips. "Hard to ignore a stunning woman."

"Oh, you do flatter me." Bea rolled her eyes and pointed at her drink. "Weren't we getting another one?"

"Hell yes."

*the best things
happen while you're
dancing*

piper

Piper led the way onto the dance floor. She needed to move more than Bunny could ever truly understand. The energy from their show still itched beneath her skin. Sweaty bodies parted to make way for them to pass without losing their momentum. Piper's smile stretched over her face as her hips swayed to the beat, her shoulders joining in on the next step.

It had been easy enough for her to carve out a space for them to dance in. People assumed because of her long legs and equally long torso that she needed a lot of room to throw her body around.

When she was young, she would often take advantage of that, using the space as a stage to show off her skills and get noticed. Now though, she danced primarily for herself. The energy that fluttered beneath her skin needed a way to escape.

Tonight she leaned into people's assumptions a little more. She wanted Jo to have space enough to not be touched.

If she had known Jo a little longer, she might not have worried about it so much. Despite how well they clicked instantly, she was well aware that not everyone was as comfortable as she was at touching when they danced.

Flicking a look up at the band, Piper nodded in appreciation for the three figures moving to their own music. They were androgynous and synchronized, and Piper's chest swelled with the recognition of her community, of being part of the family.

She had always understood Bunny's reasons for staying in the closet, and she had agreed with them just as readily. But the world was changing, and sometimes she wished they could as well.

Pushing away the maudlin thoughts, Piper focused on the music the band played. They were good. The music was always good at Julianna's. You didn't get to play there if you weren't.

"Show me what you got," Jo spoke loud enough for Piper to hear her over the thrum that poured from the stage.

"Excuse me?" Piper turned from the band and focused her gaze on Jo. She raised her eyebrows and stretched her lips into a cheeky grin. She had used that smile on enough men and women to know it worked in wonderful ways. Right now, she had no idea what turn the conversation had just taken, but she buzzed with excitement at the energy that flowed from Jo. It had been rare to find anyone who could come near to matching her own level.

Jo laughed, a full-bodied sound that tinkled imaginary wind chimes in Piper's mind.

"Bunny said you're the dancer." Jo spread her long fingers wide and palms up, moving them out from each other, encompassing the floor between and around them. "Show me what you've got."

"Care to join me?" Piper held out her hand, and Jo took it eagerly.

Before Jo could even think about taking the lead, Piper pulled her in. Her smile widened even more as Jo stepped into the move, twirling her body along Piper's arm until her back rested snugly into Piper's front. Her movements were graceful, with the ease of practice.

"How long did you dance for?" Piper asked.

"Oh, I see." Jo laughed and shook her head. Her blonde curls brushing Piper's chin. "A little tit for tat is it?"

Piper's hips moved, and Jo swayed along.

"Just wondering how you moved from trained dancer into a punk rock band?" Piper asked as she turned Jo around in her arms with the lightest touch.

"Have you looked me up, Piper?" Jo's eyes twinkled with excitement.

"Sorry to burst your bubble," Piper spoke as she curled her fingers around Jo's hips. She didn't need to put any pressure into her touch, though. Jo followed with ease, as though the two of them had been dancing together for years.

"Then how did you figure it out?" Jo's eyes furrowed, but she didn't miss a step.

"The way you stand. The way you move." Piper laughed as Jo took the opportunity and grabbed hold of the lead.

Jo pushed Piper back lightly with both palms against her chest, just over her breasts.

Piper's breath caught.

Oh yes, dancing had so often led her to seduction and many a near-stranger's bed. Some would even say it was the best thing that could happen when you're dancing. That flirt and innuendo of touch. The desire of bodies moving in new ways. That brush of fingers just right. Right now, Piper couldn't imagine disagreeing.

The tempo increased, and without a hitch, Jo increased the movement of their steps to match. Her fingers dug into Piper's hips as she stepped closer. It wasn't that they had been far away from each other, but now Piper could feel the softest brush of Jo's dress against the top of her thighs. The speed wasn't all that different. The movements became less traditional and taut.

"All right." Piper laughed in reply, wondering when was the

last time she had enjoyed herself this much on the dance floor. "I'll go first."

"First? With what exactly?" Jo winked, and damn it all if Piper didn't feel that heat rush through her body. But she wasn't here to get laid. She was here to find out if Siena should take on Jo and Bea as clients.

"I took every dance lesson my mom could enroll me in from the age of three," Piper said

"Three?" Jo's eyes widened, and Piper saw what others must. The sweet innocence of the girl next door. But in those deep brown eyes, Piper sensed the mischief hidden behind the innocence. She knew how easily people assumed things based on her appearance. When she danced for the first time around people, the shock and awe were written across their faces. How could such a lanky-looking girl dance with such ease and grace? She had heard it a million times before, and seen it even more often.

But she hadn't seen it on Jo's face.

"I had too much enthusiasm for my mom to handle." Piper laughed, a little surprised at the open honesty that came willingly to her lips. She had been in the business long enough to know keeping her life private for herself was vital. But she didn't want to keep it from Jo. Even in the few moments since they had met, Piper sensed that Jo would understand.

"Is that what they called it back then?"

"Oh, playing the age card, are we? We in the old-age category like to call it well-refined experience." Piper narrowed her eyes, but she smiled, making sure Jo knew she hadn't been offended. And she hadn't been, but she did feel the words like a splash of cold water. Age wasn't an issue, the idea of getting closer to a person, especially one she might end up sharing Siena with, was. And the sisters were so out and proud about who they were. While that made Piper want to get to know Jo even more, she knew exactly how Bunny would feel about it.

Without stopping her feet, Piper shuffled back a little, giving Jo no choice but to drop her hands or stumble forward.

Jo wasn't about to stumble, and Piper was relieved she had read the woman right. Jo smiled, but it didn't make her eyes sparkle the way they had previously.

"I wonder if Bunny and Bea have killed each other yet." Piper forced levity into the conversation. It had been so easy to talk to Jo, and she didn't want that to change.

"Perhaps not killed, but certainly traded a few blows by now." Jo laughed. Her eyes sparkled, and Piper relaxed into the sway of her body again.

They danced close to each other, but now there was a distinct line of air where one of their bodies ended and the other started.

"When I first found out about you two, I was certain you would have to be Bunny."

"What?" Piper laughed at the mere idea.

Jo threw her head back and joined in on the laughter.

Piper's mouth dried at the stretch of smooth skin covering Jo's neck.

"Why?" Piper's voice squeaked on the word. She swallowed and tried again. "Why would you think that?"

"Well." Jo's cheeks carried a rose pink that Piper smiled at, despite her knowing there couldn't be anything between the two of them. "She's not exactly the cute little Bunny type."

Jo smiled, letting the silence linger until Piper filled in the details Jo knew better than to assume.

"I mean, of the two of you she's definitely the more butch one. And Bunny definitely screams more of a femme, perky, cheerleader name to me."

"Oh." The blood rushed from Piper's face, cold washing through her at how close to the truth Jo was.

Jo came closer, breaking the unspoken no-touching-allowed rule of air between them. She laid gentle fingers on Jo's forearm. "Piper, I get the mainstream audiences don't know, and I'm guessing from your reaction you don't want them to, which is fine. But I mean…" She looked up at Piper beneath half-lidded eyes. "But family always knows each other, don't you think?"

"Oh." Piper breathed again, only just now realizing she had stopped moving to the music. Her mouth felt as though she hadn't had a drink in years. "It was different when we started."

"I suppose so." Jo's fingers danced slowly over Piper's forearm to the inside of her elbow. "But does that mean we can't have fun?"

Piper really needed a drink. "It's probably not a good idea, especially if Siena ends up representing you. Bunny and I don't mix business and pleasure."

"Do you think Siena will?" Jo's voice came out a little higher, the sultry quality of mere seconds earlier gone.

"Maybe. It's Siena's decision. She just asked us for our opinion. And while it would be fun, I don't do friends with benefits." Piper shivered, but she had been thinking about just that. She'd been wanting to get sideways with Jo already, but she pulled back.

"We aren't friends," Jo replied, that seductive, sultry quality back.

"But we could be." Piper turned to see Bea and Bunny leaning over the table toward each other, heated words being exchanged. But there was something in the way Bunny's shoulders sat that created a strange but intriguing thought to cross Piper's mind. Under her breath, she muttered, "Four minutes."

"What?" Jo asked, a chuckle of confusion on her lips.

"Once you get to know Bunny, the name makes sense."

"Really?" Jo's face twisted in complete disbelief.

"Oh yeah, she's the fucking Energizer Bunny. She just keeps going and going and going. What I wouldn't give to have a break every now and then without having to fight for it. She'd work instead of sleep if given the chance." It hadn't exactly been what Piper had meant, but it was a good secondary reason for Bunny's name.

"Oh Bea is exactly the same." Jo chuckled and shook her head slightly. "I keep joking to her about needing to get laid more often, or to at least get a hobby. Just anything so that maybe I can go back to the dance studio for one hour a week."

"Really?" Piper's mind sparked, and the intriguing idea took flight.

"I'm not sure I like that look."

"Do you like *that* look?" Piper nodded over to where Bea and Bunny leaned even farther over the table. She wouldn't say it out loud, but she needed Jo to see what she saw.

"I think I need another drink." Jo grabbed Piper's hand and led her off the dance floor in the opposite direction from where Bea and Bunny sat talking.

Piper walked closely behind Jo, having been given no choice as Jo kept a firm grip on her hand.

"Careful, there's a lip." Jo looked back as she spoke.

Despite the warning, Piper still managed to stumble over her feet as she reached the edge of the dance floor. If the movement of Jo's shoulders was any indicator, then Jo chuckled at Piper's new found clumsiness.

They kept their own council as they ordered drinks at the bar and went in search of a place to drink and talk.

"All right." Jo smiled at the men who shuffled away from the tall table as they approached.

There were no chairs, but Piper didn't mind. Leaning on the tabletop with both forearms took enough weight from her feet. Jo pinned her with a serious look, but the play of the smile at her lips told Piper that something else was going on.

"Bunny and Bea didn't seem to just be fighting." Jo looked

at Piper as though anticipating an answer to a question Piper hadn't entirely asked.

Piper waited, but it didn't take long before Jo had enough of the silence.

"I mean…" Jo laughed, and Piper melted a little. "Tell me if I'm wrong, but I sensed there was definitely something more there."

"You aren't wrong." The words were out of Piper's mouth before she knew it, and dread washed over her. "But Bunny isn't out."

"I know." Jo glanced at the pair again, sobering slightly. "I did my research on you two before I contacted Siena. I wanted to know exactly how she handles tough situations. Bunny refuses to talk about it. She gets up and walks out on interviews if they deviate from the music to her personal life. Siena then plays crowd control, as do you."

Piper was impressed at Jo's knowledge, even if the knowledge seemed entirely focused on the other half of her music partnership. "Go on."

Jo leaned forward, and her eyes gleamed with anticipation. Piper had to admit, Jo was far more clued in than she had previously given the woman credit for. It didn't seem fair that she should be so beautiful, a pretty good musician, and smart as well.

"I think it's time for those two to discover all the things they've been missing out on while they've been working us to the bone." Jo lifted her drink to her lips again.

"And this?" Piper lidded her eyes as she looked over at Jo. She waved two fingers suggestively between the two of them. They needed ground rules if they were going to do any kind of work together—professional or personal.

Jo spluttered some of her drink on the table and focused on cleaning it up with one of the napkins she'd shoved in her pocket at the bar. "I think this plan is more important than some fun we might have."

Piper took a deep breath and let it out. She had gotten along with Jo so easily, their energies meshed perfectly. She didn't want to lose that with her usual lack of articulation when a woman seemed a little too interested too quickly. "It can never be anything more than just a little flirting and fun. I like you, Jo, and I'd really like to be your friend. It's hard to always be around such calm energy."

"I know exactly what you mean." Jo winked, a grin playing at her lips. Did this woman ever not smile? Or was it just her pure sunshine energy pushing through every doubt in Piper's mind?

Piper closed her eyes and sighed with relief. "So, we get the two of them together."

"I think we need to do more than that."

"Oh really?" Piper could have kicked herself as the words purred out sultry and low.

"I think we get them to fall in love."

"Love?" Piper's voice squeaked, and she wondered what on earth was happening to her.

"Definitely." Jo finished the last of her drink and pushed herself back from the table. "But if we don't head back soon, Bea just might send out a search party."

Piper downed the last of her own drink and followed Jo. They weren't holding hands this time, so Piper had the privilege of getting to watch the way Jo sashayed her way through the crowds.

"What the hell?" Jo jerked with a start.

Piper had been so caught up in watching Jo's ass that she didn't realize Jo had stopped walking until she ran directly into her from behind.

"Sorry." Piper stepped back.

Jo turned around and searched for something over Piper's head.

"Where are they?"

"What?" Piper asked, looking around at Jo and seeing the empty table. "Well, maybe we don't have to focus on love after all."

"What do you mean?" Jo looked at Piper, a vertical line appearing between her eyebrows as confusion covered her face.

"Maybe they realized they were sparking for each other and went off to have a quickie in the dressing room."

Jo laughed boisterously as she shook her head. "Definitely not. Bea is not a one-night stand kind of person."

"Oh." Piper's hope deflated. Jo's plan would never work then, because Bunny didn't do love. She didn't do relationships. She didn't do anything except love them and leave them.

"No, it's going to have to be love."

"Great." Piper forced some enthusiasm in her voice. "Who doesn't love love?"

What she wouldn't give for another drink right now.

bea

"I worry about her." Bea finished her drink and sighed, looking out at her sister on the dance floor.

"It's good to worry about your business partner."

Bea shook her head, looking back to Bunny. "Not about that. I worry about her ability to hold up against the demands on the industry."

"I'm not sure I understand." Bunny looked around the room, as if scouting to see if someone was there.

"I'm worried she'll be eaten alive because she wants everyone to like her."

Bunny frowned, a deep line forming in the center of her forehead. She seemed like she was going to say something, paused, and then leaned forward, lowering her voice. "If that's the case, she needs to get out. Now. Don't look back."

Bea froze. She hadn't expected that kind of response. She'd thought Bunny would give her advice, not tell her to run in the opposite direction. "You think we should quit?"

"Being a celebrity isn't for the faint of heart. It's brutal. It will tear you apart in seconds. And if Jo is sensitive to those kinds of things, she's not built for this world."

"And I suppose you are?" Indignation rose up in Bea's chest. How dare Bunny be so judgmental about anyone? But especially Jo? Bunny didn't even know them. Thank God Siena had left, because Bea had a few choice words for Bunny, and she was about to let them fly.

"I'm not exactly soft." Bunny gave Bea a hard stare, almost a glare.

Bea swallowed, her gaze dropping to Bunny's arms, the strength in her muscles, the sharpness of her jawline. Bunny was anything but soft. Her body screamed an intensity and hardness that Bea had no hope of ever attaining. Where Bunny was toned, Bea was squishy, some would even call her fluffy. Though she hated that term. It always sent a rush of shame through her.

"No. I guess you're not. You're too arrogant to ever consider that someone else might have feelings of doubt."

"What?" Bunny jerked with a start, as if surprised by Bea's sudden change of tone.

"I see who you are now. I thought you were different, based on how you're presented in the media, but I was so very wrong." Bea pushed back her chair, prepared to stand up. "You're a jerk."

Without waiting for a response, Bea stood up and started for the back of Julianna's. She wanted to get out of there as soon as possible. Screw Bunny. Screw Siena for forcing Bunny on her. Screw the whole industry. She'd be over it by morning —hopefully—but for now, she was just pissed off. No one talked bad about her sister and got away with it.

Bea slammed her palm against the back door, shoving it open with a loud swing. It banged into the wall, a loud crack echoing through the small dressing room that shouldn't even be called that. Who was she kidding? It was a converted janitor closet, something that was supposed to make them feel good, like they were on the up and up.

But fuck that.

It was nothing more than a reminder of where they weren't.

"Don't do that."

Bea spun around, her chest heaving as she stared into Bunny's dark brown eyes. Her hair was askew as if she'd run her fingers through it in a fit of despair. Her cheeks were red but hollowed, like she was a raging bull ready for an attack.

Bea snorted and stayed still, her back to the small counter that was supposed to be for makeup. "Do what?"

Bunny stepped inside, shutting the door behind her. "Don't make meaning where there isn't any."

"You literally said we should quit."

"I said if she couldn't handle it, she should quit. I've seen far too many people fall into the pits of despair because the media and fans tore them apart." Bunny stalked forward, one step after the other, her boots silent on the carpeted floor.

"Fuck you, Bunny." Bea shook her head. This was ridiculous. "Maybe the industry has stolen your soul and you didn't even know it."

Bunny stopped just in front of her, their toes nearly touching. Bunny lowered her gaze, letting it rove all over Bea's body, consuming every inch of her in one fell swoop. Bea had never felt more exposed, more eaten alive, more turned on than she did right now. And she hated it.

"If it's stolen my soul, then you and Jo have no hope of surviving." Bunny's voice was low, dangerous. She still hadn't raised her eyes to meet Bea's gaze. She stopped, her stare directly on Bea's cleavage.

"I don't believe you," Bea whispered. As much as she wanted to, she couldn't believe that Bunny was this hardened celebrity, that she had no care in the world. Bea had seen her with Piper. She'd seen the soft looks between them, the silent communication. There was so much more to her than this—whatever this was.

"Believe it."

"No." Bea stood straight, squaring her shoulders and pushing in even more. "I refuse."

"Bea…" Her name was a curse on Bunny's lips. Or was it a warning?

"No," Bea said again, this time firmer, louder. But her entire body did what she didn't want it to do, and it listed forward. She moved up on her toes, as if begging for Bunny to just look at her again in that same saucy way she'd done before.

"I'm not soulless." Bunny's voice was almost a growl.

A shiver ran through Bea's body, her nipples hardening. She took small rapid breaths, unsure what to do or say next. They were arguing over the most futile thing, but she couldn't stop herself. She couldn't make this end. "Then prove it."

Bunny cocked her head to the side, raising her gaze to meet Bea's. "I don't think you want me to do that."

"You don't know what I want." Bea reached forward, putting her hand on Bunny's hip. Her skin was so hot through the fabric of her clothes. Bea sucked in a shuddering breath. She issued the order again. "Prove it."

Bunny's lips crashed into hers. The kiss was hot, feverish. Bea reached forward, gripping onto both of Bunny's hips just to keep herself upright while she was pushed backward until her ass hit the small counter where Jo had sat to fix her makeup for the umpteenth time only hours before. Bea stretched her hand backward, knocking off the small makeup containers. But she couldn't stop.

She parted her lips, tilted her chin up and waited for what she knew was going to happen. Bunny was going to consume her, and Bea was going to love every fucking minute of it. She scraped her hands along Bunny's back, pulling her loose tank top up and over her head to drop it onto the floor. She pulled

Bunny's face to hers, sliding her tongue along Bunny's, dueling for control of the embrace.

Bunny groaned and then growled. She rocked her hips forward, right between Bea's legs and cupped the back of her head as she plundered Bea's mouth. This felt amazing. Bea couldn't remember the last time someone had taken her so raw, the last time she'd been fucked into oblivion solely for the purpose of hot sex. There was absolutely nothing between them. There would never be anything between them. This was a pure base desire that Bea had no doubt was about to be filled.

Gasping, Bea raised her chin up while Bunny trailed kisses and small bites down her neck to the top of her chest, cupping her breast and squeezing. Bea's breath caught in her throat, and she had to double it to try and get some air into her lungs. Her entire body was ready for this. She hadn't realized how badly she'd needed it.

"Yesssssss," Bea dragged out the word, scraping her nails against the back of Bunny's scalp all the while pressing Bunny's face deeper between her breasts.

Bunny scraped her teeth along Bea's soft skin. She reached down to Bea's legs and tried to pull up the dress she wore, but it got stuck under her legs. Bunny tried again and again, growing more frustrated by the second.

"What? Too butch to figure out a dress?" Bea chuckled lightly.

"Shut up," Bunny mumbled against Bea's skin before pulling her off the counter, raising her dress and shoving her back onto it. When she emerged, she had a happy little look of satisfaction on her lips, and it was the sexiest thing Bea had ever seen. If it hadn't vanished so quickly, she might have completely melted just for that.

Bea leaned back and pulled her dress the rest of the way off. She didn't even bother to give Bunny the chance as she reached behind her and flicked the clasp of her bra. Bunny's gaze immediately locked on Bea's chest, her eyes wide, her tongue swiping across her lips.

"Do something about that already, will you?" Bea said, her tone lighter than she'd intended, but it got Bunny's attention.

Bunny grumbled, but she didn't stop. She leaned in and immediately covered one of Bea's nipples with her mouth. Gasping, Bea cupped the back of Bunny's head again, not willing to let any of this get the better of her. She was going to take as much advantage of this situation as possible.

"God, get this thing off." Bea plucked at the sports bra, already hating it. She wanted to see what was underneath. She wanted Bunny to be as exposed as she was.

Laughing, Bunny straightened her back and moved up to look square in Bea's eyes. Their lips were almost touching. "Can't decide if you want me or for me to have you."

"It's both," Bea answered smoothly.

"Oh, I like a woman who knows what she wants." Bunny chuckled as she hooked her thumbs under her sports bra and pulled it off swiftly. Her nipples were large, hard nubs that Bea wanted nothing more than to taste.

Standing up, Bea moved in closer and pressed her palm delicately to Bunny's chest. She flicked her thumb over Bunny's nipple, waiting to see exactly what kind of reaction she would get. Bunny rocked her hips forward, her hand coming up to press against Bea's back.

"Let me eat you," Bunny murmured.

"And then what?" Bea asked, her tone much softer than before.

"I don't care, just let me taste you." Bunny's eyes were all over Bea's body. It was like Bea's extra weight, the extra curves a lot of people tried to play it off as, didn't matter one bit.

Bea's heart rate picked up again. Bunny actually wanted her. This wasn't some kind of pity fuck. They didn't even have time to get to that level. This was genuine lust. Heat hit her cheeks hard, her entire body temperature rising as something that felt so similar to embarrassment hit her, but it wasn't that. It was something akin to belief. Belief that someone could actually like her the way she was, belief that she was attractive, belief that maybe—just maybe—someone might actually meet her standards.

Or at least someone was close to it in such a short period of time.

"Bea?" Bunny asked everything again with only the sound of her name.

"Yes." Bea gave her answer in one fell swoop. She pushed off her shoes, kicking them out of the way, and pulled off her thong, dropping it somewhere she couldn't see.

Bunny's mouth was on hers again, pushing her back until she was sitting on the counter one more time. Bunny skimmed her hands down Bea's body. She reached Bea's thighs and pushed them apart gently.

Anticipation built in Bea's chest, tightening it. She was so wet. She knew it. As soon as Bunny's mouth was on her, she would fall apart in Bunny's skillful hands. And they would be skillful. She gave every sign that she knew what she was doing, despite the fact they'd basically denied it every second they'd known each other, which had been all of an hour at that point.

God, she couldn't believe she was doing this.

It was so out of character for her.

She was the one who always held everything in close. She was the one who took years to warm up in a relationship. It was why she'd all but given up on them. No one was good enough. No one could get past her defenses. So why didn't she have them up now?

Bea put her hand behind her and pushed her butt to the edge of the counter. She bit her lip when Bunny got down on her knees and stared at her. She studied her. Bea shivered, more wetness pooling between her legs as she waited—desperately—for Bunny to finally touch her.

"Do it already," Bea demanded.

"You're so beautiful," Bunny mumbled as she leaned in and pressed delicate kisses along Bea's inner thighs, right along her stretch marks.

Bea moaned. She reached for Bunny's hair, threading her fingers into the silky strands and tightening her grasp. Trying her best, she moved Bunny closer to her. She wanted Bunny's face right against her, her tongue inside her. Bea didn't want to wait any longer.

"Bunny." Her name was a whine. "Stop hesitating."

Bunny laughed, the vibrations from her voice shocking through Bea's system because her mouth was suddenly on Bea's pussy. Gasping, Bea clenched. She shut her eyes tight, she doubled down on her grasp in Bunny's hair, she tugged hard.

Her head spun. Nothing had felt this good in such a long time. Bea spread her legs even more. Bunny put her hands under Bea's thighs and raised them up to get a better—deeper—angle. Bea couldn't keep track of what was going on. It was like she was going to explode already. Bunny was everywhere, her heady scent mixing with Bea's own arousal, blending with the sweat and stale scent of the room they were in.

"So good," Bea mumbled, tossing her head back and letting herself fall fully into the moment.

This was amazing. She pushed as best as she could to be as close as possible to Bunny's mouth. "More."

Bunny sucked her. She pulled back before pushing in again. Over and over, Bunny teased her into oblivion. Bea cried out, digging her nails too hard into Bunny's scalp, but not once did Bunny complain. In fact, she continued to kiss and suck and taste until Bea finally succumbed to her orgasm, her voice echoing through the small room as pleasure consumed her. And even then, Bunny didn't move. She eased Bea down with soft touches, gentle kisses, tender moments.

But it was too sweet.

Bea bit her tongue, trying to bring herself back to reality. She couldn't fantasize about Bunny. She couldn't let herself fall into what they both knew wasn't reality. Bunny was self-obsessed, opinionated, rude, and she'd been a jerk to Jo. That was what Bea had to focus on. Sex was one thing, but this wasn't Bunny being caring in any capacity.

"Pull your pants down," Bea ordered.

Bunny stepped back, an eyebrow raised in curiosity. "Not done with me yet?"

"I think I'll keep you around for a little bit longer."

Bea watched with rapt attention as Bunny reached for her belt buckle and pulled it loose, as her thin fingers popped the button and pulled down the zipper. As she shimmied her pants down her hips. Using the back of her heel, Bea pulled Bunny toward her, immediately putting her hand between Bunny's legs and cupping her.

"You're as wet as I am."

"Not quite," Bunny said through clenched teeth. "But I'll get there."

"How do you like it?" Bea asked, waiting for Bunny's next move before she did anything else.

"Two fingers and use the heel of your palm on my clit." Bunny gave Bea a direct stare.

Nothing sexier than a woman who knew exactly what she wanted. Bea eyed her firmly as she pulled her hand away from Bunny's body, sliding two fingers into her mouth and coating them generously with her saliva. It was the best she had. She didn't think she'd be having a one-night stand in here. That had never been a thought that entered her mind.

"Fuck, you still smell good," Bunny said, sliding her thumb along her lips. "Taste even better."

Almost impossibly, Bea was ready to go again. It sucked that they were still at Julianna's. that they weren't someplace where they could do this on repeat. Without waiting, Bea did exactly what Bunny had asked. She rapidly moved her fingers in, sliding them back and forth while pressing the heel of her palm hard against Bunny before pulling out and doing it again. Bunny pulled Bea's face toward her.

Parting her lips expectantly, Bea kissed Bunny's small pert breasts. She teased her tongue in a circle around Bunny's nipple. She sucked when she moved her fingers in again. She pulled away in the same rhythmic motion as her fingers before moving in again onto Bunny's other nipple.

This was glorious. Sex for pure and simple pleasure. She should have tried this sooner. Then again, no one had ever come close to pushing Bea to this kind of moment before now. Not that she'd tell Bunny that. It'd probably go to her head and inflate her ego even more than it already had.

God, what if she thinks I'm some stupid groupie?

Fuck. What if she likes fucking groupies?

Bea cringed at that thought and tried to shake it from her mind. Bunny didn't strike her as someone who would fuck random women, especially women who were fans. She hadn't even admitted she liked women out loud, when it would have been so easy to say she was queer.

"Close," Bunny said through clenched teeth. She kept her grip firmly on the back of Bea's head, and Bea didn't move. She kept doing exactly what Bunny had asked her to do. She kept everything exactly how it was.

Bunny scrunched her face, her nose wrinkling, her eyes clenched tight. Her cheeks were red with arousal. She arched her back and grunted softly, reaching down suddenly to Bea's wrist and tightening her grasp. Bea tried to pull back, but Bunny kept her hand in place. Bea continued the movement, the in and swipe and out, until Bunny finally pulled her hand away.

Wiping her fingers on her thigh, Bea stayed put, the realization of everything they'd just done washing her with cold disgust. How could she have given in to this? How could she have not cared enough about herself to allow Bunny to touch her? Bunny would never be good enough for her. No one was.

That was a hard lesson she'd learned early on in her life. Her standards were too high for anyone to reach them. Perfection was impossible. Bea held her breath tight in her chest as shame ate at her again. Bunny didn't move in for a kiss. She didn't offer any soft touches or kind words.

Instead, they stared awkwardly at each other. Neither of them knew what to do next.

"I guess we should get back out there," Bunny finally said, shifting her underwear and pants back up her hips. "They're probably wondering where we went off to."

Bea clenched her jaw, the muscles working hard before she shook her head.

What had she been expecting anyway?

She hopped off the edge of the counter and found her thong. Bunny got dressed at the same time, waiting for Bea to finish. When Bea smoothed down her dress and glanced in the mirror to look at her hair and makeup, she sighed. There was no way she was going to be able to fix that. She'd just have to make it look as good as she could.

She futzed with her hair, making it look purposely messy and then swiped her fingers around her mouth to clean up her lipstick. When she turned back around, she was annoyed that Bunny was still there. She was just about to push past her when Bunny's hand on her shoulder stopped her.

"Tell Jo that what the world says doesn't matter. So long as they buy your music, so long as your fans are loyal, people can talk shit all they want. What matters is that she believes in who she is with everything she has."

Bea drew in a shuddering breath, knocked back by the honesty in those words. "I will."

"And when she begins to doubt it…" Bunny trailed off, turning toward the door as if someone was coming. She quieted her tone even more, whispering, "Tell her to rely on you to tell her nothing but the truth, and then you give her exactly what you promised—the truth."

Bunny moved in swiftly, pressing their lips together in a sweet, tender kiss. Bea held on, lingering in the moment. She tilted back and gripped onto Bunny's sides, holding as still as she could.

"Same goes for you," Bunny added in between kisses.

Bea breathed out hope.

"Don't let them tell you anything you don't want to hear. Ignore it." Bunny kissed her again. "Because I've seen all of you. And you're stunning."

This was Bea's melting point. Her knees went weak, and she had to grip onto Bunny in order to keep herself upright. Bunny pulled away, pursing her lips and stepping back.

"Welcome to the real world, Bea."

Bunny walked out of the room, her hands shoved into her pockets. Bea was speechless. What the hell had just happened?

bunny

"You've got to be kidding me, right?" Bunny pinched the bridge of her nose. It had been a whole week since they'd met Bea and Jo at Julianna's, and Bunny couldn't stop thinking about Bea.

"Oh come on," Piper pleaded for the third time. Piper had been talking up Bea and Jo since that night, which wasn't helping Bunny forget it. "It'll be fun."

"Singing into badly wired microphones along with tinny recorded music will be fun?" Bunny wasn't convinced as she wiped the stage makeup from her face. It was always the first thing she did. No matter how much her clothes stuck to her skin or her body ached. After every set, she went directly to the makeup counter and removed the cloying shit from her face.

When they first started, she had put her foot down and insisted she would never wear makeup on the stage. But then the first questions and hushed whispers about her and Piper's sexuality started floating around, and she'd changed her mind real quick.

After a breakdown, she had given in to the stage makeup. It had been met with jumping, clapping, and a high pitched squeal from Piper. Bunny had also started talking about her workout routines and her running in interviews when the inevitable questions came up about what she does during her down time.

"Earth to Bunny!" Piper called from the other side of the dressing room where she hung up the new bold diagonal stripe shirt, ready for dry cleaning. She loved to wear it on stage, and Bunny couldn't deny how she wished she could get away with something similar. It reminded her of Iggy Stardust. Which was one of many reasons Bunny wouldn't. She didn't entirely enjoy being on stage with Piper wearing it, but she knew Piper didn't care as much about the rumors or about the things the press printed in just about a damn three month rotation.

The name Jamie Kettlehouse was a regular curse in Bunny's life.

"What?" Bunny removed the last of the makeup and turned around to face Piper.

"I want to go. Please come with me? We need to have more fun together. It's been all work lately." Piper might as well have lowered her bottom lip and let it quiver a little. But even knowing Piper's tricks, Bunny rolled her eyes and knew she would give in eventually. Right now, she was too tired to go another three rounds before she got there.

"Fine."

"Really?"

Bunny should have expected the jumping, the clapping, and the squealing. When Piper wrapped her in her arms and tried to get Bunny to jump right along, Bunny couldn't help but let the smile rest on her lips. But she refused to become a woo-girl.

"We're going to have a fantastic time."

"Sure." Bunny smiled, hoping Piper didn't see Bunny's plans for getting cramps or food poisoning less than an hour into the karaoke debacle.

It didn't take them long to get changed and ready. Piper was in charge of getting them there, which was such a relief. Bunny didn't have the brain power for it. The place was small, and the narrow staircase they walked up gave Bunny very little hope for the type of business they would find at the top. Then again, there would likely be fewer people there, which would be perfect for hiding her face in the crowd. She couldn't roll her eyes more at that.

But Bunny was pleasantly surprised when Piper opened the door to a well-lit open area.

"This is nice." Piper seemed surprised.

"Wait. Didn't you say you'd been here before?" Bunny didn't like the feeling that swirled in the pit of her stomach.

"No. I didn't say that. I said let's do karaoke. Oh look who's here! What a nice surprise!" Piper ignored Bunny's jaw drop as she waved her hand and headed over to a table where Bea and Jo sat.

Fuck!

Bunny's stomach twisted hard, and her heart beat just a little too fast for her liking. She had given Siena her impression of the band and had washed her hands of thinking about them again. Except of course for the memory of how she'd sucked Bea's clit until she came. Even now, the thought sent a shiver of arousal through Bunny. She wouldn't mind a round two.

"Hey, what are you two big shots doing here?" Jo jumped up and a dusting of pink covered her smooth alabaster skin. She wrapped her arms around Piper's neck in a quick hug and then started toward Bunny.

Bunny looked from Jo to Piper and back again before she accepted the quick embrace.

Right, *now* she understood.

This was for Piper, who was enamored with Jo. Of course. Now being subjected to constant talk about the sisters made perfect sense. Piper had a massive crush. They'd been through this before, and they'd get through it again. It would either form into a relationship or it wouldn't, and Bunny would be there every step of the way in support of her best friend.

"It seems like this is the night to sing for fun instead of fans." Bunny smiled at Jo before flicking a quick look over to Bea. How did she feel about all this? Was she as in the dark as Bunny had been just moments before? Or had she known the entire time?

Bea's face was hard, her nostrils flaring just a little.

Well, that confirmed it. Bea had been led here on false pretenses as well.

"We've booked a booth, and we're just waiting for it to be free," Bea supplied, not standing up from the table.

"We have to make a reservation?" Piper really needed to work on her acting skills if she thought for one moment Bunny was buying the uh-oh moment she was trying out.

"You do!" Jo's acting was no better. "But that's okay, you can join us."

"What?" Bea and Bunny asked at the same time, turning away from studiously not looking at each other to stare at Jo.

"We don't mind, do we, Bea?" Jo stopped only long enough to take a half-breath before barreling on before Bea could butt in. "Plus, you never know what tips you might get from singing with the great Bunny and Piper."

Bunny looked at Bea and was relieved to see she noticed Jo's tactics as well. There was no denying that they were being railroaded into this. Bunny crossed her arms, flexing her muscles as she turned a glare onto Jo.

"You've got a good angle there, kid." Bunny rocked back and forth from heel to toe, succumbing to the fact that this was what her evening was going to look like. Piper would hear all about it as soon as they left. Which would be far sooner than the hour. Bunny was going to get cramps in the next fifteen minutes, regardless of whether they started singing together or not.

"Have to think about the business, don't I? Bea taught me that." Jo shrugged, and Bunny couldn't help but remember Piper at the same age. Always hungry for what to learn next. It was as though the two of them knew what the world thought of them with their slim bodies, and perfect hair and makeup and refused to let themselves be lulled into skating by on those things. They'd forced their way to where they were today, and it had been hard-ass work to get it.

"That's perfect. Thanks, Jo." Piper smiled, and Bunny felt vindicated in her first thoughts about Piper's motivations for karaoke tonight.

"We need to go let them know we'll need some more microphones." Jo threaded her arm through Piper's and started to walk toward what looked like a bar, but it didn't have alcohol. Instead it had sound equipment, mostly cheap stuff that was easily replaceable. "You should have a seat, Bunny, we might be a while."

"Sure, sure." Bunny pulled out the seat across from Bea and plopped her ass in it, determined that the next time she stood up, she would be leaving this hellish idea in the dust. "Take all the time you ladies need."

Without a backward look, the two of them hurried off. Bunny wouldn't have been surprised if they broke out into a gleeful skip.

"Why do you keep insisting she has an angle?" Bea's voice was low and dangerous.

Bunny shuffled in her chair, taking her gaze from Jo and Piper's shrinking forms and landing directly in the stormy blue seas of Bea's eyes. "It's not a bad thing. She's a clever kid. Why shouldn't she be thinking about getting some tips when she's managed to get us here to spend some one-on-one time with you both?"

Bea shook her head forcefully enough that the loose tie holding back the dark blonde locks let a few strands fly free. "So I suppose that's why you think she set this whole thing up?"

"Actually, no." Bunny dragged her chair a little closer so they could talk quieter. She didn't need anyone else in this room overhearing what she was about to say. "I think they both set this up because they wanted an excuse to spend more time together."

"What do you mean?" Bea's eyes narrowed on Bunny's, and for a moment, Bunny wondered if the woman had X-ray vision.

"Piper likes Jo, a lot. Believe me when I say I haven't had an hour without your name and Jo's name being mentioned in the last seven days, and I'm sick of it already. But coming here tonight, I get the sense that the feeling just might be mutual." Bunny hoped she wouldn't catch one of Bea's tirades. Though to be honest, the last time hadn't exactly led to an unfortunate or regrettable evening.

"Really? I thought Piper was straight." Bea's face lit up, and she immediately looked over at her sister.

Oh how Bunny wished she had never seen Bea's smile and eyes so bright and alive. They suited her all right. So much so that heat pooled between Bunny's legs and thoughts of dropping between Bea's legs popped right back up into her brain.

"That doesn't bother you?"

"No, not at all." Bea's eyes were so beautiful. Bunny wanted to pull her gaze away, but she couldn't, no matter how hard she tried. To be fair, she hadn't really been trying all that hard. She'd much rather look at Bea than Piper.

"And you want me to think you don't have an angle?" Bunny asked.

"What?" Bea's smile disappeared, and Bunny breathed a sigh

of relief, which didn't last long. She realized Bea's hard cold edges were just as sexy as the sweet loving big sister. And the combination of the two did things to her insides that she'd long thought dead.

"You're happy for your baby sister to hook up with Piper?" Bunny asked, needing clarification.

"No." Bea shook her head, and Bunny wondered what the hell was going on? Were they even having the same conversation? "I don't want her to hook up with anyone, not even Piper. But she needs to see that people like her for exactly who she is."

"Ah." Bunny nodded with understanding. "You listened to what I said after… after the other night."

"I'm not stupid, Bunny," Bea said. The severe hardness on her face softened just enough for Bunny to remember the feel of those lips on her skin. "And I'm not cynical enough to believe everyone has some hidden angle, but I'm not going to just ignore good advice when I get it."

"Angles don't have to be hidden." Bunny was certain she hadn't said hidden. Why couldn't she just shut up sometimes? And when those blue eyes focused on her, she couldn't be entirely certain of each word she had said. Words left her brain, replaced with the hot arousal she hadn't been able to shake.

"Of course they do. The whole implication of an angle is some hidden nefarious agenda."

Bunny laughed hard, and tried to tear her gaze from Bea so that she wouldn't see her true reaction. But she couldn't move away. "Who's the cynical one now?"

"Look." Bea closed her eyes, took a deep breath, and then opened them again. The storm within had definitely calmed, but Bunny sensed very little wind would rile it up once more. "I love my sister, but she doesn't always see the value of who she is over what she can do for someone. If Piper likes her for her, then I'm willing to do my best not to go ten rounds every time we get together for Jo's sake."

"How very magnanimous of you." Bunny would have snorted, but she sensed that might set Bea off on another tirade.

"If you somehow twist this into some other bullshit angle, I'll take the whole thing off the table now."

Bunny laughed. Despite herself, she really did find Bea a fascinating woman and not just a sexy beautiful one-night stand. Bunny always was a sucker for an icy woman who knew exactly who she was and what she wanted. "I wouldn't dream of it."

"Good." Bea nodded as though that were the full stop at the end of their newfound arrangement.

"All right, well I'm going to go to the bathroom before the two of them return, and we can start singing other people's songs in small-ass booths." Since when had she decided to stay? Bunny would figure that one out later.

"Ah, there's the cynicism I've come to know." Bea pointed at Bunny and waggled her finger back and forth.

Bunny shoved her hands in her pockets, shrugged her shoulders, and followed the signs toward the bathroom. She didn't need to dip her toe any deeper into that well of disaster.

Turning the corner to hopefully the last hallway leading to the bathroom, Bunny stopped and stared.

Jo's back was pressed against the wall, pinned there by none other than Piper. Piper's hands were curled into Jo's hair, and their lips moved against each other's. Bunny failed to see exactly where one of them stopped and the other started.

She grinned wildly and quietly stepped back around the corner to give them their peace. She could hold back the realization a bit longer.

"That was quick," Bea said as Bunny sat back down.

"Was a long line. I didn't want to wait." Bunny wasn't sure

why she didn't just tell Bea what she had witnessed, but she supposed if they weren't even bothering to go into the bathroom before making out, it wouldn't be long until Bea came across them the same way Bunny had.

Or someone else did.

"You're smiling," Bea accused from across the table.

"I do actually do that, quite regularly."

"Want to share?"

If someone else did figure them out, that could cause a lot of issues for the Bunny and Piper brand. They had to be more discreet, and for that to happen, Bea and Bunny were going to have to work together. Bunny looked Bea directly in the eyes, making her point clear. "I was just thinking how I am totally up for civility between us to help Jo and Piper spend a little more time together."

"Good," Bea said, but her look said she knew Bunny wasn't telling her everything.

But Bea didn't need to know all the things that had crossed Bunny's mind. Including some personal reasons to encourage Jo and Piper to spend more time together. And definitely not including the fact that she had yet to forget Bea's tangy flavor.

Piper would owe her later.

And maybe—just maybe—this would balance out the whole sister-in-law fiasco.

bea

Bea wrung her hands together, her stomach almost in tighter knots than it had been two weeks ago when Siena had come to watch them play. They'd played phone tag for the better part of a week, and finally had a meeting set up. Bea glanced over her shoulder to check on Jo in the elevator.

Keeping her sister in line for this conversation was going to be a task, but Bea was prepared.

They walked into Siena's office and were immediately greeted by an assistant who told them to sit down and wait. Bea shifted a glance to Jo, and sat precariously on the edge of a comfy lounge chair. Jo sat down next to her, clearly resisting the urge to bounce her feet on the ground.

"Do you think this is where Bunny and Piper first met Siena? Or has she found new digs since then?" Jo couldn't stop looking around the room.

Bea winced, but since the assistant hadn't come back into the room yet, she didn't mind it too much. "My guess is she's moved up in the world right along with them."

Jo grinned and leaned in closer. "I can't believe we're here."

"Spoiler alert," Bea said with a conspiratorial look. "I can't either."

Laughing, Jo rubbed her palms over her knees. It was her nervous tic. Bea had no doubt that she wasn't the only one worried about this entire negotiation. Though Siena hadn't said it was going to be that. She'd just said she wanted to meet with them to talk. After everything that had happened at Julianna's, had Bunny told Siena about it? Had she told Siena not to hire them?

The worry slipped its way through her, and it was impossible to shove it all down and lock it in a box never to see the light of day. That would be too damn easy, wouldn't it?

"Do you think they'd ever do a show with us?"

"What?" Bea frowned and looked over at Jo.

"Bunny and Piper."

"Why would they want to do that?"

"We could be their opener or something."

Bea sighed heavily. Jo's crush on Piper was going too far. Bea rubbed her hands together, looking around the pristine office again. It was well decorated, minimalistic but still nice. If she had an office, this is what she'd want it to look like. Instead, she did most of their business off her kitchen table, which was shoved into the corner of her studio apartment because that was all she could afford at the moment.

"I don't know. Karaoke was fun, wasn't it?"

"Sure." Bea winced. She hadn't really enjoyed the night. It had been tense with Bunny there. But she'd endured it for Jo's sake and that was enough. She and Bunny had agreed to be civil, and that was all she could ask for.

"Have you thought about dating again?"

Bea choked. She spluttered and pounded her hand against her fist. "I'm sorry. But what?"

"Have you thought about dating again?" Jo repeated. "I know after Genevieve that you wanted to take a break—a well deserved break, I might add—but that was over a year ago. Aren't you ready to get back on the wagon?"

"Back in the saddle," Bea corrected, staring at the wall. How would she explain this in a way that Jo could understand, because clearly it hadn't sunk in before. "I don't want to date again."

"But you can't be celibate for your entire life. I know you. You don't want that."

"No, I don't want that." Bea lowered her voice, hoping that the conversation wasn't carrying down the hallway for Siena or her assistant to hear. "This really isn't the appropriate place to talk about this."

"I know, but you never want to talk about it."

"Why would I?" Her voice had a bite to it. Bea cringed and tried to backtrack, knowing that Jo would take offense to her tone and it would cause more rifts between them. More than they needed going into this conversation with Siena. "Look, this really isn't the right time or place to have this discussion."

"But don't you dream about it? Don't you dream about what might happen if you were to find love again?"

Bea snorted out a laugh and closed her eyes in pain. "I didn't love Genevieve."

Was that truly the first time she'd said that out loud to Jo?

"Are you serious?"

"Bea! Jo!" Siena appeared in the lobby, a grin on her lips and her hands clasped in front of her like she was going to clap at them.

How much had she heard?

"Siena." Bea immediately plastered on her business face, shot Jo a *shut up* look and stood up with her hand outstretched. They shook, and Bea immediately stepped to the side so Jo could also join in on the conversation.

"Come on in." Siena led the way to her office.

They were all seated in chairs to the side of Siena's desk, a small table between them. Bea had to work really hard to tame her nerves so that she could make reasonable conversation.

Once they were settled, with water bottles for each of them, Siena gave them a patented smile. "I'm glad I was able to speak with you today."

"We're glad we could meet as well," Bea said, taking over their side of the conversation.

"We'd love to work with you," Jo chimed in loudly. A definite sign that she was nervous.

Bea shot her sister a sharp look. "Jo's not wrong, we would love to see if we could work with you. But we understand there's a lot of conversation that needs to happen first."

"Right, there is." Siena's smile faltered. "Your show the other week was good. I'm surprised you're not represented by anyone already."

Bea shrugged slightly. "We've worked with several publicists and production managers in the last few years. None of them worked out."

"Why's that?" Siena twisted the cap off her bottle and took a long sip.

"A number of reasons." Bea sighed. "I'm sorry, but I have to ask because it's been weighing on me. How's your daughter?"

"My daughter?" Siena halted, the bottle of water right in front of her lips.

"She broke her arm?" Surely, Bea was remembering that correctly. She hadn't been able to get the thought out of her mind. Siena had looked so worried that night.

"Oh! Yes." Siena put her water bottle down. "She fell out of her bunk bed. My ex insisted that bunk beds were the only beds that would fit in the room, and of course, since Harley is older, she'd have to be on the top."

"So you have two kids?"

Siena waved her hand. "Only Harley. She's fine. She has a

bright pink cast that her friends have drawn all over, and she's absolutely loving the attention. She hates the fact that she's not allowed to do any writing at school, though. I'm pretty sure she'll figure a way around that one by the end of the week."

"Good." Bea let out a breath of relief. "I was worried it was more serious than that."

"No, just typical kid clumsiness, I suppose. At least that's what my ex keeps telling me." Siena glanced from Bea to Jo and back again. "I'm surprised you remembered."

"I'm a big sister to quite a few siblings. I think the worry comes naturally."

"Ah." Siena smiled, genuinely. "Well, thank you for asking."

"No problem. I didn't mean to disrupt our conversation."

"No, don't worry about it. You were saying that you've worked with several managers."

"Yeah. We have. None of them worked long term, and right now we're without representation." Bea squared her shoulders. Just that small interlude of the personal had given her enough strength to find her center and continue this conversation in a manner that would get them somewhere.

"What didn't work out with them exactly?"

This was where honesty could either work in their favor or not, and Bea had a strong suspicion with Siena that it would work for them. She'd told Jo as much when she'd initially brought Siena to Jo's attention.

"Most wanted us to tone down our queerness."

Siena coughed. "I'm sorry, what?"

"They said we were too gay."

Siena's jaw dropped. She focused her gaze on Bea, her head shaking slightly before looking at Jo. "Is she serious?"

"Unfortunately. The conversation always centered around one of us could be gay, the other one couldn't, or we could be out, but they didn't want it anywhere in our branding. And they really didn't want us to have any relationships that were out in the public."

"Holy shit," Siena muttered. "Talk about homophobic, especially since we live in Portland. Then again, I can't say that I haven't seen it before."

Bea nodded, folding her hands together so that Siena wouldn't see them tremble. "We'd love to work with you for that specific reason."

"Because I'm a lesbian."

"Yes."

Siena pursed her lips. "There are other queer production managers out there."

"You also represent Bunny and Piper," Jo chimed in again.

Bea really should have prepped her better for this conversation. While she wasn't saying anything outrageous, this conversation could go so much smoother in some ways than it was.

"I do represent them." Siena slowed down her speaking pace. "Which means that most of my time is spent with them."

"We won't be as busy as them," Jo said.

"But you hope to be, eventually, I assume."

"Yes," Bea answered so Jo wouldn't say anything else that might get them into deeper water. "Yes, we want to grow our brand and our business."

"And what plans do you have in place for that already?"

"We're booked after the New Year every weekend until April. And we're working on writing a new album so we can record it in late spring." Bea folded her hands together more sharply. Her anxiety was rearing its ugly head again.

"You've booked those on your own?"

"Yes." Bea had done a lot of the leg work. Julianna's had asked them back at least monthly, and she'd gladly accepted the booking. "But we're starting to reach beyond what I can do."

Siena nodded. "I've seen the numbers that you sent me."

Bea shifted a glance to Jo. Had she done that when she'd invited Siena to observe them? Damn Jo for that. Sometimes she was so much better at this than Bea gave her credit for.

"Bunny and Piper did speak highly of you."

"Did they?" Bea asked, trying not to make it sound like she was hinging more than necessary on that question.

"Yes." Siena sucked in a sharp breath. "I'm not willing to sign a full contract with you just yet. I want to make sure that we work well together before that happens. I don't do short term commitments. If we're in this together, then we're in it for the long haul."

That was exactly what Bea had wanted to hear.

"So I have a proposal for you." Siena stood up and walked to her desk, snagging a manilla folder and setting it on the small table before she sat back down. "There's a charity event that I've agreed to manage this year. It's a fundraiser for the Holbrook Foundation, which is a charity for single mothers. It's not your typical fair, so I'm not looking for your regular music."

"You're not?" Bea frowned. How would it be any kind of test for them if they weren't singing the songs they wrote?

"No. This is a Christmas fundraiser. The traditional songs, slightly non-traditional songs, those will be expected. You can add your own twist to them, for sure. But it won't be your original music." Siena spread out some of the papers in front of them.

"So we'll have to learn all new music in order to do this?"

"You will. But like I said, traditional songs, so you should know the basics already." Siena sent Bea a comforting smile. "I'll represent you for this charity event, and we'll see how we work together from there. If that goes well, we can sign a one-year contract. If after that year, we both agree to continue to work together, we'll sign a much longer contract."

"Who else is singing at this thing?" Jo leaned forward and picked up one of the papers to read.

Bea was still too stunned to say anything.

"You'd be the first to sign officially if you agree. I was just handed the contract late last week." Siena leaned back in her chair and crossed one long leg over the other. Bea gnawed on her lip as she skimmed what she could of the papers, wanting to read them in far more detail than she had time for.

"Will we be singing with whoever else you hire?" Bea asked.

"Maybe. It depends on what the other band wants to do. Would you be open to singing with other people?"

"Yes!" Jo bounced in her chair.

Bea nodded her agreement on that because what else could she do? She'd rather stick with just Jo because she knew Jo's voice so well. It would be much harder to blend with people she didn't know.

"This sounds like fun," Jo said.

"You'd have to be available for the entire week of Christmas."

"The whole week?" Bea and Jo asked together.

Siena nodded. "This is a Christmas charity event, so yes. The concert is on the twenty-fourth."

"Indoor or outdoor?" Bea found her voice as her mind ticked over the most pertinent information they would need.

"Indoor."

"Full setup?"

"Yes." Siena's lips twitched upward in a smile. "This sounds like you're interested."

"We are!" Jo squeaked. "We're very interested."

Siena nodded slowly. "Good. I'll have Marina write up contracts if you're amenable, and we can do some negotiations from there."

"I'm assuming this is an unpaid event." Bea held her

breath. They really could use the money. Especially since it was going to take a week of their time, not that they'd booked anything for that week, but there was still time to do that. "Since it's for charity."

"It is unpaid."

That might be a dealbreaker. Bea sent Jo a look, telling her as much. But this would give them the chance to work with Siena, which could potentially make them more money in the long run. But could they handle the lack of pay for a bigger pay off in the end?

Yes.

"All right. We'll do it."

"Do you agree as well?" Siena looked directly at Jo. "When I make agreements with bands, I expect every person to sign on. One person doesn't, then I won't sign the contract."

"Absolutely!" Jo was beyond excited. "I want to work with you, Ms. Frazee."

"Good. Then it's settled. We can work on the contract over the next week." Siena stood up, and Bea and Jo followed suit. "Welcome to the family."

bunny

"Why does Siena want to see us today?" Piper asked for the third time since they got out of the car and made their way toward the restaurant.

Bunny closed her eyes and took a deep breath. She could do this. All her annoyances and frustrations had been heightened since karaoke, since being stuck in that small booth with Bea pressed up against her, all over her. At least they'd been civil.

"If I knew, I'd tell you. I'm not holding anything back from you." Which was a lie, because there was absolutely no way Bunny was going to tell Piper about what happened in the dressing room at Julianna's. Piper would have her head for it.

"Sorry. You know how I hate meetings without a purpose." Piper scrunched up her nose in apology.

"It's okay." Bunny grabbed Piper's hand for a moment as they stepped into the restaurant's lobby. She gave it a squeeze before quickly dropping it and scanning the area. The restaurant screamed high-end clientele, and Bunny felt the tension in her chest tighten further. It had been bad enough that Siena wanted to meet out, but this place told Bunny more than the phone call from Siena had.

Siena wanted them to do something she knew they would push back on. And by them, Bunny of course knew it meant her. So she'd brought them here to seduce them into whatever she was going to throw their direction.

"Siena would have made sure the place was checked out," Piper said, unconcerned as always.

"It never hurts to be careful." Bunny tried to rein in her frustration, but she'd had to skip her morning run for this breakfast meeting and her patience had already worn thin. "If you'd been careful with Haylee and let me do a check on her it would've saved us all a ton of pain."

"Jesus, Bunny." Piper stopped walking, her face crumbled and her eyes filled with unshed tears.

"Shit, I'm sorry." Bunny stopped and turned back to face Piper. "My stupid mouth ran away from me again. You know none of that was your fault. I didn't mean it that way."

"It sounded like you did."

"I'm a jerk. I'm so sorry. You're my best friend, and seeing you get hurt is kind of a trigger for me." Bunny's heart was in her throat as guilt washed through her. She'd already fucked up and it wasn't even nine in the morning yet.

"No shit." Piper laughed and ran fingers beneath her eyes checking that no tears had managed to escape.

"Siena should know better than to let me talk to anyone without a run, a workout, and some damn coffee."

"You should put it on a shirt and sell it at concerts." Piper laughed, and Bunny's breath came a little easier. She hated hurting people, but to hurt Piper made her hate herself. She never wanted to hurt her friend.

"That's actually not a bad idea." Bunny smiled, not quite up to laughing yet but much further along with Piper at her side.

She hadn't meant to bring up Haylee, but Piper's new interest in Jo had brought that unpleasant issue to the forefront of her mind again. And unpleasant was being very generous, especially with the mood she found herself in this morning.

"Bunny, Piper." Siena stood as the hostess led them toward the table where Siena had been sitting.

"Hey, Siena." Bunny forced a smile and a quick hug before sliding into a chair across from her.

"Morning." Piper lingered in their manager's embrace for a moment longer, and the two exchanged air kisses before returning to their seats, Siena across from Bunny and Piper beside her.

"Do I need to know?" Siena's voice lowered as she leaned toward the two of them, forearms resting on the white cotton tablecloth. It wasn't the first time Bunny had noticed Siena's cleavage. She didn't leer or linger. She had never been that person, but it had always amazed her how confident Siena seemed in her own skin. Bunny could fake confidence when she hid behind the music and her costume, but to willingly wear tight and revealing clothes when she wasn't being forced to was a world she didn't understand. And Piper had tried to get her to on more than one occasion.

"She didn't get time for her run this morning. So she's in an extra-pleasant mood," Piper supplied with a sarcastic lilt and a smile that teased at the line of mocking Bunny. But Bunny supposed she deserved that one, after the whole Haylee comment.

"Oh, I thought I had made this meeting late enough."

"You did." Piper chuckled a little. "But Sleeping Beauty over here snoozed the alarm a few too many times, forgetting we were meeting this morning."

"Ah." Siena sat back and flipped open the menu. "Self-inflicted then. I refuse to feel bad."

"Good." Piper chuckled, and Siena joined in.

"You both suck." Bunny smiled despite herself. They knew her too well. Nothing would get her out of her mood faster than their light teasing. They both knew where the line was, and neither dared to cross it. The trust in each other reminded Bunny of why they were there.

"Siena, if you want to ask for nude shots, you're definitely going about it the wrong way. Despite the fancy restaurant, I expect to be seduced for that." Bunny raised an eyebrow at Siena, making sure that the message was clear.

"Didn't get that one past you, huh?" Siena closed her menu and placed it on the table in front of her. "Let's order first, and we can discuss it over coffee."

Bunny could hold her own with the way things worked, but today certainly pushed her closer to cracking than it should have. She had snoozed the alarm too many times because her frustration during the night had her tossing and turning, even after she had made herself come with memories of Bea's fingers inside of her—several times.

Karaoke earlier in the week had continually played in her mind, and she had slept like shit every night since. Bea's flowery perfume filled her senses even when she wasn't around.

She had enjoyed seeing Jo and Piper flirting and laughing. Piper's energy had been off the charts since she had met Jo, and it felt so good seeing her best friend happy, not just energized.

But her own enjoyment of the evening had been marred by the strain between her and Bea. She couldn't blame Bea entirely, the awkwardness had been a two-way street. What made it worse was her own body's determination to remember the feel of Bea's fingers inside her, the pressure of her palm against her clit. And no matter how much she had drunk, she couldn't get the taste of Bea off her lips.

By the time the food arrived, Bunny was on her second cup of coffee and feeling much more like herself. The food smelled amazing, and she relaxed into her chair as she picked up her cutlery.

"I want you to perform over Christmas for me," Siena said before she put a forkful of omelet into her mouth.

Bunny had always appreciated Siena's ability to get directly to the point when the work conversation started.

"Christmas?" Piper groaned, her voice edging toward a whine. "That's the only time Bunny lets me sleep."

"I know." Siena laughed and patted Piper's hand where it rested beside her plate.

"What's important about this performance?" Bunny asked, not hating the idea immediately.

"It's a charity concert for the Holbrook Foundation."

"That's for single mothers, right?" Bunny's earlier mood had lifted entirely the moment Siena had started talking about work. This was her element.

"Yes." Siena smiled, and it didn't seem to matter how old she got or how often Siena smiled at her, Bunny still got a boost to her praise kink from it.

"All right. Tell me more."

Bunny and Piper ate while Siena laid out some of the general details. A week of their time, unpaid, seasonal songs, performance on the twenty-fourth, a collection of bands, musicians, and other entertainers would be performing.

"Who is the headliner?" Bunny asked as she finished her breakfast and sat back in her chair.

"You, of course."

"Sucking up, Siena?" Bunny raised her eyebrows.

"Nope." Siena chuckled before wiping her mouth and placing the napkin on her plate of half-eaten food.

"Piper, what do you think?" Bunny asked.

Piper shrugged as she continued to pick at her plate. Then, as if an idea hit her, Piper sat up in her chair, eyes bright and a smile stretching her face. "If we're the headliners, who else have you already got on board?"

"The idea is to keep it small and intimate, so there's only two groups that'll be playing that night, assuming you agree of course." Siena waved her hand in the air.

Piper and Siena locked gazes.

Something heavy immediately sat in the pit of Bunny's stomach. Why was Siena being so cagey all of a sudden? It wasn't normal for her, and she didn't like it.

"Who else?" Piper asked, leaning forward and snagging the drink she'd ordered.

"A band who is newer to the industry than you are. They're just starting to get their feet under them, actually, so I thought it'd be a good idea to pair them with you." Siena refused to look at Bunny when she normally would have.

That was the second red flag.

"Who is it, Siena?" Bunny asked, her fingers clenching hard around her coffee cup.

"They sing similar music to you two, so your voices should blend nicely, because Holbrook will want the whole company to sing together on stage for at least two or three numbers." Siena continued to stare at Piper, who shifted her gaze back and forth between the two of them.

"Siena," Bunny said in a warning. "Who is it?"

"Sole Sisters."

That weight in her stomach solidified and dropped, squashing whatever was in its way. Bunny's stomach lurched, and she instantly regretted having eaten all of the breakfast and that third cup of coffee.

"You've agreed to represent them." Bunny asked, but it was far closer to a statement. She didn't need to know who Siena worked with, but for some reason, this time, it hurt to know.

"Temporarily." Siena's lips thinned, and Bunny knew she

was walking on eggshells waiting for Bunny's reaction. "You remember the drill and all that."

Bunny had told Siena that the sisters needed help. They had potential, but they weren't there yet. She'd thought it would be enough to deter Siena from taking them on as clients, which would push Bunny to never have to think about Bea again.

Guess not.

"So this charity event is their test?" *With a whole lot of free publicity to help them on their way if they decide not to go with Siena.* Bunny kept that thought to herself. So much for Bea not having an angle. She wouldn't be surprised if Bea and Jo had been the ones to suggest the concert as their trial period.

"We have to do it, Bunny." Piper bounced in her seat, pulling Bunny from her thoughts. "Think about it, please."

"I don't like the idea of this." Bunny shook her head in the negative as she spoke. She didn't want to have this discussion with Siena looking on, and who knew what ears might be able to hear them.

"What are your concerns?" Siena asked, giving Bunny her full attention. She always did that, and it won her many clients and a hell of a reputation in an often untrustworthy industry.

How could Bunny articulate it? She didn't want to make things worse. Even if Bea was using Siena and the concert as a leg up in the industry, could Bunny really blame her? Everyone had their angle. Bunny and Piper had their own angles while they were starting out as well. Hell, they still had them.

"Bunny?" Piper asked.

"Is it going to be a rainbow flying event?" Bunny didn't know how else to say it. She had worked too hard to get this far. Both she and Piper had. She wasn't going to just give it all up now and be lumped in with the new fashionable young lesbians who were the hot things for the next five minutes.

"Bunny," Siena spoke with a tremble on her lips. Bunny

hated seeing that. It meant she wasn't going to like what Siena said next. "You know I have many clients who identify with a range of sexualities and genders."

"I know." Bunny already wished she had kept her concerns to herself. She was making herself out to be the biggest jerk on the planet this morning, and for some reason, she kept stepping right into the dog shit willingly.

"This isn't about waving any flags, except for supporting and raising funds for the Holbrook Foundation. Which, I'll remind you, is founded by two queer women."

"It is a good cause, I get that." Bunny had no issues with that. She would support single mothers any day. Her own single mother was the only reason she'd made it this far, and she'd died an early death because of it.

"Would it really be so bad if there were a few rainbow flags around?" Piper asked quietly.

Bunny's chest ached to see Piper so still when her face had been animated so wildly just moments earlier. She knew Piper didn't have the same level of concerns Bunny always had.

They had fought horribly about it once, and Bunny had always accused Piper of not understanding because she could be with a guy in the end. Piper had accused her of being a biphobic asshole, and in the end, Bunny had been the one to apologize. Because Piper was right. Bunny never wanted to revisit that argument again, and she understood Piper and bisexuality a lot better now. But still, the gripped fingers worried Bunny.

To be labeled as queer would alienate their fans.

"Piper," Bunny started, tasting each word on her tongue before letting it touch her lips. "I know you don't always feel the same, but we agreed we can't just come out in this industry."

"Things are changing. Hell, things have already changed."

So they were back to the argument despite Bunny wanting to avoid it.

Bunny slipped a glance to Siena, hoping for some help here even though she knew she wouldn't get any. Siena had plans and backup plans for when it did come out. But Bunny was adamant about staying in the closet for as long as humanly possible—preferably until the day she died.

"Not enough." Bunny shook her head, not having to think about her answer.

"Have you even checked?" Piper looked up and met Bunny's eyes. "I hate lying, and that's exactly what we do. We have fans who love our music, and we lie to them every single day about who we are. And for what?"

"We have a right to our private lives." Anger built in Bunny's chest, folding in on itself and tightening, although it didn't feel solely like anger. It tasted of fear.

"I know, but this is more than that. You do see that, don't you?" Piper pleaded.

"Siena." Bunny couldn't look into Piper's begging eyes any longer, so she turned to Siena. "Have things changed all that much?"

Siena pressed her lips together. It wasn't like Siena to hesitate or hold back, and Bunny knew which side of the argument would win.

"No," Siena finally said. "It is changing, but it's slow. Just the other day I heard about several agents who would only represent a queer band if they toned down the queerness."

"I'm sorry, Piper. I can't agree to it." Bunny turned to Piper, who looked down at her hands and nodded.

"I know. I just wish we didn't have to lie anymore."

"I think we all wish that." Siena took control of the conversation again, spinning it back to the entire reason they were there. "But what do you think about the charity event?"

"Piper?" Bunny asked.

"I want to do it."

"For us or for… some other reason?"

Bunny kept her eyes on Piper but saw Siena's eyebrows rise at her question.

"Can't it be both?"

"Yeah." Bunny smiled on a sigh. "I'm sure it can be."

"And you, Bunny?" Siena asked.

Bunny turned back to Siena, her chest heating with the discomfort she had known all her life. "I don't know."

"Please." Piper's voice was stronger now. Her hands no longer gripped the table, and she bounced a little in her seat.

"I promise, no rainbow waving card will be required." Siena put her hands up and out, making sure her voice was quiet and discreet so it didn't carry. Bunny always appreciated that.

Bunny closed her eyes, huffed out a small breath and squared her shoulders. She'd put Piper through the ringer that day already, first with the mention of Haylee and now this. She could do this one thing for her best friend, couldn't she?

"All right." Bunny nodded, and Piper squealed with excitement. That weight eased up a little, and Bunny couldn't stop herself from smiling. When it came to Piper, having her happy mattered more than the pain in her chest. "Put us down for the headliner."

snow, snow, snow...

bea

"I can't wait to see who we're singing with!" Jo, perky as always, vibrated with barely contained energy.

Bea's stomach was a twisted tangle of nerves. It always was whenever she had somewhere new to go or something new to do, and this was so different from anything she'd done in a long time. The stage where they were set to perform wasn't available until the week running up to the event, so they were rehearsing in a small studio on the edge of town that took Bea an hour to get to.

Commuting an hour each way was going to drive her insane.

Jo bounced around as she went, acting as if none of this was a problem. The door to the studio was opaque, the glass looking almost rippled, but it was definitely the right place. Bea had triple checked the address before they'd left that morning and insisted that Jo travel with her at least for this first day.

She could do this.

Pushing the door open, Bea told herself again that she would plaster professionalism all over herself no matter who they ended up singing with. Music filtered through the studio from the piano that was staged close to the large windows on one side of the room. The lights were bright, and the acoustics exactly what they needed.

The melody was so familiar to Bea that she almost started humming along to it already. *December Prayer* was one of her favorite Christmas songs to date. If that was going to be one of the songs they were singing for the charity event, then Bea was happy they'd agreed to it.

Jo's squeal was so loud that it echoed through the studio. She raced up and wrapped her arms around Piper's neck as she leapt into a hug. The two of them embraced while Bea's stomach sank even more.

This she should have figured out.

This she should have known.

The piano music stopped abruptly. And Bunny stood up, leaning over the edge of the upright to stare at Piper and Jo before slowly sliding her gaze to Bea. And that gaze was intense. It moved straight between Bea's legs, causing a shudder to flutter through her.

"I didn't realize you were doing the charity event, too!" Jo spun around the side of the piano and wrapped her arms around Bunny, who froze. Sharply. Stiffly. She looked over Jo's shoulder and made direct eye contact with Bea, begging her to step in and make it stop.

"Jo, leave her alone," Bea said softly. "Siena put it together. It's not too much of a surprise when you think about it."

Bunny stepped to the side and moved decidedly out of Jo's reach. Piper moved in and gave Bea a half hug. "It's good to see you again."

"Did you know?" Bea murmured, keeping her voice as quiet as possible so hopefully Bunny didn't hear.

"Yeah."

"So we're the ones in the dark this time."

Piper shrugged. "I hope you don't mind."

"Can't really complain." Well, Bea could, but she wouldn't. This was probably more to her and Jo's advantage than it was to theirs.

"I've already gone through and picked out several songs." Bunny took the binders that were stacked on top of the piano and handed one to Jo before walking directly to Bea and handing her another one. Their fingers brushed, and Bea's breath caught in her throat.

This was going to be the longest fucking month on the planet.

Bea flipped open to the first page, which was the song Bunny had been playing at the piano. It was listed for just her as a solo. In fact, each song listed exactly who was going to sing what. There were duets, trios, and a few for all four of them, but absolutely none of them had Bea and Bunny singing together.

"If you have any other song suggestions, let me know," Bunny said to the room loudly, as if she hadn't already talked this over with Piper before they arrived this morning. "We can add them in if they fit."

If they fit? Bea almost rolled her eyes, but she caught herself in time. The last thing she needed was to piss Bunny off before they'd even started. And they had agreed on civility.

"Siena said we're to fill about three hours of time. There will be a small intermission in the middle. I don't want the choreography to be too complicated. I think we could all probably use the rest from memorization."

Bea pressed her lips together tightly. She wasn't even sure what to say, but the command Bunny had over the room was astounding. Not just command, but her serious organizational ability on such short notice.

"Are you two warmed up?" Bunny asked, looking directly at Bea.

Her heart skipped a beat. She was staring into Bunny's

dark brown eyes like she could be lost in them for days. She looked so relaxed in her loose racerback and jogging pants. Her tennis shoes were scuffed as if they were well used and loved.

"Bea," Bunny nudged with a gentle tone.

"Oh, um, no. We didn't." Why did she sound so breathy?

"Right. We'll do that first then." Bunny took the open binder in Bea's hand and snapped it shut. The sound reverberated throughout the studio before she sat at the piano and started playing chords.

Piper moved to stand next to the piano and Jo followed. The two of them stood on the back side, which left Bea with a choice. She could either make them squish together even more and face Bunny for the warm-up, or she could stand directly behind Bunny.

That was definitely the wiser choice. Then she wouldn't have to see Bunny's face while she sang. Bea moved into place, keeping at least a foot of space between her and Bunny's back as Bunny's fingers played over the keys. She closed her eyes, following the warm-ups easily as they went.

"All right, Jo. Your turn. Show me what you've got." Bunny nodded toward Jo, and Bea's eyes opened wide.

Bunny's fingers pressed into the keys, delicately, one after the other with a firmness that Bea understood precisely. With every touch of Bunny's finger to a key it was as if Bunny touched her, caressed her. Bea gasped as her knees went weak, the full brunt of the memory of Bunny between her legs hitting her.

She rocked forward, her front hitting Bunny and she had to grab onto Bunny's shoulder tightly to keep herself upright. Bunny turned to look up and stopped playing immediately, swinging Bea down next to her on the piano bench, a hand on her arm and a hand on her waist.

"Are you dizzy?" Bunny asked.

Bea's ears rang with a buzz so loud that she could barely make out Bunny's voice.

"Bea," Bunny said louder. "Bea, what's wrong?"

"Just give me a minute." Bea pressed her forehead against Bunny's shoulder, trying to catch her breath. But it seemed every time she was just about to grasp onto it, it would slip away from her. Why was the whole world spinning off its axis?

Bunny snagged her hand and held onto it tight. Jo fluttered around, her noises barely out of Bea's senses. She couldn't focus. Bunny said something, but Bea didn't catch what it was. Suddenly something cold was pressed to the side of Bea's face. She reached up to grab it, finding someone's hand already there, but she didn't let go.

The cold was exactly what she needed to focus, and it brought the room slightly back into view. Well, not the room, but Bunny. Bea still hadn't moved her forehead from Bunny's shoulder, and they sat facing opposite directions on the piano bench.

"Give her some space," Bunny ordered.

Heat kissed Bea's cheeks. God, she couldn't believe this was happening. It had been so long since she'd well and truly fainted, but she must have made the mistake of locking her knees, of not breathing right. She was so distracted that she hadn't been able to focus on anything other than Bunny's fingers.

Those strong fingers that traced a sweet pattern against her waist, the warm fingers that were the barrier between the cold-water bottle and her hand. Bea's heart thrummed along steadily, too fast for the beginning of a rehearsal.

"She hasn't done this in years," Jo said, so obviously worried.

"I'm fine," Bea managed to get the words out, but her voice sounded a million miles away. "I just need a minute."

"You have it." Bunny held still, unmoving, the stability and anchor that Bea needed in that moment. "Stay here as long as you need it."

Right there.

Bea nearly crumbled.

That was the woman Bea had seen at the end of that first night, the sudden softness she'd never expected. And here it was again, once Bunny pushed past all the demanding, all the skepticism, all the bravado.

Was this the real Bunny?

Bea lost all track of time. She didn't want to lift her head and move. She didn't want to face the embarrassment that she knew was awaiting her as soon as she looked in Bunny's gaze. She shifted on the piano bench, her ass starting to hurt from sitting in the odd position for so long.

"Are you ready to move?"

"I think so," Bea whispered. She took in a deep bolstering breath before she pulled back. Bunny still didn't let her go. She held onto both of Bea's hips, making sure she was steady.

"Take your time. I'm serious."

"I know you are. You're never not serious." Bea bit her tongue. She shouldn't have snapped. Bunny was just trying to be helpful. Bea knew that. But her embarrassment was rearing its asshole nature and making her even more embarrassed by the second. "I'm sorry."

"Don't worry about—"

"Will you just accept my apology?" Bea snapped again. She cringed. She had to find a way to make herself stop.

"Yes." Bunny pulled away slightly, lifting Bea's chin so she could look in Bea's eyes. "Yes, I accept your apology."

"Thank you." Bea relaxed a little more. She tried to shift off the bench, but Bunny was right there with her, an arm wrapped around her waist. Bea let her do it, because honestly, she wasn't sure if she could stay upright without it. Not right now. Looking around, she was confused. "Where are Piper and Jo?"

"Jo said something about you needing sugar."

"Oh." Bea rubbed her lips together. That was what normally made her weak like this, a dip in her blood sugar. Leave it to Jo to remember that and race after something that would help. But that wasn't what had happened this time.

"They should be back soon. Piper took her to the coffee house just down the road to get something."

"Okay." Bea tried to move again, but Bunny was right there. "I won't fall over."

"I don't believe that." Bunny pressed in a little tighter. "But if you have a problem with your blood sugar, you need to tell me. Because if we need to plan for breaks during the show for you to keep it level, then we will."

"No, I should be fine."

"Three hours is a long set, Bea."

"I'm fully aware." Bea's chest tightened under the stress of everything. They should have never agreed to do this show. She wasn't going to be able to keep up with Bunny and Piper. They weren't seasoned enough to do this. And it was already show-ing. They hadn't even made it through a warm-up.

"What's wrong?" Bunny asked, seeming genuine.

"I'm not some newb who's never done this before. Jo and I have been doing shows for years, and we deserve some credit for that."

"You have it." Bunny shook her head in confusion. "I'm not underestimating your ability."

"But you're underestimating me." Bea shook her head. Why was she doing this? Surely, she had better control of herself by now. "So stop."

"I'm not—"

"Stop denying it!" Bea raised her voice.

Bunny's lips parted but no sound came out. She dropped

her gaze from Bea's eyes to Bea's lips, causing another wild shudder to run through Bea's body and her knees to threaten to give out again.

"I don't think you're an idiot, Bea." Bunny straightened her shoulders, but she still hadn't looked back up into Bea's eyes. "But you can't deny that working with us is a boost to your ego and your image. Don't think me an idiot."

"That isn't why we agreed to this." Bea's heart was in her throat again. She turned her body, forcing Bunny to raise her gaze up to her eyes. "And if you think I'm that shallow, then I'll quit right now."

Bunny snorted lightly. "Shallow?"

"I call it like I see it."

Taking a step forward, Bunny pushed Bea back. Bea took an uneasy step, the backs of her thighs hitting the edge of the piano. When had she gotten so close to it?

"And so do I." Bunny's threat was clear. She still had a hand on Bea's side, and she lowered it to Bea's hip, giving her one good hard shove until she fell back onto the keys of the piano. The discordant notes hit the air just as Bunny's lips were on hers.

Moaning, Bea dropped her hand to the piano to hold herself up better, the noise loud in her ears. Bunny's tongue pushed against hers, and Bea struggled to breathe again, but this time for an entirely different reason. She was lost in the kiss. She dug her fingers into Bunny's hair, tightening her grasp as she sucked Bunny's lower lip into her mouth and scraped her teeth along the sensitive skin.

Two could play this game.

Perhaps this was Bunny's angle. She kept accusing Bea of having one, why should Bea be so stupid as to assume that Bunny didn't have one too? Seduce the young musician every time she dared to have an opinion.

Jerking back, Bea held her ground. She stared directly into Bunny's eyes when she said, "Stop."

Bunny put her hands up and took a step back. She swiped her fingers over her mouth, cleaning it as she took a walk toward the window. She raked her fingers through her hair, pulling at the strands. Bea watched her carefully from the piano, still leaning against the keys.

"Just stop being a jerk."

Bunny's shoulders dropped. "We agreed to be civil."

"We did." Bea stood up, finding her footing again. Bunny was right. She pulled herself back together and folded her hands in front of her. "And for that sake, let's move on. Why didn't you plan a duet with me?"

"What?" Bunny spun around. "What are you talking about?"

"There's no duet for us. There's every other pairing under the sun, but none for you and me." Bea walked closer, finally finding her confidence. "Why?"

"I didn't…" Bunny trailed off, blinking and furrowing her brow. "I didn't think our voices would blend well together."

"Don't lie to yourself. If you didn't want to do one with me, that's all you had to say."

"It's not that." Bunny frowned. "It's not that at all."

"Then what is it?"

Bunny looked stunned, fear crossing her gaze before she shook it. "Just trust me. That's not why."

"We have refreshments!" Piper said from the doorway.

"Oh, thank God," Bunny muttered as she walked past Bea.

So much for that conversation. Bea took an extra second to pull herself together before she turned around and faced her sister. She couldn't know what they'd just been doing. No one could.

TEN

"All right, what happened?" Jo asked when they got into the car to go home. Whatever was going on between Bunny and Bea—and Jo knew something was definitely going on—had left Bea bristling for the rest of the afternoon.

It was almost easy to quell her excitement as Bea's icy quiet filled the car.

But the afternoon had gone well. Jo and Piper fed off each other's energy and all their voices seemed to blend together really well once they got warmed up and onto practicing. They had only gotten through a few songs, and there was definite improvement to be made. But the excitement hummed like electricity beneath Jo's skin.

"What do you mean?" Bea asked, keeping her attention on the road.

Jo knew her sister better than Bea often gave her credit.

"You haven't had a sugar spell in months."

"Years," Bea muttered as she turned onto the highway, heading toward Jo's.

"So what's going on? Are you eating?" Jo stayed very still, afraid that she would scare her sister out of talking.

"Yes." This time Bea looked over at Jo as she snapped out the word. Turning her attention back to the road, she continued, "I'm eating, Jo. I don't need a watcher."

"I know." Jo leaned back into the seat in defeat. "But am I allowed to be a sister who cares?"

Bea let out a big huff.

Jo let it linger in the small space of the car.

"I'm sorry. It's just a stressful week. I'll keep a closer eye on my blood sugar."

"So you won't tell me why it happened today?" Jo didn't mean to pout. She'd just never been good at hiding her feelings, or her energy. "We had a fantastic first rehearsal, and you act like everything went wrong. So please, can you tell me what else is going on?"

"I told you." Bea's snappiness told Jo more than Bea seemed willing to admit with words. The pain in her chest was acute, but Jo also knew pushing Bea had never worked in the past and she knew it wouldn't work this time.

"Okay." Jo didn't bring it up again, and she spent the rest of the drive looking out the window as the city passed them.

"Are you going to see what Piper has to say about the first rehearsal? Did we meet…*Bunny's*…standards?" Bea asked the third time Jo's phone went off with a beep.

"She can wait. But if you'd like me to ask, I can." Although Jo itched to pull her phone from her pocket and read the texts, she didn't want to get Bea all prickly again. "Thanks for the ride home."

"Jo." Bea grabbed Jo's hand. "I'm sorry I'm snippy. I guess it's harder to work with other people than I realized. Makes me appreciate how well we work together."

Jo knew that Bea was still resistant to this entire idea. She didn't want to be there, but she'd agreed. And Bea wasn't someone who backed down. "It's going to be great."

"Yeah." Bea forced a smile, but Jo appreciated the effort, even if it looked more like a grimace. "It'll be great for us."

Jo barely held back rolling her eyes. She jumped out of her car. "See you tomorrow."

With the front door of her apartment not yet closed, she pulled her phone from her pocket and opened it. What did Piper have to say about rehearsal? Had they royally fucked up and pissed off Bunny or were they making progress on that front?

The door closed with an ominous thud as Jo stared at the screen. For a full minute she stood, far more still than was natural for her, and simply stared at the name lighting up her screen.

It wasn't Piper.

Why couldn't it just be Piper?

Forcing herself to take a deep breath, Jo walked to the tiny galley kitchen and pulled a drink from her fridge.

Sitting down on the worn couch, Jo finally opened the messages from her ex-girlfriend, Mandy. She really didn't want to read them. But she was compelled to. Forced by obligation, curiosity, and self-hate.

Mandy: Hey stranger. I've been thinking about you. Remember when we went to Paris? I've still got our photo kissing under the Eiffel Tower stuck on my mirror. I miss you. Xoxo

Mandy: How are you? I heard you'll be away all of Christmas. I was hoping to catch up. Maybe I can come see you where you are. I miss you so much. Have you missed me, too?

.   .   .

Mandy: I'm so sorry about what happened between us. I know we can talk this through and give it another try. We're so good together, baby xo

By the time Jo read the messages a third time, her legs jiggled up and down and her fingers trembled so hard the words on the screen jumped. Throwing the phone onto the couch cushion beside her, she stood up and paced the length of the room. It wasn't nearly big enough for her to work through any of the feelings that swirled like a dust storm inside of her.

She grabbed up her phone and quickly closed the messages.

Her finger hovered over Bea's name, but she hesitated. Bea was hiding things, things that had her in her own tailspin. The fainting gave that away, and her energy on the way home cemented it. Jo couldn't put this stress and drama onto her as well.

She paced, back and forth, back and forth, her mind racing.

She knew who she wanted to contact—Piper.

But was that really fair?

As it was, her own feelings for Piper were just one of the many feelings caught up in the dust storm.

But they weren't together. Sure, Piper's kisses had made Jo's head dizzy and her body reacted faster than it ever had. But they were friends, and neither of them had said anything about commitment or even going further than a grope here and there. It had simply been an experiment anyway. Piper had bragged about a technique, and Jo wanted to know what it was.

Well, it was amazing. That's what.

Jo wasn't even sure she wanted to get involved with Piper that way, did she?

"Ugh!" Jo screamed up at the ceiling, stopping her pacing only because she knew she'd trip and break something if she didn't. "God damn it."

Before she could talk herself out of it, Jo hit the call button on Piper's number.

"Hey, long time no hear." Piper's energy filled Jo's chest, and the emotions she'd been holding back burst free.

"Hey," Jo sobbed out.

"Oh my God. What happened?" Worry filled Piper's voice.

"I..." But she didn't even know how to say it. How to start with the whole entire mess that three stupid text messages had created.

"Text me your address, and I'll be over as soon as I can."

Jo spluttered out some sounds that didn't even remotely resemble words.

"Jo?" Piper's soft voice calmed her enough to find words.

"Are you sure?" Jo hated this. She should have just called Bea. Bea would understand everything, and she wouldn't have to explain it all from the beginning. She wouldn't have to go through the embarrassment of her past relationship.

"Yes." There was no hesitation in Piper's voice. "Now text me your address, and I'll be there soon. Okay?"

"Okay." Jo smiled though she sniffled, and the tears wouldn't stop.

"Good. I'll see you soon. Wait. Do I need to stay on the phone with you while I get there?"

Jo shook her head before she spoke. She didn't need to be more embarrassed than she already was. "No, I'll be fine. I promise."

"Okay. I'm trusting you on that."

"See you soon." Jo hung up as soon as she could. Her tears slowed as she typed her address in a text to Piper.

Once she heard the whoosh that let her know the message had been sent, panic washed over her in a different way.

What the hell was she doing?

She should have just messaged Bea, but she hadn't been able to bring herself to do it. She paced her small apartment, unable to settle the energy that seemed to be erupting from her every few seconds. It wasn't long before Piper arrived. And Jo couldn't deny how her heart beat a little faster when she opened the door to Piper with a box of donuts from Zena's and a bag hanging from her wrist. A bag that looked suspiciously like it carried ice cream and alcohol.

"I'm sorry," Jo said immediately.

"Never be sorry for giving me an excuse to enjoy great company and naughty food."

"I'm not sure I'll be the best company."

"You don't have to be," Piper said as she followed Jo inside. "I have donuts, ice cream, and non-alcoholic beer."

"Non-alcoholic?" Jo raised her eyes.

"It sounded like actual alcohol might have a negative effect, and friends don't let friends text drunk."

Jo laughed and nodded as she sat back down on her couch. Piper placed the items on the table in front of them. The table that was actually an old bookshelf lying face down on the floor.

"So, is it a you need to talk about it, not talk about it, or vent and let off steam kind of thing?"

Jo still couldn't find the words, so instead she picked up her phone, opened it to the texts and handed it over to Piper. Jo's legs bounced up and down, her fingers picked at her nails, and her teeth gnawed her bottom lip while she waited for Piper to say something. How long did it take to read three small messages? What could Piper be pondering that took this much time before she responded?

"Mandy? Isn't she the one who ran off with that one-hit wonder from Chicago?" Piper asked as she gently placed the phone between the box of donuts and the plastic bag of goodies on the bookshelf–turned–coffee table.

"That would be the one." Jo's laugh came out in a more hysterical tone than she felt comfortable with.

"Well, I guess the first question…" Piper leaned forward, flipped open the box of donuts and asked, "Is it donuts first or ice cream? If it's donuts, we better put the ice cream in your freezer."

Jo laughed, and she threw her head back. When she brought her head forward again, she noticed Piper sticking the tip of her pink tongue out and gliding it over her lips as though she hadn't had a drink in years. Had Piper been staring at her neck?

Jo's cheeks heated at the very idea.

Piper was gorgeous, no doubt about it, but they had only been having some fun. A little Christmas fling while they dove into the thing they both loved. Which, in this case, was singing.

"I'm half tempted to put the ice cream on top of the donut just to get the full effect." Jo jumped up, relieved to have something to do with her hands. Instead of sitting down after opening the donuts and handing Piper a drink without meeting her eyes, Jo grabbed the ice cream and walked away from the couch. "I'll pop this in the freezer for later."

"I mean, we could stack it. It sounds interesting." Piper's voice was soft and a little raspy. Jo turned to her. When their eyes met, the dust storm of confusion in Jo's head whipped itself up into another frenzy.

"Just be a second." With her head inside the freezer, Jo decided to keep that last detail to herself. And she did indeed follow the tub of ice cream into the almost empty top freezer.

By the time she came back out to her living room, Piper was sitting with her back against the arm of the couch, her knees bent, and her now bare feet tapping out a rhythm on the couch cushion.

Jo took the time unnoticed to really look at Piper. It was obvious to just about anyone with a pulse that Piper was stunning. Her lankiness just seemed to add to her charm, especially when she danced. She had reminded Jo of Danny Kaye the first time they'd danced together.

"Ice cream has been rescued just in the nick of time." Jo forced herself to step out of the kitchen and back into the living room.

"Excellent. Nothing is worse than comfort ice cream turning into soup. Though I think I want to try the ice cream on the donut thing at some point."

"Agreed," Jo said as she took the other end of the couch and mirrored Piper's position. "Also, I'm crazy, aren't I? For even letting these stupid texts get to me."

Piper leaned to her side and reached for a donut, picking a chocolate covered mousse filled variety. Jo's favorite as well. "I think that depends."

"On what?" Jo leaned over and picked up a plain glazed one for herself.

"On whether you want to get back together with Mandy." As soon as Piper had spoken, she took a big mouthful of the donut. Mousse spurted out the sides and landed on Piper's chest. "Oh shit," Piper mumbled around her full mouth.

Jo laughed and squirmed a little more into the couch, though she asked. "Do you need some help? Tissues or something?"

"Nope." Piper's grin made Jo's stomach tighten. All right, it was a considerable distance lower than her stomach. "I've got it."

Jo gulped and swallowed audibly when Piper used two fingers to scoop up the first and then the second splat of whipped mousse.

Putting both fingers in her mouth, Piper looked up to see Jo staring. Her eyes widened, and she pulled her fingers out quickly.

"Sorry, I'm a slob. But can't waste the mousse. It's the best part." Piper's cheeks pinked as her words filled Jo's home. Jo laughed, and Piper shook her head, laughing along. "You're a bad influence."

"I know. I know."

For a while, they sipped their drinks and ate their donuts in a silence Jo had never known before. It wasn't awkward or tense. It just was.

"So, do you?"

"What?" Jo looked up at Piper's question. Had she missed something? Had the silence only been in her head?

"Mandy." Piper smiled, but it wasn't the same infectious smile Jo had gotten to know. "Do you want to get back together with Mandy?"

"No." The word came too quickly, and Jo groaned. "I don't know. She's not wrong. We weren't just good together. We were amazing together."

"Maybe that's the first thing you need to work out." Piper's sad smile still rested on her face, and Jo wanted to have her Piper back. The one who understood her more than anyone else had before.

But she wasn't Jo's Piper. And honestly, Jo didn't know if she wanted her to be. Even if she did have a chance with her, which of course she didn't because she was Piper, of the freaking Bunny and Piper. *The* Piper.

Jo blew out a heavy breath.

If Bea found out about the texts, she would go insane. She hadn't liked Mandy even before she had hurt Jo.

"Want to watch something with me while I pretend I'm not having a slight meltdown over here?" Jo looked up at Piper.

"That's what friends are for, right?"

Friends, right. The word lodged itself in Jo's throat.

"I don't have many friends," Jo confessed as easily as she had with everything else that had come up in discussion with Piper.

Sure, they had made out, but Jo was just confusing a friendship for something more. She needed to have a serious conversation with her libido, because this kind of reaction wasn't the one she should be having over a friend wrapping her lips around the neck of a non-alcoholic beer bottle and taking a deep drink of the amber liquid inside.

"Thanks for coming over." Jo's voice came out raspier than she would have liked.

"You're welcome." Piper looked up, her regular smile back in place.

"Now, what crap can we watch and mock?"

Piper laughed and wrapped those lips around that bottle again.

Yep, Jo definitely needed to give her libido a stern talking to. Thank God Piper had brought non-alcoholic beer.

bunny

"We need to change the lyrics if we're going to sing that."

Bunny tensed at Bea's voice. Ever since that kiss on the piano, Bunny had been on edge, and it seemed like nothing made a difference for Bea. She was cool, calm, and collected. Bunny however? She was on the hot mess express, and no matter what she did, she couldn't get off. She'd tried. Nothing could get the feel of Bea under her fingers out of her mind.

"What?" Bunny snapped.

"We need to change the lyrics."

Bunny wasn't even sure what song Bea was referring to because she was so damn distracted by Bea's scent, by the extra-low-cut blouse she was wearing that day, by the way she kept fidgeting with her hair and pushing it behind her ear, by the way her lips formed an almost permanent smile that she seemed determined to push down into a frown when it would be so much more natural for her—

"Bunny?" Bea asked, setting a hand on Bunny's shoulder. "You still with me?"

Fuck.

"Uh, yeah." Bunny cleared her throat. "You were saying we needed to change the lyrics."

But to what fucking song?

Bea sighed heavily. "You said you wanted to change them, and I've seen different versions here and there since the original ones are so sexist and non-consensual, but these ones are just lacking."

Bea pushed the paper with lyrics that Bunny had written up in front of Bunny's face. Well, at least she knew which song Bea was referring to now. But that didn't help the fact that she didn't want to rewrite the lyrics again. And they weren't bad.

"I think they should be gay."

Bunny coughed. "Excuse me?"

"I mean, if you and I are going to sing them, then shouldn't they be written for two women?"

"Absolutely not." Bunny shot up from the piano bench and shoved her hands in her pockets. They were in a small practice room, barely big enough for the upright piano and the two of them to have any space.

"It'd be weird for one of us to pretend to be a man, wouldn't it?"

"We're not pretending. We're just singing." Bunny crossed her arms and paced the small room.

"It's not just singing." Bea stood still in the middle of the room, standing her ground.

Bunny shot her a glare. Didn't she understand what she was asking? Bunny wasn't out. She wasn't going to brand herself as the lesbian singer. She wasn't going to feed into the rumors that she and Piper were a thing. And she damn well sure wasn't going to do it with her one-night stand from the other night.

"This is only about singing." Bunny froze in front of Bea. "It's about doing this charity event and then going our separate ways."

"Gee, tell me how you really feel." Bea shook her head and snorted. "Not that I needed you to spell it out for me."

"What are you even talking about?"

"Look. I get how much you find Jo and me annoying. I get that you have zero desire to even do this event with us. I don't understand why you're still here. But I'm not going to half-ass this concert just because you don't want to put in your full effort." Bea crossed her arms, pushing her breasts up in the super-low-cut shirt, which made the skin on her smooth breasts all that much more enticing.

Stepping closer, Bunny halted. She couldn't think like this. She couldn't breathe with Bea so close to her, with Bea so stunning and amazing. She didn't want to do this event, but it wasn't because she was singing with Bea and Jo. It was just Bea and her damn presence that kept distracting her.

"I'm not going to back down on this," Bunny ground out. "I'm not going to out myself to the world because you have some whim about making this a queer song."

"That's not what I'm saying at all."

"That's exactly what you're saying!" Bunny's voice echoed in the room. She hated hearing how afraid she sounded. How scared she was to even just be standing there.

"No. It's not!" Bea yelled back. "Would you just listen for once?"

"I'm listening." Bunny's voice was tight with anger. Because she was listening. Bea was the one who was ignoring everything Bunny said.

"Not with that tone, you're not." Bea raised an eyebrow at Bunny, staring her down like she was a bug to be squashed.

"I am."

"You know what. Whatever. I'm about to give up. You can't be moved, so why even bother. And what's wrong with coming out, anyway? Don't you think it's a hell of a lot better to live authentically than to live in a constant state of fear?" Bea moved toward the door.

Bunny ran forward and slammed her hand against it, pushing it closed again. Her heart raced, her stomach twisted tightly. "I don't live in fear."

"Like hell you don't." Bea turned her back to the door and canted her head to the side. "Can't you see what you're doing?"

"I live my life exactly how I want to live it." Anger burst in Bunny's chest. She stepped close to Bea, pushing her against the door. "And I don't intend to live it any other way."

"Because you're letting fear run you over like an eighteen-wheeler."

"Fuck you, Bea."

Bea laughed coldly. "You wish."

Bunny's jaw dropped.

Bea clasped onto Bunny's cheeks and pulled her in hard. Their mouths slammed together in a fiery kiss. Bunny tried to pull away, but Bea held her tightly. She was so strong, and Bunny didn't really want to leave. She wanted them to stay right where they were, mouths together, bodies together. Bunny's knees weakened. She pushed harder into Bea to keep herself upright.

Bea slid her hand from Bunny's cheek to her neck, parting her lips and sliding her tongue against Bunny's. It was a plea to give in. It was Bea begging for Bunny to tell her that she was right.

But she was so wrong.

Bunny didn't need the world to know who she was. No one needed to know except her. Moving in swiftly, Bunny tried to take control, but Bea flipped them, pushing Bunny's back into the door. Bunny groaned, her hips jutting out until Bea pushed her thick thigh right between Bunny's legs. Bunny groaned, her eyes fluttering shut as sensations took over her.

"Fuck," Bunny mumbled. She gave in. She pushed her hands into Bea's hair and pulled her in even closer. Their lips melding together in a desperate kiss.

This was all she needed to know that she was gay. A woman in her arms, someone who was hot and heavy, someone who would melt as soon as she touched her. She slid her hand up Bea's back, finding her bra strap and snapping it for good measure. She needed more of those amazing tits. Perhaps she could press her face between them and forget there was a world outside that existed.

Bea bit her lip as she smoothed her hands down Bunny's front until she reached the button and zipper on Bunny's jeans. "Do I get a taste this time?"

"If you want," Bunny answered, enjoying the sly look in Bea's eyes.

What had gotten into them?

They couldn't keep apart. They couldn't even stop touching each other. From that one night, to the insane kiss at the piano, to this? Bunny sucked in a sharp breath and pressed her shoulders against the door. Did she even care if Bea managed to plant her face right between Bunny's legs? Nope.

Get fucked.

That's all Bunny cared about right now. Shutting Bea up about living out in the world, and getting fucked good and hard. Bunny shoved her pants down her hips to her ankles. She didn't even get a chance to take off her shoes before Bea was on her knees and her hot mouth was on Bunny's clit.

"Holy crap." Bunny gripped onto the doorknob to keep herself upright. She bit back her moan, not wanting it to reverberate around the room and alert everyone in the building to what exactly they were doing.

Bea laughed, the vibrations rolling through Bunny's clit to her stomach to her chest. Her nipples hardened instantly. She wanted so much more than this, but this was all she would ever allow. Bunny pushed the back of Bea's head, moving Bea harder into her. Bunny clenched her jaw.

"Your tongue is wicked," Bunny said with a laugh. She couldn't help herself. If she and Bea only ever did this one more time, she'd be happy as a clam. The first time had been so good. This time was bound to be better.

Bea said nothing as Bunny ground her pussy against her face. The sucking became harder, more frantic. Bea's breathing was sharp, but she didn't let up. Bunny rutted against her, needing Bea to keep going. Needing this moment to never end. Here, with a woman between her legs, was exactly what Bunny needed. This and her music and she would be the happiest person on the planet.

Bunny halted.

Piper's voice filtered down the hallway as she chattered with Jo. They were coming. Bunny froze. She pushed Bea's face away, but Bea didn't get up and move. Bunny threw her thumb over her shoulder and raised a finger to her lips. Piper and Jo's voices grew louder as they walked by and then softer as they left.

Bunny couldn't do this. She couldn't let Piper find out any of this. Bea looked at her inquisitively.

"Continue."

With a small smirk, Bea planted her face back between Bunny's legs and picked up right where she had been forced to leave off. Bunny tightened her grasp on Bea's hair. She was so close. Gasping, she crumbled. Bea clutched onto her hips, keeping her upright from the force of her orgasm. Bunny clung to the doorknob, needing it now more than ever.

Bea breathed deep, sliding up Bunny's body and dragging her shirt with her. She cupped Bunny's breasts and flicked her nipples. "See? Don't you want to be able to do that every day?"

"I can do that every day." Bunny locked her eyes on Bea's soft blue eyes. Where was this argument even coming from?

Bea knew nothing about her or about their band. Yet she had the audacity to tell them they were doing their business wrong. Bunny had been incorrect before. Bea didn't have an angle. But she was assuredly obnoxious in her convictions. "And even better, I don't need the world to watch me while I fuck you."

Spinning them around, Bunny pinned Bea to the door.

"Or did you have a better idea for how to end this little tiff?" Bunny started undoing the buttons on Bea's blouse, finally finding her push-up bra right in place on the soft mounds of flesh she'd been longing for. Pressing kisses to the tops of Bea's breasts, Bunny waited for an answer.

"I didn't realize this was a tiff." Was Bea's voice breathy? "I thought this was how you did foreplay."

Bunny snorted, pressing the flat of her tongue along Bea's breast and sliding it under the fabric to find her nipple hard and ready for her. Bea chuckled, her chest rising and falling with the sound.

"Oh you're a feisty one."

"Are we fucking or fighting?" Bunny retorted.

Bea snorted. "It seems both."

"Then shut up." Bunny froze. She sighed heavily and pressed her head to Bea's chest. "That was uncalled for."

"It was." Bea breathed deeply and let it out on a sigh. "So are you going to apologize?"

"Are you going to stop trying to force me to do something I don't want to do?"

"Touché." Bea smiled saucily. "But I don't understand why you won't—" Bea gasped, her mouth parting. She glanced down.

Bunny's fingers were under her dress, two fingers deep inside her. "You were saying."

"Clever." Bea laughed. "I don't understand why—"

Bunny started sliding in and out, moving her fingers back and forth and pressing the heel of her palm into Bea's clit. The distraction was working. Because she didn't want Bea to finish that thought. She didn't want to have to answer the question.

"Why won't you just admit it?" Bea said between gasps.

"Admit what?"

"That you're scared!"

Bunny paused all movement. She shot Bea a glare and pursed her lips. "I'm not afraid or ashamed about being gay."

"I beg to differ."

"You don't know me." Pulsing her fingers between Bea's legs, Bunny put as much focus as she possibly could into making Bea come apart on her fingers. Bunny held Bea close, pushing her fingers in harder, faster. "You won't know me. Ever."

Bea groaned, her eyes clenched tight. She had to be close. Her breathing was rapid. Her cheeks red. Her body tight. "Challenge." Bea breathed heavily. "Accepted."

Bea tightened around Bunny's fingers. She wrapped her arms around Bunny's shoulders as her knees gave way. Bunny had to work to keep them from tumbling hard to the floor. She stumbled on her way down, her knee cracking into the hard floor as she softened Bea's fall.

Bunny winced, but she held onto Bea until she was sure Bea wouldn't hurt herself. Then she slowly moved back, wiping her fingers on her shirt. She was just about to move to pull her pants up when Bea grabbed hold of her shoulders and dragged her in for a kiss.

This time it was slow. Bunny slid into the embrace, their mouths melding together. She breathed deeply, smelling nothing but Bea. The scent of sex filled her nostrils. No doubt the entire practice room reeked of it. Bunny pulled back slightly, needing to breathe. She had to figure out what the hell they were doing because sex twice was out of the question. This couldn't happen a third time.

Bunny swallowed hard.

Bea looked around them and hit her head lightly against the door. "What are we doing, Bunny?"

"Hell if I know." Bunny moved, pulling up her pants and doing up the button and zipper. She sat on the floor next to Bea, her legs stretched out. If she looked over at Bea, she still got to look at her perfect breasts, just begging to be touched again.

"I won't have a hidden relationship."

"Good. Because I don't want a relationship."

Bea's lips parted in surprise, but she shrugged slightly. "Then we're on the same page."

"At least about this. I'm not making the song gay."

Humming, Bea breathed deep, her chest rising and falling slowly. Bunny couldn't take her gaze off Bea's tits. Her stunningly beautiful, perfect tits. Bea put a finger under Bunny's chin and lifted her gaze.

"My eyes are up here."

bea

The door to the rehearsal room opened sharply. Siena walked in, followed by a tall, thin, absolutely stunning woman. She looked like she could have walked right off the runway. Bea sucked in a sharp breath, straightening up. She wasn't ready for this—whoever this was. She was in her grungy clothes, barely made up.

Bunny had told her they were going to work choreography that day, so she'd dressed down, needing to make sure she could move instead of look good. Bunny stood up immediately, walking over to Siena and the woman, shaking their hands and lingering with the gorgeous woman.

"Bea and Jo, this is Allegra Ilic." Siena grinned.

Jo immediately bounced her way over to meet this woman, but Bea stayed behind, stomach queasy after what she'd just witnessed from Bunny. She didn't like how Bunny was eyeing Allegra up and down. Bea was just about to move toward the crowd of people when Jo's phone buzzed.

"Mandy?" Bea stared at it in confusion a split second before the anger hit. With one glance to her sister, she unlocked the phone and pulled up the text messages. Her stomach instantly churned with bile.

"Bea!" Jo called, a light in her eyes until she saw Bea on her phone.

Pursing her lips, Bea straightened her shoulders and walked directly toward the small group of people. She stood between Jo and Bunny and extended her hand to Allegra. "Hi. It's good to meet you."

"You as well," Allegra said with a patented smile. "I was so happy when Siena shared that you both had agreed to join in our charity event."

"We love giving back to our community," Bunny chimed in, practically drooling over Allegra.

If they were alone, Bea would have some sharp words for Bunny. Something about not falling on her face on the way out. Bea clenched her jaw, knowing that her face didn't match the calm, smiling ease that the others had managed.

Why was Mandy texting Jo again?

"That's something Jo and I would love to do more of, so the opportunity was perfect." It wasn't much of a lie. They had talked about it. They just hadn't planned on it happening yet. Jo slid Bea a curious look.

Was Jo looking to start up a relationship with Mandy again? Because that would be a bad idea. Hands down. The devastation Jo had experienced during their last breakup was enough for one lifetime.

"Perfect. Well, I thought I should tell you a bit more about the Holbrook Foundation so that you know exactly what we're raising funds for." Allegra looked at each of them, making eye contact.

Oh, she was good at this. Schmoozing. It was exactly why she was in the executive director position, wasn't it? The muscles in Bea's shoulders tightened even more. She didn't like it. It felt so underhanded, and the way Bunny was all over Allegra in an instant really put Bea off of the whole situation.

Maybe Bea really was just another notch in Bunny's belt.

Allegra gave the spiel. Bea only half listened, making eye contact with Siena and nodding toward the door. Siena raised an eyebrow at her and shook her head.

"We're wanting to help the people who need it most. Research shows that a stable mother relationship with any child will propel that child forward on the right foot when they hit adulthood. So we try to help single mothers as best as we can to give them a hand up in finding their place and stability in this current culture."

Bea stepped closer to Jo and touched her arm lightly. She hated that they were stuck here and couldn't talk. She really needed to ask Jo what the hell was going on.

"They make such amazing waves for mothers," Bunny jumped in, turning to Bea and Jo. "My mom was a single parent. It's tough out there. Next to impossible to survive."

Bea stilled. Bunny came from a broken home? She cringed. Why had she thought that? Some crass crap her father would say, and she hadn't managed to break free of its grasp on her completely yet.

"We're working with Holbrook on a different fundraiser next year." Piper jumped into the conversation. "It's for some work with soldiers."

Bea was impressed. It seemed the Holbrook Foundation was doing a lot of work. But she still had a sense of unease in her belly, something she couldn't shake that had absolutely nothing to do with Holbrook and everything to do with the gorgeous woman that Bunny couldn't stop fawning over. And the fact that Mandy was texting, again.

What the hell did she want?

Bea hung to the back, letting Bunny and Allegra chat away.

She eyed them carefully. Jo came to stand next to her, giving her a funky look.

"You look like you want to murder someone," Jo muttered under her breath.

"Why are you texting Mandy?"

Jo sighed heavily. "I'm not texting. She's texting."

Bea turned and stared at her sister, her strong, hurt, and manipulated sister. Jo had fallen head over heels in love with Mandy, and she'd never managed to untangle herself from the woman despite their multiple breakups. Bea pushed her fingers through her hair.

"I don't like it," Bea said.

"Well, neither do I, frankly."

"Anyway, I just wanted to express my gratitude for your volunteering to work this event. It'll help us raise the funds to meet our goal for the next year." Allegra folded her hands in front of her. "But I know you have a lot of work to do, so I'll let you get back to it."

She said her goodbyes and walked out with Siena. Bea shot Jo a sharp look before following behind. She would take care of the Mandy problem if it was the last thing she did. She allowed the anger to surge into her, needing it to make clear to Siena how dangerous this woman could be.

Bea trailed Siena, waiting until she'd said goodbye to Allegra. Siena turned around, facing Bea with a confused and curious look on her face. "Did you need something?"

"Yes." Bea bolstered herself. Jo was going to be so ticked off at her for doing this, but something had to be done. And it was Bea's job to protect her little sister in every way possible. "There's a woman, Mandy Obrist. She's harassed Jo for years, and she's popped back up recently. She has a way of… getting into places she shouldn't be allowed."

"Oh?" Siena stepped closer now, her entire body movement shifting into one of concern.

"I thought she was finally gone because she left the state, but Jo said she's been texting again." It wasn't wholly the truth, but Siena didn't need to know that. "I don't want her at the event."

"What kind of harassment has she been doing?" Siena flicked her gaze to something behind Bea.

The hairs on Bea's neck stood up. Was Jo back there? Ready to pounce on her for spilling such personal information?

"Any and all." Bea winced and turned around, finding Bunny standing right there.

Well, at least it wasn't Jo.

"From text messages, to stalking tendencies of being at our gigs when she's not welcome, to coming backstage. She's very good at figuring out how to get close to Jo."

"Who is this?" Bunny immediately stepped in closer, lowering her voice in a dangerous tone.

Was she just as protective as Bea was? A shiver of pleasure ran through Bea.

"No one of your concern."

"Mandy Obrist," Siena supplied. "Does the name ring a bell to you?"

Bunny shook her head and shoved her hands into her pockets, rolling up on her toes. "You said she's stalking Jo?"

"Well, she was kind of. We've mainly called it harassment."

"You haven't filed police reports for stalking?"

"Jo won't go for it."

Bunny pressed her lips together hard, pushing them out. "Take care of it, Siena."

"I'm planning on it already. Bea, I need you to send me what you have on her. Pictures, but also her birthday and any other information you have. Address, phone number, and any methods she's used to get close to Jo."

"Okay." Relief flooded Bea's chest. Were they really going

to work on this together? She hadn't imagined Bunny wanted anything to do with them beyond what was required.

"Do you think she'll show up here? While you're rehearsing?" Siena asked.

Bea was about to answer and then stopped. "I'm not sure. She's never really shown up outside of shows. At least when Jo wasn't letting her. But she'll come to every show of ours she can find. She just wants to be in the spotlight from what I can tell. She craves that attention."

"Then we definitely don't want her at a charity event." Siena nodded at Bunny. "I'll start working on it, and I'll see about posting security here just in case."

"We're off the beaten path," Bea objected, wanting to keep this as low key as possible. She already knew Jo was going to be massively pissed off that she'd brought it up with Siena. Adding security into the mix was only going to make it worse. "I don't think it'll be a problem here."

"It's not your choice," Siena answered. "I'll have it arranged for tomorrow. Send me that information before the end of the day. I'll talk to you later about what details I come up with."

With that, Siena left. Bea stood awkwardly on the curb, Bunny next to her in silence. Siena waved at them as she drove off, and while a slight amount of the tension eased from Bea's chest, there was another tension that she couldn't get rid of.

"I want more details than Siena." Bunny looked Bea over, down and then up. What Bea would give to fall into Bunny's arms and be held. But that wasn't anywhere near the relationship they had. Bunny was hard, stony, and the stare she was giving was one of disgust.

"It's not my story to tell."

"How dangerous is this woman?"

Bea pressed her lips together hard. "Well, she's never attacked Jo or me."

"Way to sidestep that. She'll throw Jo off her game, massively, won't she?"

"Yes." Bea sucked in a deep breath and let it out slowly. She looked around, half expecting Mandy to jump out at them.

"Then we can't have that." Bunny stepped in closer, reaching for Bea's shoulder. "She's one of us, now. And I'll do everything I can to keep her safe."

Bea's lips parted in surprise. It was her job to project Jo. It had always been her job. No one else had ever even tried to step into that role. Not any of their siblings. No one. So to have Bunny say it now was so odd. A calm washed through her in a way it never had before.

"Thank you, I think."

"It's not a problem." Bunny raised her fingers to Bea's chin, lifting it up so they could look into each other's eyes. "You should have told me sooner."

"I just found out." Bea couldn't stop looking into Bunny's gaze. Who was this woman? One minute she was hot and sexy, the next she was all control and power as their non-chosen leader, so put together as if she could do anything. But right in this moment, she was soft, caring. Like she actually did want the best for them. "Bunny—"

Bunny shook her head. "It's not a problem. I promise."

"I wasn't going to say that." Bea clenched her jaw, still unable to find words to explain what was washing through her.

"Then what?" Bunny dropped her hand, putting space between them.

It was exactly what Bea had needed in order to find herself again. "I don't get you."

"I'm sorry?" Bunny jerked her head up, suddenly on the defensive.

"I just don't. One minute you're cold and aloof, the next

you're accusing me of having some kind of agenda. And now you want to be Jo's savior?"

"I don't want to be anyone's savior." Bunny narrowed her gaze. "I'm hardly a saint."

"Well, that's clear, isn't it?" Bea clenched her jaw. "You make no sense."

"Then I guess you know me pretty well." Bunny stepped in closer, her voice dropping to dangerous levels, except this time, it was aimed at Bea instead of Mandy. "Because I'm absolutely not a saint. I'm no one to write home about."

Bunny's breath brushed along Bea's shoulder and down her neck. If Bea closed her eyes, she could vividly imagine Bunny's mouth on her skin. The press of those soft lips meant solely to incite pleasure. Bea pressed her thighs together, hating that her clit pulsed and her underwear was already damper than it had been.

"Fun fact," Bea started, turning her chin to meet Bunny's gaze. "Neither am I."

Twisting on her toes, Bea walked back into the building. She didn't stop until she reached the main rehearsal room. Piper and Jo were halfway through one of their duets, singing with grins on their faces as they spun around the room in the tango-esque dance that would be the choreography for that particular song.

Bea stayed on the edge, observing every move. If she hadn't seen the texts, she never would have known that Jo was struggling. In fact, she couldn't even bring herself to see it now that she was looking for it. Perhaps Mandy's texts hadn't been that bad. Maybe Mandy hadn't wanted anything.

Who the hell was she kidding?

Mandy only ever wanted one thing—Jo. And she knew exactly how to get Jo in her clutches and rip her to shreds, again. Bea couldn't watch that happen. It had taken months for Jo to even smile after the last time, and Jo deserved to enjoy life. Like she was right now.

"They look good together," Bunny said, her voice quiet so as not to disturb the rehearsal going on.

Bea pursed her lips, glancing from her sister and Piper to Bunny. "They do."

"I wouldn't mind encouraging that relationship to flourish. Would you?"

"With Piper? Absolutely not."

"But I come attached to Piper." Bunny looked directly at Bea. "And that's your hesitation?"

"You've not exactly been warm and welcoming." Bea bit the inside of her cheeks.

"Sounds like the pot calling the kettle black."

Bea snorted.

"I thought we agreed to civility." Bunny crossed her arms, looking back at the couple in the center of the room. "For their sake."

"That was before." Bea's body wanted so badly to turn into Bunny and push her against the wall. Just like they'd done in the piano room. Fall to her knees and have Bunny come all over her again. It had been stunning to watch that unraveling.

"And what's now?"

Well, that was the question, wasn't it? Bea sucked in a sharp breath and rolled her shoulders. She had to give an answer. Bunny was fishing to figure out where they stood together. And the pressure to actually respond instead of just avoid was so strong. But she couldn't make herself do it.

They might end up running in the same circles, but that didn't mean they had to like each other.

"Now, we get ready for the event. That is why we're here, isn't it?" Bea kept her voice as level and even as possible. Despite what her heart told her, despite what her body insisted she felt, she couldn't make her brain give up those clutches on her. Not just yet. "We've got a lot of work to do."

"That we do." Bunny looked Bea over one last time before walking toward the piano and plopping her ass on the bench.

At least that was done. Now if Bea could only convince her body to catch up with her brain, she'd be golden. She just had to convince herself that this was the right decision. Not about Jo—that was absolutely the right choice. But about her and Bunny.

They needed to stop whatever dance they'd started.

piper

Piper sat on a spare piano stool against the wall of the rehearsal room. Jo had gone to the bathroom, and Piper was taking the opportunity to have a small break before they all dove back in for several more hours.

It was Bea and Bunny's turn to run through their part of the song the four of them would all sing together. It was one of Piper's favorite Christmas songs and already her excitement bubbled up again as Bunny started playing it softly.

Bunny sat at the piano while Bea stood a little to the left behind her. Piper watched and tilted her head as Bea leaned forward, pointing to something on the music sheet.

Bunny turned toward Bea, the back of her head to Piper.

Whatever Bunny had said set Bea's smile stretching wide on her face, as her fingers gently brushed Bunny's upper arm.

What is that?

But then Bea started singing along to Bunny's playing, and Piper could imagine Bea in a formal gown, while Bunny played, all dressed up in a tux. Piper snorted softly to herself. Bunny wouldn't be seen dead in a tux, it might fuel some of those rumors she was so scared of. The ones that were always half right. Yep, Bunny liked the ladies, but Bunny and Piper had never crossed that line—let alone had a secret relationship their entire career.

"Good, you're back." Bunny looked over to the door as it opened with a whoosh. "We need to go through this song a few more times. And then I want you and Piper to practice the dance routine for the second half of the show."

"Sure, no worries." Jo walked, a skipping energy in her steps as she stood next to Bea, directly behind Bunny.

Piper stood on Jo's other side.

Jo raised a single eyebrow in question as she met Piper's eyes. Questions filled her face. But Piper smiled and quickly mouthed *later* before Bunny began playing the song, louder and with more enthusiasm for the music this time around.

Piper's smile flickered on her lips as she watched Bea's fingers brush along Bunny's shoulder while the four of them sang. Instead of Bunny ignoring Bea or shrugging to push the touch away, Piper could have sworn Bunny's head tilted toward Bea.

What the hell is going on here?

Piper shook her head after Bunny turned around at her missed cue.

"Sorry," Piper said softly.

"Come on. We're all tired, but that was the second time you missed it."

"I know." Piper shook her head again, this time determined to remain focused. But it was getting harder. Now that she had noticed those little brushes of Bea's fingers on Bunny, and Bunny not shrugging the intimacy away, Piper began noticing more soft smiles and gentle touches being exchanged between her best friend and Bea.

"From the top. And then you and Jo need to work on the choreography." Bunny raised her eyebrows as though her words had ended in a question. Piper's nod was the confirmation she was looking for.

They made it through the song while Bunny made notes on a photocopy of the sheet music, something Piper was all too familiar with.

"What are you smiling so big about?" Jo asked as they made their way over to the cleared part of the room where they'd been practicing.

"Look," Piper whispered and jerked her head back toward the pair who remained at the piano.

"What am I looking at?"

"I want to increase the tempo during the middle section of the song. Let me know if it gets too fast," Bunny interrupted before Piper could respond.

"Okay," Piper and Jo spoke at the same time.

"What was I looking at?" Jo asked again.

"Really?" Piper's mouth dropped open a little, incredulous that Jo couldn't see it. But when she looked at Jo's face she saw a twinkle in the woman's eyes and a huge smile on her face.

"You already noticed something, huh?" Piper guessed.

"Only yesterday." Jo shrugged, and the two took their starting positions. She lowered her voice to barely above a whisper, "You're only just noticing it now?"

They smiled as they danced, going through the routine with a familiarity that dance partners normally wouldn't have had until they had been dancing together a lot longer than a handful of rehearsals.

"Something's going on between them." Jo seemed to be as intrigued as Piper was with how well Bea and Bunny were working together. Piper had even noticed several other little touches and blushing cheeks between the two of them. She wanted to know more, but pinning Bunny down to get actual answers was next to impossible. She always found out after the fact what Bunny had been up to or who she was interested in.

They had managed to hit the new tempo with every step on the third time through. "Something's there, but I can't figure out exactly what it is," Piper murmured as they stopped, her breath heaving from the exercise. She wasn't sure how much longer she'd be able to keep moving like this. Her age was wearing on her in ways it hadn't before.

"Something is definitely going on." Jo nodded in agreement.

"Bunny isn't exactly the *something is going on* type." Piper half-hated herself for the words that had already passed her lips and looked to be on her way to full hate as she couldn't stop the rest from coming out. "She doesn't do relationships. The closest she's gotten to one is a few hours."

Minus Piper's sister-in-law. That had been years worth of infatuation despite the feelings not being reciprocated, which only added to the problems. Piper had hated every moment of watching Bunny go through that.

"A few hours?" The line between Jo's eyebrows deepened as she tilted her head.

"Um, yeah." Heat spread over Piper's face as she kept her eyes on Bunny and Bea as they laughed about something Piper couldn't hear. "About the time it takes for… um, her and the hookup to finish."

"Oh." Jo's eyes widened, and she laughed. A moment later her face fell, and this time the word carried deeper thought than amusement. "Oh."

"Oh?" Piper wanted to ease Jo's concern, if that's what it was. But she had to know exactly where she had traveled to from one thought to the next.

"Bea hasn't dated for a while. She said she never wants to date again."

"Okay." Piper still wasn't sure where this was leading.

Jo's face scrunched up as though she were working through a database of evidence before she committed herself to words.

"Okay, thinking about my sister like this is just wrong, but I mean look at them."

Piper smiled, a small chuckle escaping her lips. "You've got to fill in the gaps. I don't understand."

"All right." Jo nodded, as though resigning herself to an annual exam. "She said she never wanted to date again. I just thought that meant until she was ready, but maybe that isn't what she meant at all."

"You mean she's ready to date now?" Piper asked, still unsure as to where Jo was going with this conversation.

"No, definitely not." Jo shook her head. "But maybe she's looking for exactly what Bunny is willing to offer."

"Oh." It was Piper's turn to let the information wash over her. She didn't want Bunny to be stuck in the perpetual hell of never finding love or a deeper relationship. Piper still wanted that proverbial break she was always whining about. "Well, I think maybe we all deserve some relaxed time off together."

"Another karaoke night?" Jo all but bounced beside Piper.

"Nope." Piper couldn't hold back the laugh. It was loud and bounced around the room. As the echoes came back, Bea and Bunny's eyes followed the sound to Piper.

"I want to go through the final song one more time before we call it quits for the day," Bunny called out to them, no doubt trying to interrupt whatever she thought was going on over there. Bunny had never had a subtle bone in her body.

"Shall we?" Piper offered Jo her elbow.

Jo laced her hand through the gap and rested her fingers softly on Piper's forearm. The touch sent a shiver through Piper's body, turning to heat as it settled in her lower belly.

"So if not karaoke…" Jo asked as they walked toward the two at the piano. "What then?"

"I have a much better idea. And maybe, just maybe, the two of them might realize they both want something a bit more than an orgasm." Piper wasn't entirely sure why she was determined for Bunny and Bea to have more than the usual fun Bunny allowed herself, but the idea weighed with importance in Piper's chest. And it had nothing, absolutely nothing, to do with her own desire to have Jo longer and more permanently in her life. Nope, not at all.

"Do you think Bunny is really capable of that?" Jo asked, her teeth pressing into her lower lip.

"I think the two of them will either kill each other or be so utterly devoted it'll leave every sapphic relationship either of us have ever known, heard about, or read about in the dust."

"I'm betting we'll have to buy funeral clothes." Jo laughed just before they reached the piano.

It was a grueling hour, going over the finale again and again. This time a fraction faster, this time slower, the next time working on blending this section more seamlessly between voices.

By the end, Piper was wondering if maybe they should simply give up on the idea of encouraging whatever was blooming between Bea and Bunny. But one look at Jo made her energy return in abundance, and there would be no going their separate ways tonight, even if it was the last thing she did.

"All right, we'll meet back here tomorrow at eight," Bunny said as she tapped the bottom edge of her music sheets against the now closed lid of the piano.

"Bunny..." Piper started with a warning that she knew Bunny would recognize in an instant. "We need dinner and some down time."

"What?" Bunny turned to Piper, arguments against the idea all but written on her lips already.

"The rehearsal went well, didn't it?" There was worry written in the lines of Bunny's face, and Piper knew she had to get a handle on this quickly.

"Yes, but—"

"No, that wasn't an open invitation," Piper singsonged. "It

went well, and we've all busted our asses off this week. We need a break."

"We really have," Jo said, clearly catching on and adding in her support.

Piper had never known anyone who could keep up with half her own energy and enthusiasm. But she had to admit, Jo might even have her beat. She made the Energizer Bunny appear cool, calm, and collected instead of the hyper-focused workaholic Piper knew her best friend to be.

"We've done an amazing job of coming together to get these songs ready." Bea's voice was soft, and in that moment, Piper could have kissed her. But, of course, she wasn't the sister Piper wanted to kiss. Besides, the plan was to have Bea kissing Bunny.

"If I say no, are you just going to bug the shit out of me until I end up giving in?" Bunny sighed, closed her eyes, and shook her head back and forth a little.

Piper beamed, knowing without a doubt Bunny would be able to hear the smile in her voice. "You know me too well."

"Oh, and I plan to be just as persistent!" Jo added.

Piper and Bea laughed. Bunny narrowed her eyes at Piper.

Piper saw the small twitch at the corner of Bunny's lips and barely resisted the urge to pump her fist in the air. This had to be one of the easiest times she'd ever had convincing Bunny to do something other than work.

"Fine." Bunny groaned. "What torture are you putting me through this time?"

"The new piano bar and fondue place over on third," Piper said confidently. They'd talked about going there so many times before and had never made the effort to make reservations. Well, Piper was already on her phone and clicking through the links to get a table for them.

"What the hell?" Bunny stared at her, displeasure plastered over her features.

"You don't like fondue?" Bea asked

"It's a restaurant and piano bar." Bunny wrinkled her nose in disgust. "And it's not exactly somewhere you can wear jeans and a T-shirt."

"Oh, a dressy kind of place?" Jo squealed as she clapped her hands together. Piper winced. That would make Bunny back out if Jo kept it up.

Piper nodded. "It's about time we spoiled ourselves a little. We can do dive bars anywhere anytime, but tonight is going to be a get dressed up and spoil ourselves sort of evening."

"That sounds like a nice idea, Piper." Bea smiled and gave a small nod, but Piper detected a hint of worry in her gaze. She'd have to ask Jo about that later.

"Did you already have all this planned before now?" Bunny eyed each of them in turn.

"Neither of them knew what I was proposing until right now," Piper said, automatically defending the sisters. She wouldn't let them fall into Bunny's trap of annoyance if it was the last thing she could do. At least not tonight. They all needed this. Let loose, burn off some excess energy and frustration, have some fun, get to know each other that much better.

"You seriously want me to dress up?" Bunny whined this time.

"It's mandatory." Piper sang as she walked to her bag and flung it over her shoulder. "I'll make a reservation for tonight. How does seven sound?" She'd already made it, but that didn't matter. They were coming with her one way or another.

"Sounds like I have time to start feeling sick," Bunny muttered under her breath, but it was loud enough for Piper to hear.

"I'll carry your corpse in there if I have to," Piper replied firmly. "And best friends don't let each other try a new place alone. Besides, don't you owe me something?"

"Not that again," Bunny growled. She grabbed her bag as she headed for the door.

"It'll be worth it. I promise!" Piper said louder.

"I'll believe it when I see it."

Piper heard Bunny's grumble, and Jo and Bea's chuckles, as they walked out of the studio.

"See you all in a few hours." Piper slid into her car, pride and excitement swelling inside of her as she started the engine.

She would enjoy seeing Bea and Bunny as they tried to pretend nothing was going on between them when they were outside of the studio. She grinned with satisfaction as she drove home. Of course, the last time they had socialized outside of work, Piper had gotten to know personally just how soft and delicious kissing Jo was.

She definitely wouldn't say no if Jo wanted another night of drunken fondling along with the taste of lime and salt on her tongue.

i'd rather see a
minstrel show

bunny

Bunny pulled on the vest she wore, trying to keep it from bunching up on her breasts. Piper had made her dress nicely for tonight, and she was far more made up than she would be on any given day, but it was a nicer restaurant than they would normally patronize. Her muscles burned from her evening run.

She'd taken to those, too.

Because she had to burn off the sexual energy that Bea set off in her somehow every time they were in the same room together. And it had been bad the last few days. Bunny had resolved herself not to kiss, touch, or fuck Bea again. They had to stop this nonsense. It wasn't good for either of them.

And tonight was going to prove that. They were here for Jo and Piper, nothing else.

Bunny stepped out of her car, pocketing the keys. She'd driven herself that night, needing the space away from everyone else. It was hard being in constant contact with two extra people every day. She wasn't good at socializing, and being thrust into a room with Bea made it that much worse.

When Bunny stepped into the piano bar, she froze. Bea was at the front, a stunning little black dress wrapped around her beautiful curves, highlighting every single one of them. Bunny groaned, shoving her hands into her pockets and clenching her fists. She did not need Bea to look so fuckable tonight because she really didn't need the temptation.

Then again, Bea always looked fuckable. Even when there were no innuendos or heated looks, as they talked about music, or about Piper and Jo. It had shocked Bea the first time she realized they had more than sexual chemistry between them.

"Hey," Bea said, her voice tight. "Jo said she'd meet me here."

"Same with Piper." Bunny clenched her jaw. Were they being set up? Was this Jo and Piper's ultimate plan?

Little did they know.

"Think this is all some elaborate plan of theirs?" Bea shifted her body, sliding one hip down and putting her fist on the other one.

Bunny had to swallow the lump of arousal that caught her. Her voice broke when she said, "Uh…yeah."

"Wonderful."

"My thoughts exactly." Bunny had meant that to come out annoyed. Instead, it sounded like she was drooling over Bea. Which… she was. Bunny snapped her gaze from Bea's breasts, pushed up so delicately and scrumptiously in the dress she wore, to her face. "I—"

"Your table is ready." The hostess appeared in front of them.

Bunny flicked her a glance, really wanting to clarify to Bea what she'd meant, but she just couldn't make herself do it. Bunny put her hand on the small of Bea's back as they were led toward their table. They were set up right next to a grand piano that was cordoned off. The seats had low backs, connected like an uncomfortable couch from the seventies, and a round table in the middle of them. The fondue was already set up, with tastes of different items all around.

"Carrie will be your server. She'll be over to ask what drinks you'd like."

Bunny sat down, Bea next to her, despite the fact that she really didn't want to be that close to Bea. She needed the extra inches of space.

"Here they are," Bea said.

Bunny looked up to see Piper and Jo coming toward them, both grinning from ear to ear. "Thank God."

"I didn't realize my company tortured you so much." Bea raised one eyebrow, looking directly into Bunny's eyes.

"In more ways than one," Bunny answered, giving back a look that was all fire and desire. If she was going to be forced to sit next to Bea all night, then they both deserved to be tortured. Bunny slid her hand against Bea's knee under the edge of the table so the other two didn't see. She shifted the edge of Bea's dress up, and played her fingertips lightly over the soft skin on the inside of Bea's thigh.

Bea dragged in a shuddering breath.

Exactly, Bunny thought before moving her hand. At least she wasn't the only one struggling with this.

The meal went quickly, and with drinks flowing, Bunny finally found a way to relax. She finished off her second drink for the night and eyed the piano. For a piano bar, she really expected there to at least be some music.

Carrie came by, taking another drink order and dropping off some more items for the fondue. Bunny glanced at the piano again. "Will there be music tonight?"

Carrie sighed heavily before shaking her head. "Unfortunately no. Our pianist called out sick."

"Do you mind if I—"

"It's all yours." Carrie grinned broadly. "I'd love the music."

Bunny immediately scooted out of their table. She needed the break from Bea. She needed space between them to clear her head, refocus, and maybe make the night go a little faster. She moved the piano bench out and sat down. The keys were cold under her fingers, and she closed her eyes to think.

What songs did she actually have memorized that weren't her own for the set list of their current concerts or those damn Christmas songs they'd been practicing nonstop? Something classical for sure. Something from when she'd been a teenager and forced to practice hours on end.

Instantly, she knew what she was going to play. The soft melodic tones of the *Moonlight Sonata* echoed throughout the building. The chatter from all the patrons turned into a duller, quieter noise in the background. Working solely from memory, Bunny worked her way into the second movement. She only messed up once or twice, but hey, it'd been decades since she'd played this properly.

When she opened her eyes, Bea was standing next to her, phone on the piano and turned sideways with the sheet music on it. "Piper said you could probably use this."

"Thanks." Bunny squinted at the screen, trying to pick up where she was at. Bea flipped the page and suddenly she found her place.

"Could you use a page turner?"

What was she supposed to say to that? Bunny nodded as her fingers continued to fly across the keyboard. Bea scooted next to her on the bench, the warmth from her thigh seeping into Bunny's leg. Every time Bea leaned forward to hit the phone and turn the electronic page, Bunny would get a whiff of her perfume, of her scent, and it sent a shiver through her. She couldn't make herself stay there. She had to get out.

Bunny finished the song and then shifted as if she was going to get up.

"Would you mind playing this one?" Bea held out the phone.

Bunny froze. What was this? Torture by proximity? She

couldn't handle it much longer. Biting her lip, Bunny skimmed the music. It was a jazz piece. Jazz wasn't something she played often. In fact, she couldn't remember the last time she'd tinkled the keys to that kind of tune.

"Are you going to sing?" Bunny asked, locking her eyes on Bea's blue ones.

"If you'd like. This is one of my favorites." Bea leaned in closer.

Bunny closed her eyes, trying to center herself, but no matter how many times she tried, she felt as though she was in a proverbial imbalance, always leaning toward Bea or away from her. "I didn't realize you were interested in jazz."

"I like all kinds of music, don't you?"

Choosing not to answer that one, Bunny sat back at the piano. "But you don't play."

"Piano was never really my forte. I can play, but not well. Guitar is far easier for me."

"It's not quite the same when it comes to jazz," Bunny murmured.

"It's not," Bea whispered back. "That's why I leave it to the real piano players."

"Why Bea, is that a compliment?" But Bunny started to play, not wanting to turn the pleasantry into another heated discussion.

Bea's reply was a smile as the notes filled the room and Bunny's chest. Bea hit the first note in the song, her voice pure and strong as she sang out. Surprise ricocheted through Bunny, and she had to work hard to keep her gaze on the music in front of her and not look at Bea because then she'd be completely lost. Bunny divided her focus, listening to Bea's amazing voice and keeping her fingers moving on the keyboard.

The lyrics filled her soul.

Good Morning Heartache but with a modern twist, with Bea's pure angelic voice pulling the notes and the lyrics together like the worst heartbreak song on the planet. Bunny blinked back tears. She couldn't dare herself to look at Piper because she would completely lose it. She would break down from the amount of emotion in Bea's voice, in the way she moved through the melody.

When Bea finished, Bunny sat back, awash with awe. "You're amazing."

"I've always had an affinity for jazz."

"Based on what I've heard you sing, I think you could sing anything you set your mind to."

"High compliment coming from you." Bea beamed.

Bunny snorted lightly and rolled her eyes, but a smile played at her lips. "It's well deserved."

"Sing with me then."

"I don't know about that." Bunny's stomach roiled. There was no way she would be able to match Bea's talent. Bunny had a voice, but more than anything she had the business mindset and acuity to get her to the top, or at least closer than she had been when starting out. That was what had propelled her and Piper upward. Not because of her abilities but because of her tenacity. Bea didn't need that. She had the fucking raw talent that Bunny lacked.

"Please." Bea pulled up another song and set it on the piano.

Bunny stared at it, narrowing her gaze in curiosity. What the hell was Bea up to now?

"You start. I'll follow." Bea rested her chin on Bunny's shoulder as they reached the first line of lyrics.

Bunny took the alto lower part to *Shallow.* She sight-read the music as best she could, but she knew this song well enough to not feel chained to the music like she had with the last one. When Bunny finished her part, Bea immediately started, changing the lyrics slightly to be about two women instead of a man and a woman. The hair on Bunny's neck stood straight up, but she ignored it.

No one would notice, would they?

They kept singing, their voices blending after the nearly full week of practice. They could hear each other in ways they wouldn't have been able to before. Bunny instinctively knew when Bea would breathe and when she wouldn't.

They finished the song, and a round of applause erupted around them. But Bunny couldn't tear her gaze away from Bea. What were they doing here?

"Come home with me."

"What?" Bea wrinkled her nose.

"Come home with me. Tonight."

"I thought we weren't going to do this again." Bea lowered her voice so no one else could hear them.

"I changed my mind." Desperation clung to Bunny. She couldn't say why she wanted this. All she knew was that she had to have Bea, all of her, every inch that she was willing to give. And worse than that, she wanted Bea, not just her body. But maybe her body could ease some of this confusion bubbling up within her.

"Why?"

Damn her for asking the one question that Bunny couldn't answer. Dashing her tongue against her lips, Bunny dropped her gaze to Bea's mouth, to those scrumptious lips that would feel so good, taste amazing. Slowly raising her gaze up to meet Bea's eyes, Bunny said the first thing that came to her mind. "Because you deserve to be worshipped."

Bea gasped. She held Bunny's gaze, her lips slightly parted, her breathing in short rasps.

"Tonight."

"Tonight?" Bea repeated as a question.

"Yes. Right now." Bunny couldn't explain why she needed

this to happen immediately. But something had changed. Something was different.

"Bunny."

"I'll be outside waiting. If you want to *come*—" Bunny put a specific emphasis on that word "—then get your things and meet me."

Without another word, Bunny grabbed Piper's phone and headed for the table. She left Bea on the piano bench to make her decision. Bunny dropped her phone right in front of Piper, leaned over and whispered into her ear, "If you disturb me tonight, I'll kill you."

Bunny couldn't look at her. She straightened up, slapped some bills onto the table to pay for everyone's meals and walked out. She couldn't take the close proximity anymore. She needed to breathe fresh air, she needed to figure out what she'd just done.

Running her hands wildly through her hair, Bunny pulled at the strands as she asked for the valet to bring her car around. She was an idiot. Bea wouldn't want her. Bea wouldn't want anything with her. A quick fuck was all they'd agreed to, nothing more. In fact, they'd hardly agreed to that. It had been during little moments of anger.

The rain was cold against Bunny's skin, but it was a good reminder of what idiotic decisions she'd been making lately. Bea wouldn't want her. Bunny had nothing to offer other than quick moments of sex. There was nothing more that could be between them.

She was chilled to the bone when the driver brought her car around and handed her the keys. She stepped around the driver's side and opened the door.

"Bunny!"

Bunny froze. Looking up, she stared directly at Bea as she walked toward her, one heel in front of the other, dress perfectly cut for her curvy figure. It showed off everything Bea had, everything Bunny wanted. Bunny's heart was in her throat. She put both feet on the ground and faced Bea as she walked around the hood of the car and shut the driver's door.

"You invite me with you and then leave without me?"

"What?" Bunny's brow furrowed in confusion.

"That's pretty rude, don't you think?" Bea clasped her hand around Bunny's upper arm, pulling her in. "And I don't like it when people are rude."

Their mouths pressed together. Bunny's knees went weak. She sucked in a sharp breath and stepped closer, pulling Bea in by the small of her back as she parted her lips and slid her tongue against Bea's lower lip.

"But I think you can make it up to me," Bea murmured, kissing Bunny again quickly. "What do you say?"

Bunny had no idea what to say or think. She'd never been this thoroughly seduced before, and hell, it felt amazing. Bunny wanted this to happen every day. She moved, pushing Bea back toward the hood of the car and around the front of it.

She opened the passenger side door and held onto it firmly while she gave Bea a long and deliberate once over.

"Get in the fucking car," Bunny ordered.

FIFTEEN

Jo

"Bea?" Jo turned and looked up as Bea slowly returned from the piano. Concern filled Jo in an instant. She hadn't expected them to fight in public like they did at the studio, but she also hadn't expected Bunny to just up and leave so quickly.

"Um." Bea's face was flushed as though she had run a few times around the block before returning to their table. But she didn't sit down. "I think I'm going to call it a night as well. I'm exhausted after this week."

"Is everything okay?"

"Yes." Bea smiled. It was a smile that Jo wasn't sure she had ever seen before. "I think I will be. I just need some rest."

"Okay. Be safe and call if you need anything."

"Thanks for a lovely evening, Piper." Bea's soft voice was filled with emotion, and Jo wasn't sure the plan had actually worked the way they had wanted. Something new washed over her sister, and she had no idea if it was good or bad. "I'll see you both back in the studio tomorrow."

Silence settled over the table for a moment.

"Well, that happened a lot sooner than expected." Piper leaned over to Jo after both Bunny and Bea had left. "For a successful evening, I get the impression something else is going on." Piper lifted her eyebrows in Jo's direction. The soft touch of a smile on her lips soothed Jo instantly.

"I'm just worried, I guess. Bea and I are close, but sometimes she forgets she isn't actually my protector. And keeps me a little at arm's length when I think she could actually use someone to talk to."

"Ah." Piper nodded and picked up her drink, taking another sip. Jo now couldn't remember what round of drinks they were up to or what she and Piper had been drinking.

"I guess we'll have to see how it all shapes up tomorrow." Jo forced a smile on her face.

"But you and I still have the rest of the night together." Piper's voice held a low huskiness that sent a shiver through Jo's body.

"Yes, we do. Should we head out and go for a walk maybe?"

"I like that idea." Piper waved down the server. While she asked for the bill, Jo's phone vibrated in her purse.

"Bea?" She swiped without checking the screen.

"Hey stranger, you finally decided I was worth your time again, huh?" The purr turned into a pout. Jo's blood drained from her body and settled somewhere in her feet. Immediately, she looked at Piper, begging for help, for anyway out of this torture that was about to happen.

"Mandy?" she choked out.

"Of course it's me, sweetheart. I've missed you so much. I can't wait to see you again."

Jo didn't know what to say. Mandy's chuckle came through the phone, but still Jo couldn't find the words.

"Jo?" Piper's voice was coupled with a gentle shake to Jo's bare arm. How many times had Piper tried to get her attention?

Jo looked up, blinking as she tried to process what was happening.

"What's wrong?" Piper skimmed her hand up and down Jo's arm in comfort.

Tears filled Jo's eyes. Piper took the phone from her, not hesitating. She glanced at the number on the screen and cringed.

"Jo can't speak right now. She'll call you back *if* she wants to." Piper hung up and scowled at the phone. It had been a private number.

"What did she want?"

"Probably to get back together with me." Jo twisted her hands in her lap, staring at the edge of the table.

"Come on. Let's get out of here." Piper stood up and offered Jo her hands. Jo looked up, hating herself as she saw pain and anger in Piper's eyes.

"I'm sorry."

"Nope, none of that." Piper's eyes softened, and she indicated her hands once more for Jo to take.

Jo took them, and when she stood up, Piper pulled a little harder than Jo had anticipated. They pressed together, chest to chest.

"Hi." Jo looked up into Piper's eyes.

"Hi yourself." Piper smiled as she tucked a stray strand of Jo's hair behind her ear before stepping back. As she did, Piper twisted her hand in Jo's and entwined their fingers. "Now let's take that walk."

For a few minutes, they walked past people and restaurants. The silence between them didn't quite feel as comfortable as it normally did. Jo cursed herself and then huffed in frustration. She shouldn't be angry at herself. It was Mandy who had once again barged into her life to try and… what? Jo had no idea anymore.

"Are you okay?" Piper asked as they pushed past the last of

the restaurants, the crowd thinning out as the path curved down toward the river.

"No," Jo said. "No, I'm not okay at all."

"Do you want to talk about it?"

"I'm so angry. I cared about her, I really did. But she never treated me as anything important until something big happened. Every time Bea and I got in the papers for something, every time we moved one step toward the big goals, Mandy would dote on me. I would think, finally she realizes what I'm worth and how much she cares about me." Jo wiped angrily at the tears that escaped.

"I'm sorry," Piper said as she squeezed Jo's hand in her own.

"And now, I've had such a fun night. I always feel like I'm someone important when I'm with you, you know. And here I am ruining it all."

Piper pulled on her hand, and Jo had no choice but to stop walking. There were people still around, but none were close to them anymore. "You *are* important. You're also wonderful and deserve to be treated like a queen every day, not just when you take another step forward toward your career."

"See!" Jo smiled despite her need to sniff and the watery haze she saw Piper through. "Even now when I must look like a raccoon with rabies, you always say nice things."

"You're beautiful. And you haven't ruined anything." The warmth in Piper's eyes made Jo's stomach muscles tense.

They stepped in together, closing the gap between them.

It wasn't their first kiss, but it felt deeper than any they had shared before now.

"I like you, Piper," Jo whispered, eyes closed as she rested her forehead against Piper's and smiled as their noses brushed each other. "And I would really like to take you home tonight."

Piper's sharp inhalation made Jo's smile stretch wider as she pressed her lips against Piper's once more. The smooth softness of Piper's lips opened at the smallest touch of Jo's tongue.

A moan escaped Jo, and Piper laughed as she pulled back.

"I think we'd better get back to your place before Bunny kills me for being arrested for public nudity."

Jo laughed and couldn't believe how much her heart raced and her stomach fluttered with nerves and anticipation as she pulled Piper back to the restaurant. Piper had the valet retrieve her car as soon as they arrived.

The ride seemed to take twice as long as the drive to get to the restaurant. Though Piper's hand on the inside of her knee tracing spirals on her pants might have had something to do with that. By the time Jo had managed to get the front door to her apartment open, their lips were on each other's in a heated and inciting embrace. Piper was behind Jo in a second as she turned to lock the door behind them.

Jo gasped as Piper's hands found her hips while her mouth found the soft skin where her neck met her shoulder. She whimpered and leaned her forehead against the now locked door.

"You're so sexy," Piper whispered in Jo's ear before taking her lobe between her lips and gently sucking on it.

"Oh fuck." Jo moaned as she pushed her ass hard against Piper's crotch.

"Yes," Piper whispered, her breath sending shivers down Jo's body.

Piper untucked Jo's shirt from her pants and slid her hands beneath the released fabric. Her fingers danced up Jo's stomach, making Jo's legs quiver a little. When she found Jo's breasts, strong fingers pinched the already erect nipples that strained through her bra.

"Fuck." Jo gasped between breaths. "Bedroom. Now."

Piper laughed and spun Jo around so they faced each other. This time, the kiss wasn't soft and sweet. It held the fire Jo had always held back. The fire other lovers had shied away from whenever she showed any kind of dominance. Apparently being an overall happy and enthusiastic human being meant she couldn't possibly be the instigator in the bedroom.

But Jo didn't fear that reaction or assumption from Piper. She had no reason to think Piper would be different—except, of course, she had been almost the opposite in every other way to any other woman Jo had fallen for.

Fallen for?

No.

This was fun and freeing. This wasn't the time to fall for anyone. Bea and Jo were just starting to make a name for themselves, and she couldn't be distracted with emotions and the encompassing nature of falling.

Jo forced her thoughts back to the gorgeous woman in front of her who kissed her as though it was their last day on earth, and she wouldn't waste a second doing anything else. Jo gently encouraged Piper to walk backward toward the bedroom. Her heart beat faster as Piper trusted her to take control, to lead her safely to the bedroom. By the time they had reached it, Jo's entire body buzzed with the thrill of arousal and power.

"Take your clothes off," Jo rasped out. Hoping she didn't sound too bossy, or as nervous as she still felt beneath the thrill.

"Yes, ma'am." Piper winked and slid the strap of her dress off one shoulder, revealing smooth skin beneath. How had she not realized Piper hadn't been wearing a bra? She bit her lip, wetness soaking into her underwear. Watching Piper slowly undress herself would have made her body react, but having her do it without losing eye contact had Jo's clit pulsing, and her breath close to gasping. She wouldn't last long if her body didn't calm down soon.

"Do I get the same show?" Piper asked as she stood naked in front of Jo.

Jo swallowed and hesitated.

"Hey." Piper stepped forward, as though her own nakedness meant nothing, and cupped Jo's cheek in her palm. "Are you nervous?"

"I'm always a little nervous." Jo shrugged, the confidence she had found earlier seemingly disappeared in the light of her bedroom, staring at a masterpiece of the human body.

"We don't have to." Piper tilted her head until she met Jo's eyes.

It had been all Jo needed for that energy and desire to come rushing back through her. Jo pushed forward, devouring Piper's mouth with her own and dragging Piper onto the bed with her. Her hands roamed over Piper's smooth skin, causing goosebumps to rise in her wake. Piper's hands were on her again, hands beneath her shirt, dancing over her back, and in a moment, flicking the clip of her bra, releasing Jo's breasts.

"I want to do this," Jo muttered between kisses.

"I want to, too." Piper grinned as Jo stripped herself of her shirt and bra. "But you set the pace, and you tell me to stop anytime you want, or if there is anything you don't like, promise?"

For a moment, Jo was overcome by this amazing woman. She had her energy, and she truly understood. But this was a whole other area Jo had never experienced before. Someone who cared as much about her pleasure and comfort as their own. Maybe even more. The idea unsettled Jo for a moment. It must have registered on her face.

Piper propped herself up on her elbows and looked closer. Not at her exposed breasts, but at her.

"I promise. But only if you do it, too." Jo said.

"Guaranteed." Piper winked at Jo.

"All right." Jo bit her lip, fear and excitement warring with each other. Could she really explore those things she had always been shamed for wanting? Would Piper really not think less of her for wanting them?

"What do you like?" Piper whispered as she reached forward, taking Jo's hands. They shuffled up together farther up the bed. One of Jo's knees, still dressed, pressed right between Piper's legs.

Jo ignored the question, unable to voice what she wanted. As though sensing her hesitation, Piper flipped her over onto her back and kissed her hard, bruising her lips in ways that sent shudders rocking through Jo's body.

"Do you want me inside you?" Piper straddled Jo and ground her pussy against Jo's stomach.

"Yes." Jo hips bucked up.

"Can I take the rest of your clothes off?"

"Yes," Jo said. How were questions making her breath increase and her clit throb?

Piper took her time as she kissed her way over Jo's breasts, stopping long enough to suck on each nipple until Jo grunted, before working her way down Jo's stomach.

Her fingers were fast and furious as they undid the pants and rid Jo of the material.

"A thong?" Piper moaned as she placed a kiss on Jo's mound through the cloth.

Jo's breath hitched, and her hips bucked.

"You're so receptive." Piper laughed, nudging Jo to lift her hips so she could slide the thong off.

Piper's fingers slipped through Jo's folds, and Jo moaned, rocking her hips up, begging for more pressure. Piper circled Jo's clit as she pushed herself into the space between Jo's thighs. Jo wrapped her legs around Piper's hips, pulling her in closer.

Piper leaned forward and pinched Jo's nipple with her free hand. Their hips rocked together, pressed harder and harder as the scent of arousal filled the room.

"I want..." Jo started but stopped before she got any further.

"What do you want?" Piper's voice was filled with curiosity and softness.

"Top drawer." Jo covered her face with her hands as Piper got off the bed and walked to her dresser.

"Is it sterile?"

Of all the things Jo had expected to be asked, that hadn't been on the list. "You mean you don't mind?"

"Why would I mind?" Piper faced Jo, the strap-on already looped into the harness. Piper's eyes smoldered as they stared at Jo.

"It's sterile." Jo swallowed and forced herself to keep eye contact with Piper. "It's never been used."

"What?"

"I was told it was disrespectful to ask a lesbian to use one."

"Who the hell told you that? Also, not a lesbian." Piper slid the harness onto her body, her lips quirking to the side. "Definitely pansexual. Every moment of every day."

Jo was not answering that question. "And you really don't mind?"

"Do I mind making a gorgeous woman come the way she wants to?" Piper walked around the bed and got back on her knees between Jo's legs. "Never."

The first cold touch of the dildo caught Jo's breath, but soon her juices coated the toy. Jo pushed her head back into the mattress as Piper's fingers opened her up and Piper pushed inside. Slowly at first, a gentle pull back before sliding in again. The stretch was such a tease of untold pleasure to come.

Jo cried out as she pushed against Piper's increasingly faster thrusts. She lifted her shoulders off the bed as she reached for Piper's hips with her hands, pulling Piper into her harder and faster.

Piper leaned down and kissed Jo's lips as one of Piper's hands cupped the back of Jo's head, the other slipping between them. Piper circled Jo's clit as she continued to thrust.

"Fuck!" Jo screamed out as she came with a shudder.

Piper chuckled into her mouth as she helped ease Jo back down to the bed. She didn't pull out or move her fingers off Jo's clit. Jo's aftershock shudders were met with the strong touch still on her and in her.

It might have been delirium from post-orgasmic bliss, but Jo had all the confidence in the world for a few brief seconds. "I want you to sit on my face."

"Really?" Piper's eyes opened wide as she asked.

"Surprised a girl like me wants that?"

"No." Piper shook her head as she gently eased herself out of Jo. "Not surprised, just extremely glad."

"You like riding faces?" Jo asked as she hurried Piper out of the harness herself.

"Well, yes. But I like you telling me what you want."

A wildness inside of Jo woke up, and she pulled Piper back onto the bed. As soon as Piper was in place, she pressed hard against her clit with the flat of her tongue.

"Oh fuck, yes." Piper growled gutturally as she fell forward with the sensation. Jo didn't wait to feel Piper's body land on the mattress above her head before she covered Piper's clit with her mouth and sucked hard.

Piper moaned unintelligible things while Jo sucked, flicking her tongue over the sensitive nub in irregular patterns. She gripped Piper's ass and pulled her into her face harder as Jo's own pleasure peaked again.

"Fuck me while I fuck you." She grabbed Piper's hips and shoved her away enough from her mouth so she could speak.

"How?" Piper barely got the word out.

"Turn around."

It took Piper a second before she understood the command. With her back arched high into the air, Piper lowered her face to Jo's throbbing clit while Jo circled Piper's entrance with her fingers.

"Can I fuck you inside?"

"Yes." Was all Piper got out before Jo pressed two fingers into her, only to remove them and add a third.

Piper's groan sent a wave of pleasure through Jo as it vibrated over her clit.

They sucked and licked while their fingers fucked each other faster and faster, as though racing each other to release first.

Piper collapsed over Jo's body, half rolling off as they both came within moments of each other.

"Fuck." Piper let out with a chuckle.

Jo laughed and shuffled herself on the bed until they laid side by side. Piper opened her arms, and Jo quickly moved into her embrace, head resting on Piper's shoulder, her eyes watching Piper's perfect breasts as their movement eventually slowed with the evening out of her breath.

The last thing Jo remembered before she fell asleep was Piper's kiss pressed to the top of her head, a mumbled thanks whispered into the quiet room.

bea

Bea blinked slowly, warmth surrounding her in the big bed filled with soft fuzzy blankets. Who knew Bunny would have such a heavenly bed? Turning on her side, Bea reached for Bunny only to find that part of the bed empty.

Frowning, she looked around the room and found herself alone. she rubbed her eyes before stifling a yawn behind her hand. She wouldn't let waking up alone be the undoing of all the warm and satiated feelings that swayed inside of her.

Bea took her time luxuriating in Bunny's shower, imagining a future where it wasn't just Bunny's. She laughed, and the sound echoed around the tiles, mixing with the rush and pound of water. She couldn't remember the last time she had felt so relaxed, even after the other times she and Bunny had sex. This had outdone all of them.

Taking her time, she allowed herself to linger in the memory of Bunny worshiping her body, as though she were the goddess Aphrodite herself.

Bunny still hadn't returned when Bea got out of the shower. Refusing to let that take away her happiness, Bea got dressed, double checked she had all of her things and pulled the door locked behind her. As soon as she did, worry washed over her. Had Bunny left without her keys, assuming Bea would still be there when she returned?

Bea shook her head. She hadn't seen any keys in the bowl near the door.

Almost skipping her way to the curb where her ride waited for her, Bea decided she would take a detour to the studio this morning and grab coffee on her way for everyone.

Using her back to push open the studio door, Bea carried a tray of coffee in her hands. Music filtered down the hall, and she smiled as she walked, her feet automatically stepping in time with a familiar song she couldn't quite pin down. It would bother her later, or come to her later. Either way she stopped at the threshold of the piano room and took a deep breath.

Bunny sat on the piano stool, her body moving with the music she played. Bea took the moment to watch her unnoticed. She had become addicted to the shape of this woman, her strong wide shoulders, the muscles that rippled under her short-sleeved shirt. Bunny rocked into the music, and Bea's hips swayed in time of their own accord.

"A really good job, Bunny."

Bea startled a little, splashing a few drops of coffee over the tray, thankfully missing her own skin. She regretfully turned her eyes away from Bunny, and for the first time, noticed Siena sitting on the floor against the wall. She wore dark slacks and a tailored button-down shirt with sleeves that were cut angularly from beneath her elbow and down to her wrist. Siena sat with one leg stretched out in front of her while the other bent at the knee, her bare foot flat on the ground. On the thigh of her bent leg rested a folder with sheets of paper on it. Siena flicked through the pages as though she had done it several times and looked up at Bunny. "These lyrics are fantastic."

Bunny spun around on the piano stool and stopped before she reached Siena. She had turned toward Bea, and as their eyes caught, Bea's heart fluttered and her smile spread wide over her face.

"Hi." Bea dipped her head and tucked hair behind her ear with a hand. The tray wobbled in just the one hand, and Bea quickly returned to holding it properly. Since when had she ever played the demure role? It didn't sit well with her. "I brought coffee."

"Bea." Siena jumped up and strode forward.

Bea squared her shoulders. Professional—despite everything, she would remain the consummate professional. Always. Despite the wobble she felt in her legs as Bunny's eyes raked over her body.

"Perfect timing." Siena leaned forward and brushed her lips against Bea's cheek. Maybe it was the corner of her lips and not her cheek. Bea had no idea and quite frankly didn't care. Her eyes remained fixed on Bunny until Siena moved back, and Bea forced herself to return Siena's look.

"Bunny's reworked the song *Baby It's Cold Outside*, and the lyrics are brilliant. This song will be the perfect duet for the two of you as the finale for the show."

"We're doing a duet?" Bea asked, her heart speeding up. The set list she'd seen so far still hadn't included any duets for them. Every other combination was there except that one. Bea had tried to bring this up to Bunny, but she hadn't thought her words had made any difference.

"It'd be a waste not to show off all the combinations of voices we have between the four of you. Wouldn't it?" Siena voiced Bea's very thoughts. Then again, maybe Bunny would actually listen to Siena.

"Well, yes." Bea nodded, blinking in confusion. Had Bunny listened to her after all? Or had she only reconsidered after they had slept together? No, she shook the idea away as soon as it entered her thoughts. Bunny was a professional. Despite what they did away from the studio, or at least away from other people when in the studio, she wouldn't do a duet just to keep Bea happy. She must really believe in the strength of their voices combined.

"Yeah." Siena drew out the word, looking at Bea and then Bunny. Oh shit, had Bea missed something while she worked through things in her head? "So, are you okay doing it with Bunny?"

Bea's eyes widened, and she snapped them back to Siena, having allowed them to drift over to Bunny once more.

"Umm." Bea studied Siena's face. Did she realize what she'd just said? Did she know? Her face gave away nothing, but Bea wondered if that glint in Siena's eyes told more than what the woman was saying. "Yeah, as long as the lyrics have removed the lack-of-consent issues, then I'm absolutely fine with singing it with Bunny."

"Great." Siena clapped her hands and nodded. "You two can work together on the lyric changes."

"Enjoy your coffee." Siena laid a soft hand on Bea's forearm for just a moment. Bea found that she didn't really care one way or the other if Siena did know about her and Bunny.

What would it even matter? Bea wouldn't go back into the closet for anyone, and while she tried to understand Bunny's perspective on coming out, not even Bunny would make her hide who she was. Besides, she would get to sing with Bunny on stage. Even with the song still reeking of heterosexuality, it couldn't take away Bea's excitement about the duet.

"Thanks for the feedback." Bunny smiled as she took the offered folder from Siena.

"Anytime. Glad I popped in." Siena turned and gave Bea another smile, this one feeling a little more intimate than the previous one. "Can't wait to hear you and Bea sing together."

"Thanks, Siena."

Siena nodded and left. She didn't seem like one for big fanfares. And Bea could appreciate that.

"Oh my God. Is that coffee for us?" Piper walked directly up to Bea. After Bea nodded, Piper found her order written in the shorthand codes of the barista and smiled at Bea. "You're my new favorite person."

"Hey!" Bunny called from the piano chair.

Piper shrugged, taking a big sip from her cup. "Bring me coffee and you might be able to win back the title of best friend."

"Oh, it's conditional now, huh?" Bunny's amusement colored the words, and Bea wanted to dive into this moment and let it wrap around her forever.

"There's coffee?" Jo's squeal interrupted whatever Piper's answer might have been as she rushed into the practice room, tucking her pockets into her jeans.

Had she gotten dressed in the car? Worry ate at Bea's stomach.

"Thank God." Jo kissed Bea's cheek as she grabbed her cup. "The line for coffee up the road was too long and there was no way we were going to be late again."

We? There is a we? Bea looked at Piper and Jo and back again. Neither seemed fazed by Jo's words or focused on anything except the coffee they consumed like starving lovers.

Bea placed the tray on the small table near the piano where Bunny had put the clipboard down next to a stack of papers. The top sheet was covered in Bunny's small messy writing. Bea was glad she had a cup in each hand so the temptation to trace the words with her fingers couldn't be acted on.

"And this one is yours." She handed out the cup to Bunny, who remained seated at the piano stool.

"Thanks." Bunny reached for the cup, but was that a slip in her stoic gaze?

Their fingers brushed, and Bea's breath caught in her throat.

"So, what's new?" Piper smiled as she pushed herself up on an empty table a little away from where Bunny and Bea both still held onto Bunny's cup.

Bea swallowed, let go of the cup and turned to the rest of the small room.

"Yeah." Jo's lying face had never been good, but Bea shook her head. The frustration she had felt over it last night had subsided into a gratefulness she wished she could scream about from the rooftops. "Everything okay?"

"Everything's fine." Bunny stood up, placed the coffee on the table untouched and collected the stack of papers. She divided them up and handed them a relatively equal pile each. "These are your own personal lists. If you aren't singing in one of the songs, it's not in the list."

They all thanked Bunny and instantly flicked through the music. Even Bea refused to linger on Bunny's face as she took her sheets. She could be just as professional as Bunny. More so. Even though another kiss against the piano wouldn't be unwelcome. She was a professional, sure, but she definitely wasn't dead. Any thoughts of her libido being dead had fled the moment Bunny had first laid those smoldering eyes on her.

"Let's get into rehearsing the first half hour of the show right through. I think we've gotten far enough to be able to do that. I've set up a timer so we know exactly how much time we need between each song to work out if we are going to do costume changes."

"Really?" Jo and Piper's eyes widened as though it were already Christmas morning and beneath the tree was a pile of gifts with their names on them.

"Only if we can get our timing right." Bunny pursed her lips and looked at Piper and Jo with such serious teacher eyes that Bea had to press her own lips together so as not to laugh at the two nodding with their big puppy dog eyes.

"Of course." Bea said, clearing her throat and nodding. "Shall we start warming up then?"

"Sounds like a good idea." Bunny nodded.

The rehearsal was brutal with Bunny making them run through the first half of the show three full times, including multiple pauses to fix mistakes. Each time she gave critiques to each of them and, surprisingly to Bea, asked them all if they noticed anything she could improve in her own performance. The critiques were minimal and even Bunny seemed to relax into the joy of it all by the end of the third run through.

"We can do at least one costume change in the first half. If it runs as smoothly as that on the night, there will definitely be enough time." Bunny nodded at them, still serious as she ever was.

Bea's cheeks heated as Bunny's gaze rested on hers a little longer than necessary before roaming down her body and back up again. How could her eyes have such power to make heat pool between her thighs?

"So, ideas for costumes?"

"Well." Piper flicked her look to Jo and then back to Bunny. "Jo and I have a few ideas. Can we work on them together after rehearsal and bring them to you both tomorrow?"

"Sounds good." Bunny nodded. "Shall we start on the next section of the performance? How are the dance routines going?"

"They're going great." Jo's energy bubbled up, and it made Bea smile. "Piper and I work really well together. The choreography we've chosen isn't too difficult. Simple, but still enough to make the crowd go ooh and aah."

"Ooh and aah?" Bunny asked, raising her eyebrows, but Bea saw the pull of her lips as she fought back the smile.

"It's the professional term for it." Bea smirked, unable to help herself.

"Oh well then, who am I to criticize?" Bunny smiled outright this time, and Bea didn't care that Jo and Piper were still in the room. She couldn't pull her eyes away from Bunny's lit up face.

"Take a break, get some lunch."

Jo's easiness was so nice to see. Bea wanted to bask in it a little longer, so she pulled Jo toward her. It had been a while since the two sisters had given in to their sibling squabbles, and Bea missed the playfulness between them.

Things had been a little tense, more than normal. Ever since Jo went and begged Siena for a chance to represent them. And then to top that off, the secrecy about Mandy contacting her again.

They hadn't spoken about it. Bea avoided the topic as best she could even though her worries gnawed at the back of her mind. Jo was her responsibility. She was the older sister, and she had to make sure Jo was safe, despite her seriously shit choices of women in the past.

Jo nudged Bea's shoulder, and they smiled at each other. Bea's worry eased a little, and she would make sure they got some time soon to really talk about what was going on with them both.

The way Bea felt right now, she might even be willing to tell Jo about Bunny.

Maybe.

bunny

"We've got the finale songs figured out as well." Bunny swallowed over the lump in her throat as Piper and Jo sat down, both sweaty and reaching for their water bottles.

They had all moved to the large dance room. Bea seemed as keen as Bunny was to see how the dance routine for Piper and Jo's duet was turning out.

"That was fantastic. You weren't kidding. The effect will be stunning, and your voices work beautifully together." Bea rushed on with her praise before either Jo or Piper could respond to Bunny's announcement.

Was Bea not as okay about the duet as she had told Siena? Truth be told, Bunny had only agreed to do the duet, she hadn't even suggested it be the final set list. It didn't sit right on her shoulders not to have the four of them signing together to wrap out the show.

She would talk to Siena about it later, and hopefully be able to convince Siena that all four of them should sing the final song, and it not be her reworked one.

"Are we all singing the finale?" Piper asked, her cheeks still red but her chest rising and falling a little slower now.

"Um, no." Bunny would not show weakness or doubt about this. "Siena made the decision. The finale will be a duet between me and Bea."

"Really?" Jo squealed and clapped her hands together excitedly. "Excellent. I was wondering why you two didn't have a duet together."

"We do. And we'll be ending the show on it, apparently." Bunny couldn't look Bea in the eye. She distracted herself by looking at her cuticles.

"You didn't ask for it to be the finale?" Bea asked.

Bunny shook her head, trying and failing to read the look that flashed over Bea's eyes. "No, Siena makes all the final decisions on the set list. She has to run them by Allegra as well. So we don't have much say ultimately."

"So the order we're practicing has already been approved?" Jo asked immediately. Bunny liked Jo. Despite the energy it took to put up with two high energy extroverts, she enjoyed seeing how quickly Jo's mind worked behind the girl-next-door look. She couldn't deny she had worried when they first met. Piper had a similar look, but with her long gangly height, Bunny had never mistaken her for an airhead. When she had first seen Jo, those thoughts had flitted through her mind, and they had definitely not been kind.

"The order of the first half has been approved. I'm waiting for Siena's confirmation of the second half."

"So we might not be the finale after all?" Bea asked, and this time the sadness in her eyes was obvious.

"Siena seemed pretty convinced that was what she wanted, but nothing is set yet," Bunny answered, still trying to read in between the lines for what Bea wasn't saying. Surely she understood that their time together was just that and nothing more.

"Can we hear you two practice it?" Piper asked, a far-too-innocent smile on her face. Bunny knew her too well, and didn't like the look at all.

It's a trap! flashed through her brain several times.

"Yeah! What song is it?" Jo asked, sitting on the floor criss-cross applesauce, an expectant look on her face.

Bunny never supposed she would ever find another human being as constantly in motion as Piper, let alone another musician.

"*Baby, It's Cold Outside*," Bea answered before Bunny could, her gaze locked on Bunny's face. They were trying to read each other, but they didn't know each other well enough yet.

"Ew." Jo looked as though she had just tasted something foul as she glared at Bea. "You hate that song. It's horrible."

"I've changed the lyrics. There will be no dubious consent in it."

"Oh," Jo and Piper said in unison. They looked at each other, smiled and then returned their gazes back to Bunny.

"So do we get to listen? Your voices are a brilliant combination. The perfect couple to end the night."

Bunny's breath caught in her chest.

"We haven't tried it together yet," Bea answered quickly. "Maybe after we've had some run-throughs alone first."

Bunny furrowed her brow. From the beginning, Bea had been willing to dive into the rehearsals as though her life depended on it.

The thought stopped Bunny.

Because her livelihood, her plans and hopes, did rely on this event.

So why was Bea hesitating now?

"All right. Well, I'm done with this rehearsal then. Are we good to leave, Bunny?" Piper jumped to her feet as she asked

"Yeah, we've done enough for today." Bunny nodded and shoved her hands in her pockets. She couldn't tear her gaze from Bea, still trying to figure out what the hesitation was for. She couldn't be embarrassed. They'd both fucked up enough songs by that point to know they weren't perfect when it came to singing. So what else could it be?

"Excellent." Piper spun on the balls of her feet until she faced Jo and offered her hands. Jo took them without words and let Piper pull her up.

"Jo, can I talk to you for a second?" Bea said, and after a strange look between the sisters, the two left the room together, Piper calling out that she would catch up in a moment.

"What are you doing, Piper?" Bunny asked as soon as the door closed.

"What do you mean?" Piper furrowed her brow.

Bunny looked Piper directly in the eye. They both knew exactly what she was talking about, but Bunny didn't have the heart to say it. She'd already held Piper back enough when it came to her personal life, and she didn't want to add more grievances to Piper's list.

"Fine. Don't tell me. But be careful, and don't do anything I wouldn't do."

"Wouldn't dream of it." Piper winked. "And just what *have* you been doing?"

"None of your damn business," Bunny growled. She'd walked right into that one, hadn't she? Her cheeks burned with embarrassment. But she'd never been one to kiss and tell. And she certainly wasn't going to do that if Piper and Jo even had a chance at becoming something.

Piper laughed, knowing full well that Bunny would keep her mouth shut. She shook her head as she headed for the door. "You're so easy sometimes."

"Me?"

"Oh yeah." Piper's laugh echoed through the room as she left. Her departure left a hollow feeling in Bunny's stomach.

"Hey." Bea returned on her own. She stood still as the door closed behind her.

Bunny ground her molars, her entire being trying to

convince her feet to move and plant her body against Bea's. But she held back, remembering the firm look that Bea had given her. The one that Bunny couldn't read. They needed to resolve that.

"Why don't you want to practice the song?" Bunny asked.

"You looked horrified, Bunny. I did it for your sake." Bea spoke with her cool calmness. Did she not have any conflicting feelings about the song, about the two of them at all? She hadn't seemed this icy since the first time they met. Bea reached forward and picked up the sheet music. "Are we going to practice it now?"

"Yes." Bunny could be professional. She could be stoic. She could brush off Bea with the best of them. She'd had decades of practice already. And Bea wouldn't be any different from any other woman she'd been with, right?

They ran through the song several times. Each time their voices leaned more into each other, and Bunny felt that free lightness that music gave her.

"That was beautiful," Bea spoke softly, as though she worried talking too loudly might steal the beauty of the music that seemed to linger and hum around them. Bea leaned in closer on the piano bench where she'd eventually sat. It had been such a long day, and Bunny couldn't blame her.

"It is. Siena's right. This will show the true extent of your vocal range. Far more than the rest of the night."

"She said that?"

Bunny nodded. "She did. But are you sure you're okay to sing this song?"

"Your changed lyrics definitely remove the issue of consent, so I'm okay with it. Plus, I like the jazz beat you've added into it."

It was just a compliment. Bunny kept telling herself that repeatedly. Bea hadn't meant anything more by it. There wasn't anything more between them other than sex.

But she was wrong.

Bunny knew it deep within her soul.

Raising her gaze up, she met Bea's eyes. All words caught in her throat. The music stopped. She couldn't hold back anymore. Bunny leaned forward, brushing her lips against Bea's.

The softness sent a bolt of fire into her chest. It wasn't entirely bad, but fear filled her at the same time. She didn't want the softness, or the sweet desire for Bea that lingered after they had woken in her bed that morning. She'd left for a long run because she couldn't handle the desire to stay warm under the covers with Bea wrapped around her. She couldn't stop dreaming about waking Bea up, mouth between her legs, and the desire to do that every morning.

She had to stop this before it continued. Bunny had to be the one to put her foot down, because she could see the path they were headed down. And it wasn't the one she wanted for herself. It wasn't the one she could live with.

Bunny pulled back, forcing the fear back as far as she could. But she saw the concern in Bea's eyes. And she longed to lean in again and put that concern to rest. Bunny's lips were still damp from Bea's mouth. Her chest was still tight because it was hard to breathe. Arousal still coiled through her uncontrollably.

Clearing her throat, Bunny said, "I've got some work to do this evening, so I'm going to head out. I'll see you tomorrow."

"Sure," Bea answered, her voice wavering with uncertainty.

Before Bunny could give in to the urge to explain or say anything else, she grabbed her things and walked out, refusing to look back.

———

"What the fuck is that?" Bunny's voice boomed around the rehearsal room days later. The mock-up costume designs didn't match the drawings nearly close enough.

Bea, Jo, and Piper all jerked with a start and stared at her, jaws dropped. Confusion and even a touch of fear lit up their faces.

The whole day had gone well up until this point. Now, Bunny was pretty damn sure this whole charity event was a disastrous idea. She shouldn't have agreed to work with two out queer women. They were going to drag her down with them.

The first two costumes had been acceptable, with maybe just a little too much color for Bunny's usual look. But the last costume was completely over the line.

"They're the costumes," Piper spoke softly, and a new rage built in Bunny's chest at being treated like a wild animal.

She wasn't being unreasonable. They were. "Am I really the only one professional enough here to know these costumes are anything but acceptable? Is this a joke?"

"Stop being such an asshole," Bea snapped out, and the two of them faced off eye-to-eye and glared at each other. "The costumes look amazing, and they'll be perfect for the finale. You got your way in keeping the song heterosexual. In fact, you've gotten your way this entire time. Collaboration means give and take, and it's your turn to give the rest of us a chance to be genuine human beings."

"We're not going out on stage at a Christmas charity event wearing *those* outfits." Bunny pointed angrily at the outfit on the table. "Make it Christmas, Santa rip-offs, warm, cold, whatever you want. I'm not wearing a rainbow."

"*Those*..." Bea snarled back "...are the costumes Siena and Allegra have agreed on."

"What?" Bunny's face grew cold as all blood rushed to her feet.

"I ran them by Siena this morning, and she sent photos to

Allegra. They both gave them the thumbs up." Bea's face was hard, her eyes narrowed.

Betrayal snagged Bunny's heart and gave it a tight squeeze. Bunny shoved herself back from the table, stood up, and turned away. She stalked toward the back wall, her hands pushing through her hair.

What was Siena doing? She couldn't wear *that*. None of them could. It was completely off-brand.

"What's your actual problem with them?" Piper called out.

Bunny spun around instantly.

"Piper, don't be dense. This is a Christmas event, not a rally. Those costumes will out all of us the moment we step on stage."

"So?" Bea and Jo said together.

"I'm not having my music become the sidenote to my personal life and the rumors those piranhas keep going on about. I'm not parading around up there, taking away from everything I've worked toward. You think I've gotten this far in my career by waving that flag? It's a target on our backs, not some claiming of identity." Bunny waved her hand at the outfit again, and the snarl she gave it might stay on her lips forever.

"*We've* worked hard," Piper snapped back, and for a moment, Bunny froze as though caught in the headlights of a vehicle racing toward her. Piper rarely used that tone with her. So rarely in fact that Bunny could count on one hand the number of times Piper had truly yelled at her. "*We've* climbed through every loop we needed to get here. But things aren't the same as they used to be, Bunny. Times have changed."

"I refuse to believe you. The same asshole bigots still run the show. They might say the right thing, but when it comes down to it, none of them would think twice about getting rid of us for less controversial artists." She scowled at all of them, narrowing her eyes harder at Bea. She'd gone over Bunny's head and gotten the costumes approved by Siena and Allegra, knowing Bunny wouldn't agree with them. Of course she had. Bunny had fooled herself thinking that Bea might be the first person she'd met without an angle. Of course she had an angle, and here it was, holding a sword over everything Bunny had worked toward.

None of them said anything, and Bunny turned her back on them. Fear raced up her spine, and she dropped her head forward, trying desperately to catch her breath, to see some way through this nightmare. She needed some way through that didn't leave her career and her life in a pile of cold ashes.

"Asshole bigots like me?" Siena's voice had Bunny spinning around so fast her equilibrium shifted, making it impossible for her to focus her eyes.

Bunny hadn't heard the door open. When she focused, she took in Siena, standing with her arms crossed just inside the door, a scowl to match Bunny's on her lips, and a hurt look on her face.

"I didn't know you were here." The words rushed from Bunny's lips.

"Would it have mattered?" Siena nodded over at the three others.

"I'm sorry," Bunny muttered.

"Sorry for what?" Siena walked slowly toward them. Each click of her heels against the hard floor sounded like a nail in Bunny's coffin. "For screaming at your fellow musicians while trying to bully them into your opinion?" *Click, click.* "For screaming so loud, I could hear you from the front of the studio?" *Click, click.* "Or for calling me a bigot?" *Click.* "Or sorry that I heard you?"

Bunny ran a hand through her hair, tugging at the ends sharply. "I didn't mean you. You know I would never mean you."

"I would hope not." Siena pinned Bunny with her eyes, and for a moment, Bunny felt like a child more than a veteran in the music industry. And then it found its way into Bunny's fears.

"These costumes, Siena." Bunny wanted to shut up, but she couldn't. It was bad enough she had all these sensations pulling her toward Bea, she didn't need this complication as well. "I can't wear them."

"I came down here to check how everything was going," Siena said, keeping her voice steady though Bunny could hear the anger wavering beneath. "Seems like a good thing I decided on a site visit today."

"Siena," Bunny tried again.

"We'll talk about your *issues* with the costumes later." Siena cut her another sharp look, thoroughly scolding Bunny. At least Siena was consistent. She never did take shit from anyone.

Bunny couldn't handle it. She turned on her toes and shoved open the door as hard as she could. She needed some air. She needed the fucking run of a lifetime.

She needed to escape.

bea

"Jo," Bea called down the corridor of the studio before Jo could leave. Piper had left following Bunny's outburst with the promise that things would be all right. Bea, however, had her doubts.

Siena hadn't looked impressed, and Bea's heart hadn't stopped stuttering since Bunny had walked out.

"Hey." Jo stopped walking before she reached the main door. "What's up?"

"I thought maybe we could grab a pizza and have dinner tonight."

Jo nodded, threading her arm with Bea's as they stepped outside of the studio. Bea shivered as the cool evening air embraced her. The parking lot for the studio wasn't well lit and only one other car remained besides her own and Jo's.

"Want to follow me to mine or will I follow you to yours?" Bea laughed as they nudged closer together as they walked across the loose gravel. The crunch sounded loud in the dim light, and Bea wished she hadn't spent last night watching reruns of an old crime show, or that Bunny's outburst hadn't affected her so much.

Her heart sank.

After some discussion about logistics, Bea left with Jo following behind her. Thankfully the drive was against the main flow of traffic, so it didn't take them as long as it usually took Bea to get home.

Once the pizza was ordered and drinks poured, the two sat on cushions on the living room floor, the coffee table between them.

"So." Jo smiled, her eyes wide with questions as she looked at Bea. "What inspired this sisterly get together?"

"What do you mean?" Bea knew exactly what Jo meant. They spent a lot of time together—they always had. But Jo had never been oblivious to Bea's inability to just say what was on her mind.

"What's going on?"

"I need to tell you something I did, and I'm not sure how you're going to handle it."

"Okay." Jo's smile spread across her face, and she leaned forward, eager to hear what Bea had to say.

Bea ran the pads of her fingers over her palm, trying to work out the best way to word why she had gone to Siena.

"I might have crossed a line." Bea started, and Jo's smile grew. "But I'm worried about you, and I felt it was important to let Siena know."

"What?" Jo's smile vanished in an instant. She leaned away from Bea, eyes blinking as though she had just been woken in the middle of the night. "What are you talking about?"

"I told Siena about Mandy."

"What? Why?"

"Because I'm worried she's going to worm her way back in and make trouble again."

"You mean for us." Jo rested against the couch, her shoulders slumped and her head dropping forward.

"My biggest concern is you." Jo knew that, didn't she? Had

Bea really gone on about the band more than her concern for Jo?

"I know." Jo nodded and lifted her head.

Bea had to give her credit. She'd imagined Jo going off at her about interfering in her life again. She even managed a weak smile for Bea. The tension Bea had been hoping to ease hadn't, and she couldn't put her finger on what was still holding her in this place of stress. Bea clenched her jaw and sucked down a big gulp of beer.

"There isn't anything else you want to tell me?" Jo's lips quivered, trying to find that big smile again but not quite managing it.

The rapid knocking on the door saved Bea from having to answer immediately, but as she grabbed her wallet and paid for the pizza, her mind whirled about what Jo might want her to talk about. What had that big grin been expecting to hear?

Food and napkins sorted, the sisters sat more comfortably, relaxing into memories of when they had shared an even smaller apartment than Bea's current one. They were halfway through the first slice, and Bea still couldn't place that tension. She hated it. She wanted the ease that they used to have together. She wanted her sister back.

"Jo, what did you think I was going to tell you?" Bea put her food down and grabbed her drink. She'd do anything to mend what she'd so clearly broken.

Jo's smile returned as she finished her current bite of pizza. "I thought maybe there was something you were going to tell me about." She let the word linger in the air between them.

"Tell you about?" Bea loved her sister, but this was not one of the things she particularly enjoyed. "Just spit it out."

"I was kind of hoping you'd tell me what's going on with you and Bunny." Jo wrinkled her nose before taking another bite of her pizza.

"Oh." Bea's stomach flipped over at the mixed thoughts speeding around her mind like race cars on a track.

"Oh?" Jo smiled. It was the smile that reminded Bea of the early years. Of nights lying awake, talking about dreams for the future, touring the world as a famous band and truly living the life they both wanted.

"I really like her," Bea said.

"Yes!" Jo fist pumped the air, and Bea rolled her eyes, though the smile lingered on her lips. Just saying those words out loud brought a happiness to her that she hadn't felt in ages. "But it's crazy and stupid, and I don't know what the hell is going on between us. And after today… I just don't know."

"So there's something going on?" Jo wriggled around, crossing her legs and giving her full attention to her big sister.

"Yeah." Bea bobbed her head back and forth, unsure if the answer to that was a simple yes or no. "But I have no idea what it is."

"Do you *like* like her?"

"Oh my God." Bea laughed, her cheeks burning as the memories of Bunny's face between her legs multiple times resurfaced. "Are we teenagers again?"

"Lately, I've wondered that." Jo's face pinked, and Bea smiled. It wasn't too hard to see where Jo's mind had led.

"But maybe? No? Yes?" Bea didn't want to push, even if talking about Bunny wasn't exactly what she thought the night would be focused around.

"It's not like you not to know."

"I do like her, more than I should. But her reaction about the costumes…" Bea shook her head and used the seat of the couch to rest her head. "I could never be serious with someone who's so set on being closeted. A simple rainbow outfit had her losing her shit. And to change the lyrics to make it about two women instead of a man and a woman? Hard no for her."

"I guess so." Jo nodded, her eyebrows furrowing. "Piper did

tell me that Bunny had some major hang-ups about either of them officially coming out."

"Oh yeah?" Bea tried to reel in her curiosity, but she was also too exhausted to care all that much.

"Yeah. Back when they started, there were a few bands who came out and their careers were entirely killed by it. But I think there were some threats to both Bunny and Piper too, because of the rumors."

"That's terrible." Bea tried to imagine seeing anyone be destroyed by being authentic. Theoretically, she knew it had happened, and she wasn't blind to any of the underhanded bullshit. There was more than one manager they had refused to be represented by, for that reason. But to actually see the fallout?

Had she been too hard on Bunny?

"Yeah, but who knew she was capable of having such a huge meltdown. Piper is a bit worried about her, actually. This hasn't apparently happened before. Not like this. And according to Piper, Siena is pissed. Like *pissed* pissed." Jo shoved another mouthful of pizza between her lips.

"You and Piper seem to be getting close." Bea eyed her sister carefully, taking in all the changes to see if she was on the right track or not.

"We are. She was there when Mandy started texting again." Jo chewed slowly, her cheeks paling just enough for Bea to really know just how much those text messages had affected her.

"Oh." A sliver of pain made itself known somewhere in Bea's chest. She hadn't been there when Jo had needed her. She was an awful big sister, and all because she'd been distracted by whatever was going on with Bunny. Swallowing her pride, Bea asked, "And did she help?"

"She really did."

"And do you *like* like her?" Bea genuinely wanted to know.

It had been a long time since Jo had talked about having a crush on someone. Since Mandy, actually.

Jo giggled, the sound so pure that Bea couldn't deny the happiness that Piper had brought to her.

Bea picked up the TV remote and flicked on some late-night reruns. It seemed to be the only thing she watched nowadays, and it was one-hundred-percent only because the murmurs of the characters helped to lull her to sleep.

Bea jumped up and offered her hands to help Jo to her feet. They sat back on the couch, a routine that used to be a far more regular thing, and leaned into each other.

"Bea?"

"Yeah?" Bea asked as she stifled a yawn.

"Do you really think Mandy is going to do something stupid at the charity event?"

"I want to say no. I really do. But honestly, I have no idea. I have a pretty strong feeling that she's going to try. But with Bunny and Siena on the case, whatever she's planning on trying, she won't get very far."

"I suppose not."

Without looking, Bea knew Jo was chewing nervously on her bottom lip.

"What did Piper say when you told her about it?"

"She told me I deserved better than someone who only wants me when I'm in the spotlight." That spread of color dotted over Jo's face once again, highlighting the ever-present freckles that Bea was secretly jealous of. It gave her the perfect girl-next-door look that Bea had never managed to have.

"I like her even more now." Bea smiled at both Piper's advice and the effect she seemed to be having on Jo.

"She's unlike anyone I've ever met before."

"Good." *I know just how you feel,* Bea thought. "Now stop worrying about Mandy. We'll take care of it if she dares to come around."

"I'm trying not to worry. But I don't want my stupid mistakes to ruin this event. I've been looking up the Holbrook Foundation, and it sounds pretty amazing. And this is such a big deal for us, you know?"

Bea cringed. She had to distract Jo as best as she could. She had to stop the bad thoughts from consuming their entire night, and while she couldn't stop her own turmoil over Bunny, she could certainly distract the both of them with whatever budding relationship was happening with Piper and Jo. "Well, why don't you tell me more about Piper? I'm sure that'll help keep your mind off the crazy one."

"I miss this." Jo almost bounced out of her seat as she spoke.

Bea smiled, letting the statement wash over them for a moment or two. She didn't turn to Jo, and Jo seemed to remain staring straight ahead as well.

"I miss it too, baby sis."

Thankfully, neither of them needed to be anywhere in the morning, and studio time hadn't been available until the afternoon. They could stay up late, eat junk food, and sleep in all morning.

"Do you ever think you might one day just call me sister, or better yet, just Jo?"

"Probably not." Bea chuckled as she tried to work out what the characters of the scene were talking about. Her emotions were too much, and the conversation had taxed the last of her energy reserves.

"Thanks." Jo laughed, and she all but vibrated as she spoke about Piper with the energy of youth and affection.

Once Jo had gushed about the main points of Piper's brilliance several times, she finally stilled enough for Bea to relax into the couch.

"I like Bunny, too," Jo added. "And you seem different since we've started working with them."

"Is that good or bad different?" Bea stiffened unexpectedly. She should have been able to hide her discomfort better, but it was so hard with Jo.

Jo shrugged as a yawn took over, but she didn't answer. Which left Bea in even more turmoil. Crushing on Bunny was probably a bad idea. And if her temper was anything to go by, Bea really needed to stay as far away as possible. The last thing she needed was to fall in love with someone who couldn't even love themself. But Bea hadn't really considered what Bunny had been through, what Bunny had seen and experienced herself.

Another hour passed before Bea realized that Piper had fallen asleep. Leaving the television on, Bea sauntered to her room and changed her clothes. So much for a late night. Maybe they were getting too old for those kinds of things. Burrowing under her blankets, she stared at the ceiling. Her thoughts swirled in so many spirals she couldn't untangle them.

But one thought was clear.

What the hell was wrong with Bunny?

mandy

bunny

Bunny hadn't slept.

She had gotten a meeting request from Siena for ten in the morning the next day. Her body and mind had taken turns tormenting her throughout the evening with fears and doubts colliding with anger and frustration.

At three in the morning, she had given up. She stood in the shower, letting the sound of the water lull her into calm. It was nothing but a false one for sure, but the relief made her almost weep. By eight, she felt like she'd run a marathon. By nine, she'd been ready to go for an hour, and she stepped out of her door to head to Siena's offices.

The world bustled around her, people pushing and shoving on their way to their jobs or lives. Her irritation at those completely lost in their own world took on a whole new level of annoyance as Bunny pushed her way through.

At one time it had annoyed her that people didn't recognize her and Piper when they were out in public. But it turned out, most people never expected to see anyone even remotely famous in their day-to-day lives, and it had just been her big fat ego talking. Today, Bunny had never been more grateful for the complete ignorance of the human race.

Before pushing open the door to Siena's offices, she stood still and took a deep breath in and then let it out slowly, forcing her shoulders down from around her ears as she did.

Gripping the coffee cup as tightly as she dared in her right hand, she finally pushed open the door with her left. No matter what happened today, she wouldn't walk in, or out for that matter, with her tail between her legs and the weight of the world visible on her countenance.

"Morning, Bunny." Paula, she was pretty sure her name was Paula, greeted her the moment she stepped into the reception area of Siena's office.

"Morning Paula. I have a meeting with Siena."

"Oh, it's Polly, and absolutely, I have you down here in the calendar. Just take a seat, and Siena will be with you shortly. Can I get you a drink?"

Bunny lifted the cup and shook it a little only to discover that there was no longer any weight in it. When had she finished it?

"Oh, that would be great." Bunny felt her insides deflated like a flower in the summer midday sun. So much for not having her tail between her legs.

Polly was up out of her chair and taking the cup from her in seconds. "Coffee as usual?"

"Yes, please." Bunny forced authority back into her voice, but she suspected not even Polly was fooled by the false bravado. Surely Siena had filled her in on the disaster yesterday. Who was she kidding? It wasn't a disaster. It was a full-on tantrum, and everyone had known it.

Seven minutes and thirty-three seconds later, with a fresh coffee in hand, Bunny followed Siena into her office. The door shut with a resounding finality. Bunny had fucked up royally. And she was about to hear about all of it.

Bunny opened her mouth a few times but closed it again before she said anything. It wasn't like her to be nervous or unsure of herself. It had been years since Siena had intimidated her. Years since she had wondered about the security of their business relationship, or friendship for that matter. But now Bunny felt as though she walked a tightrope that had just been jumped on. And the worst part was, she had been the one to string up the rope in the first place.

Siena tilted her head, seeming entirely comfortable to sit in the silence.

"I'm sorry." The words weren't easy. Bunny had fought hard alongside Piper to get to where they were. It wasn't that she didn't acknowledge or appreciate Siena's work. The woman was incredible at her job and had opened many doors for them over the years. But that didn't mean they had sat back and let others do the heavy lifting.

Siena continued to look at her, and Bunny slumped back into her chair.

"I don't know what to do," Bunny confessed, fearing she might actually choke on the words.

"All right." Siena nodded, finally giving Bunny a break. "I'm not entirely oblivious to your concerns. I never have been."

"I know," Bunny conceded.

"But this isn't just about you. It's not even just about you and Piper." Siena waited for Bunny to lift her head and meet her eyes before continuing. "When you started, you made the conscious decision to keep all of your private life private."

"It was either that or fall into the pit of ruined artists."

"Yes," Siena said the word slowly, and Bunny knew without a doubt that she would not like where this was headed. "But that was quite a while ago. You've got to admit things have changed and continue to change, especially where we live."

"But it's not enough." Bunny twiddled her thumbs, not

sure where to go from here. She was trying to get her point across, but it was like Siena was only half-listening to what she was saying.

"Are you sure about that?" Siena asked.

Bunny could have hugged her if she were the hugging type. There had been no judgment in her question, but a pure curiosity.

"Is it really worth the risk? I get them wanting to be out from the start, but we aren't starting. Piper and I have been around long enough to see the other side of it. They get our songs, Siena, isn't that enough? We put our hearts and souls into them. Can you honestly tell me we won't be hurt if we confirm our sexuality and start letting our fans into our day-to-day personal lives as well? Not to mention, we don't only perform in Portland. I have to be sure that we're safe wherever we go, and we have enough issues existing in this world as women. Now you expect me to risk our lives because we're queer too? Can you tell me that we'll be safer being out?"

"No." Siena shook her head and rocked back in her seat.

Relief washed over Bunny as she read the posture as the hard part of the conversation was over. As Siena conceding to her point.

"No?" Bunny wanted the verbal confirmation.

"No. I can't promise you anything like that. But I've never promised you anything I haven't been able to deliver. What I can promise is that wearing rainbow pride costumes for the finale isn't going to automatically out you and Piper. No more than about half of your songs do."

"But singing *that* song with Bea as the finale and in *those* outfits is." Bunny said it with so much certainty. She truly believed this. She had no doubts in her mind that to do both would be the end of life as she knew it.

"You haven't checked your email this morning." Siena was

back in work mode as she shuffled and clicked keys on her computer.

"No. Why?"

Swiveling the monitor so Bunny could see it, Siena showed Bunny the set list.

"Oh." Bunny's fears slipped away a little bit. Not entirely, but at least the last thing people would see wouldn't be just Bunny and Bea in that rainbow getup, singing a love song to each other.

"So that helps a bit then, yeah?"

"Yeah. I still don't think a duet with Bea is a good idea." Bunny's stomach twisted hard, bile rising up in her throat and she was regretting that coffee.

"Bunny. Don't let your emotions and personal relationship interfere with what'll be an amazing performance."

Bunny closed her eyes. She couldn't blame Siena for picking up on the chemistry between the two of them. Piper had done the same. She and Bea hadn't even done a damn thing to try to hide it. They'd practically been making out at the piano bar.

"So are you feeling better?" Siena asked. After a small nod from Bunny, Siena continued. "Now, before you do anything else about it, because I know you."

Bunny chuckled low and let her head nod a little bit.

"Now, before that, think about this. You had a choice and no one has forced you to go against that. Even this performance doesn't give any more or less confirmation about you and Piper. Jo and Bea have a choice, and they have chosen that instead of going through managers who have demanded they tone down the gay, have searched for someone who will allow them the same right I have always given you."

Bunny's head swam, and she knew this was the speech Siena had wanted to make. She wondered again if Siena practiced this one and wouldn't have been surprised if she had. After a few minutes, Bunny looked up into Siena's face once more and nodded. Because what the hell was she supposed to say?

Pick me over them?

Save me from this fucking choice?

"I'll think about all of it, I promise," Bunny finally managed.

"Before you try to convince them to change the outfit?" Siena raised a perfectly sculpted eyebrow.

"Yes." Bunny rolled her eyes playfully. "Is that all you wanted to see me about?"

"Actually, no." Siena chuckled low and not for the first time Bunny wondered what had happened with her and her ex-wife. From what Siena had told her, Tori was an amazing human. The idea that great people still couldn't make it work gave Bunny little hope for a future where she might one day settle down. Not that she had ever really considered doing that before. "We have some more events to go through. I've sent the list to Piper, and she told me which ones she would be okay with as long as you are on board as well."

"You didn't send me the list."

"I did. But you ignored my email as usual."

Bunny's ears burned. She vaguely remembered an email she had marked as important and would get to as soon as she could. She had then promptly forgotten about it.

"Sorry. I do try."

"I know." Siena smiled, and they dove into the list of potential opportunities that Siena had gotten for them.

By the time Bunny left Siena's office, the weight she had been carrying on her shoulders had definitely lightened.

But Siena had been right, once again. Bunny wasn't prepared to roll over on the idea. Not when there was still more she could do to make them see reason.

It took her until the end of the block to pull her phone from her pocket, scroll through her contacts and find Jo's number.

"Bunny? Is everything okay?" Jo's voice was higher than Bunny remembered and vaguely she wondered what else Jo did apart from singing in the band with her sister. Had she interrupted? Well it was up to Jo to say so.

"I was wondering if we could talk about the costumes." Bunny and small talk weren't good friends, and even less when stress overtook her.

"Oh." Jo's voice dropped lower and the return to the more familiar tone encouraged Bunny to continue.

"I know I didn't react very well to the last of the costume changes." Bunny took a deep breath and refrained from presenting her point of view. It wasn't necessary. "But I was wondering if you would be willing to negotiate."

"What kind of things were you thinking?" Jo's voice crackled a little, and Bunny cursed the phone she pressed against her ear as she stepped around a couple using the sidewalk as their stage for a domestic argument.

"It would be much easier for me if we could talk in person. I hate talking on the phone. And texting. Could you meet me?" Bunny worried her fingers.

"Um, sure," Jo said.

After agreeing on a place and time, Bunny hung up with a relieved sigh. One hour, that's how long she had to get ready for this conversation. And she knew exactly how she was going to spend that hour.

By the time Bunny arrived, Jo was already seated in a small booth at the back of the cafe. She shouldn't have been surprised, seeing as Jo had gotten better with arriving early for rehearsal over the last week. But still, Bunny had to give the woman some credit. She had always shown professionalism during rehearsal. A little more than Bunny had managed.

"Thanks for agreeing to meet."

"No worries." Jo smiled. She thanked the waitress who followed Bunny to the booth. The waitress placed a drink in front of Jo.

"Anything for you, love?"

Love? Bunny wanted to hiss at the woman, but it wasn't her fault.

"No, thanks. I'm fine for now." Bunny slid into the booth and swallowed down her frustration as she noticed Jo's drink.

"So, what were your thoughts on the costumes?"

"I want them to be subtle." Bunny enjoyed Jo's direct approach. She had worried it would take fifteen minutes just to get her on target. "And I want them for just the last song."

"You want me to tone down the gay?" Jo's narrowed eyes shocked Bunny, and for a moment, she worried she misjudged who would be best to talk to about the costumes after all.

"This is a charity event for the Holbrook Foundation, not some gay pride event. And wearing those costumes, as intense as they currently are, for the last song is only going to take away from the actual charity."

"Why haven't you spoken to Piper and Bea about this?" Jo asked, sipping her drink as she held Bunny's eyes.

Bunny had definitely misjudged Jo's strength. She should have known better. How many times had Piper expressed frustration at people underestimating her because of her looks? And here she was doing the exact same thing to Jo.

But she couldn't just roll over on this one.

"Could you please consider it?"

"I can consider it, but this is something everyone will have to agree on."

"I know." Bunny nodded. "But seeing as you're the main designer, I thought checking with you first would be the right way to go about this."

"The main designer?"

"Piper said you had most of the ideas already sorted before the two of you even began discussing it." Bunny furrowed her brows.

Had Piper lied to her?

"Wow. I didn't think she would have mentioned that, let alone credited me with so much. I just had a few ideas I sketched out."

"Well, she seemed impressed by your involvement. And I figured you would be the best person to speak to Bea about it as well. We tend to clash a bit." Bunny shrugged, relieved that Piper hadn't lied, and inwardly smiling at the pink blush that scattered over Jo's nose and cheeks.

"Ah, yeah, you do." Jo pinned Bunny with a look. "Just what is that all about?"

"Nothing," Bunny muttered sharply. Now she really wished she'd had a drink so she could distract herself with it. "But I thought it'd be best coming from you."

"You're not scared of Bea, are you?" Jo playfully waggled her eyebrows.

Bunny snorted. "Absolutely not."

Except she was.

Or more to the point, she was scared of herself when Bea was around.

"Talk to her for me, will you?"

"You said this was a negotiation. What do I get out of it?"

Bunny pursed her lips as she thought. She'd hoped to slip right by that one and not come back to it. Again, she'd under-estimated Jo in ways she really shouldn't have.

"I'll change the lyrics to *Baby, It's Cold Outside* to be queer inclusive."

Jo's eyes widened. "Are you serious?"

It wasn't what Jo had wanted, Bunny was sure. But she was betting that Bea wanted it enough that Jo would agree. Because that's what sisters and business partners did, wasn't it? Bunny held her breath, waiting for Jo's answer.

"Yes."

Jo grinned broadly, her lips curling upward and her eyes lighting as if she'd just won the prize of the year. "Deal."

piper

"So you had coffee with Bunny?" Piper slid Jo a curious look before turning back to the stove. She wished she could look at Jo to get the full reaction without burning their lunch, but that would be impossible.

"Yeah. It was weird and awkward." Jo groaned, stretching out on the counter and pressing her cheek to the cold marble. "Is Bunny ever *not* awkward?"

Piper laughed lightly and wrinkled her nose as she flipped the French toast in the skillet. She could cook—breakfast, that is. Anything else and she was lost. So she'd offered to make breakfast for this impromptu lunch date with Jo. "Bunny is always awkward."

"Why? I mean, I get there are awkward people in the world, but she's so smooth on stage."

"It's a well-practiced skill that she's taken great pains and decades to master."

Jo frowned, a line furrowing in the center of her forehead before she smoothed it out with her hand and glanced at her phone as it buzzed on the counter. Piper suspected it was

Mandy, that her advice of *don't contact or text back* had been ignored, and that Jo was falling back into the trap that was her ex-girlfriend willingly.

Being with someone who was still hung up on their ex wasn't something Piper wanted to throw herself into again. Been there and done that one too many times with women over the years. Men seemed to have fewer issues with that.

Still, Piper wasn't ready to give up on Jo yet. If only because it was clear that Mandy wasn't suitable for Jo in the least. Plating up their breakfast, Piper slid it across the peninsula counter and snagged the butter, powdered sugar, and maple syrup. Once they were set up to eat, Piper joined Jo on that side of the counter, sliding into the chair right next to her.

Just in time to see Jo's phone buzz with another text.

From Mandy.

Piper chose not to comment on it, yet.

"So what did Bunny want?" Piper asked, sliding a fluffy piece of bread between her lips.

"She didn't tell you?"

"No." Piper sent Jo a direct look. "She doesn't tell me everything."

"Interesting." Jo played her fingers over her fork, but she hadn't eaten anything yet.

Piper made sure to take note of that. If Jo was anything like her, then when she was emotionally distraught, eating was the last thing on her mind. Then again, Jo could be the complete opposite to her. They were still getting to know each other, after all.

"So what did she want?" Piper finally broke the silence right when Jo's phone went off again. That was going to get annoying.

"To negotiate."

"Negotiate?" Piper shoved another large bite between her

lips. Fuck, she loved her French toast. She'd forgotten because it had been so long since she'd made it. No one to cook for and Bunny preferred coffee and more coffee prior to eleven in the morning. Maybe they should do breakfast for dinner one night.

"The outfits for the charity event."

"Oh." A cold shiver ran through Piper. She'd known that was going to be an issue, but she hadn't expected Bunny to be so forward in fixing her fuckup either. Normally, she cowered in the corner for weeks afterwards. Then again, she had mentioned something about a meeting with Siena, hadn't she? Piper would have to flip through her phone to see if that had actually happened or if she was just imagining it.

"She still doesn't want to wear them."

"I've got news for you, Jo, Bunny doesn't do out-and-proud events, and those outfits, as amazing as they are, weren't ever going to go over well. She never would wear them." Piper moved her food around her plate, her appetite slowly easing away despite how good the food tasted. What had upset her so much? Was it the fact that Bunny was having these conversations without her?

No, that couldn't be it. They had worked well together for years, and they each knew what the other wanted at this point and where the other stood. They'd worked their asses off to build that kind of business partnership. So what was it then?

"She told me to tone down the gay there, but that she'd tone it up in her duet with Bea."

"What?" Piper's fork clattered onto her plate.

"She's going to change the lyrics to be about two women, explicitly." Jo finally took a bite of her food.

Piper was too stunned to even think about eating again. Bunny was willingly doing something gay? Something out there where other people could see and not just behind closed doors and hidden away in closets?

"She's making a song explicitly gay?"

"Yeah, that's what she said. If we toned down the gay in the outfits." Jo shoved another forkful of food between her lips, powdered sugar catching on her chin.

Had Piper not been so shocked, she probably would have leaned in to kiss it off. Instead, she sat in silence, still trying to wrap her brain around the fact that Bunny was doing something queer. Willingly. Without much arm twisting… Wait. Siena. Snagging her phone, Piper immediately texted Bunny.

Piper: How did the conversation with Siena go? We changing the entire set list?

Focusing back on her guest, Piper smiled. She would get as much information out of Jo about this *negotiation* as possible. Especially because she now wanted to go into the conversation with Bunny as informed as she could be. What the hell was happening with her best friend?

"How is she changing the lyrics?"

"I don't know. I didn't see them." Jo finished off her first slice of French toast. "Lyrics are more Bea's thing anyway."

"Bea?" Piper furrowed her brow.

"She writes all the lyrics to our songs."

"Huh." Piper played with the food on her plate. Maybe Bea and Bunny weren't as different as they initially came off. "She hasn't said anything about the set list. Not really anyway."

"They're Christmas songs. It's not like there's much to write or change. This isn't our normal music."

"That's true." Piper gnawed on her lip, mulling everything over. "Do you write all the music, then?"

"No, not all of it. We tend to write together."

Piper really should have done some more of this basic conversation before now, shouldn't she? She'd just been so enamored with them, and watching Bunny try to fight her own base urges whenever Bea was in the room. That had been amusement enough for Piper.

"Same with Bunny and me."

"Bunny writes with you?" Jo gave her a disbelieving look. "I'm pretty sure she's even more of a control freak than Bea."

"That very well may be true, but when you've been around her for decades, she eases up a bit."

Jo squinted, still not believing Piper. "I'm pretty sure Bunny doesn't know how to let loose, ever."

"Oh, you'd be surprised." And Piper was. Because Bunny giving in at all on the queer thing was huge. Piper and Siena had been battling that one for years at this point, and Piper had all but given up on the possibility of making any headway. Yet somehow, one suggestion of an outfit from Jo had Bunny questioning something.

"Does she really?"

"Get her drunk enough and she'll let all the gossip slip about the industry in this town." Piper laughed.

"How much does it take to get her drunk?" Jo glanced at her phone as it buzzed three times in rapid succession.

"A lot, unfortunately. Are you going to answer her?" Piper couldn't hold back anymore. She wanted to know what was going on with Jo and Mandy. In part because they'd slept together, and in part because Piper really cared. From everything Jo had told her, Mandy was bad news, and yet here Jo was, still getting texts from the one person she said she didn't know how to deal with.

Jo sheepishly snagged her phone off the counter and opened up the texts, sending a short one, and then putting it on *Do Not Disturb.* "I'm sorry."

"Don't be sorry for answering a text. I just want to know

what's going on." Piper was back to playing with the food on her plate. "Are you two getting back together?"

"No." Jo frowned, her jaw clenching. "I don't want to get back together with her."

"Then what are you doing texting her?" Piper nodded toward the phone. "Because that's only going to send her mixed signals."

"I know. But if I don't text her, she just continues to bug me."

"Jo." Piper pursed her lips, her gaze dragging up Jo's body and then back down to her hands. "You know what I'm going to say, right?"

"What everyone else has said?" Jo asked it like a question, her gaze glued to the plate in front of her. She didn't want to hear what Piper had to say, that much was clear.

Piper rubbed her lips together, debating whether or not to continue. "I have an idea."

"What idea?" Jo didn't seem too thrilled.

But perhaps the change in conversation would help. "I think Bunny likes Bea, and I think, if we get out of their way, they'll be more inclined to get over themselves and get together already."

Jo narrowed her eyes. "You noticed it too."

"Oh yeah, and I'm pretty damn sure it's the only reason Bunny was willing to *negotiate.*" Piper giggled and snagged a piece of French toast. This she could talk days about. Convincing her new friend to give up her old relationship and leave it in the past where it belonged was something she'd much rather avoid.

"What did you have in mind?"

"Well, it might also help solve your other little issue." Piper pointed to the phone, wriggling her fingers.

"Now I'm really interested."

"Let's fake a relationship." Piper grinned broadly. "Let's pretend we're together, make a semi-big deal out of it. Bunny will have to face up to the fact that at least one of us isn't straight, and Mandy will back the fuck off because you're with someone."

Jo's face pinched in doubt. "I don't know."

"Well, what about Bea? Do you think it'd help her to get over whatever's holding her back?"

"I'm holding her back."

Piper canted her head in confusion. "You?"

Jo nodded. "She doesn't want to be in a relationship if I'm not taken care of. She's always been like that. She's my big sister who took the role a little too far if you ask me."

"Oh, I get that." Piper was thinking of Bunny exactly. The two of them really were similar. "So let's have you be taken care of by someone else, someone who definitely can take care of you, and then it eliminates the issue."

"It might." Jo worried her lower lip. "But I'm not sure it'll solve the Mandy problem."

"You never know. And if I get to kiss you more often, then I'm also going to take that as a win." Piper smiled to ease the discomfort.

"If you get to kiss me?" Jo's cheeks flushed. "What do you get out of it, though? I don't want to put you out to fix my problems."

Piper laughed. "You think I don't get anything out of kissing you? God, you're stunning. Any girl would be lucky to kiss you."

Jo blushed furiously. "We're talking seriously now."

"Fine. I get a break from Bunny. She's been riding my ass for months now, and I just need a break to have some fun. I promise I'm not going into this blind."

"I'll think about it."

"Good." Piper turned back to her breakfast. "If we want, I can ask Siena to set up a little press release."

"Oh God. How much thought have you put into this?"

"More than I should have," Piper mumbled. "But it'll be worth it."

bea

Bea's heart hammered a little too hard as she opened her eyes and failed to recognize the clean uncracked ceiling above her. Memories floated back in slowly, and the smile spread like molasses over her lips. Thick and slow. Bunny had brought her home.

No, she definitely wasn't in Kansas anymore. Or her shitty little apartment either.

Now that she knew where she was, Bea's body felt more rested than it had in months. More months than she cared to admit. She had slept so soundly after last night's activities. The soft bed beneath her didn't make it such a hard wake-up either. Though actually getting out of the bed might prove another hurdle. Especially with the weight of Bunny's arm stretched over her stomach.

How had she missed that earlier? Smiling, Bea shifted a little closer to Bunny's heat that radiated from beside her.

Beneath the crisp linen, the scent of arousal washed over her. She burrowed herself a little deeper into the warmth and the scent memory. The soft material brushed along her naked skin, and idly she wondered where her clothes might be. She hardly remembered taking them off. Then she remembered she hadn't been the one throwing them across the room. Bunny had been ravenous, and Bea had been more than willing to comply.

"Didn't you get enough wiggling around last night?" Bunny's husky, sleep-riddled voice was half muffled as her breath brushed across Bea's shoulder.

The hint of frustration at the wake-up was underscored by the hint of a challenge. A challenge that sent Bea's body into high gear. Bea would have been more than happy to take Bunny up on that challenge immediately if her bladder wasn't screaming at her.

"Hold that thought." It turned out to be quite easy to get out of the bed once the hope of a replay of last night's events was on the cards.

Washing her hands and looking at her reflection in the bathroom mirror made Bea pause for a moment, even as her body ached to be touched again. No, not just touched, touched by Bunny. Damn it, she looked happy, genuinely happy. Something hard rested behind her ribs, and she rubbed at her chest.

"How long am I supposed to be holding onto this thought?" Bunny's voice called through the bathroom door.

Bea smiled and nodded. Orgasms had a tendency to make her look happy, she reasoned as she stepped back into Bunny's bedroom from the attached bathroom.

A master bathroom.

Bea had been excited when she'd found an apartment she could afford without sharing with Jo, even though it was a studio and everyone could see everything at once. Bunny was living in luxury already. Bea smiled seeing Bunny stretched out on the bed, covers now kicked off, lying in disarray on the floor at the foot of the bed.

"So what thought was I holding on to?" Bunny yawned behind one hand while the other beckoned Bea toward her.

Bea moved slowly, enjoying the sudden stillness in Bunny's chest, as she held her breath and watched Bea's swaying hips draw closer.

"I believe the thought had something to do with wiggling."

"Wiggling?" Bunny gave a cocky grin as she lifted up on her elbows to see more of Bea as she stepped up to Bunny's side of the bed.

Bunny lay back, one hand behind her head while the fingers of the other reached out and brushed against Bea's naked hip. The touch was firm but soft, just the way Bea liked it, making her suck in a breath, quickly checking in with her body.

She wanted it, that wasn't the issue, but she hadn't had so many orgasms in one night in a very long time. Perhaps ever. And checking in was never a bad idea as things usually went. Her body was good. Her mind however was another thing, and now wasn't the time to worry about that.

"Oh yes." Bea crawled onto the bed on her knees, shuffling to straddle Bunny's hips. "It was definitely about wiggling."

"And you think this is how it's going to play out this morning?" Bunny's hips rose, causing Bea to let out a small squeal that filled the luxurious room with laughter.

She stilled and blinked down at Bunny. Bunny's eyes met her own, and she blinked back. Did she realize how very strange that noise had sounded, even to Bea's own ears?

Bea shook her head and her thoughts. There was only one thing she would think about right now.

And that was wiggling.

"You mean…" Bea slowly moved in a circle over Bunny's crotch. Bea was already wet, or maybe still wet from last night, which was more likely earlier this morning. Either way the feeling sent a bolt of electricity through her body, a flood of new arousal rushing through her. "…this isn't the kind of wiggling you'd like me to do?"

"Hmmm." Bunny's growl was paired with gripping Bea's hips and pulling her down hard.

"Is that a yes to the wiggling?" Bea laughed.

"Mm-hmm." Bunny's voice remained husky as her breath grew louder and faster.

Bea leaned forward and took one of Bunny's already hard nipples in her mouth. Alternating between biting and sucking, Bea maintained a steady rhythm of her hips against Bunny's.

"Bea." It wasn't a demand but a plea, and only then did Bea give in to Bunny's grip. She told herself it wasn't the begging in Bunny's voice, but her own need for release.

She didn't believe the lie.

"Oh fuck." Bea panted as she pushed herself back up, hands gripping onto Bunny's, which continued to dig into her hips.

"Lift up." The demand in Bunny's voice was back, but this time that wasn't what bothered Bea.

"What?" Bea couldn't have heard that right. She needed more friction against Bunny, not less.

"Just a little." Bunny laughed as she slid a hand out from beneath Bea's grip.

"Oh," Bea said, the word breathy with understanding as soon as Bunny's fingers brushed against her stomach. She lifted up, letting her knees take her weight as Bunny's hand slipped between them.

"I want to be inside you." Bunny struggled to form the sentence.

"Yes," Bea answered immediately.

Bunny pushed two fingers inside with little resistance. But the sensation pulled a groan out of Bea, and she eased herself back down until the heel of Bunny's palm was against her clit.

"How about that wiggling now, Bea?" Bunny's voice was filled with all the right kinds of mischievous intentions.

Bunny and Bea locked eyes. Bunny's shit-eating grin grew

with each groan and pant she pulled from Bea. Her hips pushed up in unison with movement of her palm. The extra pressure pushed Bunny's fingers deeper, pulling pleasure from places Bea didn't even know existed.

Bea's legs shuddered against Bunny's hips, sweat beading down her back as she rocked harder and harder against Bunny's fingers.

"Come for me," Bunny demanded, and Bea couldn't fathom arguing as her body tensed and that delicious coil unfurled inside of her.

With a scream of curses and guttural grunts, Bea's orgasm washed over her. After another moment of tight muscles, she uncoiled and collapsed on top of Bunny. Panting heavily on Bunny's chest and trying to catch her breath, Bea closed her eyes and breathed in the scent of Bunny's sweat and their combined arousal. While Bunny's fingers were still inside her, Bunny's other hand caressed Bea's hip, running over the side of her body in a gentle lover's touch.

No. This wasn't love. This couldn't be love. This was Bunny. A brilliant fuck, but no. She couldn't have actual feelings for her. Could she? What a ridiculous notion.

"Are you good?" Bea asked once the power of speech returned and to distract her from her terrifying train of thought.

"Oh, I'm always good watching a woman come apart when I fuck her."

"Oh." Bea slapped herself for having even let that previous thought enter her mind. She'd been right—this wasn't love. It couldn't ever be that. "But would you like more?"

"I'm good." Bunny gently eased her hand out from between the two of them.

Bea rolled over and stared back up at the uncracked ceiling. She'd never been more grateful for her ability to keep her thoughts inside her head, even after mind-blowing sex.

Without any other words, Bunny pulled the sheet up from the end of the bed and laid it over her own and Bea's hips, keeping their breasts open to the cool air. It danced over Bea's overheated skin and sent goosebumps across her skin.

"I had a chat with Jo the other day." Bunny interrupted the awkward silence, surprising Bea.

"What about?" Bea's hackles rose instantly. She bit back any more words and tried to push aside instinctual worries about Jo. She knew she had to stop being the protective big sister, but she'd never really managed that. Even if they were only eleven months apart, she took her role as big sister seriously.

"She hasn't talked to you about it?" Bunny shifted, looking at Bea directly.

"No." Bea pulled the sheet over her chest as she turned on to her side, using one elbow to prop her head up.

"No big deal." Bunny shrugged.

"Is it about Mandy?" Bea's panic grew.

"No." Bunny's eyebrows pulled together as she turned her head to look at Bea again, sincerity in every line in her face. Despite being unbalanced, Bea eased a little just knowing Mandy wasn't causing drama yet.

"So what did you two talk about?" Bea asked and the idea that she deserved an explanation rubbed something raw and uncomfortable inside of her. If it were business stuff, of course she had a right to know. But why hadn't she been involved to begin with?

But this was Jo, of course she had a right to know. The small voice in the back of her head telling her she knew that wasn't where her demand had originated was easy enough to ignore, for now.

"I've decided to change the lyrics to *Baby, It's Cold Outside,* so it can be explicitly queer, like you suggested."

"Really?" Bea pushed herself up to sitting with more

energy and excitement than she had thought possible just moments ago.

"Yeah." Bunny's lips pulled up to one side in that sexy, cocky smile Bea loved. But something in her eyes pulled Bea's excitement down and the cynic within her rose.

"Why do I get the feeling there's something else in there?" Bea asked as she sat, feeling more exposed with the sheet pressed over her chest than she had been sleeping naked and wrapped up around Bunny all evening.

"I think you and Piper will be better suited to sing the song," Bunny stated simply as though telling Bea it was cold outside, in the middle of winter.

"What?" A twist of nausea in Bea's stomach caught her off guard. "But our voices work amazingly together."

"Look." Bunny sat up, not bothering to cover her own perfect curves with the sheet or blanket. "Your voices will work just as well together, and you're both better suited to the *message* of the song."

"The *message*?" Bea's body coiled with an entirely different tension than it had only moments earlier. The way Bunny had spat out that word had carried a weight of disgust with it.

Yep, staying over had definitely been the wrong idea, despite the morning orgasm.

"Piper's been bugging me to come out for years, but I haven't wanted to. Now she can get what she wants, and I don't have to be involved." Bunny raked her fingers through her hair, snagging on the tangles that she gave a half-hearted attempt to release before giving up.

"No one should ever need permission to come out. Jesus, Bunny. Besides, you're involved with the entire show, whether *we* do the duet or not." Bea's chest heated with frustration and anger.

A hard silence filled the room, no longer awkward but angry.

"What are we doing?" Bea's voice still carried a hard edge, but she had managed to pull it back from screaming. Just.

"Having fun while we work together on this event." Bunny shrugged.

"Of course." Bea scoffed. "I didn't realize you were such a coward. That you're so scared that singing with me in front of an audience would somehow out you to the entire fucking world."

"This isn't a relationship, Bea. It's called fucking for a reason." Bunny's cheeks reddened as they hollowed in anger. Bea had seen this look on her before, and she knew exactly where they were headed.

"Not all relationships mean marriage, kids, and a house with a dog." Bea rolled her eyes, trying to keep her disappointment at a tenable level. "If you bothered to see things from anyone's point of view but your own, you might even notice things like friendship."

"Look, singing with Piper will get you just as much publicity as singing with me. We're bandmates, so our name recognition works together. So you don't need to get all bent out of shape over this."

"Bent out of shape?" Bea laughed, the sound cold and hard as it bounced around the room.

She looked closer at the room around her. It had seemed so luxurious to her last night. A sign of having made it, a sign of things she could strive for, things she was on the right path to achieve. But now she saw it for what it really was. All the bland colors and the lifelessness seeped into every area.

There were no personal touches, no personality in the white fluffy bed. She even turned to the headboard as though expecting to see all the notches Bunny had carved into it from all of her fuck-'em-and-leave-'em conquests. But of course not. The headboard was smooth and clean, with no hints of the women she hid as neatly as she hid herself.

"I can't believe I didn't realize you're just a closeted coward." Bea ran her hand through her tangled locks and shook her head. "If you think for one second that I am doing any of this for the publicity of riding on your or Piper's coat tails, you know me even less than I thought."

Bea forced herself out of the bed, leaving the sheet, the scent, and the memories behind.

Bunny's gaze roamed over her body. Bea felt the look graze her with each movement she made. She cringed internally as she searched the floor for her clothes, pulling them roughly over her sensitive skin. With effort, she managed to refrain from hissing aloud when her shirt brushed over her still erect nipples.

"If this is more than worrying about what publicity your little band's going to get, why're you getting so upset about it?" Bunny asked from the bed.

For a moment, words she knew she couldn't say dared to touch her tongue.

Because I'm drawn to you like no one I've ever known before.

Because you being a closeted coward is the thing stopping me from letting you in.

Because the last thing I want is to be in love with someone like you.

"Good question, Bunny." Bea opened the door and took another look around the room. What the hell was she doing? "Why am I so upset?"

She didn't bother closing the bedroom door behind her. Let Bunny watch her walk away. Let Bunny figure out why she was so ticked off in the moment. While the temptation to slam the front door reared its head, the pounding of her blood in her ears was already too loud for her to handle. Bea shut the door and closed her eyes.

Why did being free from that feel so shitty?

bunny

"This is all bullshit." Bunny paced the carpet of Siena's office as soon as she and Piper stepped through the door. Ever since Bea had walked out of her apartment that morning, Bunny had been in a funk. She couldn't shake it. And the more time passed, the more she stewed, and the more she stewed, the angrier she got.

Siena leaned back in her office chair and watched Bunny silently, the way she did when she thought Bunny simply needed to let off steam.

But this was more than that. This had all gone way too far. She should have gone with her gut instincts in the first place. But not anymore. This had to end.

Bunny'd had enough. She had tried. Hell knew she had tried. But working with Jo and *Bea* was impossible. She had to put her foot down now before it really was too late. Before they couldn't pull out of the event.

"This isn't going to work. And it's better you have a chance to figure something else out instead of having the shitshow of a lifetime blow up in your face." Bunny pulsed her hands into fists, staring at the ground. She couldn't even look into Siena's face when she said this, because she knew the storm she was stirring up. But she had no other choice. This had to end.

"What the hell are you talking about?" Piper snapped from where she had taken a seat on the other side of the room.

Bunny turned to Piper and shook her head. She was making the decision for both of them without consulting Piper first, which she never did, but this was bigger than the two of them. If they continued to work with Bea and Jo, they were going to face the consequences. "Look, I know you and Jo are getting along really well. That doesn't have to change just because we aren't going to do the show."

"No." Piper's face hardened, and for a moment, it stopped Bunny in her steps, her body losing its momentum. Piper had never spoken to her that way before. She'd never been so firm or demanding. Bunny was the unmovable one. Bunny was the hard-ass. Piper was the blessedly gleeful one who was always full of joy.

"It's not negotiable, Piper. We're pulling out." Bunny clenched her jaw, staring into Piper's eyes. Piper she could look at. She had to know what Piper was thinking, what she was feeling. Because everything ultimately depended on Piper and Bunny working well together.

"No." Piper stood up and stopped right in front of Bunny, towering over Bunny's much smaller form.

Bunny narrowed her eyes, not letting Piper intimidate her. Who the hell was she kidding? Piper like this was scary as hell.

"Excuse me?" Bunny said, deepening her voice to try and make a point.

"The world's different now. The world's changed, and continues to. We aren't going to be ruined if our fans know we're gay." Piper put her fists on her hips, continuing her stare down.

"You're pansexual." Bunny spat, her face twisting with regret the moment the word left her mouth.

"Seriously? *You* of all people?" Piper's face crumpled as though she was moments away from crying. "We've worked together for years and you still can't wrap your head around it?"

Bunny shook her head. She couldn't deal with tears, not even Piper's. "I didn't mean it like that."

Tension pulled taut between them, the threads of their relationship fraying with every second that passed. Bunny needed to fix this. She couldn't do this without Piper. They'd been so much a part of each other's lives for so long. They'd built their career together. They were so intertwined.

"That was cruel of me," Bunny murmured. "I didn't mean it like you took it. I wanted to make sure that you were included in our community."

Piper squinted, then wrinkled her nose. "I'm not giving you that one yet."

"Fair." Bunny moved her hands out to her sides. She hated living in the tension of unresolved hurt. She just wanted to make it up to Piper already. But she couldn't force Piper to accept an apology she wasn't ready to hear.

"I'm doing the show." Piper channeled her anger at Bunny's thoughtless words, her face pinching to show just how pissed off she was.

"You can't. I refuse to participate." Bunny curled her fists and dug them into her hips.

"I have no idea what's going on with you. I don't even know who you are anymore." Piper's soft words reached Bunny better than any yelling had. Piper tilted her head to the side, and Bunny had a strange sensation that her friend had gained X-ray vision and thoroughly scrutinized her in ways she didn't feel comfortable. "I refuse to continue to hide who I am. I'm doing the charity event—with or without you."

"You can't." Bunny turned toward Siena. "Our contract

says we either both agree or neither goes ahead with any event."

"It did." Siena nodded, her words carefully chosen.

"What do you mean *did?*" Bunny's nostrils flared and a pounding in her head made her far too aware of how little she had spoken to Siena or Piper lately—spoken to them in any real capacity, that is.

"Our contract ran out two months ago, Bunny." Piper's voice was softer. "And I asked for the clause to be removed. Siena agreed."

"But I haven't signed it," Bunny snapped.

"I'm well aware of that." Siena stood up, fingers splayed and pressed down upon her desk.

Now the rush of her blood pulsed at her temple. Siena hadn't treated either of them like this in years. Not since they had become friends.

"So you're dumping me?" Bunny's eyes flew from Siena to Piper and back again. "Both of you?"

"What?" Piper exploded. "Jesus, Bunny. No. What I want is to start being treated like I'm an equal part of this damn group. I have to fight with you over everything. I have to beg for time off. I have to stay in the closet while you fuck any hot chick that smiles in your direction. And then you just expect me and Siena to cover up any backlash that might leak to the press."

"So why are you still here if I'm so hard to work with?" Bunny's throat tickled uncomfortably as she forced her voice over the lump and the emotion she refused to let out.

"Because I love you, you idiot. I love making music with you. We've always worked well together. But now," Piper lifted both hands up at her side, palms facing the ceiling as she shrugged. "Now you've shut me out. You're having work meetings alone, and you think it's okay to make decisions without even talking to me about them."

Bunny couldn't argue with that.

The guilt in her chest squirmed.

Piper was right. Bunny had never left Piper out of anything to do with the band before. *Their* band. It had always been their band.

What the hell was she doing? No wonder she needed to get out of this event. It was turning her into someone she wasn't, someone she hated. Even more than she hated the closet she refused to step foot out of.

"I know you met with Jo and asked her to change the costumes." Piper's voice was filled with a sadness that just about broke Bunny's heart. It came far too close to breaking Bunny's rule to keep her emotions in check.

"I'm sorry."

"For what?" Piper asked, genuine curiosity filling her eyes when Bunny met them.

"I'm not sure exactly." The heaviness in Bunny's body doubled as the exhaustion of the confrontation slammed into her. Her arms had never felt so weighed down, not even after a second encore show.

Piper smiled. It didn't fill her face with the light Bunny had always adored, the light she had always been incredibly jealous of, but it was something. "Well, at least you're back to telling me the truth."

They looked at each other, and that lump lodged more firmly in Bunny's throat.

"And now we can finally talk." Siena lifted her fingers from her desk and grabbed her phone. After a second, Siena asked for coffee before replacing the phone.

"Care to take a seat now, Bunny?" Siena waved her hand to where Piper had already returned.

Well-chastised, Bunny sat beside Piper without a word.

Siena moved into her normal chair, away from the desk that separated her from just clients. In a silence Bunny wasn't sure was comfortable or not, they waited until the coffee was brought in.

When they all had a cup in their hands and something other than each other to look at, Siena broke the silence.

"What's your biggest concern about the event, specifically?" Siena sat a little forward in her chair, just enough to show interest without intimidating. The movement made the corner of Bunny's lips twitch. Siena's job was far more complicated than people gave her credit for. She was certain that nowhere on Siena's job description was there listed *therapist to various creative types*.

And yet here Siena was, doing that exact job as though it was her entire profession.

"I can't work with Bea. There's no way I can do the duet with her. We'll be lucky not to kill each other on stage even with Jo and Piper there."

"Okay." Siena sat back and nodded, her eyes filled with thoughts rushing past too fast for Bunny to understand. But she knew the way Siena worked, fast and effective. It was of the many things Bunny liked about the woman. "So, you and Bea have some issues. Is there anything else besides the costumes?"

"Piper talked to you about the costumes?" Bunny didn't want to look up and see the hurt in Piper's eyes again.

"Yes," Piper answered softly, but loud enough to get the attention of the others in the room.

"I'm going to grab some cookies to go with this coffee. I'm in a cookie mood. I'll be right back." Siena hopped up and was already out the door before she finished the sentence.

The silence stretched between Bunny and Piper, but it didn't last long. Piper was the one to break it.

"I did talk to Siena. That's why she set up this meeting."

"And you didn't tell me?" Bunny raised her eyebrows and stared at Piper.

Piper seemed immune to the bait. "I don't know what's

going on with you. I really don't. But I'm worried about you, and if you say you really can't do the event then okay. But I'm not pulling out now. I'm more excited about this than I've been about anything else in a while. So please, can you at least think about letting us work through it together so you and Bea don't kill each other up on stage?"

Bunny looked at Piper, and then closed her eyes.

She wanted to scoff at Piper's worry, she wanted to shrug off the hurt and the pain she saw in her best friend's eyes. But every word had hit its target, and each left her wounded and bleeding.

"I'll try. I can't promise, but I'll try. Is that good enough?"

"For now." Piper's trademark smile, filled with her excitement and bounciness, filled the room once more.

"Ready for cookies and more coffee?" Siena asked moments later as she pushed open her office door.

"Yes." Bunny smiled, pretty sure Siena had been standing at the door, waiting for it to be clear to return.

"Excellent." Siena clapped her hands together and let out a loud breath. "And now Bunny, for the love of God, come and sign your damn contract."

"You really did change it?" Bunny had been at least eighty percent convinced that the clause change had been a bluff.

"That's the only clause that is different. Piper has signed her agreement, but I stand by what I always have. I won't represent any group who doesn't agree to all the terms. The music industry might still have the Rolling Stones drama in some groups, but not in any that I'm willing to represent."

Bunny nodded. "I promise. I'll look at it tonight and send it through."

"You better. Because I hear there's this new up and coming female duo that might be worth looking into, and I might just have some extra time on my hands." Siena winked.

Piper chuckled beside Bunny, while Bunny rolled her eyes,

pursed her lips, and found herself entirely grateful for these annoying women in her life.

They finished off their second cups of coffee and nibbled on a few cookies as they discussed finer details of the event and a few things lined up for the next year.

Piper and Bunny said their goodbyes with a much calmer air than their greeting and left Siena to her work.

"Bunny." Piper stopped as they stepped out of the elevator.

"Yeah?" Bunny turned back to see worry marring Piper's beautiful face.

"You know I'm always here for you, right?"

"Yeah, I know." Bunny smiled reassuringly at her best friend, but it didn't reach her eyes. Something held her back. She couldn't deny her initial reaction to the whole ambush had been fury, but now, looking at Piper she had to admit the tough love gave her more respect for their partnership.

"Good. Now I really need my best friend."

"What?" Bunny asked.

"I don't know what's going on with you, and I know you're private and that's okay, but I could really use someone to talk to, and I don't want to talk to anyone else."

"Not even Jo?" Bunny smirked, unable to resist the temptation.

"Nope. When it comes to the big things and the little things, I need my best friend to listen to me bitch, say all the right things in the right place, and only after I've given her permission, tell me to pull my head out of my ass and get over it."

Bunny laughed and draped one arm over Piper's shoulder, which really wasn't comfortable considering how much taller Piper was, but together they walked out of Siena's office building and headed toward their favorite nearby cafe for lunch and a long overdue catch-up.

jo

"Where's Bea?" Bunny asked the minute Jo stepped into the rehearsal room. Jo's heart skipped a beat at Bunny's sharp tone. She hated that she hadn't gotten used to that yet. It was still so hard to reconcile everything from her relationship with Mandy.

"She's got a meeting that she'd already scheduled. She said she texted you, and traffic was awful today." Jo kept her distance from the energy that radiated from Bunny. It was so negative that she could barely stand it.

It wasn't angry or dangerous, but there was definitely something different in the way she held herself. It put Jo on an edge she didn't want to be on, but at least the energy wasn't pointed directly at her. Then they'd be in serious trouble—well, she would be. Bunny snatched up her phone and scowled down at it.

Jo looked over at Piper, wide eyes asking what she didn't dare say out loud with Bunny still in the room.

What's going on?

Piper smiled and bobbed her head, shoulders, and body in that way Jo had come to learn meant too many things she couldn't explain in just a look. It also meant that Jo was left in the dark about what was going through Bunny's head—and that was far more dangerous than Piper being quiet.

"Well, isn't that convenient?" Bunny muttered before she threw the phone back into her bag.

"Not really. I had to miss the meeting so one of us could be here," Jo said, hoping her words weren't as frustrated as Bunny's attitude.

To be fair, it wasn't really Bunny's fault. At least it wasn't just Bunny making her feel like she was on a hair trigger.

"Excuse me for thinking we aren't nearly where we need to be. We only have one more week for rehearsals, and we've got a lot of work to do."

"Bunny." The way Piper pulled out Bunny's name told Jo that Bunny was only just gearing up for a major spitfire fit.

"I'm sorry, Bunny." Jo met Bunny's eyes. She let her shoulders drop and took a deep breath. "It's been a stressful day and having to figure out who was going where so we didn't have to cancel the other appointment but also not abandon you both was a tough and quick decision. If Bea could have canceled, she would've."

"I know," Bunny muttered again, and for a moment, Jo wondered if she'd actually heard her correctly. "That's what her text says."

"All right then." Piper jumped off from where she'd been sitting. "Seeing as we called this impromptu rehearsal, we should really get into it."

"Sure." Jo's smile came easier when she looked at Piper. Piper's own smile helped refill her energy bar and allowed the frustration to fall away from her in an instant. Piper always managed to do that lately, and Jo had clung to her as much as possible because of it. Their energies just fit so well together, almost like they were made for each other.

"Good, let's start with your duet and dance number," Bunny said.

"Can I do a small warm-up first?" Jo asked.

"Of course." Bunny nodded, but Jo saw the muscles in her jaw tighten.

"Do a proper warm-up," Piper insisted before Jo could retract the request. "The last thing we need is for you to get hurt."

"Of course." Bunny nodded and stepped out of the area they'd been using for the two to practice their dance.

Piper joined in halfway through Jo's warm-up, though she was certain Piper would've been ready before she had arrived. It was those little things that kept Jo's body on fire and her chest in a perpetual swell of warmth and joy since getting to know Piper.

Sweat dripped down Jo's back and every part of her body pulsed with the use of energy she put into the dance. Each place Piper touched her tingled, and Jo couldn't have stopped smiling if she tried.

They finished their third run-through, and both Jo and Piper breathed heavily from the exertion and the realization that at some point Bunny had left the room for one reason or another.

"I think we make a great couple." Jo leaned into Piper.

Piper's lips met her halfway, and the salty flavor made Jo moan.

"Well, now I get it. This *thing* is why you decided I'm not good enough for you anymore?" The voice filled the room and sent a shock of terror through Jo's spine.

Mandy.

Jo jumped back and away from Piper, spinning around to face Mandy, standing in the open door of the studio room.

"What're you doing here?" Jo asked, her voice trembling fiercely.

"Catching you cheating on me, apparently." Mandy snarled as she stepped over the threshold and into the practice room.

"Cheating on you?" Piper's exasperation swiveled Jo's head to see Piper's eyes narrowed and face redder than she had ever seen it.

"It's not like that," Jo said.

"I know." Piper smiled, but the sadness in her eyes struck a sharp needle into Jo's chest.

Jo turned back to Mandy, wondering what on earth she'd ever seen in her in the first place. Everything about her was fake: the excessive makeup, the too-tight clothes, and the pursed lips of indignation she had no right to have. Even as she stepped closer toward them, her ankles wavered a little on the three-inch heels she'd never gotten used to wearing.

"I knew something was wrong when you stopped answering my messages, Jo. But I can't believe you." Mandy crossed her arms over her chest, pushing up her ample breasts.

Ah, that's right. It had been the boobs.

It was a pity Jo discovered they were fake as well.

"We aren't together. You know that." Jo kept her voice calm. She didn't like to hurt anyone, and even as misguided as Mandy might be, Jo didn't want to hurt her if she could avoid it.

"But I apologized, baby." Mandy dropped her arms, and her pursed lips turned into a pout while her eyes widened.

"Mandy, I told you. It's over."

"It's not over until I say it is." Mandy stomped her foot, looking ridiculous as she shoved her fists into her hips. Best life skill—tantrum throwing.

Jo forced herself to remain calm. It wasn't that she never got angry, but she never allowed that to overshadow the joy she let into her life. Seeing Mandy's anger flashing in her eyes made reaching that joy impossible as she remembered some of the more vicious threats Mandy's texts had contained. She hadn't even turned her phone off of silent since she stopped answering them or even reading them at three that morning. The only reason she got Bea's call was because Bea's contact had been set to bypass all silent modes after they missed out on a deal because Jo had missed Bea's call two years ago.

"Jo," Mandy purred, the whiplash of emotions sending Jo into another tailspin.

But the messages.

Jo was pretty sure most of them were just trying to get a rise out of her. Even an angry reply would be a reply and a win for Mandy, Jo was certain of that. But still, Jo had been more than a little disturbed by the aggressive detail Mandy had put into her messages.

"Who the fuck are you?"

Mandy spun around, and Bunny stood just inside the studio.

"Oh my God," Mandy squealed and turned back to face Jo. Her face was alive with excitement.

The look made Jo's stomach turn. Especially when Mandy took a closer look at Piper.

"Oh wow." Mandy's hands were up in more dramatic flare than the choreography Piper and Jo had been practicing. "I didn't recognize you on the account of you snogging my girl-friend, but wow! It really is you."

Jo flinched as Mandy squealed again and her face contorted into a lecherous leer.

"It's okay, honey. I don't mind if you want her to join us. I'm so excited. Look at us, the power couple banging *the* Piper."

"Get the fuck out of here," Bunny growled low, her face contorting into pure rage.

"Look, Bunny." Mandy turned around, her voice saccha-rine as she walked, hips swaying too far one way and then the other, back toward Bunny. "I get it. It's all hush-hush, but really, Jo and I have been together for years, and she invited me here."

"Jo?" Bunny looked over Mandy's shoulder and stared directly at Jo.

Jo shook her head from side to side, but the words failed her.

"Seems you're full of shit," Bunny said.

"What?" Mandy's fury raged back in an instant. All charm and sweet seduction, as terrible as the attempts had been, left in an instant.

"You need to leave. You're not welcome here." Bunny grabbed Mandy's arm and pulled her out of the door, but not before Mandy turned those vitriolic eyes back to Jo.

"Just you wait. You'll be begging me to come back when Little Miss Pop Star here realizes what an absolute useless freak you are in bed."

Jo took in a deep shuddering breath, Mandy's words hitting harder than she thought they possibly could. The world spun, and Jo crumpled to the floor in a tangle of legs she was no longer sure she could still feel.

"Hey." Piper's sweet and gentle breath brushed strands of Jo's blonde hair around her ear.

Jo blinked and focused enough to find Piper on the ground in front of her.

"I'm so sorry." Tears spilled over Jo's cheeks, and she dropped her head forward.

"It's okay." Piper pulled Jo into her embrace.

Being wrapped in Piper's arms felt safer than anywhere else Jo had ever known. They were a place to rest and breathe. A place she could be herself. Until Mandy's prediction came true, of course.

Jo and Piper were similar in so many more ways than Jo had been with anyone else in her life. But she had dated Mandy, and Mandy knew her far better than Piper did. And in the end, Jo wasn't enough to stop Mandy from chasing a life better than what Jo could ever offer.

For now, she let herself sink into Piper's arms. She let herself indulge in the comforts of someone who hadn't grown bored and sick of her. It hadn't mattered so much as it seemed to now. Christmas was just around the corner, and the event would be the highlight of their year. As long as Bea and Bunny didn't kill each other first.

But even as the excitement loomed closer, Jo's heart ached with the truth that had rung in Mandy's words.

They were just having fun for now.

The two of them worked well together—their music, their dancing, their bodies sweating in more naked and pleasurable ways. But in the end, it wouldn't last.

When Piper had suggested the fake relationship, Jo had instantly reared back at the idea. Her entire career, her life, was about her being allowed to be her genuine self. And even catching Jo and Piper kissing hadn't stopped Mandy from trying her best to find an angle to butt in. Jo took a deep breath and shuffled the slightest bit in Piper's arms. At the movement, Piper instantly let her arms loosen and pulled back.

The little things might just be the thing to kill Jo, but she had to do everything she could to stop Mandy from threatening any of them—Bunny and Piper included.

She dreaded how Bea would react when she found out how far Mandy had gone to get a reaction from her.

"Well, she's a bit psychopathic bathed in overpowering stench," Bunny said as she walked back into the studio.

Piper burst out laughing, and moments later, Jo couldn't help but join in.

"I'll talk to Siena again about a watch for her. You let us know if she shows up again and gives you any trouble."

"I'm so sorry, Bunny."

"She's not your fault," Bunny said, though her face showed

the pulse at her temple Piper had referred to as the pissed off pulse. "We all make mistakes when we're young."

The words stung a little, but from what she had learned about Bunny over the last few weeks, she would take the kindness behind the backhanded comment.

"I'll follow you home and make sure she isn't stupid enough to show up there." Piper stood and offered a hand to Jo.

"Is it okay if we finish up now?" Jo didn't like the way her voice quivered, but continuing practice seemed a little out of her capability.

"Yeah. Your main number with Piper looks good. I can't see there being any problem with that one."

"Thanks, Bunny. I'll call you later," Piper called behind them as she led Jo to the parking lot.

Jo wanted to say thanks, but her words still faltered and her eyes scanned the parking lot obsessively as they walked to her car. The only thing that kept her anxiety from exploding on the drive was seeing Piper's familiar silhouette in the car behind her every time she looked in the rearview mirror.

*count your
blessings instead of
sheep*

bea

Bea had told herself that when she walked out of the apartment she'd never be going back.

So why was she standing outside Bunny's door, hands twisted together, and bottom lip pulled tight between her teeth?

This was for Jo.

Bea would do anything for Jo, and after hearing all about what happened earlier that day, Bunny needed to be properly thanked. And, well, Bea owed her an apology for skipping rehearsal with no warning and no conversation. Yet she still couldn't bring herself to knock on the damn door.

What was wrong with her? She'd never been in such a tizzy over something before. And Bunny wasn't exactly someone that she *wanted* to be with long term. She was a jerk on a bad day and closed off on the rest. Bea blew out a breath, ruffling her bangs from her face.

Maybe they should just have this conversation tomorrow before rehearsal started.

Except she really didn't want to do it when Jo and Piper were around. Jo was embarrassed enough by the whole Mandy incident earlier that day, and Bea didn't want to add to that.

"Just get over yourself already," Bea said to herself before forcing her hand up and knocking quickly. The faster she did this, the sooner she could get home to check on Jo.

The door opened sharply, then stopped just as suddenly. Bunny filled the entry, shoulder to shoulder, with the door pressing into her arm as she leaned against the handle and looked Bea over pointedly. A shiver ran through Bea and ended straight between her legs. She hated that Bunny had the ability to do that.

It wasn't why she was here.

"I'm sorry to bug you at home," Bea started, biting her tongue when she started with the apology. She shouldn't have done that. She should have just stated right out why she was there and left already. She didn't need any praise or conversation from Bunny.

"You missed rehearsal."

Bea pressed her lips together hard. "I did. But this wasn't a planned rehearsal. It was an addition, and I couldn't reschedule—"

"Then you should have told me about that when we scheduled it."

"I forgot. It was a simple mistake." Bea folded her hands together in front of her. "That's not what I'm here to talk about anyway."

"Oh?" Bunny pulled open the door a little wider and straightened herself. "Did you come here for something specific?"

"Yes." *But not that,* she added in a thought. Then again, Bunny was looking marvelous today. Bea bit the inside of her cheek and glanced up and down the hallway. Bunny lived in a fairly private condo, but that didn't mean that there weren't listening ears or that her neighbors didn't have those pesky cameras to catch everything going on outside of their doors.

And she really didn't want any more drama when it came to Jo. "Do you mind if we talk inside?"

She knew that it sounded like she was implying something else, and that Bunny would definitely be thinking that, but how else was she supposed to ask?

"This is important."

Bunny's lips thinned. She raked her gaze over Bea's body and then back up to her eyes. "Sure thing, babe."

Babe? Bea pulled a face when she stepped inside. Who was Bunny trying to play now? Because it definitely wasn't who she'd been any other time Bea had met her.

Bea stepped inside and closed the door. As soon as she turned, Bunny only had eyes for her. Eyes that said she wanted sex, that she thought this was some sort of booty call. Bea shuddered. That's all anything ever was to Bunny, wasn't it? Sex.

She'd known that going in, but Bea had been stupid enough to think that perhaps she might be different or that she could be different with Bunny. She'd been wrong. And now she just had to protect her heart.

"I wanted to thank you for coming to Jo's rescue today."

Bunny halted her forward movement. "Jo?"

"Yes. With Mandy." Bea rolled her eyes and forced her lips into a curve even though it didn't feel right at the moment. "I didn't think Mandy would take it to any more of an extreme than she had before, but this certainly escalated."

"Tell me, did Jo give her the address to the rehearsal studio?"

Bea shook her head, her soft curls hitting her cheeks. "No, not that I know of. I don't know why she would."

Bunny's shoulders squared, anger pulling together. Bea could see it from a mile away. She'd seen it before, but why would Bunny be getting so pissed off now? All Bea was there to do was thank her for doing what she couldn't do. For stepping into that role because Bea had been absent.

"This is why this is a bad idea."

"What's a bad idea?" Bea asked, trying to keep all defensiveness out of her tone. She didn't need to tick off Bunny any more than she already was.

"Relationships being out in the open."

"Excuse me?" Bea frowned. "No one is out in the open."

"*You* are."

"What are you even talking about?" Bea threw her hand out to the side. "We're not in a relationship. I don't want to date you."

Bunny let out a raucous laugh. "Thank God. Because that's the worst idea on the planet. But so is being out when it comes to this business, and Jo took it too far."

"Jo's living authentically, and so am I!" Bea clenched her jaw hard. She was so glad they'd come inside for this conversation. "Why do you insist that we hide who we are?"

"Because it'll kill your career faster than you can see it fly."

"That's bullshit." Bea shook her head slowly, the full realization dawning on her. Bunny wasn't afraid of relationships, she was afraid of people knowing about those relationships. So she'd cut herself off from anything that could possibly become that. Everyone except Piper. There had been plenty of rumors about the two of them over the years. Bea had seen them. She'd wondered about them. "It's ridiculous to try and be someone you're not."

"I'm not being anyone but myself," Bunny fired back, stepping closer and coming into Bea's personal space.

They were so close. Tempers flared. Bea was ready to yell and scream. She wanted to have it all out already. She wanted to be done with what was between them. "Again, I call bullshit."

"Don't tempt me." Bunny took another step.

"Tempt you?" Bea furrowed her brow and wrinkled her nose. "Why would I even think about you like that again? It's clear you want nothing from me. You didn't even want to work with me."

"Because you're making bad decisions when it comes to your business."

"No, I'm making decisions that are right for me and Jo. We make those decisions together." Bea planted her feet. She wasn't going to let down any of her shields. She needed them up to survive this argument, and probably to be in any room with Bunny afterward. This was going to kill everything they had together.

"You're too young to understand what you're doing."

"Too young?" Bea's voice nearly broke on the word. "Did you ever consider that maybe you're too old and stuck in your ways to see that the world is changing?"

"And you call what I say bullshit?"

"Enough, Bunny. I'm not having this argument with you. I came here to thank you for helping Jo today, and I've done that." Bea took a step backward toward the door.

Bunny reached out and snagged her wrist, holding her in place. "You're digging your own grave."

Bea's eyes widened. Was Bunny even talking about her anymore? The tension in Bunny's face was so tight. She was fraught with something, but Bea couldn't name what it was. Not that she wanted to spend much time to figure it out, not after Bunny was being such a jerk about everything.

"It's my grave to dig," Bea finally responded. She twisted her hand, freeing it from Bunny's grasp. "Are we done here?"

Bunny shook her head no.

Bea stayed put as she waited for whatever reaming she had coming next, but Bunny didn't say anything. She didn't move. She didn't twitch.

"Bunny?" Bea finally asked.

"What?" Bunny grumbled.

"What else did you think we needed to argue about?"

Bunny scoffed. She raised her eyes, meeting Bea's gaze. Her jaw was clenched, the muscles bulging on the sides as she ground her molars. But she still didn't say anything. Was she trying to prevent Bea from leaving? What was going on in Bunny's head?

"Anyway, thanks for helping with Jo. She needs more people in her life who can protect her."

"She's not the only one who needs protecting," Bunny muttered.

Bea reached for the door and paused. She threw a look over her shoulder, debating whether or not to ask. "What are you talking about?"

"Don't throw away your career for a fuck, Bea. It's not worth it. You have the talent to make it."

"You're saying I shouldn't throw away my career for a partner? Or on coming out to the world?"

Bunny shook her head. "It's the same thing."

"It's not." Bea staggered back a step. If Bunny really thought that, no wonder she was in the position that she was in. "It's really not."

Bea grabbed the doorknob and turned it, but Bunny was there in a second, her hand on the edge of the door, holding it open only a few inches. Bea sucked in a sharp breath, barely able to stand next to Bunny for this long without wondering about so many things.

"Don't let personal feelings get in the way," Bunny whispered, stepping closer.

"In the way of what?" Bea was so confused now. Was Bunny talking to her or herself? Because it sounded like the latter. Bea swallowed hard. "I'm not going to tell Jo she can't date just because of a job."

"This isn't a job. It's my life."

Bea paused before responding. "Are you that scared that we're going to ruin your life?"

Bunny met Bea's gaze again, but she didn't move, and she didn't answer. They stood in silence for far longer than was comfortable. She was just about to make another move to leave, when Bunny shut the door firmly and took hold of Bea's wrist again.

"We're done talking, Bunny," Bea said matter-of-factly. She didn't want to race through any decisions, but at this point, she had nothing else to say or add to the conversation. They were clearly on opposite sides of the fence on this one.

"So we are." Bunny moved in swiftly, pressing their mouths together.

Bea squeaked before she melted. Bunny was so good at this, always able to take her by surprise, always full of fire and lust. Bea carded her fingers through Bunny's hair, moving her lips and her tongue against Bunny's mouth.

Bunny turned them, pushing Bea into the door and sandwiching her body. Bea groaned, her eyes fluttering shut as she almost gave herself over to the embrace. But something about Bunny's behavior that night made her want to hold back. She had to put an end to this. Now. Before she couldn't separate her feelings from sex.

Bea pulled back and sucked in a sharp breath. "Bunny. Stop."

Bunny halted everything. She was frozen on the spot, waiting for Bea to give the next command. Bea had to work hard to catch her breath, barely able to focus her brain after the desperation that had flowed from Bunny to her. Shaking her head, Bea slid away from Bunny's grasp.

"I'm not going to do this anymore," Bea stated simply.

"Do what?"

"Anything when it involves you. I don't live in a closet of my own making or choosing. And I'm not going to join you in yours." Bea's chest constricted from the pained expression that crossed Bunny's features. Did Bunny even know she looked devastated by that revelation?

"Get out," Bunny ordered.

"Absolutely." Bea didn't hesitate as she walked out of Bunny's condo.

She made her way back to her car and slid behind the wheel before she managed to pause. She should have waited until after the charity event to do it, but she couldn't force herself to go against her morals either. She couldn't fake being someone who didn't care, and she couldn't fight to make Bunny care either.

The end was as it should be.

They could go to rehearsals and work together from there on out. Surely both of them could be professionals when it came to the concert coming up. Bea started the engine and pulled her seatbelt on. She still hated that it hurt so much, though. She hated that she wanted to climb into her bed and wrap herself in her blanket and cry.

For fuck's sake—they weren't even dating and this felt like a breakup.

It was for the best though. Bea couldn't be with someone who couldn't even accept herself.

bunny

Bunny's head thumped, and her stomach roiled. But as usual, she was the first one at rehearsal. She was a professional after all.

She had laid out three sets of stapled paper on the rectangular table. They didn't have many practices left and the show was getting closer far faster than she would have liked. But had she panicked that not a single one of the songs was one hundred percent polished yet? No, of course she hadn't. She had spent the night forcing herself not to relive the argument with Bea yet again, and instead to list the things they needed to get perfected by the end of each remaining practice.

She took the fourth seat at the table. They still weren't here. It was less than five minutes until rehearsal time started and not one of them could be bothered to get here early enough to warm up and be ready to go by the start of it.

Using two fingers on each hand, she rubbed small circles into her temples, trying again to stop herself from reliving that fight with Bea.

It wasn't as though they hadn't fought before. But something about this time felt sharp and so final. Bunny hadn't been able to say what she wanted to say, and every time she'd opened her mouth, she had made the situation a hundred times worse than it already was.

The front door opened with the obnoxious tinkle of that damn bell on the top of it. The door hit the wall from being pushed open too forcefully, the sound echoing off the brick walls of the hallway and ringing in her ears.

The added mix of voices with the squeak of tennis shoes against the linoleum floor set Bunny's teeth on edge.

Before they could reach the rehearsal room, she stood up from the chair and rummaged through her bag she had dumped in the corner for something to dull the throbbing in her skull. She didn't like taking them, but she just couldn't shake this damn headache. It felt like forever before she finally found them and swallowed them down with several big gulps from her water bottle.

They filtered into the studio room, Piper and Jo smiling and looking at each other in ways that made panic flutter in Bunny's chest. She had known from the start that this was a bad idea. Behind Piper and Jo, Bea walked in with her face set in a perfect mask of distance.

Looked like Bunny would have to be the professional, again. It shouldn't bother her. It was the way it had always been. But this time, it did strike frustration into her heart. This was why she normally said no to working with others. Even Piper was slipping on her work ethic.

"Finally," Bunny said as a way of greeting when all three finally took their seats at the table. But Bunny didn't want to sit down. They didn't have time to ease into things, and she wouldn't lose her own work ethic to their blasé attitudes. "There are a lot of things we need to sharpen up. Jo, your movements are too soft, you need to hit the steps on the beat, not just after. Piper, your vocals aren't where they should be. And Bea, we're cutting *Baby It's Cold Outside.*"

"What?" Jo and Piper said simultaneously.

Bunny didn't look over at Bea, but she felt Bea's eyes boring into her, anger wafting off of her.

"We haven't factored in enough time to perfect it, so we'll be cutting that song. It'll work better without it anyway. The show would be far too tight if we kept it in."

"And of course it had to be that song, didn't it? Do any of us get a say?" Piper fired back.

"You'd get a say if any of you actually took this seriously enough to show up on time." Bunny crossed her arms and gave Piper a stern look.

"We were on time." Piper said, her tone holding a slight edge, but Bunny also knew when she was trying to calm tension before it rose.

"It makes sense to cut that song."

"How do you figure that? Because it's gay and heaven forbid we acknowledge something other than heteronormative society?" Piper was in a mood today. Bunny was going to have to watch out for that one as rehearsal got underway.

"It makes sense because that's the song that needs the most work done on it. We're too short on time. As it is, we're going to need extra rehearsals to make sure every single song is perfect."

"It's fine." Bea stood up, the blankness taking over the fury that had flashed moments ago. That mask caused an ache in Bunny's chest. An ache she didn't understand and didn't want to.

Almost stunned into silence by the agreement, Bunny held her ground instead of staggering back like she wanted to. She slipped a glance to Piper and then eyed Bea over. "Then let's get started."

Tension settled over the room, and everything they rehearsed piled more bricks of frustration on top of Bunny's anger.

They were all being entirely unprofessional. But she didn't want another round of Bunny is wrong. How could she possibly know what the world was like just because she'd been in the industry the longest?

"Bea," Bunny spoke softly as she moved to where Bea sat at the piano.

"Yes?" Bea looked up.

Even though she seemed to look directly into Bunny's eyes her stare didn't connect. There was no warmth, and no emotion.

"Do you really understand?" For some inane reason, Bunny had to check. She had to be sure that Bea was okay with everything going on.

"Oh, I understand." Bea turned back to the piano and gently tapped on the keys, not pressing them down hard enough to make the music, but just enough for the ghost of it to vibrate.

"You do?" Bunny wasn't stupid. She could still feel the tension like a wall separating the two of them.

"Of course, I do." Bea didn't look at Bunny, but kept her eyes on the sheet music in front of her. But the page hadn't been turned, and Bunny was certain Bea had moved long past where the current page had ended.

Pride warmed Bunny's chest. Bea's talent was refreshing. It was real and beyond a simple desire to be famous for fame's sake.

Bunny couldn't let her throw it all away for something that could so easily be kept out of the limelight. Despite what the industry often went on about, not all publicity was good publicity.

"Bea?"

"You're scared. You're afraid of being judged, but more than that, you're afraid the world might actually have moved on, and you've wasted all this time being angry and bitter at the cruelty of a world everyone else has left behind."

The words exploded from Bunny's mouth. So much for approaching this professionally. "Do you seriously think bigotry and homophobia have just disappeared? That they just went poof and vanished overnight?"

"No, I don't." Bea turned on the piano stool and faced Bunny. "That's what you're afraid of."

"You don't know what you're talking about."

"Then why are you so scared to even sing a single song about love just because it's between two women?"

Their voices had grown louder, and Jo and Piper now stared at them. Jo stopped working on her dance number for song number four, and Piper now had her headphones around her neck. The strap on the guitar hung taunt on her neck, taking more of the instrument's weight than her hands.

"I'm not the bad guy here." Bunny moved her head quickly, scanning over all of them but not settling on any of their eyes. "You're all acting like children. Young, naive, and with this fucked up notion that living your truth is going to save you from the vultures."

"You don't get to talk to me that way." Bea's mouth puckered up, her eyes squinting daggers toward Bunny. It was hardly an attractive expression, and yet somehow, Bunny wondered what it would be like to kiss every new shape of Bea's face.

She shook the thoughts from her head and scoffed at herself. She couldn't honestly be screwing this up again, and yet it was like she was watching everything in slow motion in front of her and she couldn't stop it. Bunny was on a quick spiral down to the bottom. She just hoped she reached it soon enough so she could drag herself back up.

"Not everything needs to be about people's sexuality. You say it shouldn't matter. But here you are, every single one of you, trying to make a charity about single mothers of all things, into a show all about your sexuality. If you want to be successful, if you actually want to get anywhere in this business, you have to do the work and make the sacrifices. This job is about hard work!" Bunny bit the inside of her cheek, making her stop talking before she said anything else that would land her in the hot seat. And she managed to stop herself in time and to tamp down that ego that was rising up and rearing its ugly head.

"We *do* do the work." Of all people, Bunny hadn't expected Jo to be the one to speak up, especially to argue with her. Her eyebrows were pulled down and the sadness in those wide eyes made Bunny understand just a little about the web Piper was so willing to crawl into. But those eyes and that innocence didn't work on Bunny. In fact, it proved her very point.

"Bunny!" Piper's shock was evident, but the reprimand only fueled the fire she hadn't been able to put out.

"Bunny what?" Bunny snapped right back.

"You don't have to be such a bitch." Bea's words were laced with venom. "You're getting what you want. But that's not enough is it? Even when it's your way, you just can't help making sure we know how much better you are than us. Nothing else matters but what you want out of it, and if anyone dares to do something you aren't brave enough to do yourself, you'll do whatever it takes to step on their neck."

"Is that how you see it?" Bunny's breathing was becoming too hard and too fast. But she wouldn't leave here being accused of being the bad guy. *Because I'm not better at this than you.* Those words, the ones that might have actually helped them both, died on her tongue before they could fully form.

"That's how it is." Bea crossed her arms over her chest, hip cocked out to the side.

Bunny shook her head as she took them all in. Bea with her anger and defiance on display. Jo with her head down, no longer able to meet Bunny's eyes. Even Piper glared at her. Bunny had dug her own grave—much like she'd accused Bea of doing—without even seeing it. It was three against one, and she wasn't going to be able to yell her way out of this one.

"Piper," Bunny tried. Anything to get herself to stop acting like such a fool.

Piper shook her head, arms crossed, and her shoulders set. "You're acting like a bitch. Bea's right." The parroting of Bea's words did nothing to cool the embers of shame burning inside of Bunny.

Bunny couldn't find words. How could she? She'd been exactly what they'd called her out on, and she still couldn't force her body to do anything about it. Her feet wouldn't move, her tongue wouldn't make words, and her voice wouldn't carry to their ears. Bunny was frozen in fear and shame.

Bea snorted and threw her hands up in the air. "Then I guess I understand fully now." She stood up and stalked toward the door, without even tossing a look over her shoulder.

"Where are you going?" Bunny called out, worry edging into her voice and her body. Was Bea really leaving? For good this time? Bunny wouldn't be able to handle that, would she?

"To another practice room. Any other practice room. I'm not your student, and seeing as we don't need to practice anything together, I don't need to stay and be lectured, especially by you. And who knows, maybe I'll even find a little scrap of professionalism somewhere." Bea walked out and left the other three staring after her.

Bunny ignored how dry her throat had gotten, and the hitch and wobble in her voice. She stood in silence and shock, staring at the door Bea had just walked out of. But she could barely breathe. How long did she stand there? Because when she turned back around to figure out what to do next, Jo was singing beneath her breath as she moved in step to the rhythm again and again. She didn't look up or stop.

And Piper shot her a glare while she stretched. If sewing her mouth shut for a few more practices and a one-time only show was the price to pay, she could handle that. She just needed to get herself together again.

At the piano bench, where Bea had sat, Bunny put her fingers onto the keys. As always happened the moment she heard that first note, Bunny felt the tension fall away from her shoulders. At least, she expected it to, but it didn't work this time. This was why she wasn't going to risk everything she had worked for. The life she had built up, all because the youngest new group in town decided being out was the only way to live.

Bunny kept playing and playing. Her fingers ached, but the rest of her body finally released a small amount of the tension after hours sitting there. Her mind clearer, she walked over to her bag to get a drink. Only then did she realize her headache had finally gone.

And so had Jo.

Jo had left without saying goodbye. Had Bea left as well? Had Bea even stayed? She probably hadn't. She probably stormed off in a full tantrum, which frankly, she deserved to. Bunny had been a bitch to her particularly. Bea had borne the brunt of Bunny's wrath.

Bunny was surprised Piper was still there. Surprised but relieved to see that not all of Piper's dedication and work ethic had disappeared because of some big eyes and similar energy. But also surprised because Bunny's temper tantrum had exploded on everyone that morning, and she deserved to be left in the dust that day, left and made to think about her actions and words. That shame clutched her heart again, and she couldn't shake it—not that she thought she deserved to.

Bunny went back to her music. She was still playing when Piper tapped her on her shoulder.

"Hey," Piper said, no smile accompanying the greeting.

"What's up?"

"What's up? Seriously?" Piper cringed, her face squishing up and tightening.

"Everything we do has to be done with the business and its future in mind. You know that, Piper."

"Yeah, I do," Piper agreed. "So why did you treat me, and Jo and Bea, as though we're wayward children caught sneaking out in the middle of the night?"

"Because it's how you've been acting." Bunny was too tired to be tactful. She was too defensive to even try to push into her shame and allow Piper to see it like she normally would. She was too hurt to even think about letting someone else see her wounds.

"Be careful, Bunny. Or you just might get your wish." Piper met Bunny's eyes, a sad look in her ever-youthful and happy face.

"And what wish is that?"

"The one where you're the only professional in the room." Piper stepped past Bunny after a pointed look and snagged her bag off the floor, putting it over her shoulder to carry it out. "You might want to think about what you're doing all the extra homework for, because it certainly isn't that you think we haven't perfected the performance yet. Get over yourself, and quit while you're ahead. Or no one is going to be here when you're done, including me."

"What are you talking about?" Panic clawed against her throat, and the words came out tight. Bunny couldn't lose Piper. She was the only person Bunny had left in this world.

"I'm talking about you only making stupid messes when you're in love." Piper's lips thinned and she shook her head.

Bunny's lips parted, but no words formed again. She sat

frozen on the piano bench, trying to figure out what exactly to say. But she couldn't come up with anything. Piper was right. And so were Bea and Jo. When she went to finally tell Piper that, she was gone.

And Bunny was alone.

Well and truly alone.

piper

"I wanted to run an idea past you." Piper plopped onto her couch, her thigh bumping deliciously into Jo's. She'd been stewing over the idea for a few weeks now—since she mentioned it the first time—but after the disaster that was their last rehearsal and the radio silence from both Bea and Bunny, Piper knew she was going to have to pull out the big guns for this one.

"Sure, what's up?" Jo popped a pretzel between her lips and grinned.

"I know why Bunny is all pissy lately."

"I would hope." Jo gave a half-chuckle half-snort.

Piper wasn't sure if she was amused or worried. And she didn't really want to share Bunny's secrets with the world either. Rubbing her lips together, Piper debated exactly what to say. "I love Bunny dearly. She's my best friend. We're closer than sisters."

"I get that." Jo looked up into Piper's eyes, a curious expression on her lips.

Piper knew she wasn't explaining this well, but she was trying to choose her words carefully. "The last time Bunny fell in love, it was with someone she couldn't have, someone that it would never work out with."

Jo frowned. "You think she's in love with Bea?"

Nodding, Piper snagged Jo's hand and wrapped their fingers together. "Yeah, I do. And just like last time, she's digging herself into the biggest ditch ever."

"What happened last time?"

Sighing, Piper rolled through everything in her memories. What could she share? What should she share? "Let's just say she fell hard and swiftly, and when the woman she fell in love with wasn't willing to make changes to be with her, Bunny shut down. I mean hard. She never wanted a relationship again after that."

"So this is about more than just coming out to the world," Jo concluded.

"It is, but I'm not sure Bunny will ever admit that. I didn't honestly think she'd ever open her heart again to someone else."

"But you think she has with Bea?"

"I do." Piper lifted Jo's hand to her lips and kissed her knuckles. "And Bea? What's her hesitation?"

"She's used to being in charge, and she doesn't like being told what to do, and that seems to be all Bunny wants to do."

"Hmm, Bunny's clawing at control because she's losing it so swiftly." Piper ran her fingers through her hair. "Bunny's problem is that she doesn't believe love can't be messy."

"Well, she's certainly making a mess of things."

"Yeah, she is." Piper laughed lightly. She liked this side of Jo, the side that was carefree and easy, the side that didn't worry about what other people thought, how they were judging her. "But I do have an idea, if you think that Bea might be interested in more."

"Like relationship more?"

"Yes. If you think Bea might be in love."

Jo's lower lip quivered. She didn't make eye contact, and she played with the pretzels in the bag before popping another one between her lips. "I don't want to mess with my sister's life."

"Don't you think she needs a push? Something to get her to see Bunny—who she really is?"

"I've got to say that after this week, I'm not sure I want to know the real Bunny."

"This week wasn't her. Remember the woman who saved you from Mandy? That's Bunny. She's fiercely loyal and protective. She was so pissed off that she scathed Siena for it and hired more security to be at the building to watch out for Mandy there and at the concert."

"She did what?" Jo's eyes widened.

"Bunny doesn't fuck around with the people she cares for when it comes to safety. She doesn't let abusers have their moment."

"Abusers…" Jo trailed off, the word sounding bitter on her tongue. "She thinks Mandy is abusing me?"

"Harassing at the very least. Do you really not see it?" Piper hated that the conversation was taking this turn. But she did want to make her point clear. Bunny wasn't a bad person, despite what her behavior had been the last few weeks.

"I guess I can."

"We'll work on that." Piper dropped a kiss into Jo's hair. "Bunny wants you to be safe."

"She doesn't care about me."

"She does, otherwise she wouldn't be this mad about everything." Piper wouldn't be able to convince Jo otherwise, and that wasn't really her point either. Except to get Jo to help her with this insane idea, she'd have to convince Jo to at least somewhat like Bunny. "And she wouldn't be making such a mess of things. She cares about your career and your success, otherwise she wouldn't even be attempting to give advice."

"That's advice?" Jo's eyes widened.

Piper shrugged slightly. "She thinks it is."

Jo scrunched her face up. "I don't know about that."

"Bunny is brilliant when it comes to business, but sometimes, even I can say this, she doesn't take enough risks."

"And what risk is she trying not to take?" Jo moved her hand up and down Piper's thigh in a gentle caress.

"Oh, there's several of them. And I'm going to give her a piece of my mind about it real soon. She needs to be taken down a couple more notches."

"I'm not sure I want to be there when you do that." Jo giggled nervously before shaking her head. "Is that all part of your idea you wanted to talk to me about?"

"I'm not sure it's a great idea anymore…" Piper dragged out. She rested back into the couch a little more, curling her long legs under her. "In fact, it's probably a really bad idea."

"What do you mean?"

"I thought we could fake an engagement. Have Siena do a little fake PR for it, and really show Bunny that there isn't all that much to be afraid of. Force her to take that risk because she'll be doing it kicking and screaming either way."

"And Bea," Jo whispered.

"If that's what she's afraid of." Piper slid her fingers through Jo's hair. "But it's probably a bad idea. It would mean we'd have to fake an engagement to each other."

"I don't know. It could help get Mandy off my back if she finally realized I was totally unavailable." Jo trailed her fingers back and forth along Piper's arm. "This might not be a half bad idea. It could solve a lot of problems."

"Are you sure?"

"Kind of, actually. No. I am. What would that entail?"

Jo sounded so interested. Piper held herself stiff, waiting to see if it was genuine curiosity or just conversation making.

Piper pulled her lip between her teeth and let it pop out. "Just some pictures and us telling Bunny probably."

"And Bea? Do we tell her?"

"That we'd be engaged or that it's all fake?"

"That we're engaged."

Piper squinted at Jo's turn of phrase. They wouldn't actually be engaged. It would just be to get Bunny and Bea's heads out of their asses. "Yeah, if you think that'd be best."

"I think that if I'm not someone she has to take care of anymore, then she might just free herself up for a relationship. If she wasn't worried about me, then she could focus on someone else." Jo's lips slowly turned upward into a smile. "I think it's a brilliant idea."

"There could be fallout from it."

"Then we'll deal with it later." Jo quickly moved up onto her knees and straddled Piper's thighs. "I think this is exactly the kick in the ass that Bea needs. When are we doing it?"

"Uh… tonight," Piper said, making the decision immediately. "Well, assuming I can get hold of Siena. I'm sure she's heard an earful from everyone about the situation by now."

"Really?"

"Oh yeah. She knows everything." Piper leaned over to the coffee table to grab her phone. "Pray she answers."

Hitting Siena's name, Piper put the phone on speaker and held it in front of her. It was the fourth ring before she answered, and Piper's lips curled into a smile as soon as Siena's smooth, "What's up, Pipes?" reached her ears.

"Hey." Piper's cheeks turned hot. "I have a favor to ask of you, and I want you to not kill me for it before you hear me out."

"Okay?" Siena sounded curious now.

"Do you have Harley tonight?"

"Yeah, I do."

Piper pressed her lips together hard and glanced at Jo.

"Well, maybe she can help. She is one of the best wing women out there."

"What's going on?" Siena's tone turned demanding.

Harley's playful squeal could be heard in the background. Piper grinned at it. She'd always loved that kid. "I have an idea to get Bunny to quit being such a bitch, but I'm going to need your help."

"All right. I'm in for whatever it is because she's on some kind of rampage."

"Yep. So, Jo and I were thinking of pulling off a fake engagement."

"What!?" Siena's voice rang through the room.

Piper slipped Jo a conspiratorial look. "Yeah, fake engagement. Catch up, Siena. Bunny's problem is love, and I want her to know that love isn't a death sentence. That we can be out and she'll survive. So let's show her that."

"This is an insane idea."

"But insane ideas usually work."

Piper could swear she could see Siena frowning. "No, they don't."

"Yes, they do. Welcome to this entire Christmas charity event you've dragged us into." Piper giggled, though it was on the edge of maniacal. This was a risky and crazy idea, but honestly, getting Bunny to see her way out of her own ass wasn't Piper's only motivation. She enjoyed spending time with Jo, and if this put the silly idea in Jo's head that perhaps they could be together longer term, then Piper would be happy.

"What's the idea, Pipes?"

"I want you to stage some PR photos. Harley can take them, she's amazing with a phone camera, and I want them to find their way to Bunny. Not rudely, because then she'll be worse off, but I want her to know that being queer isn't going to be a death sentence for us."

"I don't know about this."

"Jo agreed. She thinks Bea needs a kick in the ass, too."

"A swift one!" Jo chimed in.

Piper sent her a small smile. "Please."

"But no actual PR?" Siena clarified.

"No actual PR. Just make it look like that."

"I might have someone who can help us. Harley! Get socks and shoes on. We're going to see Auntie P. I could use getting my ass chewed by Bunny one more time before the year ends." Siena mumbled the last part. "I'll meet you at Eastbank in half an hour. Dress nice."

"Yes!" Piper pumped her fist into the air. "But wait, who are you going to get to help us?"

"Jamie Kettlehouse."

"You're kidding me."

"Thirty minutes, Piper. Don't be late." Siena hung up.

Piper stared at her phone for longer than she should have, confusion swimming in her brain.

"Who's Jamie Kettlehouse?" Jo asked, wrapping her arms around Piper's.

Wrinkling her nose, Piper shook her head. "She's a blogger, a spitfire, someone who is known for taking a rumor and running with it. The worst gossip monger you can think of in Portland. She runs blogs, magazines, social media accounts— so many of them we'd never be able to find them all. I have no clue why Siena would think bringing her in on this would be a good idea."

"She would know how to write it up well."

Piper scoffed. "Yeah, but Siena can do that. She writes press releases all the time."

"But if we want it to look like a rumor."

"Maybe. I don't know. But I sure as hell am going to find out." Piper moved to her feet and pulled Jo to hers. "Come on, we need to get dressed."

They were five minutes late, but Piper got them there.

Siena stood still by the bridge, her tall, thin figure hard to miss, especially with Harley running circles around her—literally. Next to her stood a short, curvy woman that Piper could only guess was Jamie Kettlehouse.

Taking Jo's hand in hers, Piper started toward them. She'd quickly snagged one of her rings from her room—one that looked the most engagement-like, though it wasn't an engagement ring at all—and slipped it into her pocket before they'd left the apartment.

"Hey," Piper said, nodding to Siena and looking Jamie over.

"It's good to meet you finally." Jamie stepped forward and put her hand out.

Piper almost didn't take it. Jamie had written some horrible things about her and Bunny over the years. She'd also written good things about them, though those had been fewer and farther between. Everything in Piper's world until now had been oriented around avoiding this woman and anything she could potentially write about them.

Bunny would burn knowing that she was the one here for this.

"Auntie P! Auntie P!" Harley jumped up and down, and Piper had to let go of Jo's hand to snag Harley and spin her in a circle or two before stopping. "It's been way too long since I've seen you kid. You've grown an entire foot!"

Harley giggled, the sound music to Piper's ears.

"How's your arm? Do I get to sign the cast?" Piper put her down and looked the cast over, the small drawings and writings from kids all over it. "Is there even room?"

"Yeah!" Harley ran to her mom and snagged a pen, bringing it back over. "Right here."

Piper grinned as she drew a heart and wrote *Auntie P* on the bright pink cast. "All right, so you're here for a reason, because I need your help."

Harley laughed. "Mama says I get to take pictures!"

"Right, you do, on her phone and my phone." Piper whipped out her phone and handed it over to Harley. "I assume you know how to use it."

"Of course I do!" Harley giggled loudly.

"All right, let's get this on." Siena stepped forward. "And Piper, you have until the morning to come up with a plan for how to tell Bunny what's going on."

"I'm working on it already." Piper sucked in a sharp breath. Why was she nervous? There was nothing real about this proposal. She shouldn't be worried about whether or not Jo would say yes, that was the entire point. Hell, she didn't even have to ask. They just had to pose for photos.

"Piper?" Jo asked, that sweet voice ringing through Piper's ears.

"Yeah. Right." Piper cleared her throat. She took Jo's hand and led her closer to the water's edge and right under the light so that the pictures would look better.

Without preamble, Piper got down on one knee and held her hand up with the ring sitting in the center of her palm. The words caught in her throat. It was ridiculous. She couldn't have made herself more of a donkey's ass. She'd proposed the idea of this fake engagement and now she couldn't even get the words out.

Jo stared at her, wide-eyed and cautious.

Piper had to stop this. She had to make this better. Standing up sharply, Piper turned to Siena and to Jamie and shook her head. "Hold on. I need a second."

She walked toward the water and let out a heavy breath.

"What's going on?" Jo ran her hand along Piper's back, small circles before she dropped it away. "What's wrong?"

"Nothing's wrong." Except everything was. She wasn't sure she wanted to do this anymore. It was a bad idea.

"Then let's go. Come on. I'm waiting for this splendid proposal you promised me."

Piper scoffed. "You're sure about this?"

"Yeah. Now more than ever."

"Now?" Piper furrowed her brow and looked Jo over. "Why now?"

"Because you're just as nervous as I am." Jo took Piper's hand and led her back to the spot they'd been in before.

Harley gave them odd looks, but she held the phone up to her face. Was she still taking pictures? God, Piper would look like an idiot running away from the first proposal. She was such a Looney Toon sometimes.

"Get down on one knee," Jo murmured into Piper's ear. "You don't even have to say anything."

"But I want to." Piper's voice caught in her throat again at Jo's confusion. Shaking her head, Piper dropped to her knee. She didn't even nod at the others to let them know she was ready. She just held out her hand and stared up into Jo's beautifully brown eyes. "I want to tell you that I love you, that you are the love of my life."

Fuck, the words were flowing now, and she couldn't stop them.

"That you're the sole reason I wake up in the morning and what I dream about in bed at night. That you're what my world is centered around. I want to tell you that we're going to build a life together, one day at a time, weaving our stories and our dances together. I want to tell you that I'm confident and purposeful and I'm not going to mess things up. I want to tell you that I'll never leave you."

Jo's cheeks pulled upward, her lips curling into a smile. "Are you serious?"

Piper grinned back. She couldn't tell if Jo was shocked or laughing at her. But Piper had never been one who was short on words.

"When have I ever lied to you?" Piper asked.

Jo laughed like a fool, bending down and pressing their mouths together, her hands on Piper's cheeks. Jo dropped to her knees, their lips still touching as she pulled back and shook her head at Jo. "You're ridiculously charming some days, Piper."

"You could do worse than me."

"I definitely could," Jo agreed. "Now let me see this ring."

"But I haven't even asked you."

"So what," Jo whispered, plucking the ring from Piper's hand. "We're getting fake engaged!"

Piper's heart sank.

Yes.

Engaged.

But fake.

This wasn't real.

bea

Bea stood, fingers still gripping the handle of her front door as she stared at Bunny.

The banging on Bea's door had pushed her heart into her throat and made her jump. She hadn't been expecting anyone, and this wasn't a polite knock.

Now, staring at Bunny, she couldn't find any words.

Bea couldn't remember seeing Bunny look this disheveled, except after one of their ill-fated fucking sessions. That's how she had to think of them. As nothing but fucking. Even now, with Bunny's lips looking inviting even as she scowled at her.

Bea's mouth remained open as Bunny's chest rose and fell like she had run up the stairs. But her hands were steady as she held up her phone. Bea forced her eyes away from Bunny's lips and took in the woman's furious eyes and red cheeks. She wasn't breathing heavily from running up any stairs, but from rage.

Bea's heart plummeted to the pit of her stomach.

It wasn't like she had visions of Bunny running to find her, to apologize and sweep her off her feet.

Had she?

Of course not.

But then, why would she be so disappointed to realize Bunny was angry? Again. The surprise was stupid. When wasn't she angry, especially lately? Bea hadn't been sure of Bunny when they'd met, but the more they'd gotten to know each other, Bunny had proven to be a kind and fiercely loyal person. But these last few days had been something else entirely—something out of left field that had thrown Bea off her feet.

"Did you know about this?" Bunny thrust her phone out, closer to Bea's face.

"Hi, Bunny." Bea found her words, and they dripped with sarcasm. Two could play at the asshole game, and Bea wasn't going to let Bunny down on her end of the deal. "How are you?"

"Don't." Bunny sneered, her cheeks reddening and hollowing. She could have raged again, but she didn't. Instead, she pushed the phone into Bea's face again.

Bea's only reply was her raised eyebrows and the crossing of her arms over her chest.

"Did. You. Know?"

"I don't know what you're showing me," Bea snapped back. "You keep shaking the phone around like it's an Etch A Sketch."

"The engagement. Did you know?" There was a quiver in her voice, and Bea wondered what on earth could truly affect Bunny. Anger was one thing, but this bordered on something completely different. Any disappointment vanished as she processed Bunny's words. She definitely should have known better.

"What engagement?" Bea's shoulders dropped as she uncrossed her arms, one hand reaching out for the phone.

The fury radiating from Bunny either cooled slightly or Bea's distraction made her less aware of it. Either way,

Bunny seemed the least of her problems as she stared at the phone.

She stared at the words and the photo.

This didn't make sense.

Bea tried to take a step and stumbled. Bunny caught her by the waist and tucked Bea into her side, holding her steady. Somewhere behind her Bea was faintly aware of her door being closed with a soft snick and Bunny's footsteps helping her inside.

Heavily, Bea sat down on the lumpy middle cushion of her couch and tried to focus on the actual words that hadn't made sense the first time she'd read them. Still she struggled to make out the words and processing them was hard.

Jo and Piper engaged!

Romantic proposal at Eastbank.

Happy couple had a few small witnesses, including manager Siena.

Photos of the happy couple…

"What the fuck is this?" Bea muttered as she read the article again before scrolling down to the photos.

"So you didn't know?" Bunny asked, hands on hips as she looked down at Bea. But the angry tone from before had tempered dramatically, and the sharp contrast threw Bea for a loop. She couldn't handle these swings of emotions.

"No." Anger boiled in the pit of Bea's stomach, but her heart ached and her mind raced just as strongly. Why wouldn't Jo tell her? Why wouldn't Jo even mention that she and Piper were in a relationship before now? She'd seen them getting closer, had hoped that maybe something might grow between them, but to be left out of the narrative completely? That just flat out hurt.

It ripped Bea's heart apart.

"This is ridiculous. You know, I caught them swapping spit once, but I didn't think that Piper would take it this far. And your sister's turning this whole thing into a God damn circus. I never should have agreed to this event. It's going to ruin everything I've built."

"Excuse me?" Bea stood, slapping the phone into Bunny's chest, forcing her to step back a little.

"Piper wouldn't do *this*." Bunny planted the phone into Bea's face again to show off the press release.

"The photos tell otherwise." Bea forced the words out as calmly as she could. "She's the one who proposed."

"Photos can be manipulated."

"Right, of course." Bea scoffed. "It's all everyone else's fault, isn't it?" Each word was harder to hold back.

"First Mandy, and now this," Bunny ranted as if she hadn't even heard Bea's scathing remark.

"Stop." Bea snapped so forcefully that Bunny jerked her head as though physically injured.

She was so tired. The exhaustion of the last few weeks—the emotional and the physical—she didn't have it in her to have another screaming match. This just needed to end before it got worse.

"You can't tell me you're happy about this." Bunny looked at her, face angled as though trying to work out what was going on.

"I'm hurt by it, yes," Bea said, "But why wouldn't I be happy about it? Would I have liked Jo to tell me herself? Absolutely. But if they're happy, then I'm going to be happy for them."

"Was this the whole point?"

"Was *what* the whole point?" Bea threw up her hands and let her head fall back as she stared up at the stained and cracked ceiling of her living room. "Stop talking around whatever you think's going on."

"The angle. Is this the angle you and Jo had from the start?"

Bea's jaw dropped. "Are you serious right now?"

"Come on. This can't just be some kind of coincidence."

"Get out." Bea stepped forward, into Bunny's space.

"I've worked too damn hard to let your sister ruin everything. And for something as stupid as an engagement, which you know won't last."

"And why not?" Bea snapped out. "Why won't it last? Because you say so?"

"Because the press is going to eat them alive for breakfast, lunch, and dinner! This industry will tear them apart in seconds with the amount of hate they'll get. They'll never be able to walk down the streets and feel safe. They'll never have a moment's peace!"

Was this what Bunny truly thought of Jo and Piper? Or was it everything she feared for herself? Bea didn't have time to dive into that vat of self-loathing, nor did she have the desire to do it. Bunny needed to take time to figure her own shit out. "Or they just might celebrate them."

Bunny scoffed.

"I need to call Jo." Bea squared her shoulders and gave Bunny a pointed look. "So if you'll excuse me, I'd like to call my sister and congratulate her on one of the happiest days of her life."

"You can't just let this go."

"Watch me," Bea fired back. "Because I'm not going to be the asshole who tears apart my family. I'm not going to be the one who is going to die on this hill. And I'm not going to lose my sister because my ego is so big I can't see anything but my own fucking nose."

Bunny stumbled back another step, Bea's anger lashing out and hitting its mark. And Bea wasn't even sad about it. Bunny deserved it, and someone had to take her down a few notches.

"So get out, Bunny. I'm done."

Silence lingered between them, as they steeped in the anger, the shame, and the broken-hearted feelings. Bea shook her head again, waiting for Bunny to turn around and walk out the door. She held her ground. She wouldn't let Bunny continue to treat her like this anymore. She couldn't control what Jo did, but she could protect herself from working with this jerk.

Bea had called Bunny that the first night they'd met, and while she'd thought she'd been wrong for a few moments there, she hadn't been. And she had to be done.

Those words settled deep into Bea's heart.

She was done.

Not just with this conversation, but with everything.

"Get out, Bunny," Bea repeated when Bunny didn't move quickly enough.

Silently, Bunny walked to the door. That vibrating anger she'd shown up with was gone, and it had been replaced by something so melancholy that it would scare Bea if she focused on it. Bunny was someone to be pitied, honestly. She couldn't let anyone else be happy because she was so damn afraid of what would happen if she truly lived into her own self.

Bunny hesitated as she reached for the door handle, looking over her shoulder and directly into Bea's eyes. Her lips parted as if she was going to say something, but she remained silent. Bea watched the walls come right back up, locking into place.

The door snicked closed as quietly as Bea had ever heard. Before she let any emotions wash over her, before she did anything but breathe, she reached for her phone and called Siena.

"Hey Bea. How's it going?" Siena sounded hesitant, more than Bea had ever heard her before.

"Do you have time for some coffee?"

"Of course." The sound of shuffling paper through the phone stopped as Siena heard something in Bea's voice. Something Bea didn't have the strength to cover. "Is everything okay?"

"I'd rather do this in person." And once she'd gotten control over herself again—at least as much as she could muster. "Do you have any time today?"

"I'll make time." Siena's voice was accompanied by the quick staccato of fingers on a keyboard. "I've freed up my only meeting for the afternoon. Head in when you're ready. Would you like me to send you a car?"

"No." Bea smiled, silent tears escaping her eyes. "I'll be there soon."

"I'll see you then."

Bea hung up, washed her face and headed out. This couldn't wait. She needed to do it all now before she lost her nerve.

"Hey." Siena stood up as soon as Bea stepped in to her office. There was coffee on the small table, cookies on a beautiful tray, and bottled water. Bea wouldn't be able to eat or drink any of it. She was still too hyped from the confrontation with Bunny.

"I can't do the Christmas show," Bea blurted out. There. It was out in the open now, and Bea wouldn't have to fumble around for the words.

"And I was thinking you were here because of the engagement." Siena gave an awkward smile, her body rigid in a way Bea hadn't ever seen before. Bea slid into the chair she'd deemed hers the one time she'd been here before. Siena slowly lowered herself opposite.

"You saw this morning's photos and release as well then. I'm surprised they didn't try and get some of the PR nightmare that this will be under control." Bea wrung her hands together. This wasn't because of the engagement. She had to keep telling herself that to make sure that she believed it. Because she wasn't sure if she did. She'd always known they'd likely break up the act at some point. She just hadn't realized it'd be so soon.

"What?" Siena twitched. "What photos?"

Bea shook her head. "Sorry, no. It's not about the engagement. Not really. But I've booked some other shows over the holidays. And I won't be doing the Holbrook Foundation's charity event anymore. There's a conflict in scheduling." She'd practiced the line. She'd practiced all the lines as she made her way over. It didn't matter that they sounded hollow and unconvincing in the warmth of Siena's office. It just mattered that they were the excuse she was running with.

"So you and Jo are out?" Siena's eyebrows pulled together as she asked.

"No." Bea lifted her hands, waving them back and forth as though scared that Siena wouldn't hear the word. She met Siena's eyes and quickly dropped them to her lap. "Jo's still in. It's just—just me that can't do it."

"Bea?" Siena asked, waiting for Bea to lift her head again and meet her eyes. "Have you spoken to Jo? She told you about the engagement?"

"No, I haven't talked to her yet," Bea said, a sharp twist in the pit of her belly tightening.

"What happened?" Siena's tone was the audible version of a child settling into their bed, prepared to hear the bedtime story they'd been waiting for.

Bea took a deep breath and let it out slowly.

She searched Siena's office for the strength to do this. She had to make sure she didn't ruin this for Jo. She wanted to believe she wouldn't ruin it for herself, but despite what Bunny thought, neither she nor Jo were unaware of the fickle nature of the business. She sometimes wondered if they didn't know more about it than Bunny.

It didn't matter. What did matter was making sure Jo didn't miss her dreams coming true because of her. Bea liked Siena.

She liked her a lot. More than any manager she'd ever met. They'd been so close to their dreams, but Bea couldn't let their dreams of a career trump Jo's dream of love. She wouldn't allow it.

Not like this.

"Bea. Talk to me." Siena's voice was so soft and kind. Bea wanted to cry again, but she couldn't do that. She wouldn't.

She would be a professional, despite Bunny's vitriol playing over again in her head. It all came back down to Bunny. Bea wanted to believe it was more than that, but the truth struck where it was.

"I can't work with Bunny." Bea was almost as surprised as Siena looked. "And I know that's unprofessional, but I think it's time for me to move on with my own things. I wanted to ask if you would still represent Jo, though." Bea's words rushed out. It seemed appropriate for her mindset lately. Either all or nothing. Ever since this Christmas event, she'd lost her equilibrium. No. She lost her equilibrium the moment she'd met Bunny in the janitor's closet that passed as a dressing room in the back of Julianna's.

"You don't want me to represent you anymore?" Siena asked. It wasn't the tone Bea had expected. Siena spoke without any inflection of judgment that Bea could detect.

"I'd love you to, but I also know that I'm blowing those chances. I don't want my actions to affect Jo's chances, however. She's more talented than me, anyway."

Siena shook her head a little, a chuckle escaping her smile. "Well, I never thought I'd hear one of my own clients downplaying their own talent."

"Clients?" Could Siena really have meant that? It had to have been a slip of the tongue, right?

"I think it might be a little too early to take that completely off the table. Especially if you'd still like me to represent you.

Although, you're asking me to take on two clients now instead of just one."

"Please don't try to convince me to go ahead with the Christmas show." Bea knew the plea was evident in her voice, but this had been hard enough.

"No, no. I won't do that. I like to pride myself on knowing when someone has made up their mind and when they're asking to be convinced to change it." Siena crossed her legs, her gaze never leaving Bea, but it wasn't judgment reflected back at her. It was sympathy and understanding.

"Thank you." Bea nodded, it had been relatively painless, but she could only hold herself together for so long. At least it had gone better than expected. "Thank you for taking time out for me today. I really appreciate it. I'm sorry to let you down and to take so much of your time."

"Bea." Siena stood up and took a step closer as Bea stood. "How about we both sit down and talk a bit about how it might work representing you and Jo individually?"

"Are you sure?" Bea never usually doubted what she could bring to the table, but nothing about her life over the last few months had felt very usual.

"Would you like some coffee?" Siena asked.

Bea nodded.

While Siena made their drinks, Bea sat back down and leaned into the chair. Could she really do this? Could she walk away and still find some of her dreams coming true after all?

She'd have to tell Jo.

Bea looked forward to that about as much as she looked forward to having to see Bunny again. Which would undoubtedly happen from time to time. If nothing else, they'd both be there for Jo and Piper's wedding, assuming Jo forgave her before the two tied the knot.

Now was definitely the time to get out.

She'd been pushing herself to get through, knowing the

event would be the last they would have to see of each other. But now. She couldn't do it. Losing Jo hurt, but if she kept seeing Bunny, kept allowing her to have this strange power over her, she would lose so much more than Jo.

"So, let's talk about setting up some individual shows to really share your ability as a solo singer," Siena smiled sweetly, but Bea could see the fear in her eyes, the worry.

"I've already booked some."

"Good. You never came across as someone who would sit back and wait to make things happen."

"No, you're right about that." So why had she waited so long to put her foot down with Bunny?

Forget that. It was now or never. And Bea was making it now.

jo

Jo groaned and rolled over in her bed as yet another text pinged through on her phone. It seemed her number had been leaked. She didn't know how it happened, though she had some suspicions.

Blowing out a puff of air, she sent her bangs flying as she picked up the phone.

"Speak of the devil," she muttered to herself when Mandy's name lit up on her screen.

Too exhausted and emotionally wrung out to ignore the text, since she would only receive increasingly hostile ones, Jo slid open the message.

Mandy: You're engaged? Since when did you move that fast?

Jo: It's complicated. Relationships aren't easy. Not even ones that are written up as fairy tales.

. . .

Mandy: Oh trouble in paradise already? Does she even make you happy?

Jo heard the tone in the words. They might appear simple enough on the screen, even caring in their own way. But behind them radiated Mandy's attitude as clear as if she stood in front of her, hands on hips and mouth puckered.

Looking at Mandy's question again, Jo thought about Piper. Her smile spread easily. She didn't need to see her face to know it radiated all the way to her eyes. Warmth filled her chest.

Jo: Definitely. She definitely makes me happy.

What Jo didn't add was the fact that Piper also made her completely crazy. When they were together, Jo was almost one hundred percent certain that Piper radiated the same affection for Jo as Jo had for her.

And they fit well together, in more areas than Jo had ever dreamed of being compatible with someone.

Her phone vibrated in her hand as the loud ring filled her small room.

"Shit," Jo startled, dropping the phone to her bed before snatching it up again and answering.

Bea's laughter came through the line. "Hey sis, did I catch you at a bad time? Should I apologize to Piper?"

"What?" Jo struggled to understand what Bea was talking about.

"Never mind." Bea's voice softened. While Jo could tell Bea was trying to project an upbeat mood, the weight pressed down anyway. "You're engaged?"

"Oh." Jo scrambled. They hadn't come up with a way to tell Bea and Bunny about the engagement yet, a definitive line of who proposed, when, and how everything happened. They didn't have their stories straight! And how did she know?

"You haven't eaten have you?" Bea barreled on.

"No." Jo sighed and ran her fingers through her hair. "I haven't even gotten dressed."

"Do I have to plug my ears and start humming? I really don't need details."

Jo laughed nervously. "As if I would give you those kinds of details. Besides, Piper isn't even here."

"Cool."

"Cool?"

"I adore Piper, but I was hoping to just have a sister brunch. I need those other details."

Jo winced. She needed to call Piper before she went into this conversation. She needed to figure out what storyline they were going to feed Bea. "Okay, give me half an hour and I'll meet you downstairs."

"See you then."

Jo hung up and texted Piper immediately, hoping against all hope that she was awake. When there was no response in the first five minutes, Jo jumped in the shower and started getting ready for this brunch. What felt like every five seconds, she'd peek her head out and stare at her phone as if Piper had just called and she'd missed it—but she hadn't. Radio silence.

Taking a few deep breaths, she stared at herself in the mirror. She usually didn't mind how she looked. She saw the flaws that no one else ever seemed to notice, but she liked those as well.

But today her reflection didn't look like her.

Well, it looked like her in all the superficial ways, but the sadness in her eyes made even her pause. There were too many thoughts swarming around inside her head. Her phone pinged, and she lifted it off the bathroom counter.

Mandy.

God, why had she replied to those texts?

But she knew why. She always knew why. The idea of being hated made the contents of her stomach curdle, despite the little she had eaten over the last twenty-four hours. She didn't want to care. And no doubt there were lots of people out in the world who thought shit things about her. But to know a person who did hate her ate away at her very self.

The phone pinged again with another message from Mandy. She had to be stronger than this. She had to find a way to live with someone hating her or with someone thinking she was a bad person. Because maybe she was.

Jo jumped as Bea knocked on her door. It wasn't any louder than normal, but she'd been so wrapped up in her thoughts. Forcing her best and brightest smile on, she pulled open her front door and wrapped her arms around her sister.

"Um… hi." Bea chuckled and hugged Jo back. As they let each other go, Bea smiled her own fake grin. Jo could tell it from a mile away, but she couldn't exactly get on her high horse and call Bea out on it.

Jo grabbed her handbag from the small table beside the front door, pulling the door closed and ensuring it was locked behind her. "Where are you taking me? And it better be somewhere nice."

"I was thinking…" Bea threaded her arm through Jo's. The action so familiar that Jo's smile relaxed, becoming more *real* Jo and less *Sole Sister* Jo. "Maybe Tanya's?"

"Oh, that's perfect." Jo leaned into her sister. Bea followed suit, and the sides of their heads pressed together for a moment, their feet not missing a step.

Tanya's was a small hidden secret the sisters had been going to for years. The bell above the door tinkled as Bea held it open for Jo. Jo took a deep breath as she stepped inside. Aromas wafted to them from the kitchen. A mixture of melting butter, glazed sugar, and fresh coffee wrapped around her shoulders and hugged her tightly.

She loved it for all of its lack of pretentiousness. There were no signed celebrity posters, no announcements of prizes won, and no pompous airs or overpriced items. Sliding into their usual booth, Jo relaxed into the softened faded fabric and sighed.

"The usual?" Bea asked, already halfway to the counter.

"Of course," Jo replied even as she picked up the menu and flicked casually through it.

By the time Bea returned, Jo had tears running down her cheeks.

"Oh, Jo." Bea slid into the booth next to Jo and pulled her into a side hug. Jo fell willingly into Bea's motherly embrace and sniffled as she failed to get the tears to stop. "What happened? What's wrong?"

"Everything's changing. Even Tanya's."

"Tanya's?" Bea leaned back a little and looked down at Jo. Jo lifted her eyes and nodded.

"Look." She shuffled out of Bea's hug and thrust the menu at Bea.

"What am I looking at?" Bea asked as she flicked through the first two pages. Jo waited, knowing she would get there soon enough. "Oh."

"Yep."

"No more butternut squash soup."

Bea laughed even as her own eyes grew glassy from unshed tears.

"I've fucked everything up, Bea."

"What do you mean?" Bea frowned and dropped the menu onto the table. "You and Piper are amazing together, and your life will be brilliant, and we'll still see each other all the time."

"No." Jo shook her head and forced the emotion back just enough to stop another flood of tears from running over her face. She'd made the right choice to skip the makeup.

"Of course we will." Bea placed her hand over Jo's and squeezed.

"It's not real." Jo's voice cracked. She hadn't expected to tell the truth, but who was she kidding. She couldn't lie to Bea.

"What?" Bea's own emotions seemed to be under control again, but unlike Jo, Bea didn't have any obvious tells. "What's not real?"

"Piper, the engagement. It's not real. We wanted to show you and Bunny that love isn't horrible or career ending." Jo twisted her hands together under the table. Bea was going to yell. She knew it. They had done something terrible, and they couldn't put the cat back in the bag.

"You faked the engagement?" Bea sat back heavily in the booth. Jo watched carefully as her sister stared off into space, blinking slowly as she absorbed the information.

Jo shook her head and refused to let the sadness take over her again. "We just wanted to try and make you two see that it's not all bad being out."

"Your idea or Piper's?"

"Both, really. And—" Jo froze. She couldn't say the next words out loud, could she? She had to find a way to avoid that a little longer.

"And what?" Bea asked. Her tone remained calm and caring.

"Are you angry at us?"

"Surprisingly, no." Bea shook her head slowly. "I'm not angry. Only you two would come up with such a crazy cocka-mamie idea as this. But I suppose I understand it, to a degree. I don't need to know that love is worth it. I just don't want to fall into a relationship that isn't good or healthy for me—friend-ship, business, or romantic."

"How're my girls today?" Tanya placed coffee and a brunch special down in front of each of them. The brunch special wasn't on any menu. It was special in that Tanya only ever made it for the two of them. At least that was what Tanya said.

The plates were piled the same. Fluffy pancakes one side, light and fluffy eggs the other.

"Miserable," Jo admitted.

Bea gave Tanya a small smile as she slipped out of the booth and took her seat back on the other side, across from Jo.

"Then you'll be needing pie sooner rather than later." Tanya nodded and wandered back to the kitchen.

"Don't be miserable." Bea leaned forward, head bobbing around until Jo finally met her eyes. "I'm really not angry. A little frustrated that you couldn't tell me what was going on. I think it speaks to a larger problem that we've ignored for a while now."

"Larger problem?" Jo choked on those words. This sounded like a breakup. What could Bea possibly be breaking up with her over?

"I can't work with Bunny."

"Bea!"

"I can't." Bea shook her head, the curls nearest her cheeks bouncing from the movement. "I've tried, and I just can't do it anymore. She's a brute. She doesn't listen. She's only in this for herself."

Panic rose in Jo's chest. First Piper and now Bea? "I can't do this without you."

"Of course you can! You don't need me to have a career."

"But we're Sole Sisters."

"We were," Bea corrected. She snagged Jo's hand. "I'm kind of sad you're not with Piper because that would make this easier."

Jo furrowed her brow. She wanted to be with Piper too, in

the real sense. She didn't want a fake engagement, but a real one, and when Piper had been down on one knee, it had felt real. The words she was saying had felt like she really meant them.

"You'd have her to support you."

"I still have that," Jo mumbled. "I don't understand what you mean. You're really leaving?"

"Yeah."

"You won't even consider doing the charity event and then talking about it after a break?" Jo knew she was clawing for a grip, but she couldn't stop herself. They'd only ever talked about the two of them building their career and band together. They'd never discussed going solo. Ever.

"I can't." Bea distracted herself with adding salt to the eggs on her plate, tearing open the butter and ruthlessly attacking the toast with it.

Jo winced at the move. If Bea wasn't mad at Jo, then she was certainly mad at someone else, and her guess was Bunny. It had been so tense in the rehearsal studio lately. No one in a ten-mile radius could miss it.

"But you're still doing the show with Bunny and Piper." Bea looked up and smiled. "And I have some great news."

"You're moving overseas, and you never have to deal with me again?" Jo tried to force her lips into a smile, but she failed.

"Jo." Bea rolled her eyes. "Since when did you ever let anything get you so down that you bought into this miserable attitude?"

Jo shrugged and shoved a forkful of her pancakes into her mouth.

"The reason I wanted to do brunch with you this morning was to tell you that Siena has agreed to represent us." Bea beamed as she spoke. "She's going to represent both of us. She isn't exactly happy that it'll be two different contracts. But she would prefer to represent us individually than not at all. Her words." Bea shoveled a forkful of her eggs into her mouth. "She'll help make sure you get those dreams."

"And what about you?" Jo worried her lower lip, eyeing Bea. How could she be so calm about this? How could she not even think that Jo would be upset over it all?

"My dreams were never as big as yours. But we'll always be sisters, and I'll be in the front row every chance I get."

"I don't want it to be fake." The words came out before Jo could stop them.

Bea stopped her fork halfway to her mouth. The fluffy scrambled eggs she had scooped up fell down onto the very edge of her plate.

"I really like her. No. I love her. I love Piper, and I don't want any of it to be fake." Jo sniffed as fresh tears rolled down her cheeks.

"Oh." Bea placed her fork down with a clatter and reached over the table to grab Jo's hand. "Was all of it fake? I mean, I knew you two were spending a lot of time together, and well, I was pretty sure you were at least sleeping together."

"It wasn't all fake." Jo wiped her cheeks with her free hand as she squeezed Bea's fingers with the other.

"Ouch." Bea flexed her fingers, and Jo eased up. But only enough to stop bruising either of them.

"Sorry."

"Uh-huh." Bea gave Jo a mock stern look, and Jo smiled, letting out a small laugh.

Even with her heart shattering inside her chest, Bea could always make her smile. Bea had always been a light to help her find that sunshine within herself.

"What am I going to do?" Jo asked, big eyes pleading for her big sister's guidance. "I don't want to lose Piper, and I don't want to lose you."

"I'm positive I'm not the right person to give any kind of

relationship advice." Bea winked. "But make sure you give Piper a big hug for me when you see her at rehearsal today."

"I still can't believe you quit." What was she going to do without her big sister?

She didn't want to be alone, not even to chase her dreams. But she could do that without Bea if she had to. She supposed she had to now. Being alone wasn't something she had ever truly reached for. Even when Bea was on her back, and she wanted a little more breathing room. She hadn't wanted Bea gone entirely. They'd been a pair, Irish twins, ever since Jo had been born and they'd been inseparable.

"Bea?" Jo asked.

"Yeah?" Bea swallowed her mouthful of food and looked at Jo.

"I'm in love with someone, and I don't think I've ever been before."

"Then maybe I'm not the person you need to be talking to about that." Bea returned to her food.

Jo forced herself to eat, and after a few minutes the two of them moved onto other topics as though Jo hadn't just smeared her heart all over the table between them. She loved her sister. For always being there for her, and for always finding a way to bring things back to a place where Jo could breathe easily again.

love, you didn't do
right by me

bunny

Bunny was late.

And she was never late for anything.

But she hadn't been able to drag her sorry ass out of her condo that day no matter what she tried to do. She'd run on the treadmill instead of outside. And even that hadn't burned away the pain in the center of her chest like it normally did.

She couldn't stop thinking about Bea, and the look of finality in her eyes when Bunny had left her apartment. God, she was such a fucking dick. An idiot. She ruined just about everything she touched when it came to personal relationships. Ever since the sister-in-law debacle, Bunny had never managed to get her head on straight again.

She snorted at that thought.

Straight.

She wasn't, and she'd never wanted to be. She just wanted the world to think she was. But now with the news running wild about Piper and Jo's engagement, it would only be a matter of time before the vultures started digging into her past and prying into her personal life again.

Bunny just wanted to make music, play music, and be a

musician with an actual livable income. Was that so hard to manage?

Stumbling into the rehearsal room an hour before they were supposed to quit for the day wasn't what she'd intended either. But here she was. Showing up for what? Because it wasn't like she was going to get much rehearsing done, and she definitely wasn't in the right mindset to be around people.

Yet she was drawn to Piper like she was every time she was upset.

Piper and Jo stopped dancing as soon as she entered. Their chests heaved from the exertion of the workout, but neither one of them looked happy to see her. Bunny immediately scanned the room, looking for Bea's beautiful face, but she found it nowhere. Her bright blue eyes were missing, along with the salacious curves that Bunny had yet to manage to wipe from her memories.

"Are you fucking kidding me?" Piper said, her voice reverberating around the room. "Did you just roll out of bed?"

"No," Bunny fired back and then winced. She softened her tone on purpose as she dragged her feet toward the piano bench. She plopped her ass on it, staring at the keys and wincing again. There was one very particular memory on that piano that she didn't want to forget. "No, I didn't just roll out of bed. I never really went to bed. That would require sleep."

"You haven't slept?" Piper was suddenly concerned.

"No." Bunny glanced at the both of them. "I haven't offered my congratulations yet. So, congratulations."

"You don't seem pleased."

"Did you think I would be?" Bunny could have said those words with so much vehemence, but she didn't. It was brutal honesty. "I didn't know the two of you were even in a relationship."

"It was… quick," Jo supplied, wrapping an arm around Piper's.

Bunny pursed her lips, looking both of them over. "Where's Bea? I owe her a wallop of an apology."

Piper narrowed her eyes. "Why?"

"Not your concern," Bunny challenged back. "I'll be back tomorrow, right as rain and ready for rehearsal."

Jo glanced up at Piper before settling her gaze on Bunny. "You haven't talked to Bea?"

"No, not since... not since the other night." Was she really going to have to tell them what an ass she'd made of herself? Because she had been the worst person on the planet by her count, and she wouldn't be surprised if Bea would never see her again. But she wanted to try and at least apologize, perhaps ease some of Bea's obvious pain.

"She quit," Jo murmured.

Bunny jerked her chin up, her gaze flicking from Jo to Piper. "She what?"

"She quit. She's not coming back," Jo said, more confidently this time. "She took me out for brunch and told me about it. I just assumed..." Jo trailed off. "Well, we both assumed you and she had talked about it."

Bunny threw her hands through her hair, tugging at the strands until it hurt. She should have anticipated this. She'd fucked up over and over where it concerned Bea. Forget the relationship they didn't have, when it came to being in business together, Bunny had been the least professional of everyone.

"What happened, Bunny?" Piper asked, her voice gentle. "Because this is more than simple acrimony."

"I..." But where would she even start? Bunny's chest pulled in, almost collapsing on herself, which made it so hard to talk or even think. Everything hurt. "I fucked up."

"No shit, Sherlock. What happened?" This time Piper sounded angrier than before.

Bunny wished she had the ability to tell Piper off, but she really didn't. Not this time. Because she deserved the anger and annoyance. "I confronted her about your engagement when I found the photos online and the chitter about everything."

"Confronted her?" Jo squeaked.

"Angrily. It wasn't her fault, I know that, but it was easier to be mad at her than you two." Bunny pointed at them.

"Why would you be mad at her?" Jo furrowed her brow, a deep line forming in the center of her forehead.

"She wasn't mad at Bea," Piper said and then scoffed. "She's mad at herself for being such a fucking idiot." The harshness was back. Bunny shied away from it even though she felt she deserved the full brunt of it. "Tell me exactly what you did."

"I yelled. I accused her of having an angle, that her whole goal was to use us to build their career, and I ruined everything, Piper. Isn't that what you want to know? I got in my own damn way and then got in our way and I ruined it all." Hot tears formed along Bunny's eyes, and they stung like hell.

"You're such a fucking idiot," Piper repeated.

"I couldn't agree more," Siena said loudly, coming into the room. Anger was written all across her face.

Bunny had been on the butt end of that anger more than once, but this was the first time she really and truly felt as if she deserved it. This was the first time she would take everything they threw at her.

"Have you told her yet?" Siena pointedly looked at Jo and Piper as soon as she reached the piano.

Piper shook her head. "We hadn't gotten that far."

"Then now is the time." Siena crossed her arms.

"Time for what?" Bunny looked at them curiously, her little band of idiots that she'd come to love. Even Jo—though she wasn't ready to admit that one out loud yet.

"The proposal was a setup," Piper said, her voice soft and worried. "It wasn't supposed to get out into the news."

"What?" Bunny stood up sharply, glaring at Piper and then at Siena. "You let them do this?"

"It was supposed to be only for your eyes and Bea's eyes." Siena put her hands on her hips and glared at the other two. "What we didn't anticipate was such a public setting and word getting out that wasn't in our control."

"Control? What the hell are you talking about?"

"Jamie Kettlehouse was there," Piper muttered. "And before you fly off the handle, we invited her. We wanted to make it look as real as possible."

"Why? Why would you even begin to think *that* was a good idea?" Bunny cut her hand across the air.

"Because you needed to realize that being queer in this day and age isn't going to be the end of our careers." Piper pointed at Bunny. "And you're such a stubborn idiot, that only something this in your face would work."

"Work?" Bunny squeaked.

"Yes." Piper put her fists on her hips, ready to go toe-to-toe with Bunny. "You've been the most ridiculous asshole the last month that I've ever seen you be. This isn't about some charity event. It's about the fact that you fell hard and fast and then you wanted to kick yourself in the ass instead of just admitting that maybe you might not want to be so stuck in the closet."

"Piper—"

"No. I'm not done yet." Piper pointed a finger at her, eyes locked on Bunny's face. "I'm tired of dealing with your mood swings, your uncontrollable bitchiness has got to end. This isn't who you are. And I'm tired of trying to convince other people of that. You're better than this. So much better. And I'm not sure what crawled up your butt to make you such a jerk, but enough's enough already."

Bunny's jaw dropped. Piper had said exactly what she was thinking about herself, exactly what she'd been berating herself over for the last week at least, if not longer.

"Where's the kind Bunny who's my best friend?" Piper asked. "Because I miss her. The one who would be head over heels ecstatic that I'm engaged."

"You're not engaged," Bunny pointed out, flicking her gaze to Siena for confirmation.

"Well, if I was!" Piper yelled. "You would be happy for me. You'd be congratulating me like it wasn't your death sentence. I want *that* friend back. Not whoever you've become."

Bunny sucked in a sharp breath and nodded firmly. "All right. I hear you."

"Do you?" Piper raised an eyebrow at her. "Because I'm not going to say this again. Your behavior's been atrocious. And I'm sick of it."

Bunny nodded again, her head bobbing. "Yes, I hear you, and I agree with you."

Piper faltered, as if she hadn't been expecting Bunny to agree so quickly. She reached for Jo's hand, lacing their fingers. Bunny wasn't sure it was entirely a setup—she'd seen them pressed together against the wall when they'd gone out to karaoke, and she'd seen the way Piper had been enamored with Jo ever since, the way they'd gotten closer.

She had to fix this.

"I agree with Piper," Siena said, stepping forward. "And what's been happening has been ripping through everything, and causing so much strain and hardship where it doesn't belong."

Bunny narrowed her gaze at Siena, at a loss for what she was even talking about.

"You're going to break everyone up if you continue this tirade," Siena clarified.

"What do you mean break everyone up?" Bunny kept her gaze direct on Siena.

"I'll stop working with you," Piper chimed in.

"Bea already has," Siena added, flicking her gaze toward Jo. "And she's not working with Jo anymore either."

"What?" Bunny's eyes widened. "She abandoned her sister?"

"She thought she was giving me the freedom to find my own way." Tears silently slid down Jo's cheeks. "She thought she was doing what was best for me to continue working with you and Piper."

"Like hell," Bunny mumbled under her breath. "She broke up *Sole Sisters*?"

"Yes," Jo confirmed. "She did."

"Fuck."

"You need to fix this." Piper was pointing at her again. "You broke it, you fix it, and I'm not going to help you this time."

Bunny's heart sank. She'd used Piper to get her out of a mess last time, but Piper was right. Bunny needed to grovel on her own, and she needed to make it worth it. Running her fingers through her hair again, pulling at the ends, she plopped onto the piano bench defeated.

"I think I need to apologize to all of you first."

"Hell yes you do!" Piper charged.

Bunny flicked her a warning glance before cowering again. She spent the next hour apologizing to all three of them, groveling, telling them how wrong she was, and by the end of it, she was so drained that she could barely stand upright to give Jo and Piper hugs. But Jo was smiling again, and so was Piper. Siena was still wearing her permanent scowl, but she didn't seem that annoyed anymore.

"Feel better?" Piper asked as Jo packed up her things to leave.

Bunny gave a half-hearted shrug. "Not really."

Piper sighed and waited for Jo and Siena to leave. Then she squatted down and put her hands on Bunny's knees, forcing

Bunny to look directly at her. "When are you going to admit it?"

"Admit what?" Bunny whispered.

"That you're in love."

Bunny shook her head. "I'm not."

"Not if you don't allow yourself to be. Let's be real here, I've seen you like this one other time in all the years I've known you, and that was with you know who. Be real. I'm tired of the anger."

"I'm not in love," Bunny said, although the words felt like a lie on her tongue. She wanted to be in love. She wanted all those feelings again, but she didn't want to admit that to anyone but herself at this point.

Piper's narrowed eyes said she probably understood that. "Then why all the anger?"

"I'm scared, Piper. I don't want to lose what we have." Bunny grabbed Piper's hand with her own and squeezed it once before letting go. "Not just our careers, but you."

"Oh, Bunny, you're not going to lose me."

"You're already changing things."

"Yeah, I am, because that's what time does. It changes things. But it doesn't have to change the essence of us. You're still my best friend. You'll always be that for me."

Bunny nodded, not sure if she could believe Piper or not. She wanted to, but it was so hard to even think about it right now. "And I think you and Jo should be together, actually together."

"We're not…"

"Don't be an idiot like me." Bunny gave her a sad smile. "Just don't. You're better than me."

"We can talk about me later. We're here for you today."

Bunny rolled her eyes. "I know what I have to do."

"Do you?"

"Yes. But I'm not sure that it'll work out in the end." Bunny twisted her hands together. She had to figure out where Bea's show was tonight and then she had to show up there and make this right. She'd call or text, but she was pretty damn sure that Bea wouldn't answer. Assuming Bea hadn't blocked her number already.

"You'll never know unless you try," Piper whispered. "And I really hope that you do try. I just want to see you happy, and there's no reason for you to think that you can't be happy, that you can't be in love and still have me and still have this job that we love. The three aren't incompatible unless you make them that way."

"I think I'm starting to get that."

"Good." Piper pulled her phone out and flicked through something on the screen so quickly that Bunny didn't catch what she was doing.

Bunny's phone buzzed in her pocket. Frowning, she pulled it out and stared at the screen which held a text message from Piper. "What'd you send?"

"Bea's show tonight is at IBT Club."

"You're kidding me." Blood rushed from Bunny's face, cold washing over her.

"No. And if you want to fix this, then you'll go there tonight, and you'll fix it."

Breathing in fresh air, Bunny nodded. "I know, but it's a gay bar."

"Then it's the perfect place for you to get on your knees and beg for forgiveness." Piper wrapped her arms around Bunny's shoulders and tugged her in for a hug.

Bunny didn't want her to let go. She held on tightly, keeping Piper as close to her for as long as possible. Finally Bunny pulled away slightly and rolled her eyes. "Then I'm going to gay up the Itty Bitty Titty Club."

"Perfect."

bea

"You know, I don't really think that you fit the right category to be singing at the IBT Club."

Bea jerked with a start and spun around, finding Bunny leaning against the doorway of the dressing room with a cocky smirk on her lips that was so damn sexy.

"What?"

"Your tits are not small, my friend," Bunny said, her lips quirking up into a smile. "That's my form of a compliment."

"Uh… thanks?" Bea clenched her jaw and turned back to the mirror to futz with her makeup a little more. She'd already done her warm-up and was just waiting for the green light to head out onto the stage. "What are you doing here?"

"I needed to talk to you." Bunny stepped inside and shut the door behind her.

"To yell at me again?" Bea pursed her lips and glared at Bunny through the mirror. She wasn't going to just stand there and be berated again.

"No." Bunny sighed heavily, keeping her distance and shoving her hands in the pockets of her loose jeans. "To apologize, actually."

"Apologize?" Bea spun around, her lipstick in her hand. She stared wide-eyed, taking in Bunny's form. Her shoulders were drawn, her gaze downcast, and her cheeks sullen. Wow. Bunny really was going to apologize, wasn't she?

"I don't even have the words to describe how awful my behavior's been lately."

"Try." Bea pushed. She wanted a proper apology. She wanted something that was meaningful and was going to make a difference.

Bunny raised her gaze, her lips parted slightly, and she shook her head. "I've been an asshole, a jerk, a buffoon, off my rocker, short-fused, and unable to listen to anyone but my own damn fear."

Bea plopped her butt onto the edge of the counter as the weight of everything hit her at once. Bunny really did mean this. Those weren't just words that she was saying, but they were actually meaningful words that carried a weight she wasn't sure what to do with.

"I'm afraid of a lot of things, Bea, and I let my fear get in the way of our working relationship."

So not their personal one? Bea paused on that, unsure if she was ready to say anything or if Bunny needed to continue to explain.

"I pushed you away at every turn, and I didn't give you the credit you deserve. I clawed for control of the concert because I saw it slipping from my fingers faster than I could breathe." Bunny rolled up on her toes and then landed heavily on her heels. "And I was wrong."

"Explain." Bea crossed her arms. She wasn't going to give Bunny a break on this one. She deserved the hell that she was about to put herself through.

"That I was wrong?" Bunny squinted. "Well, I was wrong."

"Yeah, but how?" Bea clenched her jaw tightly.

"In a lot of ways." Bunny stayed put.

She didn't move closer to Bea, which Bea was grateful for, but at the same time, she wanted something other than this stiff person standing in front of her like she was reading from a script.

"I was wrong to not collaborate. I was wrong to yell at you, so many times over. I was wrong to flip out and not trust. You were right. The world is changing. I can't look at Jo and Piper and the blowup that is their insane fake engagement—I hope you know it's fake, right?" At Bea's nod, Bunny continued, "I can't look at that and not see the positive that's coming from it."

"And the negative?"

"Fuck them," Bunny spat the words out harshly. "They don't deserve my time and effort and thoughts."

Bea pursed her lips, cocking her head to the side. "This is a sudden change from you."

Bunny shrugged, rolling up on her toes again. Was she nervous being here? Was she worried about what Bea's response would be?

"I think it's been a long time coming, and I can't deny Piper's happiness."

"But the engagement is fake. The proposal was a sham." Bea shook her head. "So what happiness are you talking about?"

Bunny's lips quirked up slightly. "I don't think it's as fake as they want us to believe or as they might want to believe."

Bea hummed lightly, but she didn't give Bunny any other indication that she agreed. She gripped onto the edge of the counter and raised her eyebrows. "Why are you here? Really and truly."

"To apologize. That's it." Bunny put her hands out to her sides, palms up. "I promise."

"What's your angle? Want me to come back?"

"I think everyone wants that," Bunny replied. "But I'm not going to try and convince you one way or another. That has to be a decision you make on your own. But you're welcome to join us again if you want to."

"I think I'll pass on that one." Bea stood up and turned around, looking in the mirror again. She double checked her makeup and hair, even though she knew it was already perfect. She wasn't someone who was ever unprepared.

"Like I said, it's your choice. I wouldn't exactly want to work with me again either. And I'm sorry that I made that experience such an awful one for you."

Bea turned at that, flicking her gaze from Bunny's eyes to her lips and back again. She hadn't expected the apology to continue.

"And I did make it a bad experience, somewhat on purpose, and somewhat unconsciously. I didn't want to work with you." Bunny's hands were back in her pockets, her fingers fisted tightly to form balls. "I didn't want anyone to be able to see through the facade that we were trying to project, and I was worried that if you and I sang together on a stage—just you and me, to be clear—that the entire world would be able to see."

"See what?" Bea furrowed her brow in confusion.

"That I'm a lesbian."

Bea wanted to applaud Bunny for saying that word out loud. It might not be her first time, but it felt damn monumental for sure. Her breath caught in her throat, and Bunny's lips pulled upward into a slight smile. The first one that she'd given all night.

"That's what I'm afraid of."

"Why are you so scared of it?"

Bunny sighed heavily. "It's more than just my career, and I've never even told Piper this. Though she might have guessed it at some point." Bunny looked around the room, as if searching for someone who was going to burst in and interrupt them. "My mom was gay, and her parents were not happy about it. She jumped into a marriage with a man to get out of their house and got pregnant with me. When I was two, my sperm donor threw my mom into a wall and shattered her face. We escaped and moved here. My mom never dated anyone else after that, but there was always this shroud of fear surrounding my life. Not just from being gay but from my sperm donor and my grandparents, and whether or not they would take me away from her."

"Bunny…" Bea's heart clenched with only a small amount of the pain that Bunny must feel.

"My mom died when I was nineteen. I'm pretty sure she just waited until I was adult enough to survive on my own And I had Piper and her family too. They saved me so much during those early years. And then there was Claire."

"Who's Claire?"

"Piper's sister-in-law, and the woman I thought I would never get over." Bunny frowned. "I fucked that up too. If it wasn't for Piper, then I wouldn't be here today."

"So let me get this straight, you're afraid of being out because you're scared your past will get dredged up?" Bea tried to follow the thread that Bunny was weaving.

"Not quite." Bunny stepped closer, her voice softening. "For a long time I was afraid my grandparents would come find me and try to dupe me into caring about them. Then I was afraid of facing the hate that my mom faced. But I can't quite pinpoint exactly what I'm afraid of now." Bunny stopped right in front of Bea, looking deeply into her eyes. "Other than I'm afraid I keep making the same mistakes over and over again."

The knock on the door was swift. "Bea, you're up!"

"Right. I'll be there in a minute." Bea glanced over Bunny's shoulder at the young man who had no clue how tense the conversation in the room was.

"You should go," Bunny said as she started to move away.

Bea snagged Bunny's arm, holding her in place. She held her breath for a second before listing forward as if they were going to kiss. Pulling back was hard, but she had to remind herself of all the drama that Bunny had caused in the last few weeks. It was reprehensible. "Thank you for explaining, and apologizing. I appreciate it."

"What are we going to do about Piper and Jo?"

"Nothing," Bea answered. "We're going to do nothing."

Bunny winced. "Don't you think we should help—"

"No. I think they need to learn to live without us barging in on their lives." Bea's heart thrummed as her gaze dropped to Bunny's lips again. "Are you staying for the show?"

"Might as well. Had to pay twenty-bucks to get in here." Bunny wrinkled her nose and broke Bea's hold on her wrist, finally stepping away and ending the physical connection. "Besides, I hear they have a hot lesbian headliner tonight, and I thought I'd see if she's my type or not."

"And what's your type?" Bea had no clue why she was asking that question. She should have quit while she was ahead. She should have told Bunny to walk out and not stay, leave for the night and forget they'd ever had this conversation. That would be the best way to protect her heart.

Bunny put her hand on the doorknob and tossed a look over her shoulder, one that was nothing but pure desire. "Icy, with big beautiful tits."

Bea laughed as Bunny walked out.

With only seconds before she had to get on stage, Bea left the room, and as many of the emotions as she could, behind her. The lights were bright as she moved onto the wooden stage. Her setup was simple because she'd been such a last-minute addition to the night. She picked up the microphone, welcomed the crowd, and started in on the first song.

Blocking the memory of her and Bunny in that small room together was next to impossible. Bea had almost kissed her. Worse than that, she had wanted to kiss Bunny more than once. She'd wanted to seal the apology with an embrace, truly let Bunny know that she was forgiven for all the awful things she had said and done.

But she wasn't ready to walk back into that snake pit.

She couldn't put herself into the line of fire again, and Bunny really had to prove that she'd changed. It needed to be far more than lip service for Bea to want to be in the same room with her longer than a few minutes.

The third song started when she finally found Bunny on the floor. She had a bottle of beer between her fingers and a smirk on her lips. Fuck, Bea wanted to wipe that smirk from her face again. Bunny moved closer to the stage, sliding through the throng of people so that Bea could more easily see her face in the edges of the stage lights.

Someone gasped.

By the time Bea finished the third song on her setlist, the crowd was cheering. But they weren't screaming for her, they were chanting Bunny's name. Bunny worked hard to ignore them, drinking her beer and not turning around to face the crowd.

There was no way she was going to be able to ignore the fact that Bunny was here, because the crowd simply wouldn't let her. Bea locked her eyes on Bunny's face, speaking into the microphone. "I see we have a VIP in the house tonight."

Bunny scowled, and a sick sense of amusement ran through Bea's chest into the pit of her stomach. Payback was a bitch, and Bea was going to have some fun while she had the power in the room. She could make Bunny do pretty much anything right now, couldn't she?

"Bunny, from the band Bunny and Piper, is here for the show, you all. Give her a huge round of applause." Bea laughed while shaking her head. "Most of you know that my baby sister and Piper have gotten closer in the last month. So Bunny and I are trying to get to know each other better, since we'll be in each other's lives for the next while."

The people went wild, having Bea finally acknowledge Bunny's presence.

"Why don't you get me a beer, love, and then you can come up here with me," Bea said the words straight into the microphone as she stared at Bunny, wanting to see exactly what her reaction was going to be.

Bunny's shoulders tightened sharply, and another thrill ran through Bea. This was a small crowd, but even she knew one person could take things and run wildly with the information. The fake engagement had shown that enough, so Bea left her comment purposely vague, to allow for whatever might happen in the future. No matter what, with as much press that had gone out about the engagement, they were going to have to issue a statement about what was going on. Bunny didn't have to move as another beer was set into her hand by a waiter.

Bea's lips bowed gently as she beckoned Bunny on the stage with a wave of her fingers. "Oh, perfect, love. Why don't you come up here and give it to me?"

Bunny scowled, but she did as she was told, climbing onto the stage to stand next to Bea. As Bunny handed the drink over, she whispered into Bea's ear, "I hope you have a damn good plan for this."

"Sometimes the best plan is no plan at all." Bea winked as she took the beer and a slow sip, completely entranced with the way Bunny's eyes trailed all over her, following the line of her neck as she tilted her head back, the swipe of her tongue across her lips as she chased the drops of beer. "Ready?"

"For what exactly?"

Bea didn't answer. She turned back to the crowd. "What you might not know is that our two bands have been in some *intense* rehearsals for a Christmas event coming up for the Holbrook Foundation. You'll get to see Bunny, Piper, and Jo there if you want to support a fantastic cause of helping single mothers. The concert is on Christmas Eve, and you can buy tickets online."

"Bea…" Bunny muttered loud enough for Bea to hear.

Again, Bea ignored her. "Can we get another microphone up here? Because I think you all want to hear Bunny at her finest. Unrehearsed and on the spot. I'll tell you that it was a pleasure to find out she is as human as the rest of us."

"Devilish woman." Bunny chugged the rest of her beer and waved to the waiter for another one. When the microphone was handed to her, she held it up to her lips. "What are we singing, Bea?"

"We?" The thrill that had only been slight became a wave that knocked her over.

"Bea and I did some tinkering with a quite popular Christmas song, and I think we might be able to manage it, just the two of us." Bunny turned to the band and bowed to them. "Not that I don't think you all can keep up, but this song was made for voices."

"What are you doing?" Bea said, moving the microphone away from her lips.

"What do you say? Sing a duet with me?" Bunny held out her hand.

Bea paused, waiting for the other shoe to drop, for the anger and fear to pull up and rear its ugly head again, but it didn't. Sliding her fingers into Bunny's hand, she laced them together.

"Give me a G, would you?" Bea said.

The guitarist plucked the note. Bea shook her head, not taking her eyes from Bunny's. She was going all in on this one.

Humming slightly, she waited for Bunny to join her in matching the note and nodding.

Here we go, Bea thought. She smiled and turned back toward the audience, leaving her hand firmly in Bunny's. The words fell off her tongue, floating through the air and the crowd. They hit her hard, and she squeezed Bunny's hand tightly.

"I really can't stay…"

bunny

"Meet me backstage," Bea had whispered into Bunny's ear so delicately.

Standing in the dressing room before the show was one of the hardest things Bunny had done. Standing there now was impossible. She'd sung a few songs with Bea to appease the crowd, but then she'd bowed and headed off the stage to give Bea the spotlight.

Bea deserved it, and Bunny didn't want to overshadow her.

But the *meet me backstage* echoed in Bunny's mind throughout the rest of Bea's set. When the show was finally over, Bunny slipped into the back again and sat down in the hard wooden chair to wait for Bea to finally make her way there.

She bounced her foot as it rested on her knee in her impatience. Their conversation prior to the show had been good, and Bunny honestly felt as though they were making steps toward righting their relationship. If Jo and Piper were going to give a romantic relationship a real go of it, then she and Bea were back to learning how to be civil with each other, and

Bunny was the one who was going to have to make the most strides toward that.

Bea stepped into the room, shut the door behind her, and locked it. She leaned against the door, hands behind her back, and she looked Bunny over from head-to-toe. Her lips pursed, her eyes alight with that energy that came from performing, the adrenaline high that wasn't easily rooted out when it started so late in the night.

"I didn't mean for them to chant me onto the stage," Bunny said, putting her hands on her knees as she stayed put. This was probably a good position for them. It gave Bea the upper hand, the power in the conversation. And Bunny wanted Bea to have every opportunity to be in control.

"I know you didn't, but I really didn't mind having you on stage." Bea still hadn't moved.

Bunny looked her over, the low-cut V-neck dress that showed off those beautiful tits she'd commented on earlier in the evening, the hemline high on her thighs. It would be so easy to sneak the hem up and touch. Bunny flicked her gaze back to Bea's eyes. That wasn't why they were here at all. In fact, it was the complete opposite of why Bunny was in this room.

She was here because Bea had beckoned her, no doubt to finish the conversation that they hadn't had time for before the show started. Because surely Bunny still had a lot of groveling to do. And she would make sure that she did it the right way so that Piper had every hope of happiness that she could attain.

"I just didn't want to take anything away from you," Bunny said.

"You didn't." Bea finally stood up straight, sauntering toward Bunny like she had every ounce of power in the room. Her hips swayed side to side, saucily moving along with the dress and necklaces she had on. "It was fun to sing with you one last time."

Cold shocked Bunny.

One last time.

Is that what this was? Bea had obviously already decided that she couldn't continue with the Christmas event, despite Bunny's apology. Sadness swept through Bunny's chest before settling in the center of her throat. She had fucked it up so bad that Bea wasn't even willing to consider it.

Piper had been wrong. There was no going back and fixing things to the way they were—not that it had been great, or Bunny's goal. She wanted to fix them to be better than before. She definitely didn't want to go back to the way she'd been acting.

"I think the crowd enjoyed it too." Bea took another step.

Bunny dropped her ankle from her knee, spreading her legs as Bea stood right in front of her. Was this just to torture her? Because she was pretty damn sure that Bea knew exactly what she was doing.

"What did you want to talk about?" Bunny finally asked, trying to get them back on track.

"We need to go back to our original agreement, I think." Bea slowly pulled off her denim jacket and threw it into the small suitcase she had in the corner of the room. Then she started stripping off the abundant necklaces that adorned her skin.

Bunny tried not to be entranced with the movement of Bea's fingers, the slide of the metal across her alabaster skin, which was pink from the energy and excitement of the day, but she couldn't. She was so in tune with every move that Bea made.

"Wh—" Bunny cleared her throat. "What agreement?"

"Civility." Bea pulled up the edge of her skirt with both hands.

Holy fuck, is she going to strip naked?

Was she seriously going to pull every piece of cloth off her body and expect Bunny to do absolutely nothing?

This wasn't going to work.

Bunny shifted in the wooden chair and was just about to get up and walk out when Bea took one step forward and then another, straddling Bunny's thighs before she sat down in Bunny's lap. Bunny's heart was in her throat, her lungs constricting tightly along with the weight of Bea's body, the heat of her skin against Bunny's thighs.

"Bea?" Bunny asked, so unsure of what the hell was going on. Was this a dream?

"If we're going to be in-laws, then we should probably figure out how to be around each other."

Bunny's mouth went dry in an instant. "In-laws?"

"I'm pretty sure that Piper and Jo are going to fall head over heels in love once we get out of their way and give them the space to figure themselves out." Bea turned to the side, the shifting of her weight forcing Bunny's thighs to press together against her already pulsing pussy. Bea put her mouth to Bunny's ear and whispered, "So yeah, we'll essentially be in-laws."

"I don't have a good track record with in-laws," Bunny answered. Her hands found their way to Bea's thighs, sliding up under the fabric of her dress to Bea's hips and finding her completely without underwear on. Bunny froze. "What game are you playing?"

"I'm not playing a game." Bea pressed a kiss to Bunny's neck, then slid her tongue up under her chin before scraping her teeth along Bunny's jawline. "And I'm not your in-law yet."

"Yet…" Bunny dragged out the word, but she was still frozen.

"Touch me, Bunny," Bea crooned softly into Bunny's ear. "I want you to touch me."

Bunny hadn't ever been seduced like this. It was always the

opposite way around, where she was the one who was doing the seducing, she was the one making the decision as to whether or not to pursue. But to be pursued? It felt amazing. Bunny gripped Bea's ass, pulling her in tighter. She lifted her face to look up into Bea's eyes.

"One last time before we're in-laws?" she asked, needing to know exactly why they were here. Why they were finding themselves in this position.

"Yeah." Bea crashed her mouth against Bunny's.

Bunny sucked in a sharp breath as she tried to catch up with everything going on. Her mind spun. Her body went into sexual overdrive. To be the focus of someone's sexual energy like this was mind blowing. And she wasn't sure she could ever go back to what it was before.

"Then we can set new rules," Bea murmured against Bunny's cheek as she pulled Bunny's shirt up and over her head, dropping it to the floor. She followed it with Bunny's sports bra. Bea cupped Bunny's breasts, flicking her nipples with the side of her thumb and grinning. "For the record, you could join the itty bitty titty committee if you wanted."

Bunny snorted loudly, her lips curling upward as a flush rushed over her chest and her cheeks.

"I like your tits, too." Bea bent down and pressed their mouths together in an open-mouthed kiss. "And I'm glad you like my perfect giant tits."

"Fuck yes," Bunny muttered, already pushing her hands up Bea's sides to find those perfect breasts under her dress. She wasn't surprised to find no bra holding them into place. The dress was designed for it, and Bunny had definitely seen the way they had moved when Bea had been on stage.

"I do forgive you, Bunny," Bea whispered into her skin. "But I'm not sure if I can allow you to do something like that again."

"I understand." Bunny bit her lip, not sure where to go from there. Was this Bea killing the mood?

As if to make her point, Bea lifted up slightly and dragged her dress up and over her head, revealing every part of her body for Bunny's perusal.

"Fuck, your tits are amazing." Bunny couldn't stop herself. Immediately, she shifted forward and pressed her lips against Bea's already hardened nipple, then she flicked her tongue over the nub before sucking it completely into her mouth.

Bea moaned, her nails digging into the back of Bunny's hair and pushing Bunny's face toward her instead of pulling her away. Bunny cupped the sides of Bea's breasts, pushing them together, and she moved her face side to side in the cushion of Bea's amazing tits. She couldn't be happier. The echo of Bea's joyous laugh was music to Bunny's ears.

"Do you like that?" Bea asked, her voice husky and full of arousal.

"Only with perfect tits," Bunny mumbled between kisses to Bea's soft skin.

"Touch me, Bunny." Bea pressed their mouths together. "I'm tired of waiting."

What are we doing? The question was on the tip of Bunny's tongue, but she couldn't force herself to ask it. Staring up into Bea's beautiful big blue eyes, she was stunned into silence. Why would Bea want this? After everything that had happened between them, why would she even consider having sex again?

Bunny simply didn't understand it.

"Bunny," Bea said again, her voice a definite warning of impatience.

"I've got you." Bunny grabbed Bea's ass, squeezing her cheeks before sliding one hand right between her legs. She almost asked if Bea wanted this fast or slow, but she already knew the answer. They were in the middle of the dressing room. And Bea had never been one to linger in sensations. Neither was Bunny for that matter.

Flicking three fingers back and forth rapidly, Bunny wrapped her other arm around Bea's back to keep her steady when she inevitably started losing control of her body. Bea threaded her fingers in Bunny's hair again, plundering her mouth like Bunny was the air that she breathed. Bunny had to work hard to concentrate, to keep the pace she'd set, to not fall into the world that she so desperately wanted to get lost in.

Bea.

"Yessssss," Bea hissed, dropping her forehead to Bunny's shoulder. "Don't stop. I'm so close."

Bunny clenched her jaw, increasing the speed and holding steady. What would happen next? When Bea was done with her? How would they part ways tonight? Truce signed or still on uneven ground? Perhaps the true answer was both.

"Bunny," Bea whispered. "Stay with me."

Bunny tensed. What kind of request was that?

"Stay with me." Bea breathed the words right before grunting, her entire body tightening as she clung onto Bunny's shoulders.

As Bea stilled, still grasping onto Bunny's shoulders, Bunny had a choice. She could either take full advantage of tonight or she could escape. Pressing delicate kisses into Bea's cheek and along her jawline, Bunny breathed in Bea's scent. Ever since they had met, she hadn't been able to get Bea out of her mind. And if this was going to be their last time together, then she was going to take full advantage.

Bunny cradled Bea's body before holding her firmly. She slid to the edge of the chair and pushed herself up, gripping onto Bea as tightly as she possibly could. Moving swiftly, Bunny aimed for the counter where Bea had been checking her makeup and pushed her onto the edge of it. Not waiting, she immediately started kissing down Bea's chest, across her breasts, over her stomach, and to her hips.

Pushing Bea's knees apart, Bunny pressed her lips to Bea's clit. She didn't want to wait or hold back any longer. She kissed before parting her lips and sucking Bea's clit gently. Bea moaned, her fingers back in Bunny's hair, this time tenderly petting the top of Bunny's head.

Keening loudly into the room, Bea pulled her legs up and planted her heels on the edge of the counter. Bunny focused everything she had on this moment, on memorizing Bea's flavor, the feel of her against Bunny's tongue, the sounds she made.

Bea said Bunny's name in a repeating chant, her hips rutting against Bunny's face. Buried between Bea's legs was exactly where Bunny wanted to find herself. Not just tonight, but more often than she cared to admit. She hadn't been able to stop thinking about the moments when they'd come together like this, when she'd been allowed to touch and taste and tease and tremble.

Standing up, Bunny pressed their mouths together. She ran her fingers soothingly down Bea's sides, slowed the embrace, and sighed heavily. She couldn't pretend. Half of her job was learning how to act and not be herself on the stage, in front of hundreds and thousands of people, and she couldn't do it anymore.

Pressing her forehead to Bea's, Bunny steadied herself. She had to end this before she continued the lie they were both standing on. Caressing Bea's cheek, Bunny kissed her nose, then her lips and then her neck. But she didn't do it to entice or seduce. She did it to give herself time.

Time to figure out what the hell she was about to say, knowing how much it was going to hurt—the both of them.

"I'll see you around, Bea." Bunny kissed her again,

lingering with their lips pressed together before moving away and stepping back.

"What?" Bea frowned, confused.

Bunny swallowed the lump in her throat as she bent down and picked up her clothes. She said nothing as she pulled them on, risking glance after glance in Bea's direction. Bea was gorgeous. Bunny had never wanted Bea more than she did right now. But it wouldn't be right. Not with whatever was between them ending.

"I promise I'll be civil." Bunny tugged on her shirt and nodded at Bea.

"Civil?" Bea's voice rose, the pain already clear.

"Yeah. That's what we need to do, for Jo and Piper, right?"

"Yeah but—"

"Then I'll see you around." Bunny nodded sharply, effectively ending the conversation. She didn't look over her shoulder as she left the room.

Wiping her palm over her face, Bunny left the club and stepped out onto the damp streets of Portland. She shoved her hands into her pockets and stared at the city in front of her. It was now or never, and Bea had been right all along.

There was nothing to be scared of.

bea

The last day had been so quiet. Bea sat on her bed, the local news on, as she spooned cereal between her lips. She couldn't believe that this had become her life. Jo had been off with Piper and Bunny doing press for the charity event coming up and trying to get some last-minute people to join them for the concert, and Bea was stuck exactly where she was.

On her makeshift couch in her studio apartment, eating cereal dry because she literally couldn't even afford milk that week. Even with the boost to her income since she'd sung with Bunny at IBTC, she was still flat-broke. And she'd left it all behind because she'd been scorned.

Right?

Bea winced at that thought. It wasn't because of that. She bit her lip and stared down at the cereal in her bowl. She'd been right. Bunny had gone off her rocker, but the last night at IBTC had been amazing. Not just because Bunny had apologized but because she'd been herself again.

The woman that Bea had seen the first night.

The one who was secretly soft underneath all her bravado and fear.

Sighing heavily, Bea shoved another spoonful between her lips. She froze mid-chew when she glanced up and found Bunny on her screen. Could the woman honestly get any sexier? She was dressed down compared to what she might wear for a concert, but Bea could still see that someone had dolled her up and just how uncomfortable she was.

The tank top wasn't a loose racerback like she preferred, but a tight white tank with the band logo across the front. Her shoulders were squared, and the push-up bra she had on was clearly uncomfortable and not well-fitting. Bea's lips pulled up to the side, and she reached for the remote to turn the volume up.

"Today we have Bunny from Bunny and Piper here to tell us about her upcoming concert."

Bunny nodded, plastering a smile on her lips. It wasn't a fake smile, but it certainly wasn't genuine either. It was one that was meant for publicity, and Bea recognized it instantly.

"Thank you so much for joining us today. I'm excited to talk to you about this Christmas concert. It seems like a perfect celebration for the year."

"It is, Heidi." Bunny smiled again. "When the opportunity came up for Piper and me to join in, we couldn't say no, even though it's so far outside of our normal music." Bunny pushed her hair behind her ear, her cheeks turning pink.

What was she thinking right then? Bea wanted to know. Because she had a feeling Bunny had about twenty other thoughts running through her head at the moment, including counting down the minutes until she could get into something far more comfortable.

"Piper and I are putting on a Christmas concert of all your favorites, and we'll be pairing with Jo from *Sole Sisters*. Her voice adds an amazing middle to our mix, and let me just say this, Jo has some amazing dance moves."

They both laughed, but it came out a bit hollow. What

would Bunny say about Bea if she was still singing with them? Would she talk about her perfect tits? Bea snorted at that idea. She wouldn't, but it was a nice thought anyway. Bunny would probably talk about her mezzo voice and how they weren't going to sing a duet together.

"Piper and Jo have gotten close during this season. How did they meet?" Heidi asked.

Bunny's face fell. Bea's heart sped up and clogged her throat. She should have anticipated this line of questioning, that the world would want to know more about their relationship because of how public the fake proposal had been. But despite Jo's confession that nothing was real and she wanted it to be, there hadn't been any movement in the last week from either Jo or Piper to solidify things.

Biting her lip, Bea was glued to the television screen, the phone in her hand.

"I think that's their story to tell, not mine."

Oh, that was a good response. *Bravo, Bunny.* Bea relaxed slightly and unlocked her phone. She pulled up Siena's number, about to text and see if she could find a time to meet with her. Bea's panic over having nothing planned for the new year was setting in, and she needed to resolve that sooner rather than later.

"Can you tell us if the engagement is the reason that Bea is no longer joining the Christmas concert?"

Bunny cringed, though it was so quick that probably no one else picked up on it. Bea leaned forward, again locked on the television in front of her.

"What I can tell you is that Jo will be joining us for this concert. I went the other night to hear Bea sing a solo event at the IBTC, and she was as fabulous as ever. Bea has always had the ability to shine on her own, and I'm very proud of the steps that she's taking to continue her career." Bunny's shoulders lifted up slightly, another sign that she was uncomfortable.

Did the newscaster just not care? Or was she bluntly ignoring the fact that Bunny kept trying to avoid answering the questions.

"But to come out as gay in such a public way. There have been rumors for years that you and Piper were in a relationship. It is a bit shocking for your fans. Are you worried you'll lose them?"

"No." Bunny gave her an honest answer. "I'm not afraid of losing fans. I'm afraid of what it would mean for Piper to not be happy. But it's none of your business, or the world's for that matter, who Piper is in a relationship with, or who I'm in a relationship with. Our sexuality doesn't matter when it comes to our ability to make good music. And we're here to make good music. That's it. Piper and I love to sing and play, and we'll continue doing that for a long time. It's one of the reasons we agreed to this Christmas concert."

Bunny was amazing at turning the conversation right back to where it should be. Bea should probably be taking notes for her own lessons later on—assuming she ever got this famous as to land on the local news.

"This concert isn't about us making money, but using our name and our talent to help a foundation continue their cause —which is to help single mothers. My own mom was a single parent. It was just her and me. She was my world, and I saw how much she struggled to make ends meet and to make sure that I had everything I could possibly want."

Heidi parted her lips to try and interrupt, but Bunny just barreled on and ignored her.

"The Holbrook Foundation was founded by Bernadette Holbrook, to help single mothers have a hand up so that they could thrive in Portland and so that their kids could have better opportunities and chances. That's what this concert is about. Raising awareness of just how hard it is to raise a kid these days, and that doing it alone is even tougher."

"It's admirable," Heidi muttered, as if finally accepting that Bunny wasn't going to slip up again.

"It is, and I'm proud to support the Holbrook Foundation and to be able to use my platform to help them fulfill their work. The concert is on Christmas Eve, and it'll have all your favorite Christmas and holiday tunes. We've been preparing almost daily for the last month, and let me tell you, Piper might even get me to dance at least once."

"And tickets are available…"

Bea tuned them out.

Why hadn't she seen it before?

Bunny was protective. Why wouldn't she be? With the way she'd grown up, the fear she'd had in her life from the time she was born. It had never stopped, had it? She'd just transferred it from her mom to Piper, and now onto Jo and subsequently Bea.

Bea blinked at the screen, watching as Bunny wrapped up the interview.

Everything was about protection.

Bea hit Siena's contact information, calling instead of texting. She dumped her bowl onto the side table and immediately stood up to pace. Energy flowed through her in an instant. She should have seen it before. Bunny was freaking out because she couldn't do what she thought her one and only job was.

But it wasn't shame.

"This is Siena Frazee, please leave a message, and I'll get back to you as soon as possible."

Was Siena with Bunny for this interview? Surely they'd had some conversation about how to navigate the questions they anticipated might come up.

"Hey, it's Bea. Um… Can you call me back, like, ASAP?" Bea rolled her eyes at herself. "It's kind of an urgent thing but not an emergency."

She hung up and glanced back at the television.

"I hope you join us on the twenty-fourth!" Bunny grinned as she turned to the television. "I know it's going to be a *family* friendly event."

The way she said that word. She was sending hints out there. Bea stared at Siena's name again. Should she call or wait? The news cut to commercial, and Bea shuddered. Energy flowed through her instantly.

She'd thought it was so odd the way that Bunny had left the club, but now it made total sense. She was protecting herself, because they were getting too close again. But Bea wanted to be close. If she didn't, she would have held her ground and kicked Bunny out as soon as she'd entered the dressing room the first time.

She couldn't wait. Hitting Siena's number again, she waited as it rang until it went to voicemail.

"Fuck," Bea muttered.

She was just about to call again, when Siena's name lit up her phone. Bea answered with a short, "Hey."

"What's wrong?"

"Uhh…" How did she explain this one? "Are you with Bunny?"

Bea looked back at the television screen, like she could see into the news studio and whether or not Siena was standing right next to Bunny.

"I was. She's just getting changed."

"I need your help." Bea moved to her dresser and immediately started pulling out clothes to change into for the day. This was going to involve an in-person meeting, and she had to be ready for it as soon as Siena had time.

"What's going on?"

"I need to sing at the Holbrook event." Bea held her breath, waiting for Siena's response.

But she was met with silence.

"Siena?"

"Hold on." Siena clearly held the phone away from her ear as she said, "Bunny, I'm going to be a few minutes. Take your time."

"I don't want to take my time," Bunny growled.

"Do it," Siena ordered. She came back louder. "One more second. Let me get… somewhere else."

Bea twiddled her thumbs as she waited, still barely breathing. Was this a good sign? That Siena was interested in trying to make this work out? Or was she moving away so that Bunny wouldn't ream her for changing her mind?

"All right. What's going on, really?"

"I…" Could she say the words? "I need to do the concert."

"I need to know why. Because after the last two weeks, I'm not just going to stick you back in it without a good reason." Siena's voice was so firm and unmoving.

Bea had no doubt that she meant business. "Because I love her."

Again silence.

Bea's heart rapped hard in her chest and then it moved into her throat. She felt like she was going to puke. She needed to get those words out for Bunny, not Siena, but panic set in either way.

"I need more than that," Siena slowed down.

"Can we meet?"

"Yes. One hour. But give me something."

"Please don't tell her. I don't want her to know without me being the one to tell her." Bea glanced at the clothes she'd thrown onto the bed. She needed to get dressed and figure out exactly what she was going to tell Siena. "And I don't want Piper and Jo to know either."

"I won't tell them," Siena mumbled, and then louder, she said, "Bunny, I told you I needed a few minutes."

"Let's get out of here. That interview was ridiculous. No one should be prying into their lives."

"I'll text you where we're going to meet," Siena said right before hanging up.

Bea stared down at the phone and grimaced before she grinned. Bunny was doing her very best to keep everything together, wasn't she? In place of the panic, nerves took root. Now all Bea had to do was explain to Siena what exactly had been going on for the last six weeks.

But she hadn't lied.

She loved Bunny.

Despite her brusque and icy personality.

Despite how quickly she got mad sometimes.

Despite the fact that they had agreed to nothing beyond one quick fuck.

Bea just couldn't stop falling in love with her. Because Bunny had been right. It wasn't about being loud and proud. It was about living as exactly who they were and telling everyone else to fuck off when they wanted more of them. And Bea had done exactly the same thing, demanding Bunny give more than exactly who she was. She didn't need Bunny to wave the flag for everyone, just for her. And she had, hadn't she? She had said it, said she was a lesbian and while Bea had felt the monumental moment, she hadn't truly understood what Bunny had done. Not until now.

This wasn't about the audience or an angle.

It was about people.

Two people.

Her and Bunny.

piper

"Got a second?" Piper asked Bunny, every single nerve that she still had left in her body firing all at once. She wasn't ready for this conversation, but it needed to happen. Time was up, and unless she made a plan tonight, then she wasn't going to see Jo again.

The show would be over, and they would have no reason to see each other after that.

Piper clenched and unclenched her fists out of nerves. Siena would probably be the better person to talk to about this, but Bunny was her best friend. She had to have some advice that would be useful. And she'd been a lot calmer and saner since visiting with Bea last week.

Bunny cocked her head at Piper and then glanced around the bus they were staging in. Piper shook her head and gestured to everyone else.

"Where's Jo?" Bunny asked.

"Warming up inside," Piper answered.

Bunny clapped her hands to get everyone's attention. "Everyone out! I need to talk to Piper."

It didn't take long for the people who had been milling around to do last-minute preparations, gather up what they needed and book it out of there. As soon as the door was shut, Bunny turned to her.

"What was so important I had to kick everyone out?" Bunny plopped down onto the bench, crossed an ankle over her knee and gave Piper a serious look.

Piper nearly trembled in her boots. She wasn't ready for tonight. No one was ready for tonight. "I don't know what to do."

"About what? Because we're about to go on stage, and we really need to have our shit together. What number are you worried about?"

Piper's eyes watered and she shook her head, pacing back and forth in the bus. The energy was coming off her in waves now, and she couldn't stop it. Even if she wanted to. But she didn't. She had to say this out loud, and she needed someone else to think for her. Because she wasn't sure how she could get back to what she'd had before.

"Piper!" Bunny said sharply.

"Right." Piper stopped, her hands folded in front of her as she stared into Bunny's eyes. "I don't want to be done after tonight."

Bunny squinted, clearly confused. She wasn't understanding and Piper wasn't explaining well. Piper scoffed at herself, took another walk through the small bus, and stopped again right in front of Bunny.

"I don't want to be done after tonight."

"Repeating yourself isn't going to help me understand what I didn't understand the first time." Bunny gave her a skeptical look.

"With Jo."

"Oh." Bunny pursed her lips, relaxing her body into the

bench even more than before. Her lips curled up, playing at being coy.

Piper was taken aback by that. She figured Bunny would be freaking out, yelling at her, telling her she shouldn't do it. "Why aren't you saying anything?"

"What do you want me to say?"

"I don't know! Something! Anything!" Piper threw her hands up in the air and spun around. Then she stopped short. The small brunette outside the bus caught her attention, the sneaky way she moved, the tenseness in her shoulders.

Bunny said something, but Piper didn't hear a single thing as she froze in place when the woman turned around at the window, her face catching the light of the streetlamp.

"Oh fuck." Piper scrambled toward the door to the bus, trying to get the damn thing open. But she couldn't remember which button or lever to push. She pressed as many randomly as she could, trying to get any of them to respond to her touch.

"Piper!" Bunny snagged her hands and held them tightly. "What the hell—"

"Mandy."

"Fuck," Bunny muttered. She didn't wait a beat as she reached for the lever and wrenched open the door.

Bunny was out of the bus faster than Piper, even with her short legs. She was always the runner. Piper swung out of the door and came to a full stop.

"I thought I told you never to show your face around me again!" Bunny practically yelled. Her chest was puffed up and she was ready for a fight.

Would Piper have to break them up?

Piper waved security over, hoping they'd get there before Bunny took to her own solutions.

"Well," Mandy drawled, "I'm not here to see you."

"You're not here to see anyone." Bunny responded instantly.

"You don't know a thing about mine and Jo's relationship. She invited me here." Mandy pursed her lips and cocked her head as though she had just played checkmate.

Piper's heart beat too hard and fast in her chest. Surely Jo wouldn't have invited her? Surely she would have told Piper?

They were engag—no, they were only *fake* engaged.

Which meant nothing in the real world of relationships, and it left Piper exactly where she was standing now. Having no clue what she needed to do or say or whether or not she needed to get Mandy out of there or let her in.

Except—Mandy was banned from the show.

"Bullshit." Piper stepped up to Bunny's side, no longer caring to wait for the security guards who were taking their sweet time getting to them. "Where's the ticket she sent you then?"

"Well," Mandy purred, and Piper knew for sure what she had only hoped earlier. Jo hadn't invited Mandy. "She doesn't need to send me a ticket. We've been talking, and I know she wants me here."

"You're so full of shit," Bunny barked out with a laugh.

Piper's shoulders relaxed enough for her to take a full breath. She gasped as though she had been drowning until then. It definitely wasn't just her wishful thinking.

Bunny could see the lies written all over Mandy's face as clearly as Piper could.

"We *have* been talking." Mandy insisted, the whine in her voice akin to nails scraping down a black board. "Look, just let her know I'm here. I'm sure she'll want to talk to me."

"I'll do no such thing." Bunny wasn't laughing now. In fact, her voice took on the rumble of a wild predator ready to rip out the throat of anyone who dared to threaten her family.

Her family.

Which now included Jo.

Piper's heart swelled, her chest feeling too small for all the emotions inside. And Piper wanted nothing less than that. But how had Bunny gone from angry jerk to fierce guardian in such a quick time? Piper was about to say something when she was interrupted.

"Is there a problem, ladies?" The security guards finally reached them. The guard who spoke, who had ever so casually drawled the question as though being told to do his job was beneath him, looked bored. Piper was certain he'd even given his colleague an eye roll meant for the *ladies* in question.

Before Piper could respond, Bunny whirled on them.

"Yeah, a big problem." Bunny snarled. "This *person* is on the no-access list."

"Is she now?" The guard was pushing his luck, and even Piper felt her spine stiffen as she pushed her shoulders back ready to attack. She flicked her gaze to his name tag, prepared to report him to his higher ups if necessary.

Ed.

But the second guard made a flutter of a clipboard, flipping pages and glancing up at Mandy and then back again.

"Oh." The second guard, Alex, turned the color of old ash, white and flaking beneath the heat of Bunny's anger. "I'm so sorry, miss. I'll take care of this right away."

"What?" Ed turned to Alex.

"She's definitely on the list." Alex squeaked a little, but Piper gave him props for standing up taller as he spoke to Ed.

"Thank you." Bunny narrowed her eyes before moving her gaze to Alex. "It's Bunny." Bunny smiled at the security guard as he placed a hand on Mandy's shoulder.

"Don't you touch me," Mandy snarled.

Piper relaxed, even though the drama wasn't over yet. She knew it'd be taken care of, and that Jo would be none the wiser, at least for now. Because if Jo knew, it would get into her head and keep her from giving the performance of her life. Piper pressed her lips together hard, hoping that none of this came out or that Mandy didn't try to call or text her and that Jo didn't answer. Hell, not having her phone on her would probably be the best solution at this point.

"You've been asked to leave. If you don't want to be touched, then you need to follow my partner here without any issues."

"This is ridiculous." Mandy pulled away from Alex's hand and moved to take a step in the opposite direction she had been instructed to.

"You're leaving now." Ed grabbed Mandy around the bicep this time, her chances apparently run out. Alex, the one with cheeks still pink with embarrassment or anger, Piper didn't care which, moved to Mandy's other side, and together they marched Mandy out of the gates.

Piper crossed her arms, not letting up on her angry stance as she watched Mandy be escorted away. She'd snag Jo's phone and put it on silent as soon as she got a chance. They could tell her about Mandy after the show, or better yet, tomorrow. Bunny shifted her stance, their shoulders brushing and bringing Piper back around to what had started this entire conversation in the first place.

"I'm serious about what I said." Piper didn't turn to Bunny as she spoke. She couldn't. Concern and fear mixed uncomfortably in her stomach, but she couldn't keep it in anymore. The gates closed behind Mandy and the guards, and they continued to escort her beyond them. Hopefully, they'd take her completely off site.

"Why haven't you told Jo?" Bunny's voice was soft beside her. "That's who you really should be talking to. Not me."

"Because I love her. And I won't expect her to go into any closet and take away any part of who she is. I won't let her do that. I want to be out and free to love her the way she deserves. The world has been changing for a while, but I've been too scared to push for these changes with us. But it really is what I want."

"I'm holding you back." Bunny sighed.

"No." Piper reached out for Bunny's hand, daring to turn her head and look at her best friend. Tears were in her eyes, because there was no way to get through this without changes to their relationship. And Piper hated being the one to instigate them. But she had to, because they could navigate this. "I've held myself back. But I can't do it anymore. I'm sorry."

"I don't want you to hide any of yourself either, Piper." Bunny squeezed her hand, and for a moment, Piper imagined it was her heart. But she didn't know if it would heal or hurt her. "I don't know what's going to happen. But after tonight, I promise we'll talk about how to make sure you never have to go back to the way it was before."

"Really? Just like that?" Piper swiped one finger beneath her eye, catching the tears that were building, and threatening to ruin the makeup that she had so painstakingly perfected.

"Yeah, really." Bunny smiled, and while Piper saw her friend's old fear in those eyes, she also saw the love she hadn't seen for a while shining through on full blast. "It's been a rough few months, but I think I'm starting to understand a little more about lots of things."

"Thanks." Full tears spilled down Piper's cheeks, and she swiped them away as quickly as possible, already knowing she was going to have to deal with the mess she was making on her face. She'd have time for it.

"Yeah, yeah." Bunny bumped Piper's shoulder as they walked back toward the bus. "Enough of the emotional stuff. We need to finish getting ready, or Siena might actually go through with her monthly threat of killing us."

Piper laughed and followed Bunny inside, making sure to collect the touch-up crew on the way.

They might end up starting a few minutes late, but it was worth it. It had to be. She'd never felt freer than she did now, even though she didn't have all of the answers. All she knew was that she was in love, and she had her best friend's blessing. Now she just had to find a way to un-fake her fake engagement.

white christmas

bunny

"Here we go," Bunny whispered to herself. She smiled and gave a sharp nod to no one in particular as she walked from the bus toward the back of the stage. She had watched Piper bounce off like Tigger, too excited to walk at Bunny's forced calm pace.

Bunny knew she only had a moment or two left on her own, and she relished it. She had to get focused for this performance, because it needed to be as good as she'd promised it on the news the day before. She'd let her mind wander off in some wild and crazy ways since she last saw Bea. And she knew it was going to take some time, but she needed her world settled once more. The turmoil inside of her calm. Sad but calm—that's about where she was at right now.

Bea had left, and Bunny had very little hope of enticing her to come back.

Nervousness coursed through her system, speeding up and down her body in anything other than a comforting sensation. Except it was comforting. She had these each and every time she got on stage to perform, but especially tonight, where there were so many other people relying on her talents and efforts.

Up ahead, Piper and Jo talked animatedly with each other. They leaned into the conversation, hands flying as they spoke and fingers brushing skin without hesitation or glances around them. Was this it for them? Was Piper confessing her love and adoration? Was Jo accepting it?

After the little conversation with Bea, Bunny had no doubt that Jo felt the same way that Piper did. And she wanted this for them. She wanted them to wake up and see exactly what they had. They fit together so well, and she had never seen Piper happier. She'd been stupid to try and block it before, angry and scared, and Bea was right. She wasn't going to do anything to affect that again.

If Bunny couldn't have her own happily ever after, she wanted it even more for her best friend.

Taking a deep breath, Bunny let the tighter fit of clothing do its work. She had never felt comfortable in the skintight outfits she wore on stage, and she was even less comfortable tonight in the subtle but undeniable rainbow suit she wore. But over the years, the outfits had helped her step into the character of *Bunny the Performer*. Bunny who crooned and made the women swoon. She rolled her eyes at herself. Who had she ever been kidding? They had always had a majority female audience.

And a lot of queer women at that.

She shouldn't have been so dense as to deny that from the start. At the very least to herself. The fans would stay. They might not have all those years ago. But they would now. She had more certainty in that than ever before. Bunny tamped down her fear. Why had she still let it take the wheel?

Reaching Piper and Jo was a relief as she pushed back the churning thoughts in her mind. The two of them stood—though neither of them was remotely still, ever—near the stairs they would all go up shortly, one after the other as they were introduced.

The stairs were a crosshatched metal and clanged with the sound of their footsteps. During rehearsals yesterday, they had tried with and without shoes, but it hadn't seemed to matter all that much. No matter what, the clanging was undeniable. They had decided to bang their way up the stairs only after they were announced. It would help build the crowd's excitement and energy as they waited a little longer than normal. The crowd's inevitable cheers would also minimize the sound of the performer's stomping feet on the temporary stage.

A cold breeze picked up, biting at Bunny's cheeks. They'd barely managed to practice one night out here, and it was going to be a chilly one at best. Bunny had jackets on standby for everyone as the hours ticked by and the temperatures dropped. It had been Siena's idea to do it outside, a throwback to one of her favorite movies, but Bunny hadn't been convinced it was the greatest idea. Then again, it was a beautiful night.

As they stood at the bottom of the stairs, listening to Allegra talk about the Holbrook Foundation, the sound of the crowd moved like the roar of the sea. It drew close and then pulled back out in its own rhythm.

"So, are we all confident and ready to go?" Bunny asked, hoping she didn't sound condescending or as though she were in charge of them. It was natural for her to worry about those things. But just because certain things felt natural didn't mean she had to keep following them as though that were her only path.

"Absolutely." Jo's smile was ridiculously wide, even for Jo. She just about vibrated out of her costume. A costume that Bunny still felt queasy about, although she had now come to the conclusion that it was more a trained reaction than her actual feelings. She was glad Jo had been open to talking to her about the costumes again. She hadn't held up her end of the bargain, but Jo had adjusted the patterns anyway. These were definitely not as bright as the original designs that Jo had done and Siena had approved of.

Jo had been so kind. Hadn't scoffed at Bunny or accused her again of trying to hide who they were, trying to play down the gay. She'd simply agreed it would be better to have each costume match their individual skin tones, as though that meant something to Bunny.

Looking at Jo and Piper in their dresses, she couldn't help the pride at seeing them. Not only for their ability to embrace who they were, but how the slightly muted colors worked more powerfully against the false snow setting on the stage.

After this evening, Bunny really needed to take some time off, just like Piper kept suggesting. But for tonight, she would revel in the performance for a worthy cause.

Jo met Bunny's eyes and the continued overly stretched smile that made Jo look like the joker had Bunny squirming uncomfortably.

"What's going on?" Bunny directed her question to Piper in the hopes of some explanation, without anyone getting offended by her being too brusque or direct.

Piper's own enthusiasm and too-wide grin did nothing to ease Bunny's concern. The two of them together could charge a whole city with the energy they produced, and probably light up all of Portland with their thousand-watt smiles.

"Bunny."

That voice.

Bunny closed her eyes and took a deep breath. It shuddered, warm and wet, over her lips as she breathed out.

She wasn't imagining things, was she?

Then again, of course she would come to support her sister. Bunny should have figured that out already. If Piper was doing a solo performance, Bunny would be right there in the audience too. She flicked her gaze to Piper, wondering if Piper could read the discomfort in her body before she had managed to mask most of it.

Spinning on her toes, Bunny locked her eyes on the stunning, curvy woman standing right in front of her.

"Bea." Bunny smiled. This smile was wider than her usual *Bunny the Performer* smile, even though it still remained a weak imitation of Jo and Piper's. She didn't have it in her to try and fake not being hurt anymore.

"What do you think?" Bea flourished her hands and traced the outline of her body, not quite touching the clothes she wore.

Bunny's mouth dried instantly with the explicit permission to stare at the beautiful woman in front of her. Her eyes widened, following those hands, those wriggling fingers as they moved down to her thighs, and then back up to her shoulders.

"We're just going to check that the water bottles are stocked up." Piper rushed out her words.

Bunny forced her eyes away from the vision that was Bea and watched as Piper and Jo bounced off in the entirely wrong direction from where the water bottles were stocked.

Bunny chuckled. At least they tried to make their escape a little subtle.

"Have they finally admitted that they're not faking the relationship?" Bea scooted in a little closer to Bunny, the warmth of her body pressing into Bunny's icy skin.

"No." Bunny shook her head, rolling up on her toes and back to her heels. "Well, at least not that I've heard."

"They'll figure it out soon enough." Bea's eyes twinkled and locked on to Bunny's.

The intensity made Bunny's chest hurt. Seeing Bea filled her with bittersweet feelings. But being so close and not being able to hold her, to wrap her arms around her and breathe in everything that was Bea, was an intense level of pain Bunny didn't quite know how to deal with. She'd thought she'd left that all back at the club the last time they'd seen each other, but she hadn't. She'd never been more wrong before.

"So, what do you think?" Bea's voice dropped to barely above a whisper, and she slipped in even closer to Bunny.

"Think?" Bunny blinked. Had she been so caught up in staring into those eyes that she had missed something?

"Bunny." Bea laughed and the sound was music Bunny could fall asleep to every night.

Bunny felt her cheeks flush and wondered how people did this—falling in love and feeling all of these feelings all the time. She pulled her eyes away from Bea's, looking up.

"What's in your hair?" Bunny took a half-step forward, hand reaching up as though to touch those beautiful locks, curled and set perfectly just like the rest of them.

Bunny stepped back and stared at Bea.

"Oh, it's just a clip that I put in to represent. What do you think?" Bea gently patted her hair and the very subtle clip with a rainbow delicately painted into it.

But Bunny was no longer looking at Bea's hair. She was finally looking at Bea, all of Bea.

She had been so intent on watching those fingers as they outlined Bea's delicious body she hadn't truly taken in just what Bea had been wearing. The subdued rainbow colors that matched the costumes perfectly, the pantsuit that she was supposed to wear when she'd still been joining in the concert.

"Bea?" Bunny asked, her voice a raspy whisper.

The show was about to start and suddenly she had no voice. That couldn't be a good thing, but Bunny didn't feel the same urgency about the charity event as she had just moments ago.

"Yes?" That knowing smile hadn't left her lips since she'd stepped into Bunny's presence, and Bunny knew immediately she had missed the biggest hint of all.

"You're here? Really and truly here?" Bunny grabbed Bea's

elbow, not to keep Bea in place but to keep herself steady while her knees turned to jelly.

"I'd like to be." Bea canted her head to the side, that smile faltering slightly.

"But?"

"Are you willing to meet me halfway?" Bea took a deep breath, and Bunny noticed the slight tremble in her lips.

God, how she wanted to trap those lips with her own once more. To kiss her and never stop. There was no way to deny it, not to herself and not to anyone else. Not anymore. She'd been such a fool to think she had ever been anything but falling head over heels in love with Bea.

"Halfway?" Bunny hoped she was reading this situation correctly. It'd take a long time before she ever trusted her instincts when it came to relationships. No wonder she had always leaned into the business and ignored the personal. That was a world with rules she understood and ones that she embraced willingly.

Bea skimmed her hand down Bunny's arm, twining their fingers together. "Are we still able to use your modified lyrics?"

"Which ones?" Bunny's heart rate picked up, her ribs feeling more like a cage pressing against her organs, trying to stop her from letting her feelings or her true self out.

"That's your choice, but maybe we can sing it together? I think I understand now. There is more than one way to live authentically, and I wasn't kind assuming you weren't living your authenticity simply because it looks different from mine." Bea's lips were so close. If Bunny turned just slightly, she'd be able to press their mouths together.

"We're on in thirty seconds," Jo squealed in delight as she raced toward them, her hand in Piper's and their cheeks flushed.

"Bunny?" Bea asked, her eyes filled with so many things that staring into them was like staring into an entire galaxy of stars. Bunny was so ready to jump in and fall into everything that Bea was willing to give her in this moment. Into what she knew would be a journey of moving boundaries and change, into what she knew would be more conflict and arguments, but also so much more than that.

Touches.

Kisses.

Love.

"Sing with me." Bunny was pleased at how strong her voice came out this time. When had she finally decided that this was the direction she wanted to go? Bunny squeezed Bea's fingers as they called Jo's name on the stage and Jo pranced up the stairs, her arms waving. Bunny couldn't look away from Bea's blue eyes, from the perfection of brokenness that stood right in front of her, because that was exactly what they were together. "I promise I'll meet you in the middle."

The look they shared electrified every atom in Bunny's body, from her eyes right to the tips of her toes. Which were currently squeezed into boots with a small square heel on the back. A heel that was entirely unnecessary in Bunny's thinking, despite how small it was, though it would help her stomp out the beat during that fourth number they were singing.

"Piper!" The name boomed and the audience roared.

Piper ran up the stairs, leaving Bea and Bunny alone. Her name was next. Bunny swallowed the lump in her throat, lifting her hand and cupping Bea's cheek. Bea's eyes fluttered shut as the breeze picked up. The chill was sudden, and without warning, flakes of snow gently fell from the sky, kissing Bea's skin and landing in her eyelashes and in her hair.

Bunny's eyes teared up, but she couldn't cry now. Not when she had to get on that stage and perform.

"Bea, I—"

"Bunny!"

"You'll be amazing." Bea wrapped her arms around

Bunny's waist and gave her a tight squeeze. "Now get on that stage before they start booing because you're not there."

"Bea." Bunny's voice cracked, and she had to clear her throat. Was Bea going to sing with them or not? Or was it just the one song she'd requested at the end? Either way, Bunny was ready for it to happen. She didn't want to avoid this any longer.

Grinning, Bea stepped away from Bunny. "They're waiting for you."

"Bunny!" Siena shouted sharply from the side of the stage. "Get up here already."

"Bea…" Bunny trailed off. She wasn't ready for this. She needed more time.

"Go on, Bunny. I'm not going anywhere. I promise."

Bunny locked her eyes on Bea's once again and nodded sharply. Before she could stop herself, the words were out of her mouth. "I love you."

Bea grinned broadly, her entire body lighting up and relaxing. Bunny didn't have a chance to wait around as Siena dragged her up the steps and onto the stage. Bunny threw two looks over her shoulder until she could no longer see Bea standing on the ground below.

She had a performance to give.

But she couldn't get her mind off the fact that Bea was right there, standing and waiting for her. That she would be there when she stepped off to let Jo and Piper have their moment, and that Bunny wasn't going to give Bea a second to breathe during those breaks.

When the crowd calmed again, Bunny grabbed her microphone and prepared to introduce the first song and get the crowd riled up as the concert began. But before she could say anything else, Allegra said into the microphone, "I'd like to introduce our last singer to you tonight. The second half of

Sole Sisters, and big sister to none other than Jo. Let's give a shout-out for Bea!"

Bunny froze, her eyes wide as she stared at the stairs.

But there she was.

Bea.

bea

Bea's hands trembled as she gripped onto the metal railing for the stairs. Her shoes were heavy as she went up onto the stage, the thumps with each step she took matching the thumps in her heart. She couldn't believe she was here. Siena had been amazing, and the plans had gone off perfectly.

Jo had actually kept a damn secret for once.

Well, at least until the very end when she'd clearly told Piper what was going on, but no one had told Bunny, and that was the important part.

Stepping onto the stage, Bea held her breath. Bunny's jaw was on the floor. Clearly when Bea had asked about singing together, it had gone straight over Bunny's head. So had the matching outfit that was supposed to be exactly what they were wearing for the production itself. The entire production. No more costume changes to put unnecessary stress on the timing of the evening. Bea hugged Jo and Piper as they welcomed her onto the stage and then she moved to stand next to Bunny.

The first song was all four of them. They had three of those back-to-back before it was just Piper and Bunny. The hours of rehearsal they'd done together would come in handy for this. And she wasn't bound to forget what was involved, but they had at least eighteen minutes on stage before Bunny was going to be able to yell at her for keeping a secret off stage.

Bunny held out her elbow for Bea to take, and she moved them toward the front and center of the stage. In all their rehearsals before, Bea hadn't stood next to Bunny. Bunny had always strategically put Piper or Jo between them, not just to mix up the groups a bit more, but to put space between the two of them.

But she was going off script.

Piper took over announcing the songs, and Bunny dropped her microphone to her side. She turned to Bea and whispered into her ear, "I promise you I'm not always this dense."

"I think you were a bit distracted," Bea responded with a light giggle.

"You're definitely distracting. Perfect tits and all." Bunny backed away on a laugh and looked at Piper. "Fucking perfect tits."

Bea laughed and tried to step away, but Bunny kept a firm grasp on her hand. The music started up, and Bea focused on what she needed to do—the notes she needed to hit, the words she wasn't sure she had completely memorized, the steps she wasn't sure she was taking as they all stood together on the stage.

Bunny had the first line of music. Thank God, because the nerves that were rampaging all through Bea's stomach and chest were almost too much to contend with. She hadn't thought they would be this bad. But the crowd out there was at least ten times larger than what she was used to.

Bunny tugged on her hand, bringing her back around and giving her something to focus on. Smiling, Bea raised her free hand with the microphone to her lips and started in immediately on the harmony.

Their voices blended together so well, each of them

listening to the other and weaving the notes and lyrics around each other. Piper and Jo on either side of them, completing the music in a way that they wouldn't have been able to do without all of them on the stage. Bunny faced the bright lights, and Bea turned to follow suit.

She stared out at the dark faces in front of her, watching as they sang right along with them and hearing the off-tune music that they all made together. It was honestly the perfect metaphor for life. Bea drew in a large breath, pulling the air down into her belly, as the crescendo of the music rose, reaching its pinnacle.

By the end of the song, energy soared through Bea's body exactly like it should during a performance. She was hyped and ready for the second and third songs to hit. When it was finally time for her to step off the stage, Bunny followed her closely. Piper and Jo stayed to dance together for the first time during the concert.

"Why didn't you tell me you were coming tonight?" Bunny said, stopping Bea at the bottom of the stairs.

Bea spun around and shook her head as a shiver ran through her. "I wasn't sure you'd let me."

"Sing with us?" Bunny's eyebrows disappeared into her hairline. "What the hell would ever make you think that?"

"The last month?" Bea answered, her shoulders squaring. "The fact that you didn't invite me back when we were at the club."

"Because I didn't think you'd come back." Bunny stepped into Bea's space, a hand on Bea's hip as she pulled her in and kept her close. "And I didn't want to pressure you into doing something that you didn't want to do."

"Bunny…" Bea pulled her lower lip between her teeth and shook her head slowly. "Sometimes you have to fight for what you want."

"And sometimes fighting for it is just going to push it away."

Bunny's other hand came up against the small of Bea's back, and she was officially wrapped up in Bunny's arms.

"Don't push me away," Bea begged.

"No, I won't make that mistake again." Bunny moved in and pressed their lips together.

Bea tilted her face up, parting her lips, right when the song ended. She would have cursed their lack of timing if she had another choice other than getting back on the stage. Bunny didn't pull back though. Instead, she pressed in tighter.

Humming, Bea listed forward.

"Bunny!" Siena's loud voice boomed through the fog of arousal that coursed through Bea, and apparently Bunny, since she jerked back. "We'll talk about a press release for this later, but you missed your cue."

Bunny growled but climbed up the stairs. Piper was still up there, and Jo was at the top, waiting to come down, with a big shit-eating grin on her lips. Bunny said nothing as she walked by. Jo, however, was not so subtle.

"So you two talked it out, I see."

"Kind of," Bea said on a sigh, watching Bunny from the bottom of the stairs. Normally she'd be taking an actual break, but she'd never been this close to Bunny and Piper performing. And she couldn't force herself to be that far from Bunny. Not just yet. Not without some more answers first.

Were they dating?

Was this a formalization of their relationship?

Bea desperately wanted it to be, but they didn't have enough time to actually get those words out.

"I've been preparing for this for years, Bea. I promise you, I have it handled."

Bea looked into Siena's sure gaze and nodded. "Yeah, I didn't think you wouldn't."

"I just never thought I'd get to use any of my plans." Siena grinned. "I'm glad to have been proven wrong."

But had she been proven wrong yet? Bunny had kissed her. It was clear that Bunny was happy that Bea was there, but they hadn't talked yet. And Bea needed that confirmation of what they were doing. She needed to know that Bunny was going to meet her halfway, not just on stage, but everywhere else.

Bunny and Piper finished, and then it was time for Bea to sing with Jo. She barely got to slide her fingers along Bunny's arm as they passed by each other on their way up and down the stairs. She just wanted a few minutes. Why was her timing always off when it came to these kinds of things?

Sweat poured down the small of Bea's back when Bunny and Piper finally came back on stage for the final few numbers. She had wondered if she was going to be freezing tonight since the forecast had shown the weather to be questionable, but with as much moving around as they were doing and how much energy that she was pouring into the performance, it wasn't as bad as she thought.

Straightening her shoulders while Bunny introduced the next song, Bea stilled. The snow started falling again. This time in big, gorgeous flakes, ones that drifted down slowly. She caught Jo's eye and held up her hand to catch the next snowflake. Together they started moving toward the center of the stage and laughed while Bunny stood in front of them, still talking.

Did she ever shut up sometimes?

Then again, it was probably a good thing in times like this. Siena grinned at them from the edge of the stage. They were so close to being finished with the concert. It was dark outside, save for the lights from the venue, which lit up the snow like a soft blanket coming down to cover them. It made the sky look like it was filled with a million stars that they could reach out and touch.

Bea moved up close to Bunny and touched her arm lightly,

a smile on her face. Bunny paused, and Bea leaned in close to whisper. "I thought we were going to sing our song."

Bunny scrunched her face up. "Are you serious?"

"Yes," Bea laughed. "Kick those two off the stage, and let's do it. Meet me halfway, remember?"

"Yeah." Bunny pulled up her microphone. "Change in plans. Bea, here, has a brilliant idea since the temperatures are dropping and the snow is falling. She and I are going to sing one last duet before we get to the big finale."

Piper and Jo gave them both curious looks, but stepped off to the side with Siena. They didn't go far, probably just as curious what was up their sleeves as everyone else.

"Oh, and we'll do it acapella." Bunny pointed at the drummer and backup guitarists and pianist behind her. "Just give me a G."

Bea smiled, humming to herself. This would be so much better than when they'd sung the song the other week. It would have so much more meaning now. They were ready now. She and Bunny were ready for the commitment that this was going to take, and for the reasons they were there. And they were both finally starting on the same note.

Bea couldn't stop staring at Bunny throughout the entire song. Their voices wove together, the magic of the snow and the conversation she was still waiting to have breathed life into every word she sang. Bea stepped in closer, toe to toe with Bunny, as they came to the conclusion of the song. The last note left her lips, and Bunny immediately dropped Bea's hand and grabbed her by the back of the neck.

Bunny pressed their mouths together, bending Bea backward and holding her firmly as Bunny kissed her deeply. Bea clung onto Bunny's arms, holding as tightly as she could while their tongues tangled, heat rising between them, and hope bursting in Bea's chest.

When Bea finally figured out what was happening, and

Bunny pulled her upright, she didn't want to let go. Leaning up on her toes, she pressed her entire body against Bunny's, keeping their mouths connected, lips touching.

She couldn't believe this was happening.

Bunny was kissing her, on stage, in front of a live audience. Bea's heart nearly burst from the joy. This wasn't halfway. This was way the hell more than halfway. Bea wrapped herself around Bunny while the crowd cheered them on, growing louder and louder as each second passed.

When Bunny eventually pulled away, a few soft kisses on Bea's lips, Siena's angry voice finally reached Bea's ears. She tensed.

"Oh yeah, she's going to be pissed a while about this one," Bunny muttered through the grin and kissed Bea again. "And I don't fucking care."

"She said she had a plan."

"I'm sure I just ruined it." Bunny kissed Bea again, cupping her cheeks and holding her before pulling away. "I'll take the brunt of it."

Bea laughed lightly. "I think we can handle this one together."

"Sure." Bunny slid her hand down Bea's arm and laced their fingers together. She nodded at Piper and held up her microphone again. "I'm going to let Piper and Jo sing one more song before we come together for the finale."

Bunny didn't wait as she dragged Bea off the stage. Piper did exactly what she should have done and took over the concert. Bea was amazed at how well the two of them worked together, though she shouldn't have been because they'd been together for so long. She and Jo were the same—for the most part.

Bea stopped at the bottom of the stairs when Bunny wrapped an arm around her waist and pointed at Siena with her free hand. "Yell at me later."

"Fine. It'll be a good reaming, and you owe me a bottle of tequila."

Bunny raised her eyebrows at Bea, and Bea instantly knew there was something she was missing, something that only the two of them understood from their long acquaintanceship.

Bunny faced Siena again, a serious look gracing her features. "Tequila? Are you sure?"

"Yes. I'm going to need that after this." Siena pointed between the two of them. "Some warning would have been nice."

"Says the woman who tells me I never take risks."

"Bunny," Bea said, interjecting. "Now isn't the time."

Bunny pursed her lips and then focused back on Bea. "Fine, but only because you're a really good distraction right now."

Bea snorted out a laugh. She caught Bunny's full attention, flicking her gaze between Bunny's dark eyes and her thin lips. "I love you."

Bunny's lips pulled upward. "Finally."

"It's not like you waited that long!" Bea complained.

"Long enough." Bunny pulled her in for another kiss.

Bea was completely wrapped up in her when Piper and Jo called for them to go back on stage. Bunny followed her up the stairs, the stage now completely covered in a fine layer of snow. Would it stick? Would they wake up to a white Christmas tomorrow? Bea wrapped her arm in Bunny's, walking together.

She never wanted to let go. She never wanted to forget this moment or let it end. Then again, tomorrow would probably be just as good, right? If not better? Tomorrow would be the two of them and no one else in the world. They'd be able to start fresh right before the new year, making their lives what they wanted them to be.

"It seems most fitting tonight, that the song that'll be our last is *White Christmas*." Bunny grinned as the crowd went wild again.

Bea couldn't wipe the smile from her lips. She couldn't imagine being happier than she was now. She'd needed this, more than she knew. Piper and Jo locked arms together, standing next to Bunny and Bea. They faced the concert goers as the music started up. Bea took a deep breath, finding her center and focusing on the musical notes.

She never could have dreamed this up.

It had to be real.

THIRTY-SIX

Jo

The roar of the crowd buoyed Jo off the stage, down the stairs, and right into Piper's open arms. Piper laughed as she swung Jo around.

"That was amazing," Jo squealed as Piper put her back on her feet.

Piper's hands were still warm and present on Jo's hips, and it took everything in her to resist placing her own hands over the top of Piper's. She met Piper's eyes, and the electric energy that crackled beneath her skin from the charity event multiplied by hundreds.

"You're incredible." Piper smiled as one hand lifted from Jo's hips and brushed an escaped curl behind Jo's ear.

"You too." Jo's voice croaked out.

Time froze for a moment until noise behind them interrupted.

"Brilliant show." Allegra was beautiful, and the personification of poise and class. Jo wished they could get to know each other better, but she wasn't sure if she was prepared for that.

Allegra's words meant little when Jo could still feel the heat radiating from Piper. So close but suddenly entirely unreachable. They had touched so many times, and it had never been an issue. And now that the world still believed they were officially engaged, why would they pull apart at having someone closer to them?

"Thanks, Allegra." Piper stepped forward and offered Allegra a hand. "I hope it was a success on your end."

"Oh, it was. I don't have the final numbers, but it looks like we matched our last fundraiser."

Jo watched, in awe of Piper's ease and grace. She was everything Jo could ever dream of in a partner. Brilliant. Strong. Empathetic. Energetic. Joyful. Kind. Compassionate.

"Have a fantastic evening. Merry Christmas." Allegra shook Jo's hand as well. They exchanged similar pleasantries and well wishes.

Jo watched as Allegra moved to where Bea and Bunny stood, close and warm in each other's embrace.

"Want to get changed and see if we can't convince the two lovebirds to come dancing and drinking with us?" Piper asked as she turned her entire body away from Allegra's moving form.

"Okay." Energy buzzed through her body, but beneath it a sadness settled behind her ribs.

This was it. The show was over, and while it was a brilliant event—easily one of the highlights of Jo's career thus far—there was no reason to see Piper every day anymore. There was no excuse to talk and text.

"Besides, I think we need to talk about a few things."

"Oh?" Jo started that same old panic she hated to feel.

They clicked so well, and Jo had never felt such ease with anyone before in her entire life. And she knew they would try to stay in touch, but life would get in the way. Who knew how long it would be before they stopped chatting on the phone, or catching up when they were both in the same city? Or when one of them found someone else to date, to get engaged to for real.

The sadness behind her ribs turned into a pressure of pain.

"Are you coming?" Piper asked, the smile evident in her voice, though Jo noticed how her eyes didn't quite settle onto her own.

Had Piper just worked out the same thing?

Jo forced the thrill of the event back into the forefront of her mind. Focus on that and maybe she could avoid the pain she was facing as soon as she left tonight.

"Of course." She bounded after Piper, and together they walked back to the bus, arm in arm. "What did you need to talk to me about?"

"Two things really. The first is that I put your phone on silent because Mandy was here, and I didn't want her to upset you."

Jo stilled. She furrowed her brow and looked up into Piper's eyes. Her chest was tight, but not because she was afraid. She was in awe. "Mandy was here?"

Piper nodded. "She tried to sneak onto the bus when you were meeting with Bea."

"Oh." Jo pursed her lips and shook her head. "She was probably upset."

"Why would she be upset?" It was Piper's turn to frown.

"Because I blocked her number, and the second number she had. She couldn't have gotten ahold of me if she wanted to."

"What?"

Jo shrugged. "I want nothing to do with her again, and it's time I put my foot down about that. I don't want her disrupting my life anymore."

She hadn't realized how quickly she'd come to trust Piper with everything, and just how easy it was to talk to Piper about all the dirty details of her life. The idea of it ending left a shard of glass in her heart.

"After you." Piper swept her hand out in front of the bus stairs and waited, and Jo bounced up the stairs. Once they were inside, Piper stopped and shook her head. "I'm really proud of you."

"Thanks." Jo grinned broadly. "Was that the only thing you wanted to tell me?"

"No."

"Then what?" Jo faced Piper fully, staring with wide eyes as Piper pulled her dress off.

She stood with her back to Jo standing in a pair of panties and nothing else. Goosebumps covered Piper's bare back. Jo wanted to warm that skin, put hot-breathed kisses over each bump and smooth away the cold. She shivered despite still being entirely dressed in the warm clothes they'd planned for the outdoor event.

When Piper didn't answer her question, Jo hesitated to ask it again. This felt like by far the more serious topic. She rummaged through her own suitcase, turning her back on Piper. By the time she found the perfect pair of pants and the long sleeve blouse to wear beneath her jacket, she turned back to Piper, intent on just snatching one more quick glance. "Do you think we'll actually be able to convince Bunny and Bea to come out tonight?

"Oh, I'm sure we can talk them into it." Piper chuckled, pulling down her shirt to cover the last of her bare skin. The pants she wore flowed around her legs and from a distance might even be confused for a skirt.

Taking a deep breath, Jo turned back to her own task at hand and smiled as she noticed the shift of weather outside the small high window.

"Even with it snowing again?" Jo asked as she slipped out of her own dress, letting it fall to her feet in a pile of rainbow colors. She stared out the small window, leaning closer to see the tiny flakes sticking to the outside of the glass as she unhooked the bra from her back.

"It's snowing?" Piper was beside her, leaning against Jo's bare arm as she reached her delicate fingers toward the window, as if to caress the snowflakes on the other side.

Jo turned her head, and Piper followed the action until they were face to face and eye to eye.

"Hey." Piper smiled, reaching up and gently cupping Jo's cheek in her palm.

"You're all dressed," Jo said, as though Piper couldn't possibly be aware of the clothes she had pulled on, or like Jo hadn't tried to sneak just one more peek at the perfection beneath.

"And you're not." Piper's voice was rough and low.

"Um. No, not yet. I got a little distracted." Jo's cheeks heated, and she half hoped Piper knew the distraction had nothing to do with the snow. "I'll just—"

"Jo." Piper stopped her with the lightest of touches along her arm.

Jo's skin tingled under Piper's fingers. But this reaction had absolutely nothing to do with the chill in the air. "Yeah?"

Piper stepped in to Jo's space, her arms slowly wrapping around Jo's hips, giving Jo the opportunity to back out of the embrace or to tell her to stop. Jo wasn't going to tell Piper to stop. She would take every last second she could get.

"Damn it." Piper wasn't one who normally stumbled on her words. She threw her head back and huffed her breath up to the low roof.

"What's wrong?" Jo reached up a hand and eased Piper's chin down as she cupped Piper's cheek.

"What if it didn't end?" Piper's words rushed out.

"What if *what* didn't end?" Jo's heart beat a little harder and faster. Had she heard that right? Why had she repeated it if she wasn't sure? But the energy in the air crackled, and even if she had heard wrong, she knew Piper wouldn't make her feel stupid or ridiculous for the question.

Piper spoke after a deep breath that seemed to help calm her. "When I proposed, I said a lot of things."

"They were beautiful things. Pity it wasn't real." Jo remembered the words and being swept up so easily in the moment. In the beauty of the wind that kissed her cheeks and gave Piper's words the perfect background beat. But she didn't want Piper to be held accountable for words that had been fake for the whole *get Bunny and Bea out of their own heads* idea.

"They weren't just words." Piper swallowed audibly, and Jo felt the tug at the corner of her lips. Could Piper really be saying this? Was it really what Jo was hoping to hear?

"They weren't?" Jo encouraged, not holding any of her smile back.

"No, they weren't." Piper's face lit up with joy. "They were how I feel. About you, Jo. What… What if none of it was fake? What if you really said yes to my proposal?"

"You really want to be engaged to me? For real?" Jo was almost certain that was exactly what Piper was saying, but she had to hear it. She had to have the clarification. She didn't want to let all this joy inside of her swell larger if she was hearing only what she wanted and not what Piper was actually saying.

"Yes," Piper whispered as she stepped a little closer, her arms snugging Jo a little tighter.

"Yes," Jo replied, her breath ruffling the now loose hair that hung around Piper's face.

"Yes?" Piper's eyes were alive with a mix of emotions, and Jo couldn't wait to dive into every one of them.

"Yes." Jo closed the gap, pressing her lips against Piper's. When she pulled back, Piper groaned in frustration. "Yes, I want to be engaged to you for real. I want you, Piper."

"I love you," Piper said the words as she stared directly into Jo's eyes.

Jo caught her breath, the emotions welling up inside her chest and bursting in blurry vision before she could stop it. The tears spilled over her cheeks, even as she laughed.

"I love you, too."

"Happy tears?" Piper's face scrunched a little, worry marring her joy.

"Of course happy tears." Jo pulled Piper in for another kiss. "I'm marrying my best friend. What else could they be?"

Piper pulled Jo closer, lifting her slightly off her feet as she twirled around in the small space. Back on her feet, Jo grabbed Piper's hips and pulled them closer to her body. Piper didn't need any more encouragement than that. She pulled Jo's body even tighter into her own and leaned down to kiss Jo's lips.

At first, the kiss was filled with joy and love, but after a moment the joy and love were joined by hungry arousal.

Jo moaned, opening her mouth, willing and eager at the light touch of Piper's tongue on her lips.

"Are you still cold?" Piper asked, catching her breath,

"Not so much, all of a sudden," Jo mumbled against Piper's lips.

Piper laughed and spun Jo around before pulling her ass back into her crotch.

"Oh God," Jo groaned as Piper ground hard and firm against Jo's ass. She could feel Piper's heat against her.

"Fuck yes." Jo leaned her head back on Piper's shoulder and was rewarded with a half upside down kiss.

"Bend over the table," Piper purred into her ear even as she took Jo's earlobe and sucked gently on it.

Jo groaned as she leaned forward, heat pooling between her thighs. She spread her legs wide as Piper continued to grind in slow circles against her. The change in position made Jo gasp.

"Please," Jo begged.

"Please?" Piper chuckled, deep and throaty.

The sound sent another wave of arousal heating up Jo's body.

"Yes, please. Please, please, touch me," Jo begged, pushing her ass against Piper as hard as she could. Her fingers flinched, tempted to reach down and tease her clit herself.

Piper chuckled and leaned over Jo's body. The weight of Piper's body on top of her was delicious.

"All in good time, my love," Piper purred in Jo's ear.

Jo felt so close already. The truth of Piper's feelings made her senses heightened in a way she could barely remember ever happening before. Even with the fun she and Piper had previously had. Because this time she knew it wasn't just surface level.

The pressure from Piper lifted, and just as Jo was about to complain, wet hot kisses began from the top of her spine down to her panties. Piper eased them slowly down Jo's legs.

Her legs shuddered, and her body screamed for release. Jo bit down hard on her lower lip, trying to stop herself from begging and pleading again. Except, Jo couldn't hold back any longer. She shoved her ass backward and into Piper.

"Do you want me?" Piper asked, her voice deeper than normal.

"Yes. Oh God. Please fuck me."

Piper grabbed Jo's hips and pulled her hard against her crotch once more.

Jo groaned and ground her ass in hard circles, gasping each time Piper's surprisingly naked pussy brushed her own.

"Oh." Jo giggled and heard Piper laughing back.

"You don't mind?" Piper asked.

"I demand getting to feel you as much as you feel me." Jo smiled as she rested her elbows on the edge of the table. With all her pushing backward, she was no longer pressed against the wood top.

"Good," Piper said in a heavy breath.

Jo closed her eyes. When she felt one of Piper's hands snake around her hip and dance across her stomach, the speed of her hips increased. Piper found Jo's clit and stroked gently for a moment before speeding up to the same pace as Jo's furious grinding.

"Yes," Piper groaned out as she rubbed rapidly on Jo's clit, pushing into Jo harder with each rotation of their hips.

Jo was panting, unintelligible sounds escaping her mouth. She shuddered, her legs fighting to hold her up. Piper's other hand moved from Jo's hips and wrapped around Jo's stomach, her other fingers still rubbing. With another hard thrust, Piper's fingers swiping hard over the tip of Jo's clit, Jo screamed and felt her body stiffen and convulse.

Piper held her close, holding her up as she shuddered through the aftershocks of the orgasm.

"Oh wow."

Piper laughed in response and helped turn Jo around in her arms.

"I love you." Piper smiled and kissed the tip of Jo's nose.

"I love you, too." Jo knew she had a wicked gleam in her eyes. "But you haven't finished yet."

"I'm okay," Piper said, her pink cheeks growing darker.

"Well then…" Jo gently pushed Piper back until her legs hit the small couch that ran along the side of the bus opposite the table. "I'm not finished yet."

"What?" For a moment, Piper looked genuinely confused before Jo slid to her knees and gently parted Piper's knees.

"Oh," Piper said as Jo began to kiss the inside of her thighs. She started at one knee and worked her way up, stopping just before reaching Piper's pussy. Piper squirmed as Jo moved away and began the same trail up the other thigh.

"You sure you're okay?" Jo asked, looking up at Piper through lowered lashes.

"Definitely." Piper laughed.

"Good." Jo giggled.

The smell of Piper's arousal filled her as she thrust her tongue inside Piper's hot center. Piper's legs wrapped around Jo's head, hands tangling in her ruined curls as Jo alternated between thrusting and licking and pressing the flat of her tongue against Piper's clit.

When Piper screamed out, her thighs shuddering and stiffening against Jo's head, Jo stilled her movements, enjoying the sensation of Piper's pussy shuddering around her face.

"Come here." Piper dropped her legs and motioned for Jo to join her on the narrow seat.

Piper's legs stretched out across the bus and her chest rose hard and heavy. Jo curled up against Piper and kissed her on the cheek. Piper turned her head, and they kissed, full and hard.

"I love you," Piper said again.

"I love you, too." Jo mumbled into Piper's shoulder as her fingers found Piper's hardened nipple through her shirt, idly playing with it.

"If we're ever going to let Bea and Bunny back in here, that's not helping." Piper laughed, lifting Jo's hand and kissing her fingers softly, one at a time.

"All right. But just a few more minutes." Jo sighed as Piper threaded their fingers together.

"Just a few more minutes then," Piper whispered.

"Also, random question, I know, but have you two always shared a bus? Or would you be opposed to having your own?" Jo scrunched her nose.

Piper's full laugh was exactly what she'd been hoping for.

bunny

"Seriously?" Siena approached the table where Bunny sat. "You chose a table outside?"

Bunny chuckled and stood. "Merry Christmas to you, too." Bunny opened her arms and gave Siena a warm hug.

"Merry Christmas." Siena returned the greeting as she untangled herself from the hug. Her eyes narrowed at Bunny as they took seats opposite each other.

"It's not outside."

"You could have fooled me." Siena turned her head from one open side of the cafe's veranda to the other.

"All right, so it's a little outside." Bunny chuckled. "But I wanted to see the fresh snow."

"Wasn't the other night enough for you?" Siena's shoulders relaxed, and she broke into a far friendlier smile.

"What can I say?" Bunny shrugged and brought the cup to her lips and downed the last of the coffee, already gone from hot to just warm in the few minutes she had been nursing it before Siena arrived.

She was early, just like she had always been for her whole career. It was nice to be embraced for who she was, and encouraged to remain the person she had always been despite the world-shattering changes that had consumed her life the last three days.

Siena still stared at her, but her smirk and the twinkle in her eyes no longer held the suspicion that had lingered there when she had first arrived.

The cold air bit into Bunny's cheeks and froze her nose. But she still couldn't shake the happiness that shone brightly within her. She knew so much of it could be attributed to Bea. But since the show a few nights ago—had it really only been a few nights?—she realized this happiness was so much more than having Bea in her life. This was what everyone kept going on about when they rejoiced about living their own truth. The weight of hiding had lifted, and she reveled in the cool crisp air.

She also enjoyed being outside because she was still adjusting to the onslaught of recognition and celebration queer fans were giving out freely now.

"This suits you," Siena interrupted Bunny's silent thoughts.

"What does?" Bunny looked down at her outfit. Comfortable yet stylish, and loose. Nothing unusual. In fact, she was certain Siena had seen her in the exact same outfit more than once before.

Siena chuckled and reached over to place a hand over Bunny's, on the table beside her empty cup. "Happiness. I meant happiness looks good on you."

"Oh, thank you." Heat warmed Bunny's cheeks at the compliment and at her complete misunderstanding.

"Now…" Siena stood again. Her grace flowed from her with such effortless ease. It always had. "…I'm going to get us drinks. And then we need to talk."

"All right." Bunny was impressed the words came out normally even though they had to push past the instant lump in her throat.

It didn't take long for Siena to return. Not nearly long enough for Bunny to work out how much she would have to suck up to Siena, or for how long.

But she knew there were going to be problems. There always were in cases like this, right? When Siena sat back down, Bunny didn't hesitate before jumping right in. "All right. What's the damage?"

"Damage?" Siena asked, her face scrunching in confusion and curiosity.

"For my colossal spontaneity."

"Oh." Siena smiled and nodded. "To me, to your reputation, or to the Holbrook Foundation? Which one are we talking about?"

"Oh shit. Did they lose supporters because of me?" Bunny slumped in her chair, deflated. She hadn't thought about them suffering and what a disaster her decisions could mean for them.

"Yes, they did." Siena moved back slightly in her chair for the waiter to place their coffee on the table. She waited until he had disappeared inside before continuing, "But none that anyone from the Holbrook Foundation is going to miss. Especially considering the Christmas Eve spectacular is officially their highest earning fundraising event."

"What?" Even Bunny was surprised by how loud her voice was.

"I'm sorry." Siena chuckled, belying her words. "I couldn't resist letting you worry for a second."

"You're evil." Bunny pursed her lips before lifting the fresh cup of coffee to her lips. The warm steam swirled in front of her, filling her nostrils with the strong bitter taste. She sipped the drink more because she wanted to hide her grin. She had never bought into the whole floating-on-cloud-nine thing, but she certainly understood it a lot better now.

"Well, karma had to get you sooner or later, and aren't you

lucky it was me?" Siena looked far too pleased with herself. Her eyes twinkled, and her grin couldn't be hidden by her own coffee cup.

Bunny probably hadn't successfully covered her own smile either. But that was all right. She didn't have to hide her happiness or enjoyment of any of this. She didn't have to hide at all.

It would take some time to get used to that idea, but Bunny pushed back the lifelong fear of showing emotions and clung to this blissful sensation.

"Now." Siena placed the cup down smoothly. Her face no longer lit up with the joy of the moment.

Bunny knew Siena's business face better than she knew her own reflection. Especially now with her fight to stop smiling any time of the day. But she wasn't so far gone she didn't know how to muster her professionalism.

She took a deep breath and put her own cup down. It clattered with an almighty rattle, spilling a few hot drops onto the back of her hand.

Pulling her hand back instinctively, she hissed in a breath.

"Are you all right?" Siena leaned forward in her chair, her body almost covering the circumference of the small outdoor dining table.

"Yeah." Bunny shook her fingers before rubbing the affected area with the fingers of her other hand. "I'm fine."

Siena took a moment to make sure before she continued in her thoughts. "What you did was completely unlike you."

"I don't regret a single second of it."

"I need to know. I need to hear you say it. And if you want to get mad at me that's okay, but I need to know the truth."

"The truth?" Bunny didn't understand what Siena wasn't getting at. "The truth about what?"

"Is it real?" Siena asked slowly.

Bunny could see the worry and concern now, behind the twinkling that still lingered in her eyes.

"I'm missing something again." Bunny frowned into her coffee, trying to figure out exactly what Siena wasn't saying, but she couldn't figure it out.

"Was it a stunt? Or are you and Bea actually together?"

"What the hell?" Indignation rose in Bunny's chest, shocking her system like she'd been plunged into a cold ice bath.

"Okay." Siena sat back, both hands raised with palms facing Bunny. "I know it might seem stupid to ask. But I need to hear it."

"Why?" Bunny didn't understand why Siena was being so insistent. She wouldn't make these decisions lightly. She wouldn't do what she'd done without just cause.

"Because I'm not the only one who noticed what a drastic change doing this was for you. Your reputation has… quite frankly been very buttoned up and private. You bleed for your fans through your lyrics, and I know they should never ask for more than what you're willing to give. But please try to see it from the outside looking in."

Bunny rolled her shoulders and let her head drop back. For a moment, she kept her eyes closed. She had to process all the emotions in such a short time and work through them as quickly as possible before she acted stupid again. Before she acted as though she always knew what she was doing, even if she had no clue whatsoever and made a complete fuckup of everything.

The first cold touch on her cheek made her flinch. The second made her open her eyes.

She smiled as she watched the first flakes of snow coming down.

Stop overthinking it, Bunny.

She scolded herself and brought her head forward to look at Siena. She smiled, and the relief in Siena's body was obvious as she sighed, her face relaxing.

"It wasn't a stunt. And it wasn't something I'd planned either."

"So you really do love her? The happiness isn't some fake publicity thing like Jo and Piper?"

"No." Bunny chuckled. She understood it as best she could. "I suppose asking you when I had ever lied would be the dumbest thing to do. But I've never lied to you, Siena. You always knew who I was. Right from the start. And I wouldn't be faking this for you."

"I know." Siena smiled. "But this business makes people like me wary. It's why I initially asked you to see the Sole Sisters and get a feel for them for me."

"You thought they might be lying?"

"I thought there might have been the potential." Siena shrugged. "But I didn't want to say that and have you go in with any preconceived ideas."

"Oh." Bunny blinked as she truly processed what Siena was getting at. "That's the thing you needed to know? If they were genuinely gay?"

"Yes and no." Siena bobbed her head from side to side. "I wanted to know if they were truly who they presented themselves to be. Their sexuality was only part of that."

"Ah." Bunny nodded, not even trying to stop the smile from spreading across her lips once more. "And now you've made your decision?"

"I have." Siena didn't continue but instead lifted her cup and took a slow sip.

"Siena." Bunny snapped, but they both knew there was no malice in the tone. "Have you signed them or not?"

"I couldn't possibly say. NDAs and all that." Siena shrugged and laughed, seemingly unable to keep it together any longer. "All right. I got permission from them both first. We signed the contract earlier today. I will be representing them as of the new year."

"Yes." Bunny cheered. "That's amazing. Can you make sure I actually get some time to see my girlfriend while you're scheduling our lives now?"

Siena laughed. It was a laughter bigger than Bunny deserved with anything she had said.

"What's so funny?"

"Bea said the exact same thing once we'd signed."

"Really?" Bunny's smile spread farther over her face.

"Absolutely. Then of course Jo was very eager to ensure she and Piper still got to see each other regularly as well."

"Oh, this is going to be a whole new kind of hell for you, isn't it?" Bunny chuckled, finally relaxing properly and putting one ankle up on her knee as she drank her coffee and watched the snowfall grow heavier. The soft silence hadn't yet covered the world, and she hoped by the time it did she was curled up in bed with Bea, naked and working on being satiated, and satiating.

"It is. But talking about business and scheduling." Siena relaxed in her chair as well. Not quite mimicking Bunny, but crossing her legging-clad legs, the skirt she wore riding up a little just above her knee.

"What hell have you planned for us now?" Bunny asked, her face relaxed and her worries not a real concern.

"Holbrook Foundation has requested a repeat performance."

"What?" Bunny wasn't entirely sure she understood what that meant.

"They would like to know if you, Bea, Piper, and Jo would be interested in performing again next year for a new Christmas Eve event. New songs, new costumes, no spontaneous kisses to out yourself."

"Oh, I can't promise the last one." Bunny chuckled. "And I can't say yes."

"Why not?" Siena asked, shock and confusion crossing her face.

"I won't do it unless all of us want to. And I won't make them feel like they have to agree because I already have."

"My my, Bunny. It looks like love really has softened that icy heart of yours."

"Well, turns out the heart itself was fine. It just needed the right person to melt the ice it was encased in."

The right person with perfect tits, Bunny added silently to herself, knowing Bea's tits were only one of the myriad things Bunny loved about her.

"You should use that in a song." Siena crinkled her nose.

"I already have," Bunny said, face heating, and the urge to roll her shoulders needling at her again.

"You're writing again? Love songs?"

"Well, maybe a little more love in between the angst."

"I can't wait to hear them." Siena smiled, drinking the last of her coffee and setting the cup back down. "And I'll talk to the others shortly about the Holbrook Foundation's offer for next year."

"Thanks, Siena." Bunny stood up, and when Siena opened her arms for a hug, Bunny embraced her warmly.

"It's going to take a while to get used to this."

"Tell me about it." Bunny chuckled as they both stepped back from the embrace.

"You'll get used to it. Just don't beat yourself up too much when you sometimes slip back into control-and-in-charge Bunny."

"Oh, she's not going anywhere. Dickhead-and-bad-decision Bunny, however, is going on a very short leash indeed."

"Excellent." Siena buttoned her coat up again and turned around. "I'll see you in the new year. Say hi to Bea for me."

"Will do." Bunny waved, and Siena returned the gesture before turning around and walking away briskly.

Bunny didn't bother sitting back down. She drank the last of her coffee standing, laughed as it clattered again when she set the cup down, paid, and left. Heading home had never felt so wonderful and warm.

Even on a cold snowy afternoon.

bea

One Year Later…

The high Bea was riding wasn't going to end with the final song of the charity fundraiser. Bunny's fingers clenched in her own, were exactly what she needed to remind herself that even though it had been one year since the last fundraising concert, this wasn't going to end.

The ring on her finger didn't feel new since it had been there a few months already, but Bunny squished it against her hand hard while they stood together on the stage and sang the encore. This show, while similar to the one last year, was also vastly different. They were ready for it without even having to try, although Bunny did make them rehearse endlessly.

It'd be too easy to get out of that.

Bea laughed when Bunny spun her in a circle on the stage, her eyes alight with a mischief that Bea knew all too well by this point. Bunny dipped her down and kissed her, the cheers roaring wildly. Bea threaded her fingers through Bunny's hair, keeping their mouths pressed together until Bunny lifted her up.

"I love you," Bunny murmured.

"Love you, too," Bea said with a grin and a laugh. "Come on, I want to go home."

"Soon." Bunny winked.

The show was over. At least mostly. It wouldn't take long for Bunny to drive them home and Bea could find herself encompassed in Bunny's comfortable bed—her comfortable bed. Even though it had been two months since they'd tied the knot at the courthouse, it was still hard to believe that this was her life.

Touring.

Concerts.

Marriage.

Bea wrapped her arm around Bunny as they walked off the stage together. Piper and Jo followed closely behind, the giant rock on Jo's left ring finger a warm reminder of just how far they'd come in the last year. The wedding was next week, on the first of the year, and Bea was ready for it to be over and done with.

She wanted some calm, some time they could all spend together just lingering in the family that they were creating. Bunny wrapped her arm around Bea's back and kissed her cheek. "What do you say we get into our clothes as fast as possible and burn rubber on the way out."

"I like this idea," Bea teased. "But you'll have to deal with Siena first."

Siena was headed in their direction at a quick pace. Bunny pushed Bea toward the bus and put her hand up to stop Siena in her tracks. Bea followed the silent instructions from Bunny and walked toward the bus. By the time she and Bunny were in the car and headed home, it had been another thirty minutes.

Leaning into the seat, her eyes half-closed, Bea melted into the moment. She'd never wanted anything more than this. She had love and she had hope. They had never done a major press release about their relationship like Siena had wanted to, but it was enough. Bunny's hand against her thigh caught her attention, and Bea turned her head, lips curling up at Bunny's glance.

"Everything okay?" Bunny asked.

"Everything is perfect." Bea's voice was soft and gentle, satiated almost. And perhaps it was because of that. She was comfortable and settled, and it was perfect—truly. Bunny scrunched her face up, and Bea caught her before she could run down that train of thought. "No, you don't. Tonight was a good night. Stop analyzing how it could be better."

"Tonight was good, I'll give you that one." Bunny's fingers tightened on Bea's thigh. "It'll be even better when we get home."

Bea chuckled lightly. "Oh, do you have big plans for when we get home?"

"All day every day." Bunny lifted Bea's hand, kissing her knuckles briefly.

"Too bad we have these things called jobs."

"And annoying friends and siblings who have the worst timing on the planet."

Bea laughed fully this time. Piper and Jo had interrupted them on more than one occasion over the last year, but Bea was hopeful that it would happen less once the wedding was over and Piper and Jo were figuring out their own lives.

Bea stayed half a step behind Bunny as they walked to their condo. Bunny slid her key into the lock, and within seconds they were inside. Bea leaned against the door, locking it behind her as she eyed Bunny over. The way she moved so much more confidently now, the way she didn't hesitate when they were out on the town together. She had come into her own so quickly.

"I love you," Bea said, her voice carrying through the living room.

Bunny furrowed her brow as she turned around, keys on the tips of her fingers as she went to drop them on the kitchen table. "I love you, too. Why the sudden sentiment?"

Bea shrugged and bit her lip. "Because I have big plans for tonight."

"Oh?" Bunny's eyes widened, and her entire focus was centered on Bea.

"I like that look." Bea's lips curled up, her eyes softening. She wouldn't have her life look any other way right now. The two of them, together, spinning in each other's orbit and nowhere else.

"What look?" Bunny frowned now, a deep line creasing in the center of her forehead.

"The one that says you want to eat me up."

Bunny snorted, immediately grinning. "Maybe it's because I do."

"Good." Bea took a step away from the door. She started with her shirt, pulling it up and over her head and dropping it onto the floor behind her. Sending a saucy and expectant look over her shoulder, she reached behind her back and unhooked the strap on her bra. She wanted her message to be clear as day. "You coming?"

"Fuck yes," Bunny muttered, following her into the bedroom like Bea had her hook, line, and sinker.

Laughing, Bea undid the button and zipper on her pants and shoved them over her broad hips. She was just about to push them to her ankles when Bunny's hands on her sides stopped her. Leaning back into Bunny, Bea hummed her contentment.

"Did you ever think this is what your life would look like?" Bea asked.

"Not for a second," Bunny answered, skimming her hands up and down Bea's sides.

She touched Bea's breasts lightly and briefly before sliding her hands down, across her belly, and between her legs. Bea was wrapped in Bunny's arms like a hug, her back pressed to Bunny's front. She never wanted to give this up.

"I figured I'd be gone on tour all year, barely even home," Bunny stated, slipping two fingers through Bea's slick, wet folds. She pulled Bea's juices upward, sliding the pads of her fingers against Bea's clit. She pinned Bea's clit tightly between her fingers and then scissored them.

Bea groaned. She reached back, wrapping her arm around the back of Bunny's head and tried to keep herself upright. Bunny pressed kisses against Bea's neck, small nibbles here and there. Bea gasped, rocking her hips into Bunny's hand.

"I love that you know how to touch me," Bea whispered, her voice gravelly.

"I asked Siena to do something different this year."

Bea winced. She really didn't want to talk about Siena when Bunny's hand was doing delicious things to her. She really didn't want to talk business when her head wasn't completely in the game. Bunny might try to sneak something in there that Bea would normally push back on.

"I asked her to set up a joint tour."

Bea whimpered, clenching her eyes shut as Bunny continued the same pattern as before. She wasn't sure she had heard right, that she'd followed Bunny's line of thought.

"J-joint tour?" Bea finally managed to ask.

"Yes." Bunny scraped her teeth over the cord of muscle along Bea's shoulder. "If you'll agree to it."

"Agree to what?" Bea asked, nearly out of breath. She was so damn close, and Bunny's inane questions about business weren't helping her get there.

"Going on tour with Piper and me."

"I—" Bea stopped, words disappearing from her brain as Bunny brought her up and over the edge of orgasm. She clenched at nothing, wishing Bunny's fingers were inside of her to add to the pressure, wishing that her brain wasn't going wild with sensations and pleasure so she could answer Bunny's crazy question.

Bunny's kisses were warm on her shoulders and upper back. Bunny held her until Bea was ready to turn around. She sat on the edge of the bed, gave Bunny an odd look, and then started pulling her shoes off to divest herself of the rest of her pants.

"You want Jo and me to go on tour with you?"

"Yes." Bunny grinned widely.

"And you already talked to Siena about it." Bea pressed her lips into a thin line, wanting Bunny to sweat this one out a little. She kicked off her pants and pulled herself into the center of the bed. Two could play at this game, and she wasn't going to let Bunny be the only one to get away with it. Spreading her legs, Bea planted her hand right between them and slowly swished two fingers back and forth across her clit.

Bunny's eyes were glued to her body. Her cheeks grew pink with arousal, her lips parted as if at any moment she was going to bed down and take over what Bea was doing. Bea reached behind her head with her free hand to lift her head up slightly to be able to see Bunny's reaction better.

"You didn't think you should ask me or Jo if we wanted to tour with you?" Bea kept her tone firm but her fingers moving. She knew she was making it hard for Bunny to concentrate, but payback was a bitch, and she wasn't willing to let this one go.

"I uh…" Bunny swallowed audibly. "I thought you uh…"

"Finish your sentence, Bunny." Oh, Bea was enjoying this far too much. She should have tried this earlier.

"Damn you," Bunny muttered.

"Oh, I like the sound of that tone."

Bunny stripped off her clothes rapidly, dropping them next to the bed. Then she clambered onto the mattress and had her hand against Bea's in an instant. "Will you go on tour with me, Bea? With me and my crazy bandmate, Piper, and her insane soon-to-be wife?"

Bea's eyes crinkled at the corners as she grinned. Bunny stared at her directly, sliding two fingers inside her and curling them delicately.

"What do you say?"

"Yessss." But was she answering Bunny's question or begging for Bunny to keep touching her? Bea wasn't entirely sure.

"We'd be stuck together for months on end. I guess the question is how many times will I stick my foot in my mouth?"

"Not enough," Bea whined as she lifted her hips up, trying to get Bunny to touch her more. "I think everyone will say it won't be often enough."

Chuckling low, Bunny bent down and immediately covered Bea's clit with her lips. Bea cried out in surprise, arching backward into the heavenly mattress. She couldn't speak. Her entire body was hot. All her nerves were electrified with pleasure. She was already so close to her second orgasm and the first had barely even ended.

"Bunny," Bea whimpered.

Bunny's laughter ricocheted through her with vibrations against her clit, and it sent another shockwave of pleasure through her body. Bea wasn't going to be able to hold back. Not that she'd want to and not that Bunny would ever ask her to. Bea groaned loudly as she reached down and dug her fingers into Bunny's hair and pulled tight. She cried out, her voice reverberating around the room as she crashed through her second orgasm of the night.

Clasping her thighs together, she turned onto her side as Bunny backed away. She needed a few minutes to get control of herself again, to find her center and calm her body. She worked to settle her breathing while Bunny lay behind her and ran soothing fingers over her side from her shoulder to her thigh.

"I think I can work to keep myself in check."

Bea laughed, full and hard. "If you say so, love."

"I love when you call me that."

"Well, I love you, too." Laughing, Bea shifted away, turning on her back. "Come up here."

Bunny complied, straddling Bea's hips. They pressed their mouths together in a deep embrace before Bea beckoned Bunny to move farther up her body. With Bunny's pussy right in front of her face, Bea couldn't resist.

"I'd love to go on tour with you, for the record," Bea said right before latching her mouth around Bunny's clit.

Bunny gasped, lurching forward. Bea grinned as she sucked, creating an optimal amount of pressure. She wanted Bunny's first orgasm to be just as hard as hers had been, one that would blow her mind, one that would take her minutes to recover from. Bea wrapped her arms around Bunny's toned thighs and kept her in place as she started to get wild with her movements.

"Bea," Bunny said, and then mumbled something unintelligible afterward.

Crying out, Bunny grunted and then collapsed onto the bed next to Bea. Curling around Bunny, Bea gave her the same care that Bunny had given her. They stayed together, wrapped up in each other's arms for at least thirty minutes. There was silence between them, nothing but soothing, calm silence.

"I should tell Siena she can start planning—"

"It can wait until next week," Bea said, her tone gentle.

"I'll just text her tomorrow."

Bea grinned. "Tomorrow is Christmas. You won't be texting her."

Bunny wrinkled her nose, but settled back in. "Fine, I'll text her on the twenty-sixth."

"That's Boxing Day."

"We're American, Bea!" Bunny pinched Bea's nipple as if to make her point. "We don't celebrate Boxing Day."

"My point is, it can wait until after the wedding." Bea lifted up on her elbow and stared down at Bunny. "We've got too much to worry about right now and we can ask Jo and Piper what they think about a joint tour after they get back from their honeymoon."

"Right… we should probably ask them first."

"Yes, we should." Bea pressed her lips to Bunny's neck, trailing kisses down to her chest. "We don't need another blowup like last year."

Bunny hummed. "Fine, but what exactly are we supposed to do for two weeks with no work?"

Bea laughed. "Fuck, and fuck some more."

thank you!

Dearest Reader,

Thank you so much for reading this book. I absolutely fell head over heels in love with these four characters. I've wanted to write a sapphic queering of _White Christmas_ for years, and now I can say that I finally did it!

This was so much fun, and the research for it (watching the movie a million times) was such a blast. I'm so glad you took a chance and joined me for this journey!

I really hope you enjoyed these four as much as I did. I'd love it if you'd leave a review or a rating for this book, every review and rating helps!. And I'd love it if you'd sign up for my newsletter.

You'll get a free copy of **Made You Look** when you do sign up for my newsletter, a novella all about Aili and Birch, and just how their love story starts.

I am planning on publishing Siena's story next. Curious who she falls in love with? Make sure you sign up for my newsletter to keep up to date, you can do that by going to: https://qrco.de/MYLnewsletter

or scanning the QR code with your phone

I love keeping in contact with readers, so send me emails or get hold of me on social media anytime.

And I always love a good dad joke. Send me your best!

Til the sun shines again,

Eada

about the author

Eada Friesian is an author of snarky sapphic women who fall in love hard. She loves all the characters and relationships she gets to play with and the best friends she makes with each new book she writes. She fell in love with the genre years ago and could never leave it. Who would? Now that she's authoring her own books, she hopes to bring a fresh flair to the sapphic book world.

Eada lives in the mountains, camping her life away with her partner and horde of animals. She has her family right by her side as she strives to live her best life authentically as an author, a parent, a spouse, and weird person. She loves the smell of campfire, the taste of a completely charred marshmallow for a s'more, and living off the land with very little people around her. Of course, none of this last part is true, because Eada is a pen name, and the identity of the person(s) behind her remain hidden.

 facebook.com/sapphicsnarks

 instagram.com/sapphicsnarks

Do you believe in soulmates?

Tori Frazee is unapologetic when it comes to falling in love before she's thirty. When her marriage ended amicably, she knew she had to get back into the game to find her soulmate and have the family she wanted. Running face first into a cold but frazzled funeral director and a rebellious toddler at the grocery store isn't how she expected to find love, and Miranda certainly isn't her soulmate. Or is she?

Miranda Hart doesn't believe in love. When she's saddled with her flakey sister's kid, she has a choice to make—step up to break the cycle and keep her niece from being another victim or continue to live through her work. When she meets the cute, down to earth Tori, she can't help but wonder if maybe she does want more than her career.

When opposites attract, steam rises, especially with an ice queen in the mix. Will these two single parents break down their preconceived notions enough to find a family they can rely on?

If you love sensual, steamy age gap, ice queen, sapphic/lesbian romances, then this is the book for you.

One reserved professional. One bubbly long-term temp. One gala to unite them.

Haylee Coleman can't lose another job. Flat out broke, she's desperate to turn her life around, pay her bills, and keep her job. But more than that, she's found a place she might belong for the first time in her life. She can make a difference here. If only Cherish would like her. If only Cherish would help her figure out how to not get fired. If only Cherish wasn't so distracting.

With a bark that rivals the boss's, Cherish Barkley lives and breathes her job. She's loved Febe Aarts for decades. When the annual gala for the Holbrook Foundation looms, Cherish begs for Haylee's help. It has to go off without a hitch, unlike last year, when Febe…Cherish can think about that later. Right now, she has to protect Febe.

Will they put aside their differences long enough to ensure their boss survives the gala unscathed? Or will the mounting tension between them erupt in unsuspecting ways?

Find out what happens in this sapphic age gap, workplace romance, with an ice queen in love with her boss and a curvy new assistant that won't give up on her dream.